For Jeffrey N Baines
and
to remember
Jeremy J Beadle and Denis Lemon,
regular reviewers of murder mysteries
for Gay Times

Also edited by Peter Burton:

Bend Sinister: The Gay Times Book of Disturbing Stories

First published 2003 by GMP (Gay Men's Press)

GMP is an imprint of Millivres Prowler Limited,
part of the Millivres Prowler Group,
Unit M, Spectrum House, 32–34 Gordon House Road,
London NW5 1LP UK

www.gaymenspress.co.uk
www.gaytimes.co.uk

A CIP catalogue record for this book is available from the British Library

ISBN 1-902852-46-X

Printed and bound in Finland by WS Bookwell

Distributed in the UK and Europe by Airlift Book Company,
8 The Arena, Mollison Avenue,
Enfield, Middlesex EN3 7NJ
Telephone: 020 8804 0400
Distributed in North America by Consortium,
1045 Westgate Drive, St Paul, MN 55114-1065
Telephone: 1 800 283 3572
Distributed in Australia by Bulldog Books,
PO Box 300, Beaconsfield, NSW 2014

DEATH COMES EASY:
THE GAY TIMES BOOK OF MURDER STORIES

Edited by Peter Burton

Contents

Introduction by Peter Burton   vii

And the Band Played On by Robert Cochrane   1

Best Eaten Cold by Tim Ashley   5

Pisspants by Sebastian Beaumont   27

Takey's War by Perry Brass   41

The Collection Box by Scott Brown   53

Beyond the Reef by Jeffrey Buchanan   71

Pop Goes the Weasel by Richard Cawley   85

Dead & Gone by Bryan Connon   109

Strangers on a Plane by Jack Dickson   115

Two Birds, One Stone by Simon Edge   131

Breach by Joanne Elliott   153

Direst Cruelty by Nigel Fairs   161

Canvas by Steve Ferris   169

L & I by Hugh Fleetwood   181

The Mirror's Kiss by C. J. Fortesque   209

Little Jimmy by Christopher Francis   221

The Excursion by Patrick Gale   237

The Pitch by Drew Gummerson   247

Britain's Fattest Killer Tells All by Michael Hootman   261

Love and Hate and the Scent of Almonds by Randall Kent Ivey   275

Bala the Woodworker by Alan James   293

The Sitting Tenant by Francis King   333

Poison Pen by Simon Lovat   347

Into the Cold by Anthony McDonald   361

Still There by Joseph Mills   371

The Murdered Child by Patrick Roscoe   379

Death by Eros by Steven Saylor   399

The Haunting of James Elstead by Michael Wilcox   423

Jolly Well Played, That Man by Graeme Woolaston   435

Acknowledgements   451

Further reading   453

About the authors   455

Introduction

At the beginning of his famous essay 'Decline of the English Murder' (1946), George Orwell paints a picture of an archetypal British Sunday afternoon of the period; 'The wife is already asleep in the armchair, and the children have been sent out for a nice long walk. You put your feet up on the sofa, settle your spectacles on your nose, and open the *News of the World*. Roast beef and Yorkshire, or roast pork and applesauce, followed up by suet pudding and driven home, as it were, by a cup of mahagony-brown tea, have put you in the right mood. Your pipe is drawing sweetly, the sofa cushions are soft underneath you, the fire is well alight, the air is warm and stagnant. In these blissful circumstances, what is it that you want to read about?

'Naturally, about a murder ...'

Although many of the details Orwell delineates have changed (who, these days, could enjoy 'suet pudding ... driven home ... by a cup of mahagony-brown tea'?), that reader's interest in murder remains.

Why?

Murder fascinates because from the comfort of that soft-cushioned sofa, the reader can indulge themself in the spectacle of others of their kind sunk to the basest levels of depravity – depriving another human being of their life.

Orwell's essay then poses the question: 'But what kind of murder?' and answers with the suggestion that 'our greatest period in murder...' so to speak, seems to have been roughly 1850 and 1925, and goes on to list murderers 'whose reputations have stood the test of time' (in a list that includes Dr Palmer, Neill Cream, Mrs Maybrick and Dr Crippen) and indicates that most of these celebrated murders were 'essentially domestic'.

Perhaps a reminder is timely. 'Decline of the English Murder' (basically a review of R Alwyn Raymond's *The Cleft Chin Murder*, 'it is difficult to believe that this case will be so long remembered as the old domestic... dramas, product of a stable society where the all-prevailing hypocrisy did at least ensure that crimes as serious as murder should have strong emotions behind them') was written in 1946.

Now here is a major change. We no longer live in a stable society and it seems in the de-stablising wake of the genocide which has gone unimpeded since the mid-twentieth century and of which the Holocaust is but the most well-documented and, thus, the most well-known, murders have become increasingly more horrifying and murderers more horrifyingly reckless. It is as if the practitioners, in the face of a world, gone increasingly mad, feel they have to try ever harder if they are to attract and, importantly, retain public attention and, by a curious kind of default, public affection.

What would George Orwell have made of Ian Brady and Myra Hindley, the Moors murderers? Of Fred and Rosemary West? Of Dennis Nilsen or Jeffrey Dahmer? Of gay serial killers Dean Corll (27 victims identified from remains found at his Houston, Texas home, possibly as many as 32 victims altogether), Patrick Wayne Kearney, 'the trashbag murderer', who dumped the remains of his 32 homosexual victims on the highways between California and the Mexican border or Chicago's John Wayne Gracy, 'the fat man', who had at least 33 victims. They do things big in America. Numbers are lower in Britain. Colin Ireland strangled five men whom he had first spotted at Earl's Court's famous gay pub The Coleherne; Michael Lupo had four known victims.

And though there's no reason to suggest that gay men and gruesome murder have an affinity, it might be argued that because gay men are so often threatened with violence (still) they may possibly be more at risk than heterosexual counterparts. That said, it would be possible to endorse Orwell's intimation that domestic life is conducive to murder – as anyone who has ever spent Christmas with the family can attest.

Murder fascinates – be it in factual or in fictional form. Murder mysteries are an immensely popular form, be they in print (newspapers, magazines, books) or on screen (film, television) or on stage (plays, opera). And it must be remembered that many celebrated murder cases have inspired extraordinary novels. Within a gay context there can be few murder mysteries more terrifyingly enjoyable than Poppy Z Brite's *Exquisite Corpse* (1996), in which two of the most notorious serial killers team up: 'Imagine meeting Nilsen and Dahmer in a bar, being invited, home for coffee...' the cover copy suggests. British writer Simon Lovat utilized the Moors murders in his disquieting novel about an unhealthy teenage obsession, *Disorder and Chaos* (1996) and Meyer Levin's *Compulsion* (1959) is but one of many fictional and dramatic recreations of the sensational Leopold/Loeb killing in Chicago in 1924. Dennis Cooper's *The Tenderness of the Wolves* (1982) was inspired by the case of Fritz Haarmann, 'the butcher of Hanover', the werewolf of Hanover, who, in 1924, was convicted of the murder of 27 youths but who had admitted to slaughtering more than 40. Mass-murderer Gilles de Rais, aide to Joan of Arc, has been the subject of at least one novel and Britain's gangster twins, the brothers Reggie and Ronnie, have made frequent fictional appearances, notably in James Barlow's *The Burden of Proof* (1968), filmed and reprinted under the title *Villain*, and Jake Arnott's *The Long Firm*. The 1997 murder of fashion designer Gianni Versace was the fifth and final slaying in a rampage by Andrew Cunanan and inspired Gary Indiana's novel *Three Month Fever* (2000).

But murder mysteries inspired by gay murders and gay murderers aren't the end of the story. Effeminate men and mannish women are littered throughout the work of those long since mummified Queens of Crime Agatha Christie and Dorothy L Sayers; gay villains flicker through the work of John Buchan (*Greenmantle*, 1916), Raymond Chandler and Dashiell Hammett. And just what is one to make of Rex Stout's orchid-loving detective Nero Wolfe? However, these are all writers from the first half of the twentieth century.

More recently, almost any of the murder mysteries of the likes of Patricia Cornwall, Joseph Hansen (his series involving insurance claims investigator Dave Brandstetter), Patricia Highsmith (particularly the five novels featuring the seductively amoral killer Tom Ripley; 'Part of one of my theories is that a person who murders has something mixed up in his or her sex life and does not get a moral or even happy sex life,' she told me in 1986), Val McDermid or Ruth Rendell will include gay characters, motives, perpetrators, victims. Others operating in this field would have to include 'Nathan Aldyne' (Michael McDowell and Axel Young), Michael Nava, John Preston's gay avenger sequence and Steven Saylor.

The sheer volume of lesbian killers and lesbian detectives is overwhelmingly vast and outside the remit of this Introduction and this book.

At the commissioning stage of this present volume, one of the contributors expressed concern about the narrowness of the brief: 'Murder in all its gory forms'. He was reassured by my belief that there are many ways and means and motives for murder and that it was my view that no two stories in *Death Comes Easy* would be alike. And so it has proved.

There are stories here from across the world and set around the world and featuring work by the well-established and the just-getting-started and stories from writers working outside their usual areas of expertise (as biographer or playwright, for instance). All show imagination and flair and indicate that from there being a decline in the English – or any other – murder there has been a notable renaissance.

Peter Burton
Brighton 2003

And the Band Played On

Robert Cochrane

And the Band Played On
Robert Cochrane

It was nothing personal,
your face
your sole misfortune
on that evening
in a sweaty venue.
You didn't know
the music we listened to
were the last songs
of your life.
A random gathering
the perfect setting
for that simple act,
my slipping powder
to your drink,
the sleight of hand
in gifting death.
Like those
who scale mountains,
sail seas alone,
or infect cyberspace,
I did it because I could.
Some chances
are too beguiling
to remain untaken.
Watching your throat
drain the last from a glass
I wondered if you'd die
on the bus home
or crash your car,
or make it to bed.
A fine surprise

for your partner in the morning,
and something I may read of,
learn from the radio.
You wore a wedding ring.
I have an eye for detail,
and when you left the building
it was raining.

Best Eaten Cold
Tim Ashley

Best Eaten Cold
Tim Ashley

I.

Iris is sixteen years old today. It is the thirtieth of April 1943, and the war has been kind to her so far. It has killed her absentee father and, more importantly, it has caused her to be evacuated from the careless hands of her mother into the oversight of Miss Arthur, a spinster who lives on a large estate in the West Country.

Independently wealthy and blessed with the greenest of fingers, Miss Arthur has lived comfortably throughout the war. What she cannot grow in her extensive kitchen gardens, she barters. And what cannot be bartered for may often be obtained by the gentle milking of her connections.

These days, her appetites run little further than food. She no longer has a taste for clothes, preferring a country drab that does not require frequent renewal. But she does possess, as a result of her parents' magpie travels, an attic filled with steamer trunks containing oriental silks and satins, fine cottons from Egypt, linens from Ireland, French velvets and toiles, chintzes and chiffons and laces from Bruges and Toledo. With these, and with the aid of an ancient Singer, she dresses Iris in colours and cuts and textures which make her strange beauty shine.

Iris is no doll, however. Nor is she a substitute child. Miss Arthur's motivation is more conscious than this: she has seen in Iris the early evidence of a particular kind of ugliness, inherited, she is sure, from the girl's parents, and she has decided to help her ward counter this influence by encouraging her to be beautiful in her appearance and in her manners. If she can achieve this, she feels, she can begin to unpick whatever damage has so far been done. She can shift the focus of the child's life, replace her naive cunning with confidence, make her somehow bigger. She believes that she can spark in Iris a sense of what is fine and eventually, she hopes, of what is noble.

Thus far, she feels that she is succeeding.

And so it is that Miss Arthur wishes, for the best of reasons, to rewrite the future. As she slips from late middle age into the violet years, she is seeking some small credit with which to redress certain balances that persist from her own past, which cannot be re-written.

Iris is joyful at the prospect of the small luncheon-party that Miss Arthur has organised to celebrate her birthday. She dresses carefully in a cream blouse and a bold, floral skirt that reaches just below the knee, then sits in front of the mirror. While she brushes her hair, she practices what she will say when she meets Robert, Miss Arthur's nephew, later that day.

'How lovely to meet you,' she recites with an almost imperceptible pout. 'I've heard so much about you.'

She repeats the phrase twenty times, applies her lips and throat to it whilst holding her head and shoulders erect so as to show off her fine, long neck, knowing all the while that when the moment comes she will deliver her line perfectly. For she has learned a simple mental trick: before greeting any of Miss Arthur's guests, she repeats a phrase to herself silently, over and over again.

'This is my home. This is my home. This is my home.'

And it never fails. She can taste assurance in every word.

Next, she takes a breakfast tray to Miss Arthur's room. Two boiled eggs, buttered toast, tea and a freshly picked daffodil framed by two of its own sword-like leaves.

With light streaming across the window-seat where Iris sits, Miss Arthur looks at her appraisingly.

'One would never guess you to be just sixteen,' she says. 'If I didn't know otherwise, I should put you at eighteen, quite possibly older. *Bon anniversaire, ma chère. Bon anniversaire.*'

'*Merci, madame,*' Iris replies prettily. '*Vous êtes trop gentille.*'

In the late morning, Iris hears the crunch of wheel on gravel and knows that Robert has arrived. She glances briefly at the framed photograph of him on the mantelpiece and then goes quickly to her room where she brushes her hair once more and pinches her cheeks.

Adjusting her timing to perfection by keeping a sideways watch out of the window, she reaches the top of the stairs just as Miss Arthur and her handsome soldier nephew walk, arm in arm, into the front hall.

At lunch, to which three pleasant neighbours have also been invited, they drink champagne. Robert shows Iris how to open the bottle in a dignified manner, and she is allowed a full glass. She sips it slowly, allowing the bubbles to explore her mouth. It is the most perfect thing she has ever tasted. When she sets the flute back down in front of her, a ray of sunlight, refracted from the mirror behind her, passes through it and sends a projection of the rising bubbles onto the tablecloth before her. Iris makes a silent vow that she will always drink champagne on her birthday.

Towards Robert, she remains entirely demure throughout the meal, with the exception of one single bold stare, which she cuts almost before it has started.

Later, after the other guests have departed, Iris eavesdrops on Miss Arthur as she serves her nephew a glass of brandy in the garden room. They believe her to be upstairs changing her clothes, so their conversation is unguarded.

'I think your Pygmalion scheme is going very well, Aunt,' says Robert. 'And she really is quite startling to look at.'

'I've been painting her,' replies Miss Arthur. 'She sits well. She is not at all fidgety. She has a certain... internality, which I find soothing. And the portrait is coming along well, I believe.'

'Well if you want to get it just right,' Robert laughs, 'you'd better use a touch of the tar-brush.'

There is a brief, embarrassed silence as Miss Arthur fails to laugh at her nephew's joke. He continues, more seriously now, trying to save the situation.

'What sort of a mix is she exactly?' he asks.

His aunt pauses, prolonging his discomfort. Iris knows that the brave soldier is blushing now. She hears him cough.

'I am uncertain,' Miss Arthur eventually replies. 'I have never asked. But I would guess that she is one quarter negro. One eighth, perhaps.'

Iris has heard the tar-brush comment before, at school in London, even from her own mother. Her cheeks colour a burnished red, which signifies fury rather than embarrassment. She slips quietly away.

Minutes later, she is back. She wears the same blouse, but has exchanged the skirt for flannel culottes. She enters the garden room brightly and suggests that she might show Robert the new extension to the kitchen-garden while Miss Arthur takes her customary nap.

Once she has seen her guardian upstairs, Iris undoes a button on her blouse, collects Robert and steps out with him into the sunlight.

As they stroll, Iris focuses on her posture. Shoulders back, chest forward. She executes a quarter-turn every few steps, in order to give Robert a flash of the same look she delivered over lunch. This time, however, she mixes in the faintest hint that she is appraising him.

Soon, behind the high Victorian garden wall and out of sight of the house, she stops walking and leans against the side of a high-built cold frame. The bricks are warm, drenched in late April sun, and she can feel their heat through her clothing.

Her hips are slightly forward and she shakes her hair as she holds her face towards the sun, as if she were a flower. She extends the moment, knowing from behind her closed eyes that Robert is staring at her. After a while, she allows her lids to trickle upwards as if she has been awakened by a kiss. She creates a tiny pout, and shuffles her breasts closer together with a shrug of her upper arms. She is ambiguously his.

Robert stands facing her. His is twenty-one, flustered, less experienced and less heroic than he looks. His eyes move from her lips to her breasts, then slide up to her lips again before flicking briefly to meet her eyes. She smiles and takes a deep, slow breath, holding it in so as to make the world silent.

The moment cannot be broken. Robert takes an entranced step towards her. His hands rise to her shoulders as his face moves to meet hers. Their lips touch.

He feels the scream rising in her throat before he hears it and in his confusion he does not feel the slap, though it paints a scarlet bruise across his cheek. He does not see her hand tear swiftly at her own blouse, causing a button to rip and fall. Then she screams again, smiles at him for one long, cold second, and runs towards the house.

Miss Arthur has reached the top of the stairs by the time Iris limps panting into the hallway.

'I heard a scream, Iris. Was it you? Whatever is the matter?' she asks.

Iris pauses, waiting for the loping sound behind her to resolve itself into Robert. As he comes through the front door, she says, 'It was a wasp. A wasp on my blouse. It tried to sting me.'

Then Iris bursts into tears and rushes up the stairs towards her room. She makes certain that Miss Arthur sees her ripped blouse as she passes her on the landing.

And Miss Arthur, looking down into the hallway at her nephew's smarting cheek, says, 'But there are no wasps at this time of year.'

II.

It is the thirtieth of April, 1945. Hitler will put a bullet through his own head later today, though Iris will not hear the news for some time. The smell of the end of the war is in the air, but other matters have her attention.

Miss Arthur is fading fast. For nearly a year now, she has been spotting fresh poppies of blood onto her bedclothes as her womb rebels against the lack of use to which it has been put. In recent days she has been taken worse and from behind her opiate haze, she can no longer see the world clearly.

Iris has telegraphed to her guardian's remaining relatives – a widowed sister and a distant cousin – but they live a long way off and it is understood that they will not arrive until it is too late.

The doctor calls before lunch but insists that he cannot stay long at all. There is an outbreak of influenza at the land-girls' billet, and he must be off. But first he fixes Iris with a careful look and says that he will help her to make Miss Arthur 'more comfortable'.

As he leaves, he tells Iris to call the vicar but Iris, knowing what Miss Arthur's cogent response would be, simply nods and sees him to the door.

When he is gone, she goes to the cellar and finds a bottle of champagne. In the kitchen, she arranges ice and two slender flutes, a crisp white napkin and a tray. Then she goes through into the darkened dining room, which has recently become Miss Arthur's sickbay.

She opens the bottle quietly and pours until both glasses are half full. Settling herself by the bed, she looks across at her own reflection, projected back at her by the mirror which hangs opposite.

'Happy Birthday,' she says to herself, taking a sip of champagne.

She feels Miss Arthur's forehead. It is cold and dry.

'Miss Arthur?' she says. 'Miss Arthur, it's my birthday. I'm eighteen today. Here, I've brought us a little champagne.'

A blue-lidded eye crawls open and the pursed skin beneath it creases into the confused beginnings of a smile, but Miss Arthur is too far gone to sip at the glass being held up for her and, as Iris uses the napkin to wipe away a bead of dribble from a corner near where the mouth used to be, she hears the hiss of a breath escaping, like the sound of a bottle of champagne being carefully opened.

Miss Arthur's head grows heavier on one side. It sinks slowly, but before it can fall from the pillow, Iris cups it gently in her hand and slides it upwards saying,

'Goodbye, Arty. Goodbye. And thank you.'

III.

Iris already knows that she will get the tiny basement flat in Fulham. The widowed sister, Robert's mother, gets the country house and the distant cousin gets a cheque. Robert, dead in the waters lapping Omaha beach, has no claim to make.

A tiny flat and two hundred pounds. Iris is free. She will never have to see her own family again.

There is no affection between her and Robert's mother, for reasons that are clear on both sides, so Iris leaves immediately after the funeral. But she does look back. As the car which is taking her to the station winds along the thin ribbon of gravel leading away from the house, she looks back over her shoulder until the last chimney-stack has disappeared and the final cedar of Lebanon has slipped into the past.

IV.

Iris enrols at the Slade, but after one term she realises that she wants to be an actress. There are several months to fill before she can take up a place at drama school and, cautious of depleting her funds, she takes a job at a Lyons. She feels that it is a little 'common' to work as a waitress – or a 'Nippy' as they are known at Lyons – but that it is also a little brave, even a little chic, especially for a girl of some independent means.

Lyons is known for treating its female employees even-handedly and for rewarding and promoting them on the same basis as the men. Iris likes this, and when her course at the Academy eventually starts, she continues to work at the Corner House in Shaftesbury Avenue on a part-time basis. Soon, she is offered the post of Junior Supervisor, if she will only work full time, but she declines this opportunity. She is in love with the stage.

During her first year at the Academy, she becomes close friends with another girl, Magda. Magda is sophisticated, bohemian, wealthy. Her parents are free thinkers and Magda herself does everything freely. She drinks cocktails, smokes cheroots, and sometimes borrows her brother's Alvis for weekend country drives. She also behaves dangerously with men and it is not long before half of the boys in her year have been toyed with and discarded. She develops a 'reputation', and some of the young men cry on Iris's shoulder when they have reached the waning point of Magda's interest. They hate her, they say, but they cannot stop wanting her.

Initially, Iris is flattered by the second-hand attention but after a while, she becomes jealous. She is more striking than Magda, she tells herself. She is a more exotic fruit – nearly six feet tall, and with the most unusual looks. But Magda is pale, affectedly wilted and droll. Magda is also unambiguously English, and that is what the young men seem to like.

The most beautiful man in Iris's daily orbit is a part-time teacher at the Academy. Clive is twenty-three, tall and dashing in a daring way. He wears flamboyant hats and scarves with the confidence of a film star, and he is kind to Iris. He often comes to the Corner House in the early evening. He is always on his own and he always orders exactly the same thing: two crumpets with margarine, a pot of tea and a ham sandwich. The bill for this menu comes to 11d and he always has the exact change with him. There is something constant about him.

Iris likes his meticulous nature, his streaked blonde and gold hair, his confident posture and his way of dressing. She begins to fall a little in love with him and she confides this to Magda.

The next time Clive visits the Corner House he is with Magda, who smiles repeatedly across the room at Iris while she works, in order to make it quite clear that she has bagged the trophy. Iris smiles back and raises her eyebrows as if to say, 'Gosh it's busy here today, I'm quite rushed off my feet.'

Magda orders a Pola Maid Vanilla Ice and Iris ensures that a small piece of broken glass finds its way into the centre of the confection. Magda cuts her lip badly, and there is a dreadful fuss.

It quickly becomes clear that Clive does not find Magda interesting. Instead, he gravitates towards Iris. He takes her to the theatre, to museums and to galleries. He treats her with dignity and respect. Magda is furious, and begins to make unkind comments about Iris's 'unusual' colouring. Then one day she fails to arrive at the Academy, and is never seen again. Her disappearance is briefly famous; the newspapers speculate as to what might have become of her. Her 'reputation' is hinted at. The police search her home. Within a few months she is largely forgotten.

One evening, Clive is waiting at the Corner House for Iris to finish her shift. He is taking her to see a preview of *An Inspector Calls*. While she is changing out of her uniform, he makes a telephone call and Iris, seeing him do so, stands around the corner and eavesdrops. The restaurant is busy, and she can hardly hear what he is saying but she does catch one phrase.

'Now don't be silly, dear,' she hears him say. 'I'm trimming my beard tonight and you know how important that is. Tomorrow, I promise.'

But Clive is clean-shaven, and Iris has no idea what he can mean.

*

A year later, on Iris's twentieth birthday, Clive takes her to see a production of *The Importance of Being Earnest*. Afterwards, at dinner, he orders champagne and while they are drinking it he prestidigitates, from somewhere near his heart, a small velvet case containing a white gold ring set with two tiny, fiery diamonds. Iris is stunned, delighted, flushed. She looks at the ring for a few moments, then raises her eyes to his and says,

'Yes. I do. I mean, I will.' Then she pauses shyly before adding, 'But don't you think it's about time you kissed me, Clive?'

He stands up, walks around the table and places his hands on her shoulders, then bends and kisses her cheek, first from one side and then from the other. Then he whispers into her ear,

'Iris, my love. You really are an extraordinary woman to take me on. You do realise that I'm... earnest, don't you?'

She nods her head to show that she does realise, but Clive has misjudged the level of her sophistication. She does not understand at all.

They are married six months later. Clive is doing well now. He has stopped teaching at the Academy and is rapidly attaining the status of Matinée Idol, and so the ceremony is quite theatrical; he has chosen the flowers, the music, the venue and most of the guests. There is even a newspaper reporter at the reception, which is held at the Garrick. Iris has never been happier.

That evening, Clive says that he must take Albert, his best man, home in a cab because Albert is really rather drunk. Clive does not return to Iris's flat until three a.m. and then he sleeps on the settee.

The next night he tries to make love to her. She has a reasonable grasp of what should happen, but it doesn't and she feels herself to be at fault. She is quite certain that things will improve – after all, they are both virgins, have both saved themselves for this. There is no rush, she tells herself over the following weeks. Love will find a way.

It comes as a surprise to her to discover how much Clive drinks and how often he comes home very late and sleeps on the settee. One morning she finds Albert there too, asleep on the floor, wearing nothing but a vest and underpants. She washes the sheets in which he has wrapped himself later that week and finds a stain on them.

But she is busy, and she puts these things out of her mind. It is her last term at the Academy, and she is preparing to audition for the senior year production of *Othello*. She is determined to win the part of Desdemona, as are all the other girls. At the audition, she gives what she feels is her very finest performance and a few days later, as she approaches the green baize board on which the list containing her hopes is pinned, she feels something close to confidence. But she is not to be Desdemona. Neither is she to be Emilia, nor Bianca. Instead, she is offered a supporting role in the secondary production, an experimental drama written by one of the tutors at the Academy. She is to play a negress.

She chews her fury silently for a few hours, returning to the flat and pacing its mean spaces while she waits for Clive to return from his matinée. But he does not come, so she catches a bus to the theatre and watches the evening show. He is magnificent, beautiful, compelling, and she feels herself coming alive again with the pride of being his wife.

Afterwards, she goes to his dressing room and finds him there with Albert. Not wanting to share the news of her failure in public, she has no clear explanation for her presence and she feels uncomfortable. It is as if she, not Albert, is the interloper. Eventually, when Clive has removed his makeup and changed into his 'civvies', the three of them leave the theatre together. There is some suggestion hanging unmade in the air that she should leave them to go wherever it is that they are planning to go, but she does not want to do so. Not tonight.

After some shuffling and coughing, Clive takes her aside and insists that she catch a bus home. He is meeting with his agent and a famous impresario. It could be a turning point in his career and it would hardly be appropriate to be accompanied by his wife. Eventually, Iris concedes and allows the two men to leave her waiting at the bus-stop but then she follows them, winding through the back streets of Soho until, eventually, in a passage off an alleyway, she sees them enter a place called the Chaise d'Or.

She deliberates. Why should she doubt him? But she does doubt him and, after a few minutes, she enters the doorway and takes a narrow flight of steps until she finds herself in the basement. There is a coat-check alcove to her right and she begins to remove her hat, but the attendant says,

'Sorry, dearie, Members Only.'

She does not blink as she replies.

'I have arranged to meet my husband here. Clive Ireland. He should have arrived by now.'

The attendant is about to be difficult, but then a sly expression wipes itself across his face.

'Of course, my love,' he says. 'Mr Clive is here. He arrived a few minutes ago, with Mr Albert. Here, let me take your things. Through there,' he says, waving her forwards. 'The bar's to the left.' He smiles again, and Iris thinks that there is something vaguely usurious about him. 'Have a nice evening,' he adds, with a flourish of his hands.

The room she enters is dark, loud and filled with smoke and music. While her eyes are adjusting someone bumps into her and spills a drink over her dress, then bustles off without apology. She stands near the door, getting her bearings, and an extremely drunken man wearing eye-liner and a matelot shirt sidles towards her and says,

'Really, my friend, that is just too, too good. Very realistic. But what the fuck have you done with your Adam's apple?'

Then he attempts to reach down between her legs, but she grips his wrist firmly and twists him around until he is facing away from her. He staggers off.

Clive is at the bar. He is sitting on a high stool, laughing and laughing as Albert runs his slender fingers up the side of his face, the inside of his leg, the width of his midriff. He leans forward and kisses Albert. They both laugh, and Clive stands briefly and shuffles his stool closer to Albert. Then they kiss again, but as they are kissing, Clive's eye wanders across the room until it comes to rest on Iris. He freezes, so that the kiss becomes a twisted sculpture, and whilst Iris is marvelling at its grotesqueness, the tableau melts and Clive's body slowly slumps away from Albert.

She walks up to them, and Clive says, 'Iris, darling, whatever are you doing here?'

She does not allow her lip or her voice to tremble as she replies, 'I simply thought you'd be interested to know that your wife has failed her audition, won't be playing Desdemona in the end-of-year production, and had hoped for some sympathy from her husband tonight.'

She is about to add, 'And now, gentlemen, I'll leave you to your important meeting,' when Albert snarls at her,

'Well, maybe you should have tried for Othello, rather than Desdemona.'

There is an ugly expression on his face.

'You certainly look right for that part at least,' he continues, 'though it seems that Clive doesn't find you very moor-ish.'

Albert laughs in a brittle way but rather than interrupting him, Iris waits until the hollowness of the sound he is making becomes embarrassing. Then she turns to Clive and says, 'We will not be seeing one another again. Do not come back to Fulham. Good night.'

As she leaves, Albert says loudly to her receding back, 'Clive darling, I always said that a beard wouldn't suit you.'

Iris takes a cab back to the flat. Time is short, but it is the work of moments to go through Clive's things and soon enough she finds the bunch of keys she needs. She puts on gloves, the darkest clothes and the largest hat she can find, and walks the mile to Albert's house off Lott's Road. The street is silent and empty, and she lets herself in quickly, goes into the kitchen, traces the gas pipe from the oven to the meter and wriggles at the connection for a few seconds until she hears a faint hiss. And as she leaves the house, she mutters under her breath,

'An honourable murderer,
One that loved not wisely, but too well.'

Clive never returns to Fulham.

V.

Iris goes on to endure a series of disappointments in the theatre, failing to win the sort of roles she had once hoped for. But she is not inclined to be a theatrical freak or novelty. If she cannot be cast, by the queer mafia that she now knows to be largely responsible for these things, into roles that suit her ambitions rather than her appearance, she will not be cast at all.

She slips into a variety of backstage jobs. Wardrobe, dresser, props. Her skills as a seamstress, learned from Miss Arthur, become more widely known, and she finds herself increasingly sought-after. For the first time in her adult life, she has a sense of being genuinely popular. She is invited to theatrical parties and, as gravity pulls her into the inner circle, she sees more of the behaviour she first witnessed at the Chaise d'Or. She is not comfortable with it at first – the echoes of Clive and his duplicity pain her – but this is the only circle she has, and it has glamour of a kind. Queers appear to adore her and though she cannot understand why this should be, she experiments with the new role until it fits her perfectly.

She becomes a sort of doyenne, advising the drag queens on their appearance, even helping to make their clothes. She is insulted the first time a man asks if he can borrow her shoes, but eventually she allows it and soon her wardrobe becomes a lending library. And as her 'boys' form pairs with each other, then split up and re-form in different configurations, as they argue and drink too much, as they have their triumphs, lose their jobs or their hair, Iris provides a reliable shoulder on which to laugh or cry. She becomes accustomed to the bitchiness, the unreliable friendships, the fact that companionship can disappear overnight when a new boyfriend is taken on, only to re-appear days or months later when he leaves or is ejected.

In many ways the fragile surface of it all suits her because, underneath the gin and the tinsel, there is a familiar despair to be found in this community of outsiders.

At a party one night, as she approaches a group of men she knows well, one of them says to her, 'And how's my favourite fruit fly this evening?'

She replies, with her trademark deadpan, 'Fruit fly? I haven't heard that one before.'

'Buzzing around the fruits,' the man replies. 'Attracted by their heady aromas. Feeding on their luscious juices.'

Another man adds, 'Or "Fag Hag", dear. You're still a little too young for that particular sobriquet but, as the poet said,

"At my back I always hear

Time's wing'd chariot hurrying near."'

Iris takes care not to show that she is goaded. She laughs and says, 'Well, given how withered the fruit is in this corner of the room, I shall buzz off to greener pastures.'

But as she is turning away one of the men, Robert, decides to launch a riposte.

'Before you go, I have a question,' he says loudly. 'What is it that makes a woman become a fruit fly? Is it a fear of real men, some dreadful, suppressed Freudian terror? Penis angst, perhaps?'

He rolls his eyes in a manner he imagines to be arch, before continuing. 'Or is it an inability to attract a straight man? Of course, there is another possibility; maybe you're really a queer man, trapped in a woman's body.'

'No, dear,' Iris replies, looking him up and down. He is plump and girlish. 'That would be you.'

There is a general hissing and meowing from some members of the group, a light round of applause from others. Iris has held her own, and is now free to leave gracefully.

Iris knows of Robert's allergy to nuts but decides not to act too quickly, lest any connection should be spotted by those who witnessed the scene. Several months later, his death is announced in *The Stage*, along with a fittingly short obituary. As Iris turns the page, she reflects to herself that she never liked the name Robert anyway.

VI.

Marty Schulman, a famous director, invites Iris to a private party at his flat in Marylebone. She is the only woman there, but despite her growing loathing for such events, she has her reasons for attending. It is her thirtieth birthday and Barry, her friend of the moment, has acquired a new beau and is consequently unable to celebrate the occasion with her at the dinner they had originally planned. More importantly, her host this evening is currently casting for a production of *Antony and Cleopatra*. Iris has not given up hope and surely, with her looks, the role of Cleopatra would be perfect for her?

She realises as Marty greets her that he is under the influence of some narcotic substance. He is renowned for his excessive lifestyle and it is rumoured that before the war, at Biarritz, he once spent over five thousand francs on cocaine in one night. But Iris can tell from his behaviour that this evening's drug is not cocaine but opium. She has seen the signs before, whilst nursing Miss Arthur.

She circulates, drinks champagne without mentioning to anyone that it is her birthday. Eventually, finding herself alone with Marty, she raises the subject of Cleopatra.

'Don't be silly, darling,' is his response. 'Everybody knows you can't act! And besides, the Antony I have in mind is only five foot six. You'd tower over him. My God, it would look like a drag revue! We'd have to put in some dance numbers! *Pas de chance*, I'm afraid. But maybe we can get you in to help with the frocks?'

Iris waits for a few minutes, then goes to his bathroom. Taking her gloves from her bag, she riffles through the medicine cabinet until she finds his powder, neatly measured into paper twists. She is familiar with the doses involved and it only takes a moment to combine two of the twists into one innocent looking bon-bon. It is just the right quantity to make him 'more comfortable'.

The production of *Antony and Cleopatra* is almost cancelled after Marty's death, but with Iris's encouragement, Barry agrees to take it on. Iris auditions and everybody is very complimentary, though in the end she has to be content with doing the frocks.

VII.

Iris takes a course at Pitman, and abandons the theatre. Soon, she is working as a Court Clerk, and through the uneventful years of her thirties and forties she sits, day after day, with the evidence of thousands of cases flowing from her ears to her fingers. After a while, she becomes one of the most experienced clerks in the service and she graduates to the Crown Courts, mostly Southwark and the Old Bailey. Here, she is exposed to the highest-ranking crimes. Fraud, violence, treachery and murder course down her arms every day until she does not hear the words any more. She has become a machine for transmitting this data from one place to another, taking it from the air and punching it onto paper tapes. But as she transmits, traces remain in her system. Lessons are learned from the mistakes of others and she comes to realise how lucky she is not to have been detected in any of her own little acts of punishment. Revenge, she learns, is a dish best eaten cold. Not because it tastes any better that way, but because no one can remember who was in the kitchen when it was first cooked up.

She cross-references what she has learned in court with an extensive study of famous cases where women have taken matters into their own hands. From Agrippina to Kate Webster, from the Countess Bathory to Mrs Vermilya, she examines not their motives, in which she has no interest, but their methods. And she concludes that they have all been guilty of a crime that is, in her eyes, far more serious than murder: they have all been careless. They have allowed their motives to cloud their ability to formulate an effective method, and this is why they have all been detected. And once detected, Iris knows, the chances of appearing before a jury as stupid as the one that acquitted Lizzie Borden are very slim indeed.

But she is briefly taken with the well-known case of Edith Thompson, who was found guilty of inciting her lover to kill her husband. Edith was careless, of course, but the case sets Iris thinking: the Perfect Punishment, as she likes to think of it, should be orchestrated but not committed by the person who has been wronged. And to be truly perfect, the person who actually commits the murder would not even realise that they were acting under the influence of a third party.

But Iris leads a quiet life these days. It has been a long while since anyone treated her disrespectfully and, with the faintest sense of regret, she realises that her new theories must, for now at least, remain academic.

VIII.

Iris grows more striking and less beautiful as she ages. Her bearing remains perfect but her face is harder now, and her makeup a little too pale for a woman of her age. Her hair has started to curl more tightly and she resorts to increasingly drastic methods of control until eventually she appears, from certain angles, to be wearing a hard, black helmet. On her forty-fifth birthday she tries, without success, to go blonde and is so upset with the result that for the first time since her sixteenth birthday she cannot bring herself to drink champagne. It is many weeks before she succeeds in returning her hair to a natural shade, and each day is a torture to her.

In the same year, her colleagues decide to put on a revue for their staff Christmas party. Iris declines to take an active part. She dislikes Norman, the auteur behind the event. Like her, he once had ambitions for a career in the theatre and his failed hopes now manifest themselves in a gruesome camp. Larry Grayson is popular on the television, and this brand of humour is now considered publicly acceptable, but Iris has grown to find it repulsive.

On the night of the production, she is horrified to find that one of the sketches portrays her, not as a court clerk, but as a judge. The joke centres on her haughty bearing and her blonde, wig-like hair. She braves it out beautifully.

Three years later, long after he has left the court service, Norman is found naked and quite dead at a 'beauty spot' in Hertfordshire. Iris has never been to Hertfordshire, and she counts this punishment as her finest achievement so far, though it was very difficult to arrange.

In court, the paper tapes are slowly phased out, replaced by magnetic reels and microphones. In 1983, at the age of fifty-six, Iris leaves the Old Bailey for the last time.

She has been careful with her money and has long-since moved from her tiny basement, which is now one of many properties she owns, into a charming house nearby. Her accountant has insisted that her property investments be held in an offshore nominee company, since there are tax advantages to be had from this structure. It is certainly not illegal, but ownership of the properties cannot be traced to her and it is her choice as to how and where the income and the capital gains are declared. Iris sees certain other potentialities in this arrangement.

She no longer needs to work, but she wants to. She takes a job as Practice Manager at a clinic in Earl's Court where, when the opportunity arises, she re-arranges used needles. There is so much disease about, and the incubation period is so long, that she knows she will never be discovered. Like many people, she sees the illness as a punishment, and she is happy to play her part in the enactment of justice.

IX.

Iris learns to play bridge. Her hair becomes grey, then blue, and finally age whittles the last vestiges of her mixed descent from her features.

She marries again. Phillip is a pleasant widower with two children who are kind to Iris, and for several years she is content. But in her seventy-second year Philip dies, naturally, of a heart attack. The children and grandchildren live abroad and Iris is lonely again, has time on her hands.

She decides to write a book about the history of London's theatreland and in this small way, she finds theatrical success at last. She begins, once more, to appear at thespian parties and soon Iris becomes something of an institution. Her wit and style are more in demand now than they ever were in the nineteen fifties, and she makes many new acquaintances.

In order to help her with the research required for her next project, she takes a course for 'Silver Surfers' and becomes an internet adept. She spends a great deal of time on-line.

Iris's second book, she has decided, will be an unveiling of the secret gay lives of some of the most famous actors of her generation. She is looking forward to setting their various records straight.

Her intended subjects now being dead, the internet provides her with an invaluable resource when it comes to tracking down old playbills and film credits. She uses email to contact people whose recollections might be of some use to her, then interviews them by telephone or sometimes, particularly for those now living abroad, via on-line chat.

The chat system, in particular, fascinates her. It offers possibilities for inventing and sustaining new identities that she finds extremely appealing, since she realises that she can now play any role she chooses. She explores the chat rooms more deeply, and as her curiosity and disgust lead her to places she had not originally anticipated, Iris discovers things about homosexuality that she never knew. Masters and slaves; bare-backers and bug-chasers; fetishists and perverts of every hue, bored on-line and up-for-it-now. Most of all, she realises that whatever their preferences and practices, however unacceptable and unnatural their behaviour and desires may be, these men have one thing in common: a form of risk-compulsion that has been made unfettered by the new technology. It took her three years to engineer a situation whereby Norman, from the court service, could lead himself to the death she had planned for him. But nowadays, the queers she has chatted to on-line will meet strange men in strange places at a moment's notice, and it occurs to Iris that one of her investment properties, untraceable to her, is currently empty.

As she taps away at her keyboard late into the night, aping the sexual distortions of her unseen partners in order to get further under their skin, learning their vocabulary and their strange abbreviations, chatting to them in private and in detail, Iris's revulsion towards these men grows. She sees that beneath the twisted personalities which have caused her so much grief in the past, behind the brittle façades, lie more deeply deviant natures than she had imagined.

The bi-curious boys and discreet married men she hates the most; there is betrayal implicit in their every self-description. She imagines wives and girlfriends, innocently sleeping whilst their men folk indulge these indecent obsessions, typing frantically with one hand in their dimly lit spare rooms.

*

One night, Iris is chatting to an unpleasant man when he suddenly says that he has to go now. Iris – or 'Kris', as she is now styling herself – asks him to stay just a little longer, and the man replies that to be honest, he is finding the conversation 'a little weird'. When Iris attempts to type a reply, she is met with a 'user unavailable' message. She has been jilted.

Iris is flooded with the cold rage that makes her feel most alive. She stares for a while at the scrolling list of suggestive pseudonyms on the screen in front of her.

It is time, she realises, to come out of retirement.

Pisspants
Sebastian Beaumont

Pisspants
Sebastian Beaumont

I stop the car by the bridge and get out onto the cinder-and-gravel drive. The bridge itself – concrete, with criss-crossed, riveted metal edgings – looks exactly the same. The river, too, is unchanged with its weir and pool flanked by beech and pine, though of course it looks smaller now that I am seeing it as an adult rather than as a twelve year old child. To the north, upstream, the river meanders through the old park. The only difference is the absence of the huge chestnut tree that stood at the first bend. How stupid to think it might still be there.

I smile with disbelief when I realise it's nearly thirty years since I last crossed this bridge, in the back of an Austin 1300GT, as I now recall, driven by my mother with frantic cheerfulness, at ludicrously high speed, and with utter disregard of the pitted drive. It was a white car with a black vinyl roof – a car I haven't thought of for years. It's strange how looking down at the river like this can spark off so many memories, like a cascade.

I look up towards the building that used to be the school. Turned first into an old people's home, then later into luxury apartments, it is now inhabited by people who have never known the bustle and chatter that rang from the old house's crenulated walls.

I am surprised by my reaction at seeing the school like this, in the distance, up the azalea-flanked drive. An odd, slightly hysterical feeling of horror shivers up my spine so that I am not sure whether I am about to burst into laughter or tears at the ghosts that I have come here to lay; at the sheer scale of what I endured – and survived – whilst I was here. I suppose I had anodised these feelings by tying them down too much with words. I remember saying to my partner, over dinner in one of the better Indian restaurants in Glasgow, 'I was relentlessly unhappy there', and sipping my lager and feeling, not even an echo of the emotion that I feel now, but a sort of lightness; a gladness at having been so completely released from my suffering. And every time I thought of Eaglesfield School, I could just label it with the words, 'I was unhappy there' and leave it at that. When I decided to train as a counsellor, I suppose a part of me was unconsciously trying to make the connection between those words and the feelings behind them.

My partner (also a counsellor) was clear that I still had unfinished business regarding Eaglesfield, and he'd encouraged me more than once to talk to someone about it as fully as I could. My supervisor was also interested in a certain unexcavated seam from my past, especially when I decided to specialise professionally in the area of bereavement, or more particularly, the bereavement of parents whose children die in childhood.

*

I go back to the car and drive up to the school. It has been tastefully converted, so that it still looks like a single dwelling. But there are too many different styles of curtains in the windows now, and different kinds of light fitting – I see a small, fussy chandelier in the large bay fronted room in the downstairs of the west wing, and minimalist faux Art-Deco fittings in the room above. When I was here in the early seventies it boasted only wooden shutters and those military white metal cone-shaped shades. And iron bedsteads, and horse-hair mattresses. And boys, of course, with incipient spots and the first trickles of testosterone.

I look up again at the window of what used to be the senior dormitory. It is the window where my nose was broken against the frame when Alan Devereaux, in high spirits, flung me from my bed; and there, below and slightly to the right, is the old toilet block where I nearly choked to death on my own vomit. I'd had my head pushed so far down the lavatory that I'd inhaled some of the flushing water. I see the window there – *that* window, the one that the senior boys sometimes used to climb from once the school had been locked up, to see if they could steal a kiss or two from the younger maids as they made their way back to the village. I can see that the frosted pane has been replaced with clear glass, and the room is now a kitchen. I can see utensils hanging by the window. I hope they've kept that wonderful stone flagging.

The toilet block has a major resonance for me, given the particular complaint from which I suffered – urinary incontinence. Because the condition was relatively mild, I was never allowed any special treatment (the kind of cheap straightforward disposable pads that would be recommended nowadays were still more than a decade away). Instead, I had to wear ridiculously bloated underwear, with an extra thick front panel. If only I'd been allowed to change this underwear daily, I'd have been okay, but 'normal' boys were expected to change their underpants only twice a week, and I was no exception. This meant that I spent two full days a week in a state that earned me my nickname of 'pisspants'. I'd tried, once or twice, to rinse my underwear out, but, because of the padding, I couldn't wring them out enough, so I would get damp stains which showed up clearly as darker stains on my light grey trousers.

In the summer holidays before I went to senior school, soon after my thirteenth birthday, I had a small operation on the sphincter at the exit of my bladder. All it took was a three millimetre incision and a single stitch to completely and permanently clear my condition. I was lucky, too, that there was no one from Eaglesfield at my next school, and so no one knew my old nickname. As I had no reputation to precede me, I discovered, to my surprise and great pleasure, that I could make friends easily and be a popular, well-liked pupil.

All I was left with, physically at least, was a tiny, keyhole scar a little below my navel. Years later, when my partner asked me about it, and I told him, and explained how my prep school life had been made such a misery by the bullying and mockery that arose from it, he actually cried and said, 'Children can be *so* cruel.'

'Not just children,' I told him. 'The headmaster thought I suffered from a weakness that required self-discipline, and even caned me once for smelling foul.'

*

I'm standing, looking at the toilet block, fascinated at how returning here can bring so much back, so vividly. Even the dark yew tree that shades the window looks unchanged, still trimmed to the same shape as it was all that time ago. I remember a fellow pupil explaining vaginas to me, illustrating his description using the plump red yew berries that, when squeezed, would ooze their clear slimy juice over our fingers, leaving us helpless with laughter and a kind of vague disquiet at our ignorance.

Lost in thought, I see a woman of indeterminate age – perhaps in her forties – coming into the kitchen. She sees me immediately and comes over to open the window, releasing the catch to push it open. As she leans forward, holding the perforated metal arm, I notice that it is the same sturdy metal window catch from thirty years before. Only the glass has been changed.

'Hello,' she says, 'can I help you?'

I smile, a little embarrassed.

'Not really,' I tell her. 'I used to go to school here.'

'That's all right,' she says, 'I could tell. We occasionally get ex-pupils coming up and looking at the place. Some of the other residents get a bit alarmed by it, but you all look so wistful, I don't see how you could ever be mistaken for burglars.'

I laugh, and she begins to close the window, saying, 'I can't let you into the building, I'm afraid, but feel free to have a wander in the grounds.'

I wave in reply, and walk back to the front of the school, and the gravel turning circle there, where we used to muster every Sunday for the walk to church.

The walk to church.

I was always being tripped, kicked or pushed into the hawthorn hedging on the lane between Eaglesfield and Middlebie, usually, but not exclusively, by either Alan Devereux or Michael Swift (by far the most handsome boy in the school). I was always nursing scratches, or the little, painful perforations made by the thorns.

Michael Swift! I haven't thought of him by name for years, though he's been present as a shadow all this time. Whereas Devereux was big and lugubrious and dumb, Swift was slender, elegant and intelligent, and even at the age of thirteen his looks were bordering on devastating. He knew that I was in thrall to him, too, in an involuntary way, and despised me because of it. He would join in any mockery of me with systematic cruelty.

My mattress was covered by a rubber sheet to protect it from my occasional bed-wetting. In the mornings, when this happened, Swift would strip the lower sheet away, and, whilst Devereux held me down, he would gingerly take the wet patch, bunch it up and force it into my mouth. When I tried to keep my mouth shut or turn my head away, he would stamp agonisingly on my foot until I cried out in pain. As soon as my mouth was open, he would force the wet cotton in, laughing triumphantly, before going off to wash his hands.

All this was deeply humiliating, but somehow the little things were even worse; the jibes and petty bullying – those agonising little punches that Devereux would deliver to my upper arm that incredibly never left bruises – and the way my classmates would join in and laugh when Swift had a go at me. This was worse because it was so constant. I suppose that was the thing, the continuous low-grade misery... And worse still was the pain of being friendless. Swift saw to that. And it was an effort for some of the boys, too, because I have a good sense of humour, and even with all the troubles that beset me, it came naturally to me to be friendly to those around me. But peer group pressure can be overwhelming.

When I think back on this, I feel a small and familiar surge of resentment against my parents. They knew how miserable I was at Eaglesfield, but they never thought to take me away and send me to a day school, where my bed-wetting and need for fresh daily underwear would not be an issue. No, my brother came here and loved it, and did well, so I was made to follow in his footsteps, even when he told my parents of my nickname (though he skirted the bullying side of things). When *I* mentioned bullying to my father, in the early days, before anything more serious had happened, he showed genuine concern, but said that I must learn to look after myself, and being pushed into hedges now and then wasn't *so* bad. He himself had been bullied a little at school and he'd eventually become a close friend of the boy who'd bullied him.

'You see,' he said, 'you can take it all too seriously if you're not careful.'

*

I walk on past the wide, bay-windowed frontage of the school. The Virginia creeper has long gone, but there is an odd mottled look to some of the stonework to show where it used to be. I carry on past the two tennis courts, which are in excellent condition now, and back down the drive towards the river. The river used to be my only consolation whilst I was a pupil here. Cheerful, somehow. Bright and babbling. Even when in spate and gushing with brick red water from the cloying clay-filled soil, there was a majesty to the water, and a power too. It was hardly surprising that the chestnut tree, on the corner of the sharp bend down by the bridge, was so in danger of falling. Every time the river flooded, a few inches of bank would be washed away, and a few more inches of roots would be undermined.

In my final year at Eaglesfield, Mr Jamieson, the maths master, and the only person at school that I liked, decided to make it his mission to save that tree. He would get groups of boys down there, digging a trench to cut off the bend in the river, and to make a rough dam of stones to divert the flow. It wasn't a big river, so I don't suppose it was too impossible a task, but even when he'd got his diversion flowing a little, and had packed piles of stones in the cavities beneath the exposed tree roots, when the next flood came, it would all be washed away, almost as though no attempt had been made at all.

Mr Jamieson liked me, and would challenge any bullying whilst he was around. He clearly felt sorry for me, and whilst I was grateful for this up to a point, there is something a little desultory about being pitied by someone you like. Still, he used to spend time with me exploring the river, talking about the strata of sediment and shingle that were revealed, or looking for the kingfisher that lived up in the bank by the red scar formed by an old landslide.

But I could never join in with the dam building projects. I simply suffered too much if I tried – I would be splashed, or stones would be 'accidentally' thrown in my direction, so that ultimately Mr Jamieson would have to send me away, for my own safety.

That was how I happened to be wandering on my own over by the bridge and the tumbling cascade of the weir one Saturday afternoon, watching and listening to the endless plunging of the water into the pool there. I was aware of Mr Jamieson and his posse in the distance, and saw that he straightened, looked at his watch and shouted to the boys to stop what they were doing and make their way back up to the school. Being by the waterfall was the only place where it was not possible to hear the ringing of the bell summoning pupils for tea.

For safety's sake I waited a couple of minutes until the boys had left the river, and then went over to see how they'd got on. When I got to the bank, Devereux was still there, seven or eight feet below me, trying to move a large stone into place at the head of the dam. He looked up as I turned away, but seemed disinterested in my presence. I turned towards the school but hadn't gone more than ten yards before I heard the sound of someone sprinting up behind me. Before I knew it, I'd been felled by one of Devereux's legendary rugby tackles. I struggled furiously, and nearly escaped his grasp, but once he'd got my arm up behind my back, there was nothing I could do.

Although I am not, and never was, a coward, I'd learned from hard experience, that once trapped like this by the physical strength of a stronger boy, the best course of action is to allow them to have their will. In this case, a dunking in the river. Devereux was not an imaginative boy, and dunkings like this were about the limit of his inventiveness. If I just let him do it, then he never gained the satisfaction he might have done if he'd won some kind of struggle.

As he was pulling me down the bank to where the dam was, he slipped. It was, after all, awkward trying to get down the slope with me in front of him like that. I fell, too, but only to the water's edge. He went over half sideways, grabbing at a clod that came away in his hand, and managed somehow to hit his head against the large stone that he'd been labouring over a few moments earlier. He immediately went limp, and came to rest in the water, which was only perhaps a foot deep at that point, though flowing fast.

Without a moment's hesitation – and I wondered about my reflexes many times after that – I leaned forward and pushed his head underwater. It was easy, there was no resistance. He never regained consciousness. I could tell when he died, because there was a strange flutter of involuntary muscle spasm that ran through his body for perhaps ten or fifteen seconds before he became absolutely still.

As soon as I was sure he was dead, I stayed down by the waterside and ran, half-crouched, along to the bridge and the weir. Then, I made my way through the woods on the far side of the drive, up by the tennis courts, and wandered to the changing rooms. As I got there, Mr Jamieson was hurrying the boys along, and he smiled at me and said, 'Have you been down by the river?'

I shook my head.

'I was in the woods, sir.'

'So, you haven't seen Devereux, then?'

'No,' I said.

He nodded and looked at his watch.

'I'll have to go down and chase him along,' he said, 'blast the boy. What a nuisance.'

He looked round and shouted, 'Right, everyone, I'll expect to see you changed and inside within the next five minutes.'

Then he left to look for Devereux.

In all the fuss that ensued, it didn't really bother me that Devereux was dead. What I bitterly regretted was the effect his death had on Mr Jamieson. He was the duty master that day, and so had been responsible for the boys. He was the person who took the blame. And someone, after all, always has to take the blame. It broke him. Ruined his career. Back then, he'd seemed old to me, but now I think about it, he can't have been as old as I am now – which is to say forty-three. But he aged twenty years overnight, and left only a few days later in a hired car with all his luggage, and we had a supply teacher in for maths after that.

We weren't told anything at first, but when Devereux didn't put in an appearance at tea and two police cars and an ambulance turned up, it was clear that something terrible had happened. It wasn't possible to see that part of the river from the school, but Matron told us when we went up to bed that they'd cordoned off the whole river bend where the dam was, and admitted – after a chorus of questions – that, yes, Devereux had drowned. His bed, by the window, seemed particularly empty that night.

There was no suspicion. The boys weren't even questioned, except in the most cursory way to establish that Devereux had lagged behind at the dam, trying to move a large stone. Nobody thought to talk to me.

*

I walk down the drive and think of Devereux, and of how he was someone's child; of how he must have been mourned by *someone*, even if not me. And as I think this, I feel a desolate beat somewhere inside me, and maybe a flicker of regret, but alongside this feeling, I also have a further vivid memory:

I am in the wash room upstairs. It is nearly lights-out and I am brushing my teeth. I am the last person there, and as I put my toothbrush and toothpaste away, I am grabbed from behind by Devereux and Swift. I struggle, but it is useless. Swift has a plastic tumbler in his hand and, whilst Devereux holds me, Swift goes to fill it at the basin. He comes back and tries to make me drink, but I refuse. Devereux twists my arms agonisingly and Swift stamps on my foot again and again until I give in and drink the tumbler of water. And then another tumbler. And another. And another. I know that, although I shall probably wake up once or twice in the night to go to the toilet, what is happening now will make me wet the bed even more than usual and that Swift will stuff my sheet into my mouth in the morning. He will have the pleasure of humiliating me in front of all the boys in the dormitory. I can see him laughing at the prospect of it.

It's odd but, until I returned here today, I'd completely forgotten about being forced to drink water like that – the 'water torture', as Swift called it. I was subjected to it four or five times in that final year, and Matron was concerned that my bed-wetting was getting worse, and told my parents that perhaps I needed to see a psychologist.

But it never came to that because, one evening, when I was in charge of tidying up, I was walking through the classrooms, checking that all the chairs were on the desks and all the floors swept, when I heard a noise from the toilet block. I went through to see what it was, and I saw Swift, dangling from the window. He'd obviously climbed out to see if he could talk to one of the maids, and on climbing back in, the blunt spike of the window catch had caught his collar as he jumped down. His shirt had been pulled tight around his neck and he was choking.

When he saw me, he beckoned desperately, and managed to whisper with a strangulated husk, 'Quick! Quick, help me!'

I walked up to him. I didn't feel triumph at seeing him helpless. It gave me no pleasure that the tables had been turned like this. But – just as I had acted spontaneously with Devereux – without thinking, I leaned forward and, taking hold of Swift's ankles, I pulled down as hard as I could.

He let out one small squeak, and his arms jerked up as I pulled, forced by his shirt, so that he looked almost crucified.

I looked once at his handsome face, now hideously bloated and pop-eyed, and I walked from the room and went up to wash and get ready for bed.

This time I *was* questioned by the police, but, again, there was no reason for them to be suspicious. The local paper had a field day about it – even *The Scotsman* and the *Glasgow Herald* ran stories. Well, it was quite a tale – boys being allowed to play down by the river unsupervised, and having the opportunity to climb in and out of dangerous windows without anyone knowing...

It finished the school. Within days more than half the boys had been taken away. There were only four weeks left of the summer term, and so the place limped on until the Common Entrance exams had been taken. I was due to leave anyway, and on the day I took my last exam, my mother came to collect me and drive me back to Glasgow. The headmaster's wife saw us off, but there was hardly anything that could be said.

My mother asked me, as we set off, 'Did you know either of the boys?'

'Not really,' I told her.

*

I am now standing on the bridge, looking down at the river. As I said, the chestnut tree has long gone. There is nothing to show that it was ever there. I look down into the water, it is summer and the water is shallow and bright.

My whole life has been geared towards understanding what I did here. Becoming a counsellor was part of that. Counselling parents who have lost children has been a part of that. I walk to the other side of the bridge and look down at the waterfall, and the pool below the weir. I realise I cannot blame myself for what I did. I also realise, with a shock, that I do not accept any blame. I have suffered enough.

Takey's War
Perry Brass

Takey's War
A Story from *Noir* New York in the 1970s
Perry Brass

Every place that my lips touched his body, I wanted it to burn slightly; to smoke.

"You glitter, you know?" I said. "You really glitter."

He did. Perspiration glittered off him in the dim lamplight, from his smooth back and then down onto his legs. He seemed covered in lustrous honey. I stroked him all the way down his back, to the white creases in the bend of each knee.

"Is sex okay?" I asked nervously.

"Sure," he answered. "I want to have sex with you. You know that." He turned towards me and picked up my cock from where it rested in the wild strands of a Greek goatskin rug. It sprang to life, getting very hard as his fingers moistened the tip with his saliva. He placed my fingers in his mouth. It was very warm. Each finger ran a velvet circle around his tongue. He guided them in, one by one, and finished with my thumb.

I turned him on his stomach and greased his ass, then carefully pushed my dick into him. He was used to much rougher stuff. "You don't have to be so easy, man. I'm not some old lady."

I agreed and really – as they say – let him have it. It was wonderful letting go inside him. I came in great hot jets. He could feel me rumbling through him like a volcano exploding into a dark ocean. He only cooled me down without quenching me. I wanted to eat each hair on his prick. I ran my tongue all the way down the ridge of flesh on the inner side of his penis that ended at his scrotum, then worked my way back up it again. I licked the mushrooming head of his cock, then sucked him off hungrily.

He tasted like rainwater, incredibly fresh, slightly salty and thickened. I had to pee. I got up and put my hand up to his mouth. "Don't move," I joked with him. "I'll be right back. Scout's honor."

I stayed hard even over the bowl. I almost had to squat to aim right. My legs shook a bit from excitement. If he were mine – if that were possible – I'd keep him in my eyes, in the depth of my mind, as if he were a rare jewel, an emerald I carried with me on a Prince Albert. I heard some noise near the door. Probably my neighbors; what a noisy bunch they were. I peed quickly and then heard a car engine backfire like thunder in the front of the building. When I returned to the living room where he was lying on the flotaki, I saw two hoods leaning over him.

One of them turned to me. He wore a black raincoat pulled up all the way to his nose. A gray driving hat covered his brow. All I could see of his face were a pair of riveting dark eyes. Another man, turned away from me, was similarly dressed.

"Don't come any closer," the first warned. "We don't get a bonus for two."

They charged out as I, naked and shocked, watched them. The door slammed.

I dove into the young man – and jumped back. They had blown a lot of the top of his head off. I became dizzy; neither my stomach or brain could hold this. What would the cops say if they found me blacked out over a young man's body, buck naked?

A minute later I was able to calm down enough to throw a bathrobe over him. It was only natural. I didn't want this beautiful creature to leave my house so soon. I pulled on some pants, found a shirt, and put a light jacket over it. There was nothing for me to carry in the house, but I remembered that my neighbor kept a small revolver in a desk in his living room. It was kept in a drawer with his other important papers: his will, some engraved Chrysler Motors stock certificates, and his gym membership. He was weekending in the Hamptons and I was supposed to feed his cat. The cat, all eyes and tail, was glad to see me. I found some small cans on the redwood counter in the kitchen, scooped out something that smelled fishy, and then went through the desk.

The Inferno, as its name implied, was the club of the Damned, if not the damned moment: huge, with several levels of assorted rooms.

Although the sun was edging up onto the horizon, it still wasn't too late for the crowd who hung out there. The music was like heroin. It ran through your blood, leached into your brain and finally settling into your dreams. Wild, repetitive disco dreams: you do the same Jerk and Hustle over and over again. I paid some money to a large, pear-shaped man inside the door . He took it mechanically. I could hardly breathe because of the smoke in the air: asthma troubles since childhood. I asked the door creep where Mr Crewe was. "He's in the back. Wha'cha want him for?"

"I'm a friend of Takey's. John Takey."

"That one? He left Crewe, y'know? Crewe don't go for that, not one bit."

"I've got a message from Takey."

"Sorry, buddy. Mr Crewe never takes messages from the dead."

"How'd you know John Takey's dead?"

"Might as well be. They leave, then they try to come back. But Crewe don't want 'em back, so he treats 'em like they're dead. I'll take you to Crewe. You can talk to him yourself."

Mr Crewe was in the back room with two of his other bouncers. A slender young boy walked in, handed Crewe a cup of black coffee, and quietly walked out. They continued watching the floor on closed circuit monitors. I wanted Crewe to myself. "You a friend of Takey's?" he asked me. I nodded. "Nice boy, he was."

"Was?" I asked.

"He left."

"But I hear they come back," I said.

"Some try, but not Takey."

"Why not?"

He took a long swallow of the coffee, then blew some smoke from a black cigar into my face. I had to hold myself back from coughing.

"How should I know? Takey was different, that's all. I admit he was a looker. Some guys when they yank out your heart, they leave a little something for you in return. But Takey wanted it all."

"Maybe he deserved it," I said.

He drank some more of the coffee.

"You were smitten, weren't you, buddy?"

I couldn't answer. I was afraid I'd fall apart. I had wanted Takey the first time I had seen him, hoped so much for him; then I had him finally naked on my flotaki rug.

I looked into Crewe's face. There was a slight gloss of tears in his eyes; hard to find in a tough guy, but easy to see why Mr Crewe was hurt enough to kill.

Crew relit his cigar and snuffed out the match. "Like I said, he was a different kind of kid. Even, special."

He aimed more smoke at me.

"Very different," I said, pulling the pistol out from the inside pocket of my jacket.

Crewe did not blink. "Why don't you put that thing down, before one of my boys turns you into peanut butter?"

He smirked at me and my jaw hardened.

"Because," I answered, "I want to blow your brains out like you did John Takey's."

"You think I'd waste a contract on a punk like him? Think so? Sure, Takey had a real kind of class. I was crazy about him, but he was the wrong kid to be crazy about. Even I knew that."

My hand started shaking; I wanted to squeeze the trigger so badly that I could taste gunpowder in my mouth. I wanted to be done with it. Crewe saw my muscles twitch.

Crewe shook his head.

"They've sent a queen to do a man's work," he said blandly.

"Shut up, asshole!" I shouted, then butch as possible, added: "Or I'll clean out your pipes from the top drawer."

His men edged up behind me. Either I had to sink their boss, or I wouldn't be around to finish the next sentence. They had the drop on me. Crewe and I both realized it.

Crewe pushed his balding head forward on his thick neck. His tanned complexion looked half olive oil and half whiskey; part Florentine and part the Boston where he'd grown up.

He smiled knowingly, then let out a little chuckle.

"Let me give it to you straight, buddy. If anyone did it, his old man did. I knew the sonovabitch years ago. Big Army colonel. Old-school Irish Catholic–col. Andrew Patrick Takey – an unfortunate example of the breed. Hell, I'm Catholic and screw boys left and right. I just don't go nuts over it."

He took another sip of the coffee, then continued:

"The old man knew John was working here, so he came over one night acting like he was going to stick the FBI on me. Shit, we've had vice presidents in here. Well, one vice president, anyway. I admit John Takey didn't last that long with us, but, buddy, it had to be his old man. He did that famous 'My son the faggot' routine. Christ, how that bores me! Why can't fathers ever learn that you can love your son, even if he's not the All-American kid you thought he was, or should be? Listen, boys –" I lowered my gun; I knew he was telling the truth. You don't chuckle the way he did when a gun's pointing at you, unless you're telling the truth "– let this nice gentleman out of here. He's had a hard blow t'himself. Come back another time, sir, and tell 'em Mr Crewe knows you. They'll let you in, and give you a drink on me!"

I left and the evening felt as if it had collapsed around me. I felt hungry; stress did that. I grabbed a cup of bad coffee and a jelly doughnut in a diner frequented by leather boys in S & M jackets with dyed-blond, stylishly cut hair. None of them seemed real to me; as I finished the jelly doughnut, I remembered how sweet John Takey tasted all over and that he never made you feel cheap, or that he wasn't worth any effort necessary to get to him. I smiled, thinking: it's funny how little real substance our life contains. Takey had that thing, that absolutely real thing I was drawn to. And now... people die as suddenly in life as they do in the movies. Or is that the other way around?

Who can explain it? I wasn't crazy about sadism in art. I used to turn away from the screen at the sight of pain. But writers, I knew, were not like other people. We bled deeper. I looked up Andrew Takey's name in the phone book. I hadn't expected to find it listed, but there it was in black and white. He was drunk when he answered.

"I'm sorry to be this way," he slobbered. "I'm not used to drinking so late. You tell me you want to talk about my son? Sorry, sir, but I don't want to talk about him."

"Then he might as well be dead," I said, lighting a cigarette in the phone booth. It was late, and I wondered what I was doing out there in the damp morning, while John Takey lay under a bathrobe in my apartment. That dampness was hell on my asthma and I should not be smoking, but truthfully nicotine did calm my nerves.

"Can I see you tonight?" I said to the old man. "About John?"

"I told you I didn't want to talk about him."

"That's all right. I'll do the talking," I said, and hung up.

I took a cab to his address. It was in an old townhouse over by the river. Not in a great part of town, but I'd lost any sense of fear. The old man, dressed in a grayed undershirt and an old pair of khaki pants, let me in. His parlor-floor apartment, which was spacious, looked like he had never really lived in it. Books were still in cardboard boxes, and garbage and dust were piled up all over the place. The colonel was obviously a pig: the sins of the fathers, I thought... but what a horrifying sin that any son had to die like that. I was getting edgy again from anger gurgling up inside me. Suddenly, I wanted to pull down the old man's baggy pants, fuck him in the ass, then kill him. It wasn't a tidy thought in this filthy apartment, but it was a feeling I could not keep down any more than my anger.

He handed me a grimy glass of watered Scotch, filled like it was iced tea.

"You a faggot, too?" he asked, once I had sunk into a heavy chair covered in peeling fake horse hide.

"You put things nicely, Colonel."

"Sorry. I didn't mean it to be mean. My son is."

"Is?"

"Sure is, unless he's gone over to the other side and become normal. He's all right." He began to drool. "I loved the boy. I want you to know that."

"So did I."

He looked at me through red, swollen eyes that were half closed.

"No, you didn't. Not like I did. In the Army, believe me, you're never very far away from fags." His face squeezed itself together like an old crab. "You just wanted his dick."

"You're right," I admitted. "Whatever way I loved him, it sure wasn't the way you did. For me to love him, he had to be alive."

His tired eyes jumped out at me, like there was a bayonet waiting inside them. It had to have been him: I could tell the way he looked at me with that glinting edge of pure hatred, sprung from its holster of fear.

I'd seen that expression too many times.

"Where are your two goons?" I demanded.

"What goons?" What are you talking about?"

"The ones who killed your son."

"You mean their brother?" he replied. "You think my two boys killed their own brother?"

"I saw it!" I shouted. "I saw them kill your son!"

A smile on his wrinkled face parted its way through a veil of whiskey and contempt.

"Life is a war, mister. You learn that in the Army. I had three sons, two a credit to me. But the third – I used to ask myself why did God give him to me. Even as a kid, he was smart but was never what I wanted. I had to make myself love him and I did. It was all a part of God's will, but –"

There was a silence you could have eaten and it would have poisoned you. I wanted to say, "But what?" Then –

"God Almighty allowed my two sons to come back from Viet Nam where they fought, while John boogied or buggered or whatever you guys do. They came back and then I had to explain to people why my third son hadn't gone. That's when I said, 'Isn't it time, boys, we finished this?' But why –" he took a sip of scotch "– why in God's name didn't they finish you, too?"

"Jesus!" I cried like any decent father should have. But there was no remorse in him, at least that he showed. How could Takey have come from such a nest? The old man was so passive, like something you'd put on weeds to kill them: blameless. Everything was caused by a thing outside him. The Army. The war in Viet Nam. And sex, I was sure. His son's forbidden kind of sex. There was a war against John Takey, and boys who were like him. What a war John must have fought. A whole lifetime of war.

No wonder he said I didn't need to take it easy.

I got to my feet and pulled the gun out. He didn't even have a moment to wipe that smile of contempt from his face. It was locked on it, and only a bullet would change it. We were so close when I pulled the trigger that the colonel's brains splashed against the wall. The body fell back. Then I fired several more rounds, until his neck looked like a severed pipe gushing with blood.

The two sons bolted in from another room. They'd been sleeping, and were only half dressed. Pasty-looking young turds, their faces looked like vultures, even down to almost identical balding heads. They saw the old man's body, then me.

"We'll get you, too!" one screamed with that sharp yipe of carrion birds.

I looked at them. All of them were creatures of filth.

"Like you did John Takey?"

"No, like we'll get all you queers," the other one said. His was the voice from my apartment. It was deeper and more threatening. But I had my gun on them, and they knew it. I backed out quickly from the room and did not stop racing until I was back in my apartment, breathless and terrified. What had I done? I was just crazy about a young man, that was all.

His body lay under the bathrobe, where I'd left it. I uncovered it and ran my hand slowly over his cold, silken chest. I knelt and cried. Nothing now about him revolted me, only saddened me. I called the police and told them that I'd passed out after what had happened. I didn't get to see anything of John's murderers, only their raincoats and something of their eyes. "It's drugs," the detective explained. "Stuff like this happens all the time." He shook his head and I knew that any further investigation of John Takey's death was as finished as he was.

I had to close off my apartment. I couldn't live in it any more. John's inquest was brief, but the tabloids got hold of the story and plastered my name and picture all over them. I was ready to go nuts, which only showed me who my friends were. A few stuck with me, but most split like flies after a flushing.

I was cleared of any part in John's death. The colonel's demise was determined to be a suicide – yes, even with four shots in his head! There were people in high places who knew about the colonel's family and his violent sons, and they wanted to keep it all very hush-hush. I didn't implicate the two boys, because I didn't want to swing for Andrew Takey's murder. Believe me, I'd already paid enough for John's.

I had to leave town. I took a plane for Lisbon. It seemed like a good place to dry out emotionally inside. After take off, I was afraid that I would look across the aisle and see one of those brutal, pale faces staring back at me. Maybe I should have tried someplace farther. Nepal? Maybe... Malibu. Someplace where you can get lost, and no one bothers to come after you. I put a grip on myself and ordered one of those canned cocktails and sipped it slowly. Its sharp alcoholic warmth spread through my body.

I remembered John Takey's long silky neck and slender build. My tongue ran over my lips, and I remembered his tongue in my mouth. I could feel the small tender domes of his nipples, then his cock. I closed my eyes and had this longing for him that you can only know when something that sparkles with beauty is taken from you. Lisbon, yes, I thought: filled with handsome, dark-eyed men. We were now over the ocean into the night, and I realized that my life was starting all over again. Soon my old life would be forgotten, washed away, like a package of old shirts loosely tied with string and dropped blindly out of this plane over the receiving water.

The Collection Box
Scott Brown

The Collection Box
Scott Brown

'God, my children, did not say that homosexuality was a sin.' Harry stood back holding his hands up in surrender and shaking his head to affirm his statement. The congregation shook their heads in agreement. Taking in a lung full of fresh church air he stepped forward once more to the pulpits edge and continued. 'God, my children, was not homophobic. Homophobia is a prejudice. God Almighty was not a prejudiced being.' Harry's voice rose as his words trailed off. Raising a hand out before him, his finger pointed across the room, pointing accusingly to anyone who should think about disagreeing with him. The passion, the anger, the love, the desire, that's what they came for, it was a show, it was reinvented religion and they loved it. They loved it all, but they loved the Reverend Harry O'Leary above all else. His eyes cast across his flock, their heads bobbing like a sea, they agreed, of course they agreed. They believed it and so did Harry. Love is love and that's what God wanted, happiness. It wasn't specific, it wasn't cross-gender. It was love, love of any kind.

Clearing his throat and coming to the end of the days sermon, he gripped the pulpits sides once more and projected himself to his full capacity. 'Gay, straight, pink or yellow, rest assured that God will love you so long as you harm no others.' Harry's arm shot forward and his fist clenched firm, he drove his point home and was met by more affirmative nods and a few quiet cheers and hallelujahs which agreed with him.

'Children. Do not sin. Do not harm others. Be a loving member of this community and God *will* repay you.' The 'you' echoed around the great church walls, the acoustics always beautiful, his voice climbing the walls and entering the soul of the congregation, it was part of the magic, part the theatre. Stepping back, he smiled and waited as they buzzed with new joy and life in their eyes, they were happy, they were content. The Reverend Harry O'Leary gave them something. His congregation grew each week, he took that as credit for his services. The gay community assembled *en masse* in his little church, listening to his humble sermon, joining in his thankful prayers and simply loving the theatre that he provided. Harry had turned the little church into something of a phenomenon in under a year and of that he was more than proud.

He gazed across the sea of faces, the men, the women, the couples, the singles. The straight ones who loved it, the gay ones who needed it. He could see it in their eyes – even from here. Hope. Belonging. Family. They wanted it, they needed it and he so enjoyed giving it. His life as a servant was all he had wanted. Harry gave his all every day of the week, and on a Sunday he gave that little bit more. He was the priest to the gay community. The *Gay Times* double-page spread had more than confirmed that to the world and had certainly done wonders for his parish.

'Children.' Harry stepped forward for a final time. The noise cut off as they noticed his deeply sad face, his quiet voice, embarrassed almost. His eyes skipped guiltily across the rows of faces, the sorrow inside him being radiated into their souls. Braving a shallow smile he cleared his throat and continues: 'Before Ian Jarvis steps up to close today with "Like a Prayer", can I just ask you all to keep in mind the church roof?' Harry pointed upwards to the perfectly good-looking roof. The congregation followed the finger and agreed that it needed changing, it was sagging, he had told them that, it was just so very costly. 'You have all been most generous in the past, what with the lawns and the donations to the charities, not forgetting the changing of the windows and the Santa project at Christmas. I have already thanked you all for the repairs to my quarters.' He nodded his thanks again, looking truly humbled and every one of the congregation felt proud for their effort. They had given something back and the Reverend appreciated that, it made them feel worthy, their disposable income only slightly dented by their time at church. 'But the roof,' he continued with pain in his eyes, 'the poor roof, is in danger of falling. The church will be ruined. Finished. Worship over. The coffers are gone. We have no money, soon we will have no church.' The words echoed around again as he raised his voice, the point was made: 'I need you to dig deep, children. Very deep. The roof is not cheap, you need to help this church run my friends. You need to invest in God as he has invested in you.' Stepping back, he smiled. 'God needs you now. I hope you can help.' He grasped the sides of the pulpit once more. 'The collection box will be where it always is. At the back, on the way out, right beside where I will be standing. God bless you all. Ian?' Harry stepped down the three steps to the pulpit as Ian Jarvis stood at the alter to the church and faced the congregation, his excitement and honour clearly showing. Harry had done his job, the threat of taking every thing away from them would be enough to ensure huge donations over the next few weeks.

As Ian began his religious Madonna remix and the congregation joined in Harry moved around the side of the church and took his place by the large donation box at the door. He stood there to say goodbye, the fact that he was beside the box prompted people to put that little bit extra in, it also made sure that everybody put something in – however small, pennies and pounds. Five pounds was usually the minimum donation, and they knew that. To be invited to his house for Wednesday supper you had to be one of the ten top donators for that week, they knew that too, and competition was stiff. Gay people are very clever, Harry knew that, he knew to play people off against each other, especially those with large disposable incomes, that's why he had such a good thing going on. The congregation in turn knew that Harry's eyes were everywhere, and that he knew exactly who put in how much and how often.

'Thank you, Father. That was beautiful.' Ten pounds in the box and a smile from Harry.

'Thank you, David.' He nodded a curt thank you

'Father. Perfect, just perfect.'

A hundred pounds and a dinner invite. 'Thank you, Aaron, I'll see you in the week for dinner.'

'Oh, that'd be wonderful, Father. Oh, oh, I'm going to cry.'

'There's no need, Aaron, it's only dinner.' And if you'd been more generous in the past you would have been to dinner before now. A smile and handshake ended that conversation. Gary Downs snuck out without a donation and was clear down the path before Harry called after him.

'Gary?' Harry trotted down the steps, leaving his post, and of course the way clear for others to escape without paying, donating.

'Did you call, Father?' Gary knew he had been rumbled, Harry could tell by the way the man had stopped in his tracks stone dead.

'You don't feel the need to help us buy a new a roof for the church you use?' Harry put on the hurt face.

'I must've forgotten, Father.' Gary dug into his pocket and pulled out two ten-pound notes.

'I'll take them in for you, my child, and pray to God for the saving of your poor memory.'

'Thank you, Father, that'd be very kind.'

'Bye. Bye, bye. Yes, thank you, bye.' Harry smiled and nodded at most of the congregation as he passed back up the steps to the church and back inside. Back into the dark church, back into his home, his work, his life. Scary St Mary's, that's what they called it, and that's where he spent all of his time. Only two or three hangers-on left inside now as he looked around. Harry slotted the twenty pounds inside the box with the rest of the money and pushed the box to the side. So much to do, he hated hangers-on, for one they might steal his money. You can't trust anyone now days.

'Father, could you tell me how much it is to use the church for a wedding? I hope to be tying the knot with Andrew and we need to get things moving.'

Ryan stood before Harry, beaming with sunshine. Harry was so happy for them. Two of his original congregation, coming together.

'Oh Ryan, that's beautiful, I'm so happy for you both.' Harry leant forward and kissed him on the cheek, noting that he still hadn't made a donation today. 'The church is a thousand pounds.' Harry held his hands up in surrender. 'I can't do anything about that, rates come from above.' He laughed for a second at his own private joke. 'Well not above, you know, God above.' Another chuckle. 'But from the boss, if you know what I mean.' Harry's Irish accent made Ryan laugh; it always did. His cheeky Irish humour was why half the congregation loved him, the next quarter found him a beautiful speaker, the blarney in him, and the other quarter found him so sexy and to die for. A beautiful, well-spoken, interesting Irish priest who was openly gay, what more could a gay congregation want? 'But what I can do is reduce my fee for you?' He touched Ryan's arm and winked as his voice sank to a whisper. 'You are two of my favourite children here at St Mary's.' Ryan got close and nodded. 'I'll charge you no more than four hundred pounds. I normally charge five hundred. Now how's that?' He stood back, still holding Ryan's arm. Ryan smiled.

'If it wasn't because you're such a wonderful priest, Father O'Leary, then I would say it was daylight robbery, but it's you and we all know you're a man of God, and I'll tell you what, it's a bargain.' Ryan shook the priest's hand.

'Well, you both drop around sometime and look at the dates for the big day.' He smiled again and took Ryan in his arms. 'I'm just so happy for you both. I knew it would work.' He pushed Ryan back to arm's-length and then motioned for him to get close so he could hear what the priest had to say. 'Just so as you know. There have been some problems.' He whispered again, so that Ryan got really close. Secrets with the priest, who could resist? 'We can't accept cheques.' He nodded and frowned, crossing himself at the same time, his voice again low. 'I have to have all of the money in cash. Someone here, in the church, no names, gave me a cheque that bounced and we lost the money.' Harry stood back and pulled a face of disgust. 'Robbing the church. Robbing God.' He nodded with anger.

'No.' Ryan was shocked. Harry only continued to nod solemnly.

'I could say no more other than once bitten.' He moved back, eyes closed, head still shaking.

'Absolutely, Father. I had no idea.' Ryan touched the Father's arm and smiled.

'I'm sorry.' Harry forced another smile out.

'Speaking of money, I should get this donation box inside and locked away.' Harry sighed and realised the box was heavy with notes. 'The poor roof is so far away.' His shoulders slumped in feigned depression.

'Oh, I haven't put anything in yet.' Ryan pulled out three notes and slid them into the box.

'Had you not? I didn't notice. God bless you, Ryan, and drop by in the week now.' Harry smiled and, as Ryan left, waved him off down the steps and then closed and locked the door behind him. It was still a house of God, but the doors were no longer open day and night. Everyone had to be careful, especially with the bashing and the robbing nowadays.

'That was a bloody good sermon, Father,' Chris said, holding the door open to the priest's office.

'Chris, this is a church – will you not swear.' Harry sat the collection box down on his desk, opened the drawer and took out his tin where his personal money was kept.

'Sorry, Father.' Chris sat down opposite the priest, suitably chastised.

'Well, don't keep swearing, that's all I'm saying.' Harry raised his hand to close the subject as he always did. He looked at the blond kid, his tight black jeans, his fitted black shirt, the scuffed shoes and the crucifix around his neck that sat on a thick silver choker. Harry licked his lips as the kid sat across from him. The blond dishevelled inch-long hair. The pretty, unspoilt face – that seventeen-year-old face probably not even shaven yet, wrinkle free, worry free, life free, no elements, no fears, just innocence – all finished off with sea-blue eyes. The impure thoughts he had about the organ player were unforgivable, unimaginable, but so very desirable. He was on a tightrope, that kid, he could be played or be a player, his life was ahead of him and in his hands without him knowing. Harry sighed and stood, took out the fifty pounds Chris got for playing the organ and sweeping up five times a week, and walked around the desk, his black robes falling around him, the eternal reminder of his position. As he got close to Chris's face, he ran his finger down the boy's cheek and along his jaw line before placing the cash in his shirt pocket as he perched on the desk in front of him.

'What do you know about being gay, Chris? You're a baby.' Harry shook his head and took the boy's hand – so soft, yet so big and masculine.

'Father?' His face puzzled at the questioning.

'Why are you here, Chris?'

'To play the organ, Father.' The boy's Irish accent reminded Harry of himself when he was younger.

'Why do you come to this gay church?' Harry liked to counsel as well as guide.

'Because I feel part of a group here, I feel like I belong. I have found people who I identify with and who I love and that's why I'm here. I love you, I love the church and I love the people. It gives me hope, Father. Hope I never had as a kid. Hope I never had last year, hope I didn't even have it last month.' Chris smiled and held the priest's hand tightly.

'Good,' Harry nodded, 'so long as you are sure that you belong, then that's good. I'm here to help, you know that.' He leant back and took another twenty pounds from his tin and slid it into Chris's shirt pocket. He then took the boy's face in both of his hands and got close to it, his eyes staring into the pale sea-blue of the kid's. 'Get yourself something nice,' he said, then winked and stood. 'Scoot, I've work to do.' He opened the door and Chris walked to it.

'Thank you, Father.' He hugged Harry, who realised he was actually smaller than the kid hugging him. God, the warmth of the teenager touching him was intense.

'Go on, will ya.' He motioned with his head and pulled away from the kid, who then turned and walked out without looking back. Harry closed and locked the door behind him. Locked himself in with the cash. Trust no one, not even the kid, not with the money about.

Opening the donation box he was pleased to see it packed down with notes. A hundred and twenty in the congregation, usual donation of ten pounds, some twenty, a percentage fifty and ten or so a hundred. It took him twenty minutes to separate, pile, count and recount the money. He then took out two envelopes from the bottom drawer of his desk. In one he placed three thousand pounds. In the other he placed three hundred and fifty pounds – his ten per cent of the takings – opening the floor safe beneath the rug he pulled the other envelopes out. Monies were collected on a monthly basis, until then they were stored in the floor safe, which only he knew the combination to. His own envelope was put in the safe in his bedroom, that's where all of his personal money was – along with the keys to his beach house, the Mercedes and the yacht that were parked there – in the office safe were the church donations for the month to date. Twelve donation envelopes from sermons totalling twenty-one thousand pounds, seventeen envelopes from weddings totalling seventeen thousand pounds and seven envelopes from funerals and christenings totalling six thousand pounds. Forty-four thousand pounds this month to date, another sixteen or so would complete the monthly takings, this was a lean month, Christmas and Easter both cleared a hundred grand. Personally, he could skim an extra ten thousand off every three months for himself on top of what he already earned – if required, which it usually was. The priesthood was the only life for him.

After closing the floor safe downstairs, he went upstairs and counted his own safe. Seven thousand pounds meant that he would need to visit the bank soon. If the church money got robbed, that was alright, but his own stash, no way, he had a lifestyle to live and he couldn't do that on a priest's salary.

Cash all counted and put away, the church all empty and locked up, Harry went to his quarters and put the telly on while he cooked his dinner. He was the best cook, classically trained and wonderfully experimental – but could never be bothered just for himself. Instead, as usual, opting to throw some pasta in a pan and whip up a quick sauce. He sat to watch some murder programme on the BBC. In his jogging bottoms and polo shirt, he was comfortable and right now he wasn't a priest. Casual clothes, dinner in front of the telly and a bottle of wine half gone – right now he was Harry O'Leary, just a regular guy, just a regular guy who was well-off and knew too much about too much. Then the beating on the door started. Sometimes the church was a scary place to be on your own. The sanctuary of the great walls in the daylight is very far from that when the world takes on a new face in the moonlight and darkness. Scary St Mary's. The statues move, the eyes in the paintings follow you and the walls creak with the horrors they have seen.

'Jesus fucking Christ,' he crossed himself and looked up for forgiveness, 'who is bothering me now at this time.' At the bottom of the stairs he found that the banging was from the back door, which at least meant that he didn't have to go through the church, doing that scared him shitless everytime he did it in the darkness. However, he still wasn't content, burglars can come in the back door as well as the front. Coming in the back just meant they didn't have to beat the priest down in front of the statue of the Virgin Mary and the baby Jesus. It wasn't the most comforting thought either way.

'Hello? Who is it?' Harry reached for the bat he kept by the door, occasionally he played cricket, that was the excuse for the protection.

'Father, it's me,' a quiet voice hissed back through the thick wood.

'Who's me?' Harry didn't recognise the voice.

'Chris,' the same voice muffled through again.

'You don't sound like Chris.' Harry wasn't convinced. The boy's voice sounded edgy. The boy knew how much money Harry held – what if he had blabbed and now was being forced to rob the church?

'Well, it is me, I can assure you of that, Father.' The boy was upset, that's why his voice was cracking

'Are you alone?' Harry set the bat down, giving in.

'Yes, Father.' Harry slid the bolt back and the door creaked open as he let Chris slip in. Immediately slamming and bolting the door closed again in one movement, so that no one else made it through with him.

'Father, are you alright? You look a little anxious.' Chris touched his shoulder. The priest was shaking, adrenaline pumping through him at the thought of defending his castle

'I'm fine.' Harry led the way upstairs and pointed up for Chris to follow him.

'What do you want at this time of the night, anyway?' he mumbled, motioning for Chris to sit as he downed his wine, easing the nerves back to their relaxed state. Trust no one, the thought was always with him.

'I've left home, Father.' The boy sat back as he spoke, tears in his eyes.

Harry shook his head. 'What did you go and do that for?' He eyed the boy up, the brat-pack look from head to toe, big boots, tight jeans, tight white T-shirt, jean jacket – all topped off with the beautiful blond hair and baby-blue eyes.

'I told my mum I was gay.' A tear escaped down his baby cheek.

'Fuck.'

'Father!'

'Jesus, I'm sorry.'

'Father!'

'I'm sorry,' Harry snapped. 'I'll say a prayer later. You threw me, that's all.' Harry got up and poured himself a whisky then, after a brief consideration, poured one for the boy too.

'Thanks.' He took the glass and drank the lot. Harry poured another before they spoke again. 'So can I stay here, Father?'

'Tonight, yes, because it's a house of God, and God loves all of his children. But tomorrow we are going to see your mum and we will sort this out. You can't stay for ever – it's my home as well as a house of God. And this is a church, not a YMCA.' He nodded to Chris, who nodded back as tears flooded down his cheeks. Harry got up and poured both of them another whisky, much larger ones this time. He handed one to Chris, who greedily took it in an attempt to stop the tears, but it didn't work.

'Come here,' Harry finally said, and Chris leapt up, finally getting what he wanted: a bit of human consolation, compassion and someone to care for him regardless of who he was. Judging by the emotion, the boy obviously felt something he hadn't felt for a very long time. Harry too felt warmth he hadn't experienced for years.

As Chris looked into his eyes and moved his lips onto the priest's, Harry was suddenly in too deep to get back out. He knew what dangers were ahead, he knew what the outcome would be. Never sleep with a member of the congregation. Never cross the line, he'd done it before and now he was doing it again. Chris led Harry off to his own bedroom, to his own double bed, to his own den of sin and wrongdoing – bringing the bottle of whisky with them. It all had an inevitable feel and would require a lot of forgiveness.

Harry was a priest and he loved it. He loved the power, he loved the joy and adored the love. He had devoted his life to being a priest, and for that he was pleased, thankful and happy. He was also a man. A man who loved sex, but with that a man who had to go without for long periods. He couldn't be promiscuous, he couldn't visit the brothels, he couldn't cruise the parks and he couldn't sit in a sauna. His job didn't allow it and moreover his conscience wouldn't let him. He was, after all, primarily a man of God. What he couldn't stop happening though was his passion. When sex was right there before his eyes, on a plate, touching him, feeling him, that's when he had no desire or conscience to turn it away. When this kid with big blue eyes, milky skin and an arse as firm as a peach had kissed him – he was no longer in moral control. He wanted sex all of the time; he was, after all, a thirty-year-old gay man. A thirty-year-old gay man, who hadn't had sex for a year. The priest was out of the window, Harry was released.

As the kid's tongue filled Harry's mouth, he worked the buttons on the boy's jeans. After a year he was actually aching for the feel of a cock in his hands. How long a year is. Then it was there. In his hands so briefly. In his mouth so quickly. Chris groaning as his priest gave him head. What a cock, what a taste, the fresh firm skin so sweet and new. Harry ached, but in those sexual moments he could almost give up the priesthood. As the boy took Harry in his mouth and blew him off with an expertise that surprised him, Harry had already handed in his dog collar and black shirt. He wanted this all of the time. The sex was blowing his mind. He had never been rimmed before and so screamed when the boy did it.

The sweat was dripping off of Harry when the boy entered him. He remembered the first time he had been fucked, it was six years ago, and he knew exactly where that boy was now, how good that had been then. How good this was right now. The boy's length filling him – fucking the priest, Harry's head bashing into the headboard as the boy spread his legs wide and rammed his beautiful cock into him. Harry's hands reaching out for the boy's shoulders, holding his strong prematurely firm arms as he smiled at him, holding the stare all the time. The smile on his face, the love in his eyes, it was sensual, heavenly, *punishable*. Harry's hands travelling up, and up, twisting the boy's choker, grabbing the crucifix, the Virgin and Infant around the boy's neck restricting the airflow, enhancing the orgasm. The boy coming, groaning, his face getting redder, redder, flushing, coming – exhaling for the last time as Harry twisted the choker tighter and tighter. The boy then laying on him, his chest no longer rising, the boy simply a heavy weight on Harry's chest, a dead weight, a real weight sat on his life. Letting go of the choker after an eternity, Harry pulled the boy out of him and pushed him to the floor. The boy's head hit the bedside table on the way down. It didn't matter though, he wouldn't have felt a thing.

'Bollocks, bollocks, bollocks.' Harry hurried into the living room, lit a cigarette, poured a tumbler full of vodka and sat in the chair. 'Bollocks,' he said a last time before draining the vodka.

His Monday sermon was delivered with all of the usual joy and celebration of being gay. The dead boy now laid in his bed. He still had all of that to do later – after he had done the collection box and counted the money. After drinking the previous night away, he had decided what he needed to do and how he needed to do it. His belly danced at the thought, but he had no choice. He was a priest, a man, a human, a murderer. There was only one way to deal with the situation, and in the clear light of day it was the only thing he could do. It was the right thing to do.

'Hello?' The voice was sharp but foggy; priests sometimes napped in the afternoon, bishops always did.

'Hi, Bishop. It's Harry O'Leary. Sorry to trouble you at home, but I need to speak with you.' Harry held a Scotch in one hand and a cigarette in the other, both trembled furiously as he cradled the phone to his ear with his shoulder.

'It's not the cash now, is it?' The bishop's Irish accent was so much thicker than Harry's, talking about the cash made the bishop's tone viscous.

'No, Bishop, don't worry, it's not the cash.' Harry knew that would have sent him over the edge. Fifty grand in unmarked notes out of the door would have been very quickly followed by Harry. The bishop's beach house was bigger than Harry's, so was his yacht. The bishop even had two Mercedes and a ski chalet. You don't fuck with a bishop.

'Good, the money's grand. So I'll come over in a week to speak to you, then.'

The bishop yawned, he had been napping.

'No. I need to speak to you today, now. I need to speak to you, Gerald. Please.' Harry was firm, but his voice was croaky.

'I'll be right over.' Gerald had heard priests on the edge before. He had heard Harry on the edge before.

Harry poured another Scotch and sat on the bed with Chris. The boy's hair so fine, his face so soft, so pretty. He looked asleep, the purple bruise around his neck now covered by the sheet. No signs of violence. No signs of a struggle. This was Harry's boyfriend and he was sleeping. It had been that quick and that easy. The sleeping angel. The bishop had to help.

'Harry, you look like shit. What's wrong? Please tell me it's not the money, is it? Tell me the truth. It's not the fucking money?' Gerald looked stern, as if he knew the money had been stolen. He looked like his world was going to drop out. As if Harry would invite the bishop over to tell him the money was stolen. That would certainly be a long-distance telephone job. 'No, Gerald, it's not the money.' Harry waved his hand in the air and smiled. 'There is forty-four thousand pounds for you in cash in the safe under your chair.' Harry smiled as Gerald visibly lost a huge burden from his shoulders.

'What is it, then?' Gerald now sat forward impatiently, uninterested, there was nothing more important than the money.

'Gerald, there is a seventeen-year-old boy in my bed upstairs.' Harry looked at the floor while he spoke.

'You didn't bring me here to brag did you, because I've left a fifteen-year-old boy in my bed to come and speak with you, who right at this moment could be...' Gerald looked at his watch, licked his lips and gave off a filthy laugh. 'Well, you know what these boys can do, Harry.' He sat back and then forward, the chair suddenly uncomfortable to him.

'No, I'm not bragging, Gerald. He's dead.' Harry met Gerald's eyes, and there wasn't a flicker of emotion in them. The bishop drew in a large lung of air and shook his head silently, Harry just stared on, waiting, hoping, needing help.

'Again?' was all he said when he finally spoke. Harry just nodded. 'One is an accident, two is silly, three is careless, four, five, six, what are you at now, Harry, for Christ's sake?' His eyes angry as they burned into Harry's face, demanding answers.

'Six,' Harry confessed, almost inaudibly.

'Six,' the bishop roared, 'fucking six.' The bishop sat back and sighed, his big belly rising, his thumbs twisting in his lap, his eyes closing in meditation. 'I'll tell you something, Harry,' the bishop finally spoke as Harry sat up, the naughty boy in trouble again, ready for his punishment, ready for his guidance, 'it's a good fucking job you bring in so much cash to the Church, otherwise I'd wash my hands of you.' He stood up as he finished speaking. Shaking his head seemed to wash the remaining anger away. He finally smiled and looked into Harry's eyes. 'I'm sorry,' he moved forward and took Harry in his arms, his tone soft now and reassuring, 'are you okay?' Harry nodded. 'You really should be more careful, Harry.' Harry nodded again. 'You're so young. So innocent.' A tear came from Harry's eyes. 'Go on, get packed, I'll sort something out.' Gerald stood aside and Harry scuttled from the room. He knew not to speak, not to question, just to go – he'd left before in a hurry and would leave again in a hurry. The whole burden had now been lifted once more.

'He's a little cutie, Harry, isn't he?' Gerald came up behind Harry in the bedroom as he packed. 'All set?'

'Yes, just about. Will you send the rest on like usual?' Harry's voice was sad at leaving another church. He hated having to keep moving on – he just couldn't help it.

'Sure.' The bishop was more than aware of the procedures to follow for Harry's moments of madness. He was aware of the procedures to follow for all of his priests' moments of madness. 'St Martin's parish in Bristol. Get away from here for a while. Father Davis is coming up, you'll be fine. You got your money?' Harry nodded again. 'Here's another ten grand to get you set.' He handed Harry a large brown envelope, which Harry took without question. He was running, he needed help. 'I'll come down and check on you next week, okay?' Gerald took Harry's hands in his own for reassurance and looked into the eyes of his indiscreet priest. 'You'll be fine, Harry. So long as you keep the funds coming in, you'll be fine.' Harry was under no illusion about the arrangements, neither was the bishop.

'Thanks, Gerald – do you need any help...?' Harry motioned to the body in the bed.

'No, no, I'll tie up the loose ends here, I'm used to it. Get yourself off, have a little break, you need it.' Gerald winked and tapped his own bag where the forty-four thousand pounds in cash sat in the big brown envelopes. 'You've been working hard.' The bishop smiled and then took Harry in his arms and held him. 'God will see you are okay.'

All the while the boy lay dead in the bed beside them. Neither of them looked at him again. Harry was the Church's biggest salesman, far too big to cut loose. Harry O'Leary was careless on occasion, but manageable. Father Harry O'Leary was indispensable, and he knew it.

Beyond the Reef
Jeffrey Buchanan

Beyond the Reef

Jeffrey Buchanan

Dedicated to Peter Burton

Robert Renton clambered down the bank and walked along the foreshore towards the shipwreck. In the glare from the sun and the sea the wreck appeared as a giant washed-up sea creature picked over by scavengers, its carcass bleached under the Melanesian sun. There was nobody else about, he felt sure of that, but he looked around him nevertheless as an edge of uneasiness sifted through him. Then the excitement sluiced back and he sort of waved as if trying to attract someone in the bones of the ship wreck. This was Robert Renton's moment of fantasy come true and he laughed out loud at the recognition of it. The *Joyita*: broken, rusted, forgotten but with so much of his own history involved in it. It lay lopsided near where he stood on the yellow sand on a remote Fijian island.

Robert Renton was a hairdresser from Auckland. He had a quick glimpse of himself back in the trendy Auckland salon telling his workmates all about this adventure. Then he turned that image off and thought: "I wish I knew who you really were, Uncle Vic." He turned again to see if there was anyone around. He wasn't used to remoteness and silence. In the salon there was the constant clatter and chatter and camp shouts of hilarity. But the village on the other side of the bank that he had just clambered down had been inhabited only by a few old people. A row of wizened females had been seated on the ground in front of a palm thatch house and when they had seen him get off the battered bus and walk into their village, the one with the high stack of grey hair had made an odd noise and got up and disappeared into the hut behind her. Filled with nerves – it had been too late to go back, the bus had departed – he had approached the row of old women. The one dressed in a bright blue and red hibiscus print laplap had stood and shuffled towards him.

"What do you want?" she asked.

"To see the *Joyita*. The wreck. They said it was here... in..."

"People used to come to visit it but not any more," she said. She seemed debilitated by that much communication and she smiled and pointed to the bank and then went and crouched down again outside the hut.

Robert Renton brushed aside the feeling of aloneness. This wasn't an experience he wanted to share with one of his Auckland friends anyway. Those queens – he saw them in the salon: dressed in black, hair stiff with toxic jellies, bitchy and hilarious in turn, complacent... Here he was alone on a remote beach in the South Pacific and he congratulated himself for having achieved that. He squinted at the wreck that Uncle Vic had sailed in from Samoa in 1956. There was a photo of Uncle Victor (he was always Victor to his parents) on the wall in the old house on Te Kauwhata Street where Robert's grandparents still lived. Uncle Victor in the spare bedroom with his short blonde hair and his eyes light, almost transparent, as blue eyes turn in old black and white photos. Uncle Victor's big ears and that boyish defiant look in his face that said: "I won't be trapped in your provincialism."

The sweat slipped down Robert Renton's face and the taste of Rosemary and Honey Shampoo filtered into his mouth with a sticky sickly taste he recognised as the defining smell of the Auckland salon. For a moment he recognised that trendiness and carry-on as too fatuous even to contemplate a return to but behind him a coconut thudded to the ground and for a second the chill of his isolation went rushing through him: "Shit," he thought, "what am I doing here alone?" He walked with some defiance towards the wreck which was lodged deeply in the sand and the lagoon stretched out behind it to the breakers. The remains of the *Joyita* were beautiful and ugly and mysterious all at the same time and the source of so much of his wonder as a child: "Your uncle was an adventurer at sixteen," his mother had always warned him. "And it did him no good, did it?"

The vessel was much smaller than Robert had imagined. It lay on its side, insignificant and broken, as if saddened by the enormity of what had happened to it in 1956 when it had drifted with no one on board onto the reef hundreds of miles from its destination. The plates on the table in the mess had half eaten meals on them. There had been no sign of a struggle. GREAT SEA MYSTERY IN FIJI ISLES. The headlines were yellowed and the papers stiff and crumbly in his grandparents' scrap book of the event which shook their lives. NEVER RESOLVED: WHAT HAPPENED TO THE *JOYITA*'S CREW? TWO KIWIS ON *JOYITA*.

Robert felt prickly all over but it was from the suspense and the excitement that he suffered and not so much the heat as he stepped into the warm lagoon and waded to the skeleton. "I don't know why Victor wanted to rush away like that and leave New Zealand," was one of Robert's mother's favourite refrains. She had a head full of such sayings about her brother's behaviour and she had used them to raise her son and to mould his character so that he would not be like his itinerant uncle: Uncle as deserter; Uncle as loner; Uncle as irresponsible. They were the fables that had been instilled in him relentlessly. It was as if his whole family had never been able to recover from one shock, from that one defining moment. That generation had been inculcated in the culture of loss and resentment. Robert Renton saw it all as he stood knee deep in the placid water. It was old stuff and he had learned to live with it. He dragged it out and made it hilarious at dinner parties but now the sour side of it resurfaced. He heard his mother telling him as a kid not to talk to strangers, not to climb fences, to follow the path of his cousin James who worked in the Taranaki Savings Bank in Wellington. And to never, never, never have a friend like Timothy Sweet.

A frigate bird swept across the sea and then another. The heat came in swells like the waves out on the reef. In that vessel thirty seven men had been travelling from Samoa to the Tokelau Islands, a journey supposed to take two weeks. For eight weeks the newspapers had been obsessed about the disappearance: *JOYITA* MYSTERY DEEPENS. Even the sound of the old newspapers had enticed Robert Renton as he turned them in his grandparents' living room. More newspapers were stacked in a big old biscuit tin. The picture of a sailing ship on the lid of the tin was a hint of the misadventure that had taken Uncle Victor. THIRTY-FIVE NATIVES AND TWO NEW ZEALANDERS UNACCOUNTED FOR. *JOYITA* SPOTTED IN FIJI ISLES. The frigate bird came in closer and circled the *Joyita* as if it too were fascinated by all that the wreck entailed. It was a dream come true: Robert looked around him: the palms, the reef, the endless skies with huge white clouds on the horizon. He thought: "I can get out of the salon." He took out his digital camera and framed the wreck with the clouds and the reef beyond it. With his feet in the warm sand and the water around his knees and the sense of freedom and accomplishment at having arrived here he felt there was another world open to him: Auckland, the salon, the world of hairdressing, dance clubs; they were now confirmed as being as shallow as he had suspected. He thought: "I'm thirty-seven, twice Victor's age, and look what he'd gotten up to…" The frigate bird swooped at something and at that second Robert caught the image in his camera.

KIWI MATES DISAPPEAR: Victor and his mate Timothy Sweet; the two of them travelling together on a rust bucket around the islands at the ages of sixteen and twenty-seven respectively. Robert Renton imagined them standing on the stern (he thought the front part was called the bow but he wasn't sure about the parts of boats). The photo of Timothy Sweet was in one of the yellow newspapers: thin, dark, his cleft chin like Kirk Douglas'. Timothy Sweet in a white T-shirt and baggy trousers and described as "Itinerant… a known beachcomber originally from Wellington." Timothy Sweet had held that fascination for Robert throughout his childhood until he recognised what it was when he was about fourteen. Thinking of Timothy Sweet the itinerant, the vagabond, the seducer as he jerked off. Robert took another photo. He imagined Vic and Tim standing together on the *Joyita* as it set sail from a quiet port in the Pacific. Then that wonder about his uncle again turned to that question about himself. What he saw he didn't like: effete, ageing, a hairdresser in a salon filled with queens ten years younger than he was. What if his uncle were there now on the beach, as if some miracle dragged him up for a chat right there in sight of the *Joyita*? What would Vic's mate Timothy Sweet have to say to him, someone who felt timid about being alone on a beach in the Fiji Islands? It was a cliché that travel broadened the mind, but this experience was painful. Robert Renton had avoided pain as much as he could during his lifetime but in a snatch of recognition he saw this as the adventure that might cut the strings from a life coloured by his mother's preoccupations about Victor: Victor was irresponsible: Look what Victor did to your grandparents: People like Timothy Sweet will lead young men astray.

Felix Tavessuka had seen the white man come into the village and ask the elders something. When the pastor's wife had stood and pointed, Felix Tavessuka knew he had come to see the *Joyita*. Visitors did on occasions. A Tahitian journalist had written a piece about the mystery for a paper and had sent it to Chief Tervanuni. But the article was in French so nobody had read it. Then that New Zealander from some university had stayed for a week and asked so many questions as if there was any more to the story than the boat just floating into their reef without its passengers. Felix Tavessuka lay back in his mattress and thought about the Tahitian journalist with the ass as tight as a girl's vagina and smiled. The village boys had enjoyed that one. "Half-castes are the juiciest," he thought. Then he got up and washed his face in the basin of water in the small kitchen. From the rafter he took down his bright blue and red laplap and wound it around his waist and he smiled in the cracked mirror: "I'm still good looking," he said to his image. He thought: "They will be angry if they know I used this water." He stood and looked at the basin for a few seconds but he shrugged and went out of the frond house defiant. As he went past the elders he heard the wife of his second cousin say something he was not supposed to hear but the venom in her voice made it all the more nasty. He spat in her direction and the wife of the deceased chief spat back. "How could you be a son of this village?" she yelled at him. "Is Fiji now like this?"

The sun burned his skin. Exposure to the sun was what the doctor said he must avoid. Felix Tavessuka laughed at the thought of the doctor in Sydney telling him to avoid the sun when he got back to Fiji on account of his condition. The doctor: tall, blonde, muscled, one of those rich Sydney queers. Felix imagined himself in Sydney and not on the top of the embankment looking down at the white man making his way gingerly to the *Joyita*. Sydney was what he wanted more than anything: a life of dignity working in a factory or a restaurant, having money, a car, a flat, something useful and not this life here in a mangy village with the thought of a germ crawling around in him. He looked back at the old women sitting outside the chief's house, all of them in a row like old chickens picking over every detail of the village. It was hard to imagine that as a kid he had gone to them, that they had cuddled him, called him sweet names and given him fruit and kisses. He thought: "I must get back to Sydney." He stretched out his arms; they were still strong enough to cut the top off a coconut. He thought: "Maybe the doctor told lies about my body. Maybe there are no germs eating me." He shielded his eyes from the sun as he went down the embankment and along the sand. He kicked an empty tin of bully beef and swiped at a plastic punnet: "This white man has small feet," he thought as he followed the path made by the intruder.

For a while Felix Tessavuka stood under the palms at the edge of the sand and watched the white man. Everything about him was rich. The camera, the cap, the bag he had slung over his shoulder. He eyed the sandals that lay on the beach where the man had left them before wading into the water. They were the sort he'd seen in Sydney shops and which cost more than villagers earned from selling a tonne of taro in the markets. The thought that he wanted to be that white man gained strength in his mind and he said to himself: "This is a shit life. In Fiji we are nothing." The thought of a good life petered out and he was again in the doctor's office, the tall, blonde, handsome man telling him that thing that Felix Tessavuka hated. He stood up and with swift strokes brushed at the white sand on his long legs. "My body is good," he thought. "That doctor is lying." Grains of sand clung shiny and beautiful to his black skin. In the next second he saw the white particles as germs that were floating in his blood and killing him. Felix Tessavuka slapped at his legs, viciously this time, scraping his legs with his fingers, brushing at the sand. He looked down the white stretch of beach and he understood that getting rid of those billions and billions of grains was the same as the impossibility of ridding himself of this disease in his body.

"You must understand, these drugs are not available to non-Australians..." Felix Tessavuka shut the doctor out of his thinking. The words were like a song that doesn't shut up in your head and goes on and on and on and on and on and on so that the words begin to drive you crazy. Words like: love, love, kisses, kisses, darling, darling, sweet heart, sweet heart always banging, banging, banging in your mind while you want those fucking words to get out. The doctor's words were his constant companion. And the woman at the Immigration Service in Sydney was a similar visitor in his head as he lay for hours on his mattress: "But you're here illegally, Mr Tessavuka. How do you expect our system to pay for your medications?" Felix Tessavuka took a final swipe at the sand on his leg then sauntered down past the sandals to the water's edge and waited for the white man to notice him. The white man was taking pictures of the frigate birds that swooped over the rusted vessel. Click click click, the man wasting money trying to take pictures of birds that merely shit into the ocean. He studied him closely: even this shirt said loudly that he had lots of money, that he had everything.

"You didn't see me," Felix yelled as he waded into the water. "I'm from..." He waved at the startled intruder and then pointed to the village. When he was next to Robert he extended his hand. When he took Robert's in his, it was soft like all the white men's hands he'd shaken in Australia. Robert's brown hair was yellow at the tips and fluffy, more like a woman's. Felix looked at the man; he was soft and pretty like the boys he'd fucked in Sydney.

The two men chatted for a minute about the *Joyita* and the uncle and the connection that had brought Robert Renton to this meeting knee deep in the warm water.

"Did you go to Sydney sometimes?" Felix asked. The lines around the white's face were deeper on closer inspection. Was he young, was he old? In the village you could tell the age of a man but with whites it was not so easy, especially with those gay ones.

"Yes, for..." Robert wanted to say Mardi Gras, but that was a giveaway. The Fijian's eyes were dark, black almost, and the whites were clouded. He was really good looking, one of those head turners. The way he wore his hibiscus laplap around his tight waist, it was knotted just below his navel. His body was hard and hairy.

"Did you go to Sydney?" asked Robert. He had once had an *affaire* with a Samoan and he'd had sex a few times with a youth from the

Cook Islands. He realised as he stood talking with the Fijian that he was a Melanesian, much blacker than the Polynesians he'd fucked with.

"I go to Sydney for vacations," Robert said. "I'm from Auckland, so it's easy."

Felix looked into Robert's eyes. The blue he saw was the same one that the sea beyond the reef turned at dusk in the rainy season. "Easy to get to Sydney," Felix thought. Easy. Easy. He rolled the word around in his head. Easy. Easy. Easy. The word an echo in his thinking. Easy. Easy. He took Robert's hand in his and squeezed it. he knew this white man was a queer. "Come up into the shade for a while," he said. "Here your pink skin is burning."

They walked together up the beach and sat under the coconuts on the little bank above the sand line and began the ritual of mutual seduction.

"What is your job?" Felix said. He was sitting crossed legged, sort of kitty cat to Robert, his legs sufficiently apart to show his inner thighs. He scratched in his thick chest hair and smiled at Robert, his eyes moving slowly from the blue eyes to the bulge between Robert's legs.

What is your job? Robert Renton heard the question and hated it. He saw the other hairdressers: Simon in his all-black outfit, sexy Steven almost identical in his; Cynthia in a flimsy black negligée thing and Alex in a little black number that most Auckland gays would think of only as a dance-club outfit. The fatuousness of it all again leapt up and grabbed him, only this time for some reason with more poignancy. At thirty-seven he was the grand old queen of the salon. The love handles and the face lines and the saggy tits were testament to that as much as the deeper understanding of things and the way he wanted the world to be both towards him and he towards it. He didn't want to be a hairdresser at that moment. In fact he didn't want hairdressing to define his life any longer. This gorgeous Fijian, the villager probably had more depth, more in him than all those other sissies in the salon put together. Here was a man who probably made a living from fishing. He lived in the very shadow of the *Joyita* which had had such an effect on him, Robert. In that moment of catharsis he said: "I'm a doctor."

He regretted the lie the moment he uttered it but it was too late to take it back and he watched the Fijian's eyes widen with some kind of recognition that here was a man of higher learning or social standing. Robert didn't tell lies normally. There was never any need to but this was one of those defining moments where you know there is no way back but plenty of room to go forward. He felt happy suddenly, about being someone else on the beach on a remote island with a handsome Fijian. He looked at the *Joyita*. His Uncle Vic was a poofter. That was certain. He had always thought that. Timothy Sweet's picture confirmed it: the look in his eyes. It was probably as a result of having to lie that Vic had buggered off from New Zealand to live another life, to hide, to take another identity. He smiled at the Fijian. Life was to be lived on so many levels. Life was more than a salon where you cut, curled and styled. He laughed. Life was bubbling. The fear of being a saggy old queen in a hair salon lifted. He reached out his hand and took the Fijian's.

For a moment or two Felix looked at Robert with something akin to adoration. The touch was beautiful. No one in the village had touched him since he had come back from Sydney. He wasn't even allowed to use the water in the washing bowl that the rest of the family used for daily ablutions. He had his own food utensils. Some of the youths spat at him. He was banned from going into the food gardens in case he contaminated the vegetables. Felix Tavessuka squeezed Robert's hand in appreciation and moved closer to him. A moment later they were kissing.

A doctor. Felix Tessavuka was kissing a doctor. This man had access to the right medicines. He could free him from the illness. The Sydney doctor had blue eyes. The Sydney doctor had been about forty. Three times Felix had been to see him after he had tested positive. The first time the doctor had explained all about T cells and how Felix's were very low. The second time he had suggested that he go to the Fijian Consulate and ask for help to obtain the anti retrovirals which were available free only to Australians. The third time, the doctor explained that he could do nothing to obtain any drugs for him. Three weeks later Immigration officials had put him on a plane in Sydney at five in the morning after stamping BARRED FROM AUSTRALIA in his passport.

Felix Tessavuka and Robert Renton stripped off, kissing as they did so. Robert kicked away a thick branch from under him as he lay down on the sandy patch under the bushes and pulled Felix down to him. They were kissing and rubbing together, excited as they played with each others genitals and sucked each others nipples. When Felix fingered inside Robert's anus Robert knew what the Fijian wanted.

"I haven't got a condom," Robert said.

"I love you," said Felix. "Let me." Gently he pushed Robert to his back and slid on top of him.

"No," Robert insisted. "Not without a condom."

"Meat on meat," Felix said. He knew the germs were in semen. For a moment he relented and lifted his weight off Robert.

"Always use a condom," Robert said. He ran his hand down Felix's chest and stomach and gripped his large penis and pre cum oozed out of it. It was probably safe, the man lived in a remote island. For a moment Robert relented, he pulled the Fijian to him, wanting his big cock up his anus.

"Fuck," he thought. "I shouldn't do this. He's been in Sydney..." He pushed him away again, this time a bit roughly. "Just kisses and playing with it," he said. "Not fucking."

"You think I'm diseased?" said Felix. He saw the Sydney doctor say that there were no drugs available for non-Australians. He heard the Immigration officials tell him it was not a concern of theirs but the Fijian Government's. He'd let men fuck his ass in sleazy backrooms in Oxford Street and no one there had used a condom. Here the village youths spat at him and his family wouldn't let him use their eating utensils. The words started in his head again, those echoes. He pushed the doctor to the ground, forcing his arms back and his head down.

It doesn't take long to kill someone when they are not prepared for violence, when they can't fight back because they are not as strong as their opponent. The stick Robert Renton had kicked away five minutes earlier was now the murder weapon. Felix Tessavuka crushed Robert's throat with the stick within a minute, a knee on each end of the weapon while the struggle desisted and was extinguished. The doctor lying beneath him, his blue eyes popping and filled with the horror of dying. Over and over in the Fijian's mind everything about the germs that were in his body and the doctor in Australia and this doctor who had thought he was diseased and wouldn't let him fuck him. The echoes hammering inside his thinking.

He sat next to the body until the night blackened the lagoon then he walked down the beach to where his canoe was hidden in the bushes. He had to paddle it down past the *Joyita* to where he had laid the body near the water. Felix Tessavuka stripped off Robert Renton's shorts, put them on, and then found stones which he stuffed into the pockets. He wondered if the sharks would get his disease when they ate him as he sank down and down into the water next to the white man's body. At night the sharks would gobble them both up quickly. He thought: "Then when the villagers eat the fish, they will get this killer in them."

There was no moon and the tide was full. Felix Tessavuka shuddered as he paddled past the ghosts on the *Joyita* and out through the lagoon and past the reef to the depths where the sharks hunted.

Pop Goes the Weasel
Richard Cawley

Pop Goes the Weasel
Richard Cawley

"A pint of Stella, please." Steven addressed the back of a shaved head, above a black T-shirt and low-slung faded jeans, which revealed a centimetre or two of white briefs.

The barman swung round even before the quiet request was completed. "Shit! I'd know that fuckin' puffta voice anywhere." Despite the obvious enthusiasm of the loud greeting, the barman's eyes instantly filled with tears. "Come here you bloody old shit."

Steven's grin turned to laughter as the barman vaulted over the bar, letting fly with another string of expletives as the hip-slung jeans fell even further down, dragging the Calvin Klein's with them to reveal a startlingly pink, hairless bum.

"Not that you haven't seen it all before," he continued as he wriggled in an extravagant fashion, whilst dragging the jeans back to their former level. "Just don't want to scare the rest of my customers."

"But there aren't any customers and I have seen your arse before, but never quite that colour!"

"Sun bed... Got to look gorgeous... Gran Canaria... No customers? Well there aren't that many piss-heads like you, who drink pints of lager at eleven-twenty on a Tuesday morning." He flung his arms around Steven's neck and hugged him so hard that Steven gasped.

Then just as suddenly the barman sprung back, holding Steven by the shoulders, at arm's length. "I hate you! Bloody Sydney's certainly agreed with you. Look at the bloody colour of you! All I get is a monkey's bum. That's the trouble with being a strawberry blond..."

"Where?" Steven gave the shaved head a playful rub.

"Cheeky! Seriously, you look even more disgustingly young than you did a year ago."

"I am only twenty-nine!"

"Yeah... and the rest."

"I am, Darren, you bastard! You know very well I was born precisely two days before you. May the twenty-sixth. You're twenty-eight, too... The same year..."

"Okay. Well as long as you admit I'm younger than you, I'll let you off."

They both grinned, fell silent for a moment, then, wrapped their arms tightly around each other again.

"Matthew!" Darren screamed over Steven's shoulder at an open door behind the bar.

"Shit! Mind my bloody ear!" Steven pulled away, shaking his head vigorously.

"Get down here immediately!" Darren shrieked again.

"I *was* down, not up," a skinny boy, wearing a tight, sleeveless, white top, announced in a cheeky voice, as he appeared in the dark doorway. "Remember? You asked me to change the Guinness barrel."

"*Told* you, not asked, you saucy little madam! Remember, you do what I tell you, when I tell you... Slave!"

"So, what now?" The younger man affected a sulky expression. "I was just going to make myself a nice cup of tea and paint my toenails."

"Don't be disgusting... Slut! Now stay here and look after the bar. I'm going out for half an hour."

"What, on my own?" The sulky expression changed to a look of mock horror.

"Yes, slave. Anyway. We're not exactly busy."

"Half an hour? It'll take you that long to get it up! Anyway, aren't you going to introduce me to the new shag." The boy eyed Steven up and down with ostentatious approval.

"Its not a shag! I mean he's not a shag. Steven's my oldest friend."

"Doesn't look that old to me. Anyway, I like a man with a bit of experience." The boy fluttered his eyelids and extended a hand, which was weighed down with silver rings, across the bar to Steven. Steven shook it roughly.

"Now I know we're not in Kansas!" Steven laughed, pulled his hand away and threw his arm around Darren's shoulder. "Where we goin', mate?" He affected an Australian accent.

"Come on, Skippy!" Darren grabbed Steven by the hand and

dragged him towards the open front door and out onto Old Compton Street. "We're in Soho now, not Summer Bay."

Steven blinked, momentarily blinded by the spring sunshine.

"And keep that bloody bar spotless!" Darren yelled back over his shoulder.

"Yes, massa." The reply came, in a high-pitched Southern drawl

"Cheeky little brat!" Darren tutted.

"Kinda cute though..."

"You haven't changed... Bloody paedophile!"

"Daniel was twenty-three!" Steven protested "Twenty-four now... Well, almost twenty-five..." His voice slowed and trailed off.

They both simultaneously stopped walking. Steven hung his head. His friend faced him and put a hand on one of his shoulders.

"Come on. It wasn't your fault. You did the right thing..."

"But..."

"No! It would only have been harder if you had dragged it out."

"But I never realised he would take it *so* badly." Steven sprang back a pace. His voice suddenly became loud and agitated, his wide eyes, wet with fresh tears. "He is better now though, isn't he? You said he was... would have stayed away longer, if I'd thought..."

"No, he really is okay. Lots better."

Steven visibly relaxed and dragged his jacket sleeve across his eyes, leaving a shiny streak, like a snail trail, on the worn brown leather and starting to walk again.

"But I have had bad news as well as good!"

Steven stopped again, shocked. "What?"

"Come on. Lets get a drink." Darren took Steven gently by the elbow. "There's lots to tell. A lot's happened in fourteen months. Let's go to Kettners. It'll be quiet in there. We can talk. Anyway, we need champagne, not fuckin' lager. This is a celebration. Come on, you ugly bastard!" The mood lightened.

*

"Two glasses of house champagne, please."

The Slavic-sounding, buxom blonde woman deposited two glasses, a slip of paper and a small saucer of olives on the table in front of them, where they sat on banquette-seating in a the back corner of the bar.

"Oh God," Darren sighed. "What a disgusting thought! Olives at this time in the morning!" He pushed the offending objects away from him, towards the back of the table. Steven quickly retrieved them and began eating one.

"Well, I'm actually bloody hungry. I love olives."

"Well you know me... Essex lad... Just like a stick of Blackpool rock... cut me in half and you'll find 'common' written all the way through. Anyway what's wrong with pork scratchings? Cheers queers!" They clinked glasses.

"So how does hospital life in Sydney compare with dreary old Saint Thomas's? What was it called"

"What was what called?"

"Your hospital... Sydney?"

"Oh, Saint Vincent's, or Saint Vinnie's, as it is affectionately called." He switched once more into an Australian accent, then straight back into his habitual English public school voice. "Come on, Darren! This is killing me. Tell me just how bad was he? I know you were shielding me from the full story while I was away..."

"Pretty bad, actually. He had a full on nervous breakdown, or whatever..."

"Doesn't matter what you call it," Steven interrupted brusquely. "Shit, I'm sorry. I didn't mean to sound ratty. Its just that..." He hung his head.

"Fuck off, stupid! You don't have to apologise to me. I'm supposed to be your best bloody friend. You've done your share of looking after me in the past." Darren closed a hand gently on Steven's where it was clenched tightly on his knee. Darren felt a large hot tear as it fell. He squeezed Steven's hand gently.

"Come on. You know there was absolutely no choice."

"It's just... it's just... it's just that..." Another tear. And another. Another gentle squeeze. "I did love him, you know. So much."

"Everyone knows that. But you weren't *in* love with him."

"No, I wasn't. I tried. I tried so hard, God knows." He leaned forward and his shoulders began to shake convulsively.

"Come on!" Darren placed his finger gently under Steven's chin and tilted his head back, handing him his glass at the same time. "Here, neck this. We need more alcohol." He had no trouble in catching the bored waitress's eye, as she had been standing enthralled, watching the dramatic little scene unfold. He held two fingers up towards her, with his palm ostentatiously turned *away* from him. She straightened herself up from her slouched position over the bar and with a somewhat guilty look, nodded back in assent.

"Here, dry your bloody eyes. Don't worry, it's clean." Darren handed Steven a folded paper tissue. "You sure you want me to go on?"

"Yes. Look I'm sorry."

"If you say sorry once more, I'll get my bloody monkey bum out again!"

Steven forced a little laugh. They picked up the fresh glasses, which the waitress had placed in front of them, along with another small slip of paper, which she tucked under the saucer of olives. They remained quiet for a few moments, both seemingly examining the colour of their champagne. Then Steven broke the silence.

"Well, come on, tell me. How bad was he? What pills is he on? Who looked after him? He's no family. Well none that will own him, poor bastard." His eyes widened anxiously again. "They disowned him you know. When he came out at fourteen."

"Don't worry. He was well looked after. He was pretty bad though... at the beginning. Luckily, he still had enough of a grip on reality, to make a phone call, before he gave up."

"Who? Who did he phone? You?"

"No."

"Who?"

"Alex."

"Alex?"

"Well, you weren't there! He did *leave* Alex for you. Look, I'm sorry. I didn't mean to..."

"No, I deserved it. What right have I to be jealous. Oh god! That's not the bad news, is it? He's not gone back with Alex? He's too..." The veins began to stand out in Steven's neck and both his fists were clenched tightly.

"Come on, Steven! Alex isn't that old. Anyway, what does it matter? Actually, you should be bloody grateful to Alex. Oh God, I'm..."

"You've every right to. I was getting completely out of order. But look, if I'm not allowed to apologise, then neither are you."

"Well, Alex apparently jumped straight into a taxi. Luckily, he still had a key to Daniel's flat..."

"Oh my God! Daniel didn't try?"

"No, not that. He was just like a zombie. I saw him the next day. He'd... well; he'd just switched off. That's what Alex said the doctors told him. It was all just too painful for his mind to cope with. So his brain just kind of fainted... Went into a kind of coma. He just switched off. The batteries ran down and the screen went blank."

"Yes, that's what happens. A very good description. He must have had a good doctor.

"Yeah. They were all really nice. The hospital was very depressing, but all the doctors and nurses were great. Anyway, he wasn't in long."

"Didn't they section him?"

"Only for a week, but Alex contacted Ray and Alison."

"His last foster parents. I never met them, but I know he was very fond of them." This time Steven caught the waitress's eye. He drained his glass. Darren followed suit, then continued.

"Well they drove immediately down from Peterborough and took him straight back with them. Apparently, he just slept, mostly, for the first couple of months. The pills..."

"Do you know what he's on?" Steven interrupted.

"Yeah. I went to the hospital to get a repeat prescription and send them on. Venla... Venla-something?"

"Venlafaxine?"

"Yeah. That's it, Venlafaxine."

"Oh that's good. Very clean drug, very modern..."

"Anyway, Alison's retired now, so she had time to spend with him. Brought him back, bit by bit. Started with little walks in the park, then shopping, then the odd film."

"When did you last see him?"

"Oh, three weeks, now. No, it'll be four."

"Is he still up there?"

"No, he came back to London a couple of months ago. He's still not working. Still on medication."

"He will be. He'll need to stay on them for at least a year."

Steven paused and his voice took on a reflective, almost reticent tone. "Do you think it would help if I saw him?"

"Well you could try ringing him."

"You mean he wouldn't want to see me?" A note of panic returned.

"No, as far as that's concerned, I'm pretty sure he'd be fine. It's just that... well he's... he's moved on."

"Moved on! What do you mean moved on?"

"Well you've got to find out sooner or later. Best it comes from me. Ouch!"

Steven realised what he was unconsciously doing and released his vice-like grip on Darren's forearm. His face had turned quite red and the veins stood out clearly on his neck and temples.

"Who?" Darren dropped his head.

"Who, for Christ's sake? Come on, I have to know!" His face became even redder.

"Fuck! You're not going to like this. I told you there was bad news as well as good."

"Who?" This time the word came out as a barely audible growl.

"Aubrey."

"Not?"

"There is only one Aubrey. Aubrey de Berg; the well-known antique dealer. Although everyone knows it's a totally different kind of dealing he makes all his millions with!"

As the waitress put down the two new glasses, they were instantly smashed to the floor by Steven's flailing hands.

"That... that cunt! No!" He buried his head in his hands, running them through his longish brown hair, then sat bolt upright, face scarlet, veins pulsing, eyes staring ahead madly. "The cunt! I'll..."

"You'll do fuckin' nothing Steven. Nothing that is, except, calm that nasty temper of yours. Shit, I'd forgotten how you lose it when you're upset." Darren suddenly glowered at the waitress who was now standing, dumbstruck, staring at them.

"Perhaps," he spoke in a slow, calculated, but obviously angry voice, "it might be a good idea to clean up the mess. Then, perhaps you'd like to replace the two glasses you *dropped*!" She flounced off, muttering under her breath in a foreign language.

Steven sat, slumped forward, clutching his bleeding hand and shaking his head slowly and repeatedly.

"Cunt... That vile cunt..."

"Here, let me look at that."

Steven relinquished his hand, like a child. Darren picked up the Kleenex from the table and dabbed at the cut, peering closely. "It's only a nick. No glass! Pretty sure... Here, hold this on it. Listen to me! You're supposed to be the doctor."

"The cunt!" This time, his voice sounded a little calmer. Darren took advantage of the lull to try to lighten the atmosphere. The waitress deposited two more glasses of champagne in a surly manner.

"Call me old fashioned, Steven, but that word really doesn't suit you. Not with your poncy accent. If you must refer to the person in question quite so often, could you substitute the word weasel perhaps?"

"Hmph." Steven almost smiled. He was visibly calming down.

"Look, get that down you and I'll put you in a taxi. I've got to get back to the pub, but Joe and Greg are on this evening, so I finish at six. I'll come round to you as soon as I finish work. Then..." He paused nervously. "If you want to try ringing Daniel... I don't like the thought of you being on your own... just stay at home and calm down. Have a sleep. I wish I could."

*

The flat still smelt of cigarette smoke, even though the boys who had rented it while Steven was in Sydney, had been gone for almost a month. There were marks on the cream flokati rug, where someone had made a half-hearted attempt to remove what was almost certainly a red wine stain. What a relief that he had decided to take the new red Arne Jacobsen swan chair to his parents, for safekeeping. With the matching footstool it had cost just over two thousand pounds. He had resisted the stool at first, but the salesman had persuaded him by saying that if he waited a year and bought it then, the dye lot of the fine tweed might not match.

Darren sat next to him on the settee, clutching a glass of strong gin and tonic in one hand, his Louis Vuitton organizer held in the other. It was open at the D pages of the neatly arranged address section.

"Go on then, if you're going to."

Steven gulped down his own strong drink and tentatively took the organiser. His hand shook. His eyes blurred momentarily. He shook his head. The number began with 0161. He didn't recognize the prefix. He picked up the phone and hesitated.

"Go on!"

He dialled and put the phone to his ear. His heart was pounding. No reply! He felt relieved. He waited for the answer machine. Then suddenly his heart leapt to his mouth. There was no mistaking that flat Doncaster accent.

"Hello, Aubrey de Berg's phone, Daniel speaking."

"Daniel. This is Steven."

"Oh Steven! How wonderful! I heard you were back. You just caught me. We're leaving for Manchester airport in about ten minutes." Daniel's guileless voice showed obvious, instant delight, without a hint of resentment, or any other apparent negativity. This made Steven feel a little more at ease. The word "we", however, caused his stomach to feel as if it was dissolving.

"Manchester? Where are you staying?" He couldn't bear to say "living".

"Altrincham. You should see the house. It's on Dunham Road, where all the footballers live. Not that you can see any neighbours! The gardens are so massive." His excited voice slowed and dropped a key, becoming very serious. "Oh look, Steven! You must have heard? Aubrey says you know each other."

"Yes, we have met… a long time ago. I'm surprised he remembers me?" He tried not to let his voice sound bitter or sarcastic. How could anyone who was recently so depressed, now sound so bright and cheerful?

"God, Steven! It's so lovely to hear your voice. You heard I've been ill?"

"Yes. Darren's kept me up with all the news. Thank God for email. He's here with me now." He tried to make his voice sound normal, but he could hear it trembling.

"Oh! Say hi to him. Steven, I'm fine now. I really am. Look, Steven! You don't mind, do you?"

"Mind? Mind what?"

"About Aubrey."

"Mind about Aubrey? Of course not! Why should I? How could I?" he lied.

"God, I've just had the most brilliant idea!" Daniel's voice became high pitched again with excitement. "Look, it's my birthday on Saturday –"

"I hadn't forgotten," Steven interrupted.

"Well I've just had a brilliant idea. We're going to Provence. Aubrey's got this amazing house. Almost a chateau! I've seen photos. It's really amazing. It's surrounded by vineyards. His own! Just by the sea, though. Somewhere called Cassis. Near Marseilles. We're having a party. He told me to invite who I wanted. So far I've only asked Allan. You know Alan from St Thomas's. And Peter, his new boyfriend. Please say you'll come. It would be perfect."

"I couldn't..." he stuttered in panic. "Anyway, what about Aubrey?"

"He won't mind. He's not the jealous kind. He knows he's no need to be."

Steven felt as if someone had just filled his whole body with molten lead.

"Anyway, he said to ask anyone. Please say you'll come! It would mean so much to me." He hesitated. "You know. Kind of closure." He waited for some kind of reaction. Steven couldn't speak.

"Look, I'm going to put the phone down. I'll have a quick word with Aubrey. Just to make sure. I'll phone straight back. Think about it. Look, bring Darren! Yes, bring Darren. Don't say no, Steven. Please!" The phone went dead.

For a moment Steven was numb. Darren looked at him anxiously, waiting for an explosion. There was none. Instead, Steven turned slowly towards him, his lip quivering, his eyes wet and blazing.

"I *am* in love with him! How can I have been so stupid? How can I have been so selfish? I've got to get him back. Oh God! It can't be too late. Tell me it's not too late." He clutched Darren's hands tightly and stared into his eyes with a frighteningly desperate, almost manic look. "He can't be in love with that... that..."

"Weasel?"

*

Darren had insisted that Steven go through, while he waited for their bags to arrive on the carousel. He had guessed, correctly, that Daniel would be waiting for them on his own, whilst his new lover remained in the car. It would give them a few minutes on their own, to get over the first difficult conversation.

It wasn't at all difficult and even though Steven was nervous, he felt oddly calm, as he walked through customs to the sparkling new entrance hall of Marseilles airport. The first thing that struck him was the unexpected absence of a smell, or combination of smells, which he always associated with French airports. The unmistakeable one of Gauloise or Gitanes cigarettes, combined with an underlying, but unidentifiable sickly-sweet caramel smell.

He didn't see Daniel at first. He was standing with his back to a doorway, so that the glaring early summer sunshine rendered him little more than a silhouette. His hair was different, much shorter and carefully waxed and twisted into little spikes. He walked smiling towards Steven. That totally guileless, beautiful smile. He ran the last few steps and flung his arm round Steven's neck and whispered into his ear.

"Friends?"

"Friends."

Daniel sprang back, grinning. "You look as handsome as ever."

"Thank you. Must be the tan." He was finding this strangely easy. "Don't look too hideous yourself." The boy was indeed looking wonderful, in beige shorts, to just below his slender knees and a white T-shirt, with a peace symbol printed on in red, to look like graffiti.

"Thank you, kind sir. Hey. Where's Darren?"

"Waiting for the bags. So's we'd have a few minutes on our own. Thoughtful old Darren."

"Well, the baggage is pretty quick here, but we've time for a beer. Look, I'll go and get us a drink. There's a money machine round the corner, if you want. Bet you didn't get any. Not that you'll need any, staying at Aubrey's."

Steven fished out his card and disappeared round the corner, trying to ignore the last sentence. He was back within a couple of minutes.

"Cheers." The boy was sitting on a shiny modern aluminium chair, grinning up at him. Steven wanted to take him in his arms and kiss him. No, he mustn't spoil everything now. He sat down. The cold beer tasted good.

"Where's Aubrey?"

"Waiting in the car. It's brand new. Wait till you see it. He's scared someone will open their car door and scratch it. Don't worry. He's got *The Times*. We got here early so I could take it out to him."

"What about Alan and Peter?"

"Oh! They got here this morning. They've stayed back at the house, making use of the pool. Oh God! Just wait till you see the pool. Crazy really. Aubrey had it put in, but he can't even swim. He says he likes to see his guests enjoying themselves."

I bet he does! Steven thought to himself. *Watching* though, not seeing.

"Peter's really cute, but I think Alan's a teeny bit jealous about me and Aubrey. It was him who introduced us.

"Where?"

"Ku Bar. It was my very first outing since..." His voice slowed and softened. He quickly regained his cheerful equilibrium. "He must be jealous. He even tried to put me off him. Suggested Aubrey wasn't quite... you know... reliable. Of course it's nonsense. He adores me. I know he does. Look!" He held out a new Audomas Piaget watch for inspection. "*And* he's promised to convert the *pigoniere* into a meditation room for me. *And*..." He paused and looked directly at Steven, measuring the effect his next announcement would make. "We're going to get married! Not yet. Maybe in a year? But a proper wedding. In a lavender field!"

Steven quickly changed the subject. "Is Alan still at Saint Thomas's?"

"Yes. He keeps trying to persuade me to go back to nursing. The thing is, I don't really need to now. Aubrey doesn't want me to. Says I don't need to earn a living. He says he's got more money than he knows what to do with. Hey look! It's Darren!" He jumped up, rushed over and gave him a bear hug.

Aubrey was standing by the car. He was immaculately and expensively dressed in Armani, with bare tanned feet in pale brown leather deck shoes.

He shook hands first with Steven, smiling broadly, but fixing his gaze with a steely glare, which Steven interpreted as a threat. "Yes, Doctor Steven Wilson. We met years ago." And then turned, smiling and hand outstretched to Darren." I don't think I've had the pleasure?"

Darren simply smiled back and accepted the firm handshake. He would have liked to reply, but restrained himself for Daniel's sake. "Oh, yes, you have. And I remember exactly where and when. It was Sub Station South in Brixton on a Monday night; underwear night!"

*

The conversation in the car during the half-hour drive from the airport to Cassis was polite and affable. Aubrey, who, Steven noted with regret, was looking exactly like a film star, did most of the talking. He acted as tour guide explaining the assets and peculiarities of this particular little corner of Provence. He also mapped out the plans for the weekend. This evening, as they would inevitably be rather tired, they were to spend quietly, with dinner at home. Then, Saturday morning at leisure, with of course, use of the pool. Then in the late afternoon they were to go by boat to something, which Aubrey referred to without explanation as the *cabanon* for a birthday picnic dinner.

The little port of Cassis is situated at the mouth of a narrow valley, just to the east of Marseilles. Every available centimetre of the valley is filled with well-established vineyards, which border either side of the narrow road, which connects the motorway with the port.

"Home at last!" Aubrey announced, as he swung the Mercedes off the road to the right and stopped in front of a pair of magnificent iron gates, which obediently opened silently, as if by magic.

The car crunched slowly up a long beige gravel drive, shaded by an avenue of dark pencil pines. On either side, neat manicured rows of vines stretched away into the distance and ahead, the house. Daniel swivelled round in his seat to look back, grinning at Steven and Darren, just to make sure they were suitably impressed. It would have been difficult for anyone not to be impressed. The house was magnificent. Seven pairs of tall French windows punctuated its honey coloured façade. The middle pair, slightly wider than the rest, provided the main entrance to the house. On the first floor, there were seven slightly smaller windows and above those, under the terracotta pan tiled eaves, seven small oval ones. Each window had a pair of open wooden shutters, painted in a faded lavender colour, which made a wonderfully harmonious contrast with the pale yellow of the sun-bleached stone. Aubrey steered the car around the side of the house and parked.

"We'll go in the back way, then you'll see the pool." The back of the house was even grander looking than the front. What had at first seemed to be a solid block of a building, turned out to be built on a delicate U plan, with two narrow wings stretching backward from either side of the front section of the house. The three inner walls, which seemed more windows than wall, protected a gravel courtyard. Between each pair of French windows stood a dark green wooden box, each containing a small olive tree. Behind the house, stretching across it's entire length was the swimming pool, and behind that the "orangery". The ground floor of this elegant building, they learned, housed changing rooms, shower, sauna and gym. The first floor contained two staff flats. One was empty and the other was occupied by Jean Luc.

Jean Luc, they learned, looked after the pool, the garden and the cars. The rest of the staff comprised of two Portuguese girls, who came in every day to look after the house, and Carlotta, the cook, who drove in every morning at six from Marseilles on a large Harley Davidson. Carlotta, who was unmarried and favoured rather masculine clothes, came from Genoa, where she had been the head chef in a very chic restaurant. Aubrey confided that he simply couldn't stand the whole French attitude to food and that if anyone else offered him foie gras or lobster, he would vomit on them.

"Mmm. I thought the boys would have been enjoying a swim!"

Aubrey seemed somewhat disappointed. "Still, they're probably having a little nap." He chuckled. "Hadn't realised how late it is! Daniel will show you where you are sleeping, then if we all meet by the pool in about half an hour for a drink... then dinner at eight? We'll eat in the dining room. Hope you don't mind. It's such a bother to eat outdoors. Bloody mosquitoes and Carlotta gets very cranky if she has to stay late and pack everything away. If we eat in the dining room, she can get away after pudding. Then we just shut the door on the mess and the girls sort it all out in the morning. Oh! Don't dress up..."

*

Daniel showed Darren to his room first, then Steven, to his, next door. It was the room at the back of the right hand wing of the house and had windows on three sides. The fourth wall, through which they entered, was entirely covered with books.

"Isn't it brilliant?" Daniel beamed with innocent pleasure as he bounced on the white hand-quilted bed cover. "It used to be Aubrey's room..." He blushed slightly. "Before me... Now we use the big bedroom at the front of the house. It's got two en suites!"

Steven instinctively knew that Aubrey would cringe at the expression "en suite" used to describe what he would probably refer to as a dressing room.

"Come here! Let me give you a hug." The boy's hair smelt different. His own heart was pounding. He had to be careful not to get serious too early. "God, what have you got on your bloody hair. You nearly had my eye out!"

"Boring old fart!" Daniel laughed. He seemed quite at ease. He couldn't be happy? It must be an act. "Oh! You know Aubrey said don't dress up? Well, he does. We don't wear shorts for dinner!" He raised his eyebrows slightly as he turned to leave. The door, Steven realised for the first time, was covered in fake books. The whole wall of books must be fake!

"Don't worry, I won't embarrass you. Okay if I wear my leather harness?"

The boy laughed heartily and closed the door behind him. Steven began to explore the elegantly decorated room. It was surprisingly plain, relying for its effect on the architectural detail and the windows. There were no pictures or curtains, only a white-painted antique wooden bed and an elaborate, heavy gilded armchair, upholstered in faded denim.

He pushed an obviously worn spot on the wall of leather book spines. Another door sprung back to reveal a dazzling white marble bathroom. It was equipped like a five-star hotel. In a recess in the wall, behind a yellow background tapestry, he discovered a row of padded coat hangers, covered in white linen. On a low marquetry table, Steven was surprised to find, among the plethora of toiletries, a very expensive looking set of binoculars. He picked them up and walked back into the bedroom. The rear windows of the room, looked out onto the pool. He put the binoculars to his eyes. He didn't need to adjust the focus. If the "apparition", which was leaning on a rake at the end of the pool, had been white, rather than golden-brown and not been wearing a minute pair of sky-blue Speedos, he would have sworn it was a statue of an ancient Greek athlete. So that was Jean Luc! He scrutinised his face. Stunning indeed, he looked like a Versace model. But he definitely didn't look happy! He was glowering up at the house. What did that look signify?

*

The dining room was a surprise. Although the pale wooden panelled walls between the floor-length windows sported elaborated gilt and crystal candle brackets, the dining table, by contrast, was a huge brutal altar of granite, supported by two more massive granite slabs. The twelve chairs were of moulded blonde plywood and were, it was explained, a classic Swedish design of the sixties. The china was large, white and totally plain, but the cutlery was of heavy crested antique silver. In the centre of the table was a large square glass vase filled with wild grasses. Carlotta, it transpired wouldn't consider scented flowers on the table, distracting the diner from the simple perfection of her food. And perfect it was. That evening's menu consisted of a salad of wild rocket and baby dandelion leaves, topped with a perfectly poached egg and a snowdrift of white truffle shavings. This was followed by poached chicken, with simply steamed waxy potatoes, accompanied by Mostarda di Cremona, a sweet Italian relish of preserved fruits in a mustard-flavoured syrup. The meal ended with a large glass pedestal dish filled with tiny wild strawberries and a matching jug of crème fraiche.

The wines were as superb and sophisticated as the food was deceptively simple. The conversation, mostly led by Aubrey, was polite, but stilted to begin with, until the alcohol began to blur the prickly atmosphere somewhat. Alan, however, hardly uttered a word all evening and looked positively sullen. His young boyfriend, by contrast, got drunk very quickly and giggled at each and every comment. Daniel seemed totally unaware of any tension and chattered away excitedly whenever Aubrey wasn't holding court and extolling the virtues of Provence. Darren was surprised at Steven's calmness and the extremely polite way he encouraged conversation from their somewhat pompous host. He suspected, that perhaps Steven was trying to goad Aubrey into making a fool of himself. Aubrey excused himself three times during the course of the evening and was absent for rather longer than it takes any man to pee. Each time he returned, his eyes shone a little more brightly and his demeanour became even more pompous.

The plans for the birthday celebration the following day were revealed, as the second bottle of Beaume de Venise was uncorked at the end of the meal. Aubrey, it transpired, had an important business deal to finalise the following morning. He suggested that Daniel took the estate car, in the morning, to give his guests a short tour of Marseilles and pick up the provisions, which he had ordered from the best *traiteur* in the city, for the evening's picnic. They were to have a light lunch in the city. Then, in the early afternoon they would set off for the *cabanon*... Aubrey paused to judge the non-comprehension the word had had on his audience. Steven obliged him by enquiring what a *cabanon* was.

Numerous small fjords, called *calanques*, indent the rocky coast between Cassis and Marseilles, Aubrey explained. Most of these, surrounded by tall cliffs, are only accessible by sea. Over the years, locals have built small rustic shacks, called *cabanons* which they use as secluded holiday homes. The previous owners of Aubrey's house and vineyard, owned one of these, and when Aubrey bought the property, this was included in the deal.

Aubrey's *cabanon* was closer to Marseilles than Cassis, but still only about three-quarters of an hour very pleasant boat ride from the much smaller port. Although Aubrey owned a motor launch, which he normally used, it was really only comfortable for four people, so he had arranged to hire a small wooden fishing boat for the afternoon and evening.

Alan's young friend, who had apparently been in a state of semi- coma for the last half-hour, suddenly sat bolt upright and piped in a shrill voice. "If there are two bishops in bed, which one wears the nightie?"

Darren tentatively filled in the embarrassed silence, which followed."Okay. Which one wears the nightie?"

"Mrs Bishop, of course!" The boy almost fell off his seat with laughter.

Daniel was the only guest to join in and then very half-heartedly. Aubrey ostentatiously dropped a crumpled napkin beside his plate, pushed back his chair, stood up, gave the boy a withering look and announced, "I think an early night might be a good idea. Everyone seems to be rather tired."

*

Aubrey didn't appear for breakfast. He always had his in bed, Daniel explained. Carlotta seemed in a much more cheerful mood than usual and was positively chatty. She was Italian it transpired. She confirmed that her parents were from Italy, but she was born and brought up in Sydney and had only moved back to Italy a year ago.

Shortly after breakfast, a shopping party of four set out for Marseilles. Steven excused himself at the very last minute. He wanted to just enjoy the quiet. It had been a busy week at St Thomas's. He wanted to finish re-reading *Rough Music*. He went very quietly straight up to his room. The flowers *and* sheets had been changed, he noticed. He heard the engine of the people mover start up and listened to the distinctive noise of heavy rubber tyres on gravel as the vehicle slowly rounded the side of the house and then fade and disappear along the avenue towards the automatic gates. He picked up the binoculars and trained them on the pool area.

Less than five minutes later he heard the gravel crunch again. This time it was a fainter sound. Feet. Seconds later, Aubrey came into view. He was walking purposefully towards the orangery. He was carrying what appeared to be a small package in one hand. He stopped in front of the side of the building, where Steven knew the doors to one of the staff flats was. He appeared to talk for a few seconds and then disappeared inside. Steven sat patiently on the broad polished oak windowsill, the binoculars trained on the spot where Aubrey had disappeared. His face appeared perfectly calm and lacking in any visible emotion.

About forty minutes later, Aubrey appeared again. He turned round and faced the invisible but obviously open doorway. He seemed agitated. Steven focused the binoculars more accurately. Heated words were being exchanged. Aubrey suddenly turned on his heels and walked briskly back in the direction of the main part of the house and disappeared from view. Steven slowly lowered the binoculars from his face to reveal a calm, confident smile.

He changed and went to lie by the pool until the others returned. Aubrey avoided any eye contact when Steven saw him next.

*

"Hate these crowds! But at least they're not quite as common as the oiks at St Tropez or Juin les Pins," Aubrey spat out as he led the small crocodile of picnickers down a narrow tree-lined street, bordered with small boutiques selling resort clothes, post cards and rustic pottery.

The compact seafront looked exactly like a picture postcard, with crystal clear blue sea, small wooden fishing boats tied up to the stone quayside and a row of jolly bars, cafes and restaurants with colourful shutters and tables spilling almost into the sea. These were crowded with noisy holidaymakers, half of who, male or female, seemed to be dressed in white cotton or linen with quantities of chunky gold jewellery. Apart that is from a smattering of camouflage or leopard prints.

Jean Luc took up the rear of procession carrying a large wicker picnic hamper. Despite the fact he was sporting what was obviously a very new Tag Heuer watch, his face looked like thunder.

*

Aubrey spotted someone through the crowds and quickened his pace towards the quayside. In doing so he disturbed a group of seagulls, feasting on pieces of croissant, donated by some late breakfaster. As they flew up around him, in a bristling cloud, he shuddered; for once his normal polished veneer showed a crack. "Vile feathered vermin!" he cursed under his breath.

Quickly recovering his equilibrium, he was soon pressing, what appeared to be a sizeable wad of notes, into the hand of the burly youth who was standing in front of a small green-and-cream-painted wooden boat. The boy grinned at Aubrey and winked.

Within minutes they were settled in the boat and the group at last began to assume a party atmosphere. Jean Luc sat in the prow, with the hamper wedged under the bench, behind his legs. Steven and Darren sat side by side in front of him on the wooden bench facing the stern. In the middle, Alan and Peter perched on the low side of the boat with Daniel opposite and Aubrey stood in the stern, one hand on the wooden tiller, where he manoeuvred the little craft carefully out of the harbour.

Even Alan was now laughing and joking. It was impossible not to be happy in such a glorious setting, with the brilliant early afternoon sun making the slightly choppy sea around them, shimmer and sparkle like diamonds. As Aubrey steered out of the protection of the harbour, the sea became even choppier and there was much hilarity as they ducked and dived among the little white horses, the spray drenching their tee shirts as they clung on to the narrow wooden sides of the boat. Darren was relieved to see his best friend Steven looking positively carefree. Only Jean Luc remained unsmiling.

Aubrey pushed the worn wooden tiller to the left behind him and the boat steered right and edged its way in towards the shelter of the tall cliffs, where there was no wind and the sea was as flat and shining as a mirror. He called out the names of the different *calanques* as they passed them on the right. For the first half hour, they were accompanied along the coast, by several pleasure boats filled with tourists out enjoying the same sights. Then suddenly they reached the spot where the pleasure boats turned around to return to Cassis and then they had the magnificent craggy coast entirely to themselves.

"Time for some birthday bubbles," announced Aubrey, who for once was smiling almost naturally. He nodded at Jean Luc, who dragged the hamper from under his legs. The lid had special compartments for champagne glasses, which were quickly passed down the boat until everyone was clutching one with one hand whilst holding on to the boat with the other. Next, Jean Luc took a bottle of champagne from the hamper's specially insulated section and wrapped it in a white linen tea towel, embroidered in the corners with blue anchors. Just as he was about to tackle the cork, Aubrey interrupted, his face now wearing an expression that could only be described as a sneer. "No, JL," he purred in an obviously sarcastic tone, "we have professional bar staff on board." He nodded towards Darren, who calmly took the linen-wrapped bottle. Verve Cliquot, he noted with approval. The distinctive yellow label showed above the white cloth. Just as he began to massage the cork out of the bottle's neck, the boat rounded the small headland, which had been sheltering them from the blustery wind. The boat began to duck and dive more and again the little party dissolved in fits of laughter as cold foam repeatedly hit their, now sun-baked, bodies.

It happened in a split second, but one that seemed to last for minutes, as if in slow motion. The cork hit Aubrey in the centre of his forehead exactly halfway between his carefully groomed, blond eyebrows. No one shouted as they watched him topple backwards into the boiling water. Champagne spurted from the open bottle, mixing with the sea spray.

The boat was almost overturned as Jean Luc jumped over Steven and Darren and scrabbled to the stern to grab the tiller. He screamed at everyone, in French, to sit still. Used to driving a car, he rammed the tiller over to the left, expecting the boat to follow, but instead it swerved instantly in the opposite direction towards the cliffs on their right and before he had time to correct the mistake, the prow rammed itself up into a deep fissure in the perpendicular cliff. The engine, which no one knew how to stop, wedging the wooden sides of the boat harder into the jagged vice.

As they scrabbled to try to release the boat from its rocky prison, no one noticed that Darren alone hadn't moved from his seat. He sat smiling and sipping champagne. No one heard him singing under his breath. "Half a pound of tuppeny rice, half a pound..." The sound was carried upwards on the wind where a lone seagull sat on the top of the cliff. The bird raised its head and let out a cry. It sounded like a human laugh. Darren looked up at it and winked.

Dead & Gone
Bryan Connon

Dead & Gone
Bryan Connon

Back in the so-called swinging 60s, I wrote a TV feature about Percy Mahon who was hanged in 1924 for chopping up his mistress at a lonely cottage near Eastbourne. He had film star good looks and at his trial he dressed smartly in a new suit and wore a tan make-up as he sparkled and charmed his way through the horrifying evidence. In his hometown of Richmond-on-Thames he was a popular attraction at the tennis club, where his prowess and well-muscled body were much admired.

I did most of my research in Richmond library browsing through the local papers for 1924 but, to my surprise, the case, which dominated the likes of the *Daily Mail* and other sensational national papers, got hardly a mention. By contrast the *Richmond Times* gave full coverage to the mystery killing of two young men on the towpath who were found early one morning by a gent 'walking the dogs'.

They had been beaten to death and one had his face battered to a pulp. Studio portraits of the boys showed Bill aged 18, an apprentice plumber, to be darkly handsome and butch, while Alex aged 19, an assistant in a menswear shop, was fair and startlingly beautiful. They were in their Sunday best and the formal suits, stiff white collars and ties with hair slicked back emphasised their good looks.

A discreet comment left a good deal to the imagination: 'their clothing was disarranged'. Several more reports followed, but after a brief account of the inquest the case was apparently dropped with the comment that the police were pursuing inquiries.

It was obviously a gay murder in a town that had a long gay history, probably going back to the time it was chosen by Henry VII to build his palace. The towpath was notorious and there was a long tradition of gay pubs. There had even been a tearoom on Richmond Hill, which had private rooms available for male couples, which was only closed down during a police purge in 1954.

Because I was intrigued by the boys' deaths, I researched their story along with the Mahon story, but discovered nothing about them. It seemed as if all trace of their families had vanished and the handful of locals who remembered Mahon had only vague recollections of Bill or Alex. Writing my TV script, the idea gradually formed that Mahon could have been their killer. Facts were lacking but coincidence wasn't. Mahon was in Richmond on the day of the murder and his police record suggested he may have been bisexual. The shop where Alex worked sold sports clothes and Mahon may have bought his tennis gear there. The motive could have been sexual jealousy. Finally, I wondered, if the police had dropped the case because they had Mahon in custody for the Eastbourne murder?

The TV feature was transmitted in the autumn and received good ratings but a line implying that Mahon was bisexual was cut. "No stained sheets to prove it, old boy," as my fiercely hetero producer picturesquely put it. But he left in a reference to the unsolved murder of the two boys which I had sneaked in as Richmond background.

Several days after transmission I got a letter forwarded by the Television Centre from a Mr Gray asking to meet me as he had information about the killing of Bill and Alex. He turned out to be a tall, well-built man, of military bearing, about sixty. He was neatly dressed in navy blazer and well-pressed flannels, with a regimental tie and a full head of white hair carefully brushed. He smelted of perfumed soap or cologne, which did not fit the straight image. He smiled a great deal but his eyes did not. He introduced himself as Jack and we settled at a table in the corner of the S and F café off Piccadilly where he had chosen to meet. This was a favourite of actors, rent boys and gays of both sexes, a sort of halfway stop before the pubs opened. Nursing a cup of coffee he abruptly announced that he was dying of cancer: "It's a matter of months. I wanted to see you because you mentioned the unsolved mystery of the towpath murders on your programme. I thought after all this time it had been completely forgotten. I know the truth and I want it told." He lit a cigarette from a pack of Capstan Full Strength. "Bill was my brother, we were both queer and we both fancied Alex. After Bill died, my family moved to

Peterborough and I joined the regular army and gave up as an apprentice butcher, which I hated. Eventually I married, most queers did in those days. The wife and I had an understanding, if I had a fling she didn't want to know. She died during the war in 1942. Then I met Jimmy in the Salisbury. We used to come in here when he worked in town. He was an actor, mostly understudying and the odd bit part in films. He was self-educated and he educated me. Should have been a star, should Jimmy."

I interrupted. "What about Bill and Alex?"

He grimaced. "Bloody Alex, a right little tart, a dab hand with the tape measure in the shop and at your service outside it. Everyone fancied him, even Percy Mahon who liked a change now and again from women. Nobody took Alex seriously, then he fell for Bill, head over heals, it was pathetic, little presents, silly notes, like a lovesick girl. Bill was flattered, and tried to laugh it off, but I could see Alex was not going to give up and I got annoyed and jealous. Bill told me not to be stupid but I couldn't help myself, I told Percy about it over a few drinks, he was a sympathetic listener, a good type, very popular around the pubs. Handy with his fists. He offered to have a word with Alex, warn him off, duff him up a bit." He grinned. "That was the time he asked me about the best butcher's knife for cutting raw flesh."

I asked the waitress for more coffee. The S and F was starting to fill up as actors came in for a snack before performances. Jack watched them. "I was hoping to see some of Jimmy's mates come in."

When the coffee arrived, I asked: "What went wrong? Did Mahon go too far and why did he kill Bill?"

Jack stared at me and laughed: "You've got it wrong. Percy had nothing to do with it. It's me who went too far. Followed Bill and Alex along the towpath and watched them make love. I can't describe the fury and jealousy I felt, I went berserk and attacked Alex, nearly beat his face in, then I saw Bill on the ground, I didn't know what happened exactly. He was still alive but he died in my arms. The police questioned me but they never guessed. They must have decided it was down to anti-queer thugs." He stopped for moment and stared at me, his eyes expressionless. "You don't get it, do you? Bill and me were lovers, had been since we were kids. Identical twins, it's not unusual. I killed half myself that night and I've only been half alive ever since. There's always an empty space in my bed where he should be."

At that moment a tall angular woman smelling strongly of Tweed leaned over our table: "Hallo Jack, my dear. How are you bearing up? I did admire you at the funeral. Jimmy was such a lovely man." She smiled a crocodile smile and moved on.

"That was Jimmy's agent." Jack took out his wallet and passed me a cutting from the *Islington Gazette*. As I read it silently, a chill spread through my body: "Actor beaten to death in Highbury Fields."

Jack smiled, his eyes still expressionless: "Funny how history repeats itself."

Strangers on a Plane

Jack Dickson

Strangers on a Plane
Jack Dickson

'Ever wondered what it would be like to kill someone?'

I looked at him, with his beige turtleneck and his long dark hair tied back in a ponytail. 'You mean, have I ever wanted someone dead?' My mind flashed to the bastard of an editor who'd dragged me half way across the world only to finally agree that yes, this draft was fine and any further rewrites could be done email.

'No, no...' A series of quick head shakes quivered a lock of that tangled hair free from its tether.

I fought an overwhelming urge to brush it gently from his pale cheek.

'... I mean, have you ever wondered what it would feel like. To kill someone.'

'Ah...' I nodded, staring into soft green eyes. I wondered what he'd look like naked.

It was one of those three-in-the-morning conversations. Around us, most of the other passengers on the redeye from Newark to Heathrow dozed fitfully. 37,000 feet above the Atlantic and I was too buzzed to sleep.

We'd got talking four hours ago, after a few smiles and glances exchanged over Continental's choice of in-flight movie: Brad Pitt and Julia Roberts in something banal and senseless. He'd said Pitt was awesome in *Snatch*. I preferred him in *Fight Club*. He introduced himself as Nicholas Straw, HR consultant. I'd smiled, returned the gesture. We exchanged business cards, chatted about his first visit to the UK and the US publication of my most recent book. And things had progressed from there.

'I think about it all the time...' He leant back in his seat, gaze focused on the panel above his head. '... I wonder if you need to be... detached.'

'Like those cold, emotionless sociopaths you see on TV?' I couldn't take my eyes off him.

He nodded, more acknowledgement than assent. 'I never buy that – I mean, just because they don't show much emotion, doesn't mean there's not stuff going on, deep down inside.'

He was American, this Nicholas of mine. A native New Yorker who lived with a boyfriend of eight years, in a loft in Chelsea – Chelsea of the Chelsea Hotel fame. He used the same deli as Edmund White, but was too young to remember Sid and Nancy. I considered giving him my 'it's detachment from the consequences of one's actions, not the act itself' speech. But I was content to let him just ramble on...

Full, bee-stung lips pursed in thought. Nicholas stretched out long, coltish legs under the seat in front.

... because as long as he talked, I could look at him with impunity.

'Those guys who go buy an Uzi then mow down their co-workers – or high-school kids, opening fire on classmates...'

He was chewing on his bottom lip now, and I would have paid money to change places with those pristine white teeth.

'... what's that all about? I mean, all that anger.'

'No clue, but people also kill all the time to... protect what's theirs.' I watched the way the fine muscles in his neck strained, and thought about tigresses fighting for the survival of their young.

'Oh yeah – that's true. Possessiveness. I wonder...'

It wasn't quite what I'd been getting at, but I was too transfixed by the way his Adam's apple bobbed lightly when he swallowed to correct him.

'What about hate? Maybe you need to really, really despise someone in order to take their life.'

'Or be really, really in love – *crime passionelle*, and all that.' .

'Cream...?' That soft green gaze swivelled to meet mine.

I smiled. 'Crime of passion, jealousy, spur of the moment thing – love and hate supposedly opposite side of the same coin.' Now that I had his attention, I was determined to keep it. 'Believe it or not, in French courts *crime passionelle* was considered a legitimate defence until fairly recently.'

'Oh...' He looked vaguely disappointed, eyes returning to their examination of the air-conditioning controls above his head. '... only in France?'

'Not sure about Canada, but like I said, even the French don't buy it any more. You could maybe swing it and argue diminished responsibility but if it's premeditated, murder's murder in most civilised countries, these days.' My smile remained fixed. I tried to work out how we'd got onto this topic. I tried to remember when subtle flirting had given way to a philosophical discussion. 'You want another drink?' I nodded to his empty Evian bottle in an attempt to change the subject.

'Far as I can see, premeditated at least means you've given it some consideration. And I kind of like the idea of that.' The tip of his tongue flicked where his teeth had been, wetting the surface of his dry lips. 'No one should die without thought...'

I watched the shadow of a yawn play around the corners of his mouth, stretching and cracking the delicate pink skin.

'... Hell, life's meaningless enough, don't you think? Death has to have a point, or why bother at all?' He smiled. His entire face lit up for the briefest of seconds, those soft green eyes glowing in the 4 am gloom of the 747's dimmed cabin lights.

Entranced, I smiled back and watched his eyelids them flutter together. My reaction to the sheer physical proximity of this pale-skinned creature in the seat next to mine outweighed the effect of any rubbish coming out of that beautiful mouth. And ten minutes later, when his dark head slumped onto my shoulder in sleep, I let it lie there, shifting only the in-flight magazine from the seat-back pocket to cover my hard-on.

We shared a taxi into central London. When he suggested breakfast in his hotel, I should have known better. Following those coltish legs towards the lift, then up into Room 302, my dick was in charge. As I pushed that dick between bony arse cheeks and he moaned beneath me, I was still telling myself Nicholas was just some stranger on a plane I'd never see again, so where was the harm? It was a hard fuck. A rough fuck. He seemed to like the way I gripped his wrists and held him down. I liked his like enough to get it up a second time. I left him curled foetally around a pillow, bruises blooming on his wrists and mumbling in his sleep two hours later. And on the Tube to Baron's Court, I threw his business card into a litter bin.

*

Tom smiled and took my kiss, then listened to me rant about bastarding American editors and the decline of New York City's gay scene, post-Guiliani. Over Earl Grey and croissants, we chatted about his week, and the leaky roan pipe which was still disgorging its contents into the stonework of this bijoux, now-valued-at-£245,000 shoe-box of a flat. Domesticity reasserted itself. *We* and *our* dotted the conversation, and I saw no point in mentioning Nicholas Straw. Easing between crisp sheets just before 11 am, I gave up fighting jet-lag and let myself sleep. Somewhere in the distance, the phone rang. The answering-machine picked up and recorded two minutes of silence.

The rest of the week passed much as it usually did: work and cosy dinners in front of the TV. Tom took another couple of those wordless phone-calls. We even did 1471, but the caller withheld their number, as that irritating recording puts it. Saturday morning, he was at rugby-practice. I was redrafting. The phone rang. I picked it up:

'Hi Jack.'

I replaced the receiver.

The phone rang again, almost immediately.

I let the answer-phone pick up.

It taped another two minutes of silence. Was it my imagination, or could I hear him breathing at the other end of the line? Maybe I'd thrown his business card away, but he'd obviously held onto mine. I worked for another half an hour or so, but my heart wasn't in it. What that fist of muscle was doing, in fact, was throwing itself against my ribs. So I called it a day, switched the laptop off and went to meet Tom from the Accies.

Nicholas called another four times, over the course of that weekend. At least he had the sense not to leave a message. In one way, it would have been easier if he had: those silences spoke of melodrama and mystery – exactly the sort of thing this wasn't. Then they stopped. One, two, three days went by, and I found myself able to lift the receiver without an icy hand clutching at my balls. He'd taken the hint.

Nicholas Straw had finally worked out I wasn't interested.

Sunday night, we lay on the sofa watching *The South Bank Show*. Tom's head was on my chest, and I was stroking his hair. We were both half asleep. I didn't quite catch what he said, when he said it the first time. 'Hmmm... sorry?'

'This really hot-looking American was chatting me up, at the clubhouse yesterday.' Tom giggled. 'I tell you, made me feel there's life in the old dog yet.' His hand, which had been resting on my thigh, slowly moved upwards.

I stiffened. Literally and figuratively.

Tom's giggle deepened into a chuckle. One finger traced the outline of my balls. 'Didn't catch his name – I think he was a friend of Roger's, or something...'

I tried not to react. I tried to play it cool. Maybe I was just getting paranoid.

'... but he was definitely giving me the come-on...'

Two fingers toyed with my zip now. Then a third joined the duo. A breath caught in my lungs, refused to be expelled.

'... said he was over here on business or something – boy, that Noo Yawk twang's really sexy...'

Tom was moving now, his body shifting beside mine. Fingers lowered my zip. A hand slipped inside, palm curling around my half hard-on. Soft words in my ear, a parody of an accent:

'... wanna fool around, buddy-boy?'

But just because you're paranoid, doesn't mean they're not out to get you. Before I knew what I was doing, I was levering myself off the couch and marching through to the kitchen.

'Jack?' Confusion in my wake. 'Jack, what's wrong? I was only joking...' Tom's voice from the living room, competing with Melvyn Bragg's.

At the sink, I turned the tap on full and grabbed the kettle. The sound of drumming water drowned the thumping in my head.

'... it was just flirting, it didn't mean anything...'

Coincidence? I shoved the kettle under the tap, to fill it. Water gushed everywhere. I tried to turn the tap off. My knuckles gleamed, pyramids of white bone under pink skin. Hand gripped my shoulders:

'... baby... come on – I wish I'd never mentioned it, now.'

I had to ask. I had to ask if his American had dark tangled hair tied back in a ponytail. If he had soft green eyes, the kind of mouth you wanted to push your tongue into. Then Tom's hand was uncurling my fist from the tap and easing fingers between mine:

'You know what I think?'

But I didn't ask. How could I? What would I say: 'Roger's American friend sounds exactly like this guy I met on the plane from Newark, took back to his hotel and fucked'? Infidelity's such a bourgeois concept, but that doesn't make it any less hurtful.

'I think you need a holiday. You're working far too hard...' Tom's other arm curled around my waist, holding me tightly.

And I didn't need to ask. I knew it was Nicholas Straw. But I had no idea what he thought he was playing at. Or how to put a stop to it.

'... what do you say? I'll take next Friday off, and we'll have a long weekend in... Paris? You know you like Paris.' Tom kissed my neck.

Slowly, the knot in my stomach began to slacken off. I nodded. Yes, a holiday. Just Tom and I. No work. No distractions. No phone calls or chance meetings.

His strong arms eased me around. 'Okay, Paris it is.' His head was on my shoulder.

But later, in bed, sleepless eyes focused on the ceiling, it was Nicholas's face I saw.

Paris passed in a blur. I made the effort for Tom's sake. It seemed to work. By the flight home from Charles de Gaule the tiny lines of concern had left the corners of his eyes. And the skinny American with the ponytail and the bizarre line in chat-up material had slipped from my mind, the way I'd slipped from his body a full three weeks earlier.

My publisher had arranged a book-signing at Foyles. I loathe these things, but I did it. Three guys in Ben Shermans, one lady librarian and a Political Science student named Marvin. And later:

'To Nicholas, from Jack. Death is only the beginning.'

The antique fountain pen trembled on my hand. Ink scuttled across the page like a frightened spider. I closed the book and plucked an unmarred copy from the pile at my side. I started to write, eyes fixed on the smooth creamy paper.

'Why won't you take my calls?'

The nib of the pen stuttered on the fifth word of the inscription. Around us, people chatted, wine glasses clinked and a coffee machine hissed.

'Tom seems very nice – how long you guys been together? Fifteen, sixteen years was it, he said?'

Somehow, I got to the end of the dedication. I snapped the hardback shut with a bang and held it out, going into the spiel. 'Thanks for buying my book – I hope you enjoy...'

'Meet me later.' He took the volume. Our fingers brushed. The cuff of his shirt slid up to reveal a ring of yellowing bruise.

'No.' Under the table they'd set out for the signing, my cock belied my mouth. I stared into his open, innocent face.

He smiled. 'Just a drink – no strings.'

'I don't think that's a very good idea.' I reached past him, to take the book from the next customer in the growing queue.

He turned side on, his slender body screening us from view. 'I missed Tom, last weekend at the Rugby Club. Roger was telling me you guys were off to... Paris or somewhere?' His voice was low. The implication was unmistakable.

'Keep away from my...'

'Room 302. You know where. I'll be there all evening.' Then he was gone, khaki-ed arse and ponytail making their way towards the cash-desk.

Two hours of scribbling inanities transfigured my panic into a slow-burning frustration. I thought about going to the police, but there was little to tell and even less they could do. When I knocked on his hotel room door, it opened under my clenched fist. He was sitting on the bed, cross-legged and naked from the waist down. His hair was loose, tangling over his shoulders in thick ropy locks. He was holding my book. I entered, locking the door behind myself.

He smiled.

I hit him.

He dropped the book but took the slap.

I grabbed him by the hair, hauled him up off the bed and glowered into those soft green eyes. 'Don't phone me again. Leave Tom alone.

Stay out of my life.' The imprint of my hand was already pinking on his pale cheek.

He gazed into my face, huge pupils ringed with jade. The smile refused to leave his lips.

So I hit him again. And kept hitting him. I hit him till my knuckles stung and his mouth was a bloody hole. I hit him till I could no longer tell if he was smiling or not. Then I walked from the room.

I threw up on the Tube home, much to the disgust of my fellow passengers, and told Tom I'd caught my hand in a door. Later, when he was asleep, I wanked alone in the shower. The motion reopened the damage to my knuckles. I came shaking and sobbing, creamy spunk reddening then fading under the pounding jets.

'Mr Dickson?'

Next morning, I stared at the two uniformed police officers on my doorstep and stuck my bandaged hand into the pocket of my trackies.

'Mr John Dickson?'

'Er... yes, that's me.' Somehow I found a voice.

'I wonder if you can help us, Mr Dickson.'

Blood buzzed in my ears. It never occurred to me he'd try to press charges. My brain roared into action. Witnesses? Fingerprints? Had I bled in his hotel room? How long did spunk stay in the body? My word against the word of a...

'A white male in his early thirties was found, sexually assaulted and badly beaten, on Hampstead Heath early this morning. His wallet was empty but this was in his pocket.'

I stared at my business-card. Something dried and dark smeared one corner.

'We think he's American: US sizing in his shoes. Five-ten, one hundred and forty pounds... long black hair. Green eyes – mean anything to you, sir?'

Relief poured from my body like a bad smell. I half-wondered how he'd got from a central London hotel out to Hampstead. I half-wondered who had picked up where I'd left off. And about the sexual assault.

'The bloke's still unconscious, and we've no idea who he is. Could you spare half an hour or so to come down to Charing Cross Hospital and take a look at him for us?' The cop who was doing most of the talking lowered his voice. 'There's been a lot of gay-bashings on the Heath recently, as I'm sure you're aware, sir.'

The irony almost made me smile. I could have refused, denied all knowledge of green-eyed Americans. But instead I nodded, kept my bandaged hand in my pocket and followed them to their squad car.

He lay on his side, tangled hair spilling ink-like onto the white pillow.

Three stitches to the lip. Another four above the left eye. Fractured cheekbone and some windpipe damage. There was also rectal trauma and bruising to the thighs, so the doctor informed me.

'Straw – Nicholas Straw...'

The police officer to my left produced a notebook and wrote it down.

'... and he is American. Lives in New York, I think. We met on a flight from Newark, last month. He's in... Human Resources, or something. We exchanged business cards, the way you do.' I didn't mention his hotel. Staring at the limp, vulnerable shape with the drip in the back of its right hand I thrust my own deeper into my pocket. 'Is he going to be... all right?'

'Cat-scan's clear, he'll have a thumping headache and a sore throat when he wakes up, but apart from that, yes – looks very dramatic, I know, but it's all fairly superficial.' The doctor replaced Nicholas's chart at the side of his bed.

'Any idea about next of kin, Mr Dickson?'

I mumbled something about a partner in New York. They thanked me for my time and left with the doctor, chatting about time-zone differences and NYC phone books. I continued to stand there, then moved closer to the unconscious figure. Asleep, Nicholas looked younger. Much younger. He also looked at peace. As I stood there, staring at his mess of a face, one eyelid fluttered, then opened. I took a step back. The second eye opened. And ruined lips began to move:

'You came. I knew you'd come.' A parody of a smile edged its way onto his face.

I turned and stumbled from the room.

*

That evening, I made some excuse to Tom and went for a walk. I needed to think. I needed to decide what to do now, if anything. In a sense, it was his move. In whatever little game he was playing. To this day, I have no idea why I didn't tell Tom the whole sorry story then and there.

Maybe I knew it would make no sense.

Maybe I knew Tom was guaranteed to get the wrong end of the stick.

Maybe I knew that forming the words would give the thing an import and significance I wanted to avoid.

Or maybe I knew, even then, that this was something very private. Something between two strangers on a plane.

Walking along the Embankment, I replayed it all in my head. The phone calls and his chats with Tom. My reaction. His face as I'd slammed my fist into it. The churning in my guts when I learned he'd gone out, later that night, and got himself well and truly fucked over.

A plea for attention?

A cry for help?

Was it worth trying something I'd not previously considered, to rid myself of all this? Was it worth attempting to reason with someone who was obviously beyond reason? Someone who had the upper hand?

Under its wrapping, my fist throbbed. My entire right arm ached from the exertion of the beating I'd given him. A few shreds of adrenaline quickened my pace.

I knew I had to try.

And I knew I had to see him again.

Three days later they released him from hospital. I'd lost track of the last time I'd eaten. Or slept. We met in a bar, in Earl's Court. I wanted people around. I didn't trust myself alone with him. He was late. I'd already consumed two stiff gins and when he walked through the door every eye in that crowded place lingered on him.

Not because of the bruises. Or the stitches. Not even because of the striking, handsome figure of a man he cut, despite the damage from my own and other anonymous fists. But because he seemed to glow from inside. His eyes were alight. I thought it was drugs. But when he sat down opposite me and reached for my bandaged hand I knew better.

'I'm sorry you hurt yourself...' His voice was hoarse. Cradling my fist in both hands, he raised it to his lips and kissed it. '... and I'm sorry for all the games. But I had to know. I had to be sure.'

Everyone has their price – even screwy guys from NYC. With my free hand, I pulled out a long manila envelope from inside my jacket. Royalties-wise, it had been a good year. Plus, it was about time the house in Baron's Court earned its keep: forging Tom's signature on the application for a second mortgage had been easy. I pushed the envelope past my glass towards him.

He ignored it. 'Remember what we said on the plane? How anger wasn't enough? Or even the urge to protect?'

I had no idea what he was on about. So I pushed the envelope a little closer to his elbow.

'And you're anything but detached, Jack. I know that now.'

'There's half a million in there. Take it.'

He pushed it back towards me and leaned in closer. 'After you left me, four nights ago? I took a taxi to Hampstead. I'd read about the gay-bashings, in your *Evening Standard*...'

I could smell the stink of hospitals on him. Clean and sharp. And beneath that, a sour, desperate odour.

'... the police want me to press charges – they think they've got the guys who raped me, there's DNA and stuff – but I told them I didn't see their faces...'

The fingers of the hand on mine were easing up the bandages, loosing the grubby wrapping and slipping underneath.

'... and it's the truth. I closed my eyes, Jack, and I imagined it was you. Your cock ramming into me, tearing at my hole. Your boot in my ribs. Your hands holding my thighs apart...'

The rasping voice broke. A thumb brushed my raw knuckles.

'... pinning me down, smashing into my face...'

He was whispering now, holding my hand. I gazed into those soft green eyes.

'... don't let it be a stranger, Jack. Let it be you. You know I'm going to do it anyway. Be with me. Make it mean something.'

You go more than forty-eight hours without sleep, strange things start to happen in the brain. I lost it, then and there. Or maybe I found it – whatever *it* was. Somehow, I stood up. Somehow, he kept hold of my hand and my fingers curled around his in return. Back out in the streets, I led the way, my arm now around his slender waist. He leaned against me, whispering in that hoarse voice. It was all I heard.

I'm not sure how long we walked. But when we reached the alley, something felt right. Pinning him against a crumbling redbrick wall, I could barely see his face in the darkness. I kissed his injured mouth hard and fast, the way I'd fucked him that one night. The whimper came from deep in his chest. His arms reached up to wrap around my neck and he returned the kiss, moulding his body to mine. I was erect. I could feel his cock arching parallel to mine. When I pulled my lips from his and nuzzled his neck, the whimpers continued. His skin tasted salty. And as I moved him deeper into the alley, an empty bottle clattered and rolled on potholed tarmac.

I had no idea what I was doing. I'm not even sure there was an *I* any more, in any real sense. Part of me knew this was about to get very messy. Part of me knew I should undress. Part of me couldn't have stopped if my life depended on it.

His fingers were in my hair now, his body so alive in my arms. I dragged him off me, held him against crumbling brick. He lolled like a rag-doll after the first blow. I lost sensation in my fist after the fourth. When I could no longer bear to hit him, I gripped his shoulders and smashed the back of his skull off the wall.

He lost consciousness a couple of times, but took a long time to die. Where the fuck had been hard and fast, this was slow. So slow. I kept groping for a pulse on his neck. His thick hair was wet and warm and stuck to my face. He kept breathing, his skinny chest rising and falling gently... only to rise and fall again.

Some time later, we were both on the ground. My back was to the wall. We'd knocked over a dustbin at some point, and I could smell rotting vegetation over the sweet perfume of his body. I held him in my arms and let him bleed all over me. When his tired, unhappy heart squeezed out its final beat, I was glad it had been me. And I finally knew what it felt like to kill someone.

*

Some glass-collector or barman's now half a million better off, because we left the envelope behind. And maybe no one noticed the middle-aged writer when he came in, that night. But they all clocked Nicholas. And they all gave statements – five picked me out at an ID parade. That, plus the inscription I'd penned in his copy of my latest book convinced the jury I was indeed the danger to society that the media had painted me. My brief entered a plea of diminished responsibility, which the judge accepted. But they were all wrong. So wrong. I could never do it again. And my sense of personal responsibility had never been stronger.

Nicholas was right. Death is only the beginning. The beginning of a life sentence in a secure psychiatric unit for me. And freedom for him.

Two Birds, One Stone
Simon Edge

Two Birds, One Stone
Simon Edge

Walter turned obituaries and felt a stab of envy. It was not the first time.

He had always liked the obits. That was the reason he bought the *Telegraph*. It horrified his angry friends. But Walter didn't read those bits. He loved to see the faces of rosy-cheeked young captains – handsome in the way of all twenty-year-olds, with so little to show that they were actually seventy-eight or eighty-three, the text devoted to their exploits on the beach at Anzio or in North Africa with Monty. As if nothing since mattered. Perhaps it didn't.

Walter imagined friends not recognising the young blade, or grandchildren bemused to see their own faces reflected in smudgy newsprint: old men half his age, youth preserved in brilliantine.

Lately, though, the obits had begun to lose their attraction. Several times he had felt jealousy on reaching his favourite page. Seventy-four, seventy-eight, eighty-one. The bastards had served their time. It was like the woman at work who got in before everyone else so she could leave early and see to her kids. She had put in the hours, but you couldn't help resenting her putting her coat on at half-past four.

Today there were two wing commanders and a minor lesbian novelist. Generic wing commanders, Walter thought, just as he thought of archbishops as parsons. True to form, neither had done anything of note since 1945. The novelist had lived with a succession of other minor lesbian novelists, falling out with all but naming a cat after each. She had died trying to sue a newspaper which referred to her as dead. Normally, he would have enjoyed this detail.

He was not depressed. He had no problems. He was just not gripped by the future. He was forty-one. He had half his life to go; all right, that was optimistic, given some of his lapses on poppers. But even fifteen or twenty years was a wearying prospect.

He had not done badly. After Oxford, he had joined the civil service and progressed. He was now special adviser to an obscure minister of state. He was reasonably paid, and once he had accepted that he was never going to fly high, he was satisfied. Admittedly, his job did not impress anyone else. Friends from the media acted as if they were doing the world a favour by sharing their office gossip, and there was always an audience. But nobody ever wanted to know about Walter's job. He said he was a civil servant, and the questions stopped. Once, early in the Blair era, his minister had been caught in a cash-for-something shock, and there was surprise when Walter said he knew the man well. The clamour went up for more, but Walter had been a civil servant too long and could not. Everyone forgot about his inside track. He returned, mainly with relief, to the role of listener.

Civil service discretion worked the other way too. He thought most people at work knew, but he rarely volunteered that he was gay. There were two others in his department, Darren and John; the three would lunch or meet after work at a pub in Victoria Street where disco was played. Darren was young and fleshy. John was older, straight-laced in the office but camp in safe company. Walter would not say he liked them, but held them in a certain affection. They were where his two lives, work and gay, came together.

His heterosexual colleagues were another matter. Walter knew gay men who regurgitated every blow-job at work. One of them, an architect called David, led office outings to leather clubs. He said it was political, and it sometimes shamed Walter. But David did not work with Mrs Janet Rimmer from Banstead, three years from retirement and unaware that her surname could reduce a gay bar to giggles. (Dennis, Walter's fondest ex, referred to anilingus as "janetting".) It would also have been easier to fly the rainbow flag over Whitehall if he had someone to talk about. "Andrew/Peter/Steven and I went to Brighton for the weekend" might be acceptable, even to Mrs Rimmer, in a way that "I went to a sex club where I licked the private parts of several men whose names I don't know" was not.

The absence of Andrew/Peter/Steven was another disappointment he had resigned himself to, and even come to prefer. He had had many flings – sometimes with men called Andrew, Peter and Steven – and two or three relationships. The longest was with Dennis. It had threatened to become permanent until Walter asked him to move in. The problem was Dennis's cat, and Walter's allergy. It was not an issue when they lived apart – they just spent more time at Walter's. Then Dennis needed to move, and Walter decided it was time to live together. He convinced himself he could make it work with determination and antihistamines. He spent the first week sneezing, the second sneezing and snapping, and the third hinting that Dennis might like to give Elaine (as in Paige, the queen of *Cats*) to his sister Paula, who shared his passions for pedigree Burmese and musical theatre. Dennis spent the fourth week looking for somewhere new, and moved out two years to the day after their first meeting – neither of them noticed in the upheaval. Dennis was reluctant to return to Walter's to stay the night, and they stopped sleeping together. They discovered they were relieved.

But the friendship survived. Dennis was a tower of strength on Walter's thirtieth birthday, helping him fend off the miseries of being single and old. By his fortieth, at a private club on the Embankment, Walter had realised that he was one of life's bachelors – not just as a euphemism. He sold his two-bedroom flat on the Northern Line and moved into a Bloomsbury mansion block. It was handy for one-night stands – "I only live round the corner" worked wonders in Soho after the Tube – but it was cramped if a stranger stayed beyond a chivvying cup of coffee. He realised that was how he wanted it.

He still went out looking, and was capable of excitement if he found someone he didn't regret in the morning. There were also lows. The worst part was returning alone to the flat he had tidied before going out, the plumped cushions taunting his failure.

Dennis admitted to summoning the boy-whores who displayed their wares in the back of the free listings magazines. What You Saw Was What You Got – although not in all respects, since the photos never changed from year to year. Dennis, who was in the City, said it saved going out. But it was not for Walter, even if he could afford it. He had tried it once, when he was young enough for it not to mean anything, and spent the whole time worrying if his pierced, plucked, shaved visitor would have been there without the money. On the evidence, he seemed to like Walter. But that was probably professional skill. Walter knew this was not the point, but it bothered him all the same. It made him realise that sex, for him, was about self-esteem not gratification. He needed to know his market value, and cash distorted this market.

Not that it was worry-free when the transaction was cashless. If he picked up someone better looking than himself, he spent the whole time, before and after lights-out, wondering when they would realise their mistake. Would they be polite enough not to show it before leaving? It was not worth the stress. If he had to go to bed with someone in a different league, he preferred looking down not up. It was more reassuring.

He could still hold his own, albeit on the senior circuit. He had joined a gym and discovered he could bulk up. His head was too round, and he had never been handsome. But very short hair counteracted baldness, and the muscles were a definite asset. He was faring better than many contemporaries. The beauties of his twenties and thirties were suffering facial landslides, or getting fat. Age had levelled the field he was still able to play on.

He could rely on a degree of success at the Eagle, a late-night bar south of the river. Stripped to the waist, mooning out of leather chaps, he could grope other shaven-headed, bare-chested, moon-buttocked men of his age. Occasionally, he went back to their home or invited them to his. Other times he cruised the chat-rooms, calling a cab in the small hours and putting tipsy faith in a photo online.

It was a life, a perfectly good life. He had a few close friends, a central flat, and money to eat out and sit in the stalls at the theatre. He had two proper holidays a year – Italy in the early summer, for the wine and frescoes, and Gran Canaria in November, for the gin and sex – and had just had a long weekend in Warsaw, where an ex of Dennis's showed them around. He had done everything he had ever wanted to do. He had tried a quantity of drugs and a variety of sex more associated with rock stars than middle-aged civil servants.

But one night when he was thirty-seven, he had ended up in a foursome after the Bolt. Disconnected from his body, thanks to whatever was up his nose, he realised he had two men in him at the same time, and that he liked it. He was aware – the impression lingered when the drugs wore off – that life could only go downhill.

Other people never seemed to weigh the pros and cons. Did the good outweigh the bad, or even the indifferent? Half an hour's good sex, versus an inside-out umbrella drenching him on the way to work. An hour trudging to and from the supermarket, shirts still to iron. There were moments of bliss and misery, and ages of neither. Why not add them up? Other people had relationships or children to divert them, perhaps, but he didn't see the difference. Surely it was no more enriching to spend years fretting over some junior version who would hate you when it was old enough. And you still sagged and decayed – faster, even.

The wing commanders and the lesbian novelist could jack it in without anyone thinking the worse of them. Everyone else had to bide their time.

The phone rang.

"How was the Eagle?" said a Scottish voice, ominously chirpy. Dennis.

"I didn't go. I was knackered."

"I know the feeling."

Walter waited. Dennis only asked how his night had been when he wanted to boast about his own.

"Aren't you going to ask why?"

"I was assuming you were going to tell me."

"Oh, all right. You drag it out of me. He. Was. Stunning. Six foot two, German, enormous tits and perfect teeth. I tell you, we were at it. All. Night."

Walter grunted. Was he the only person who ever had bad sex?

"He had the best Es with him. Really strong, like a blast from the past. I told him, I said, I don't just want you, I want your dealer as well."

Walter did not share Dennis's excitement about dance drugs. He did not like jumping up and down for hours, and they stopped him concentrating at work for days. It never failed to surprise him how Dennis could do it in accountancy.

"And are you seeing him again?"

"Am I! Tonight. He's going back on Monday, so I want to make the most of him."

"He doesn't live here, then?" Walter had hoped for this.

"Here on business, the bastard. From Berlin."

Walter relaxed. Happy as he was being single, he preferred it when Dennis was too.

"Make sure you get his address. I haven't seen the new Reichstag."

"Well, I'll have somewhere to stay. What about you?"

"I'm sure he's got a spare room."

"In your dreams, darlin'. We're going to be fucking in every square inch of his flat. If last night's anything to judge by."

"Not to mention tonight."

"Exactly."

There was a change of gear at the other end.

"So anyway. How are *you*?"

"I'm all right."

"That good, huh?"

"Oh, I don't know. I'm fine, really. Just a bit... I don't know."

"You don't sound fine to me. Do you want me to come over?"

"I need to go to the gym. I didn't go last night."

"Go this evening."

"There's a film on TV."

"Tape it. I bet it's some black-and-white rubbish that you've seen tons of times before. I know what you're like."

"I keep telling you the old ones are the best."

"That's lucky for you then, isn't it?" said Dennis, on cue. He was five years younger than Walter, and never tired of mentioning it.

"Why don't you come round tomorrow?" Walter relented. "Come for lunch."

"I may still be lunching on my hot, meaty German. Cook me supper instead."

"All right, supper. About eight. Bring your own key. My buzzer's broken, and I'll only have to come down to let you in."

"Those stairs can't be easy at your age."

"Do you want supper or not?"

"Yes, I do. I do. I'll see you tomorrow at eight."

"See you tomorrow. Oh, and Dennis..."

"What?"

"If you talk about your bloody German for longer than five minutes, you won't get any pudding."

"Pudding's fattening," said Dennis, and rang off.

*

He got round the gym before the steroid brigade arrived. He knew the other solitaries by sight. Today two of them were talking to each other. It was a betrayal, like your first and second choice in a bar going home together. He took it out on the chest press.

As well as solitaries and talkers, he divided the gym crowd into unattainables, possibles and non-starters. Today there were two unattainables, five non-starters and a possible. This was a slim boy ('boy' meant anyone under thirty-five) called José – Walter had seen it on his membership card. He had smooth pecks and dimpled cheeks, and was thinning at the crown. He probably couldn't see this tonsure, which explained why he seemed unaware he was a possible not an unattainable. He was on the machines when Walter arrived, and ignored him the whole time. At the end, Walter managed to be in the changing room with him. He allowed himself a glance as José dropped his towel after his shower. To his surprise, the boy swelled under his scrutiny. José turned his back, presenting a lesser but welcome view, tangling in his elastic as he struggled to make himself decent. He finished dressing, refusing eye contact, and hurried away. Walter was as pleased as if they had had sex.

He picked up some food from the overpriced local supermarket on his way home, checked his messages as he let himself in – there were none – and undressed for a nap. He lulled himself to sleep with smug thoughts of José.

It was dark when he awoke. He lay there for a while and realised he was starving. It was later than he thought. He got up and made pasta with sauce from a bottle, poured a glass of screw-top wine in front of the television. He watched the film – it was just as Dennis had guessed, and all the better for it – and it was time to get ready.

He liked getting ready for Saturday night. Once upon a time, he had tried a fashion phase, buying something new every week and taking as long as possible in the bathroom before putting it on. He played music as he went, but these days it was Wagner not Abba, and what to wear needed no thought. The places where he was still below the average age were all leather. The dress code saved ringing the changes. As his mother said of school uniform: cheaper in the long run. Walter had his chaps – with jeans on the Tube, without once he arrived. What took the time was shaving. It improved his definition, but it had to be done properly. Wisps gave the game away, and once he had gone out with just one armpit shaved. It was like going to work in your pyjamas.

Sitting in his bath, he pushed his stomach full out to get inside his navel, and used his finger to judge what he could not see as he squatted over his razor. He thought of Mrs Rimmer.

After a lot of lacing – chaps, twelve-hole boots – and a quick tidy, he only just caught the Tube. It was packed. He was nervous among the shouting kids, some of them half his age. On his right was a buzz-cut blond, coldly handsome, a ring in his eyebrow and a girl on his arm. He tried not to look, embarrassed because the youth could be his son. Not that straights felt such qualms. One man's pederasty was another man's mid-life crisis.

He felt exposed in the carriage. To those who knew, he was a middle-aged homosexual heading for a leather bar. But not everyone did know. Did he look tough? Or just weird. He stared at an advert for period pain relief, then glanced at the boy. The girlfriend caught him. He looked away. He was relieved when they got off, watching the boy disappear down the platform. He was bolder with the doors shut.

The club sucked him in. Its shadows were warm, kind. The place was a comfort blanket really; the muscles and the paraphernalia of aggression were not to be taken seriously.

In straight pubs, there was a ritual of apology, a ballet of "sorry mate"-ing if one man brushed against another. Maybe it was necessary, but here it was not. The testosterone was make-believe, an accessory like the bikers' caps and riding crops. The only arguments were over the Coliseum versus Covent Garden.

He put his clothes in the coat check and laced himself back into his chaps. He waited at the bar and measured himself against the rest. He was not embarrassing. As he picked up his beer, a bare-chested boy – hairless not shaved – jogged him. He shook the beer off his arm; no chance of a "sorry mate" there. But the boy touched his skin. "Did I get you wet?" he said, keeping his hand there. His eyes were smiling. Walter searched for a double entendre, but the boy was off into the crowd.

"I thought you were in there for a second," said a voice.

"Bloody hell," said Walter. It was John from the office. "What are you doing here?"

"It's a free country, dear."

Walter had never seen John out. He tensed, not wanting to peck on the cheek; it would be like kissing Mrs Rimmer. But John was clearly of the same mind, and the danger passed. Walter took in this new aspect of his colleague. A leather waistcoat flapped at a white paunch, with greying chest-hair in wisps. Walter was repelled, but reassured. No competition here.

"I've never seen you out before, that's all," he said.

"I could say the same to you."

"But this is my local."

"It may become mine, dear, if it's always like this." John made play of salivating as a beefcake specimen pushed by, showing everything off in leather shorts and boots.

"Dirty devil. Wait till I tell Sir Anthony." Sir Anthony Pembridge was their permanent secretary.

"Tell him yourself, dear. He's on his knees in the corner."

He had Walter for a second. "Don't say that, even as a joke," he protested. "I've got a meeting with him on Monday morning and I'll never keep a straight face."

"There's never been anything straight about your face, dear."

"The old ones are the best," said Walter. He wished he could do repartee, but it was like singing, or getting straight out of bed when the alarm went off. You either could or you couldn't.

"Well that's lucky for you, then, isn't it?" John obliged.

"You're older than me, or had you forgotten?"

"It must be the Alzheimer's."

Dennis said it was not being exposed to Bette Davis as a child. Perhaps. He just couldn't banter. He didn't see why you had to. What was wrong with talking about the weather or television – or single entendres? But there seemed to be rules.

Someone slapped his rump. He found himself looking up at the giant figure, stripped to the waist, of James, another ex of Dennis's.

"James! I haven't seen you in ages."

James was Australian. "Sexually incompatible," was all Dennis would say when they parted. Walter suspected water-sports had been attempted, or even fisting. He was pale and broad, with an expensive tattoo reaching over his shoulder and across his right breast. Walter would have flirted, if he had any hope of success.

"You hardly come here any more," he said.

"And you don't go anywhere else in your old age," said James. Why was everyone talking about his age? He introduced John, explaining the work connection.

James gasped. "That means you must know Janet!"

"You know Janet?" said John.

"No, but I feel like I do," said James. "I'm dying to meet her. When are you going to introduce us, Wally?"

"When hell freezes, or when a handsome stranger with perfect teeth wants to have your babies, whichever is the least soon," he said, surprising himself. "And don't call me Wally."

"You're so educated. I'd never have known to say 'least soon'," said James. "It's what impresses us convict races so much." He turned to John. "Do you talk like that too? Be honest. Have you ever split an infinitive?"

Walter stared at James's pierced nipples. They stuck out proud, from years of tugging. He imagined chewing on them.

"No, but I've boldly gone to a few places where most men wouldn't dare," John was saying. "What has he told you about Janet?"

James mimed with his tongue.

"She's never a lesbian!"

Walter groaned. "He just means her surname. Ignore him. It's not his fault he has a mental age of five-and-a-half."

"Do five-and-a-half-year-olds know about rimming?" said John. "I certainly never did."

"You Poms clearly have the wrong kind of primary school."

"Tell me what goes on at the right kind."

With horror, Walter realised they were flirting. He looked at the blond trail from James's navel to his waistband, and John's pudgy gut. God and monster. But there was no doubt, and he wasn't prepared to watch. They barely noticed him go.

The club was a railway arch vault, divided into two rooms. In the front, customers talked around the bar, a bikers' cocktail party. The back room was darker, and nobody talked – they prowled. The successful clutched one another, trousers around ankles against the walls. In a corner was a scrum of those who didn't care who was attached to what. Walter nosed around the edge of this group, thinking of Sir Anthony. The boy who had spilt his drink was centre of attention, poppers in hand – naked and adored from all angles. Walter got an amyl smile, and thought of pushing through. But these men, slobbery before the boy, knew he was their best chance all night. Like early flag-wavers at a royal procession, they would give up their prime spot to nobody.

Walter continued around the less crowded corners, brushing off unwanted hands and wanting ones that stayed in pockets. He saw a familiar face: José from the gym, sleek under a complicated harness. Walter changed course and stared blatantly. José looked at the ground. Playing hard to get? Deluded old fool. The body language said he wasn't interested, because he wasn't. Walter was just another monster to ward off.

Further along, a skinhead eyed him up. He was borderline fat, but Walter was grateful. He stared his admirer in the eye and grabbed his crotch. Lips parted. Some men would let you suck them off but not kiss; tenth base was easier than first. But this one kissed with passion. Walter let him go down, but it was one of those encounters that was better for his confidence than his libido. After a decent interval he patted the skinhead on the shoulder and pushed himself back into his jock-strap. They each muttered "see you later", knowing they would ignore each other if they did.

John was alone at the bar.

"What happened to James?" Walter asked.

"He went off looking for dick, I suppose. I'm not his keeper."

"And there was me thinking it was Tom or Harry he was after."

"Very good, dear – for you."

"You looked like you were getting on well."

"Oh?"

"You just seemed to be getting on well, that's all."

"Please! I should be so lucky."

Walter did not contradict.

"And what have you been doing?" John asked.

"This and that. I made a new friend."

"Just the one, dear?"

"So far."

"Name?"

"We weren't introduced."

"You young people!"

"Do we know any young people?"

"When you get to my age, dear, everyone's chicken. How old are you, as a matter of fact?"

"Old enough for it to be rude to ask, grandpa. Let me get you another drink."

He got two pints, and they stood examining the talent.

"Look at that one," said Walter. "Has he no shame?"

A greying man shuffled around the bar, scrawny buttocks on show. A jock-strap, also greying, was all he wore.

"I bet he's a judge in real life," said John. "Secretaries and ushers running around, people calling him sir. He likes this place for the degradation."

"Sir Anthony again."

"Yes, except this one's really here."

"How about this one?"

"Fuck me!"

"Don't say it too loud or he really will."

He was about fifty, shaven-headed, in a leather waistcoat, with an enormous erection pointing out under it. He stared as he passed, daring them to look again.

"There's nothing like showing off your best asset," said Walter.

"It's so much harder when your best asset is an arse the size of a windsock," sighed John.

"You poor thing."

"Me? I was talking about you."

José appeared. John saw him too. "Yum," he said.

"Pricktease," said Walter. "Waste of time."

"At least you're not bitter."

Walter did not answer.

"Don't look now," said John. "Your Australian friend has noticed him too."

James was talking into José's ear, closer than the music required. Walter's stomach tightened. Did the old men in the obituaries still feel jealousy? It would be nice to think they didn't, that it disappeared with desire. That would be something to look forward to.

John was still scanning the room.

"Hel–lo! There's someone to take your mind off your little pricktease. He keeps staring at you. Three o'clock."

Walter looked. The man against the opposite wall was not his usual type – too rough, too bulky. But there was something about him. Amid the studied glowering, he was smiling, just slightly. Not at anyone else, but to himself. He looked self-contained, confident. Also, amid the tattooed and pierced flesh, he was still wearing a green padded bomber jacket.

"Not bad, but cofar," said Walter.

"Cofar?"

"Coat On For A Reason."

"You think he's got something to hide?"

"Could be fat."

"Not necessarily. It doesn't work the other way round. Just look at me." John slapped his own belly.

It was true – bodies around them cried out to be covered. Walter looked again, and their eyes met for a second. Knowing he had Walter's attention, Bomber Jacket rubbed the back of his neck, then pushed himself off from the wall and wandered towards the back room without another glance. Cocky bastard.

"Don't let me stop you," said John.

"It doesn't matter."

"Go on. What are you waiting for?"

Walter drained his glass and set off as casually as he could in the same direction. It was more crowded now, and he had to push through a group of leather-men, all muir caps and cigars. He bumped into James, who leant down conspiratorially.

"Want some smoke?"

This close to James, Bomber Jacket was forgotten.

They headed into the back and found a corner away from heaving bodies. The air was already clogged with cigarette smoke and poppers. James retrieved a cigarette case from his boot and took out a joint. He lit it and passed it on.

"Hey, look," he said, as Walter took smoke down. "There's a couple of guys janetting."

Walter spluttered it out. "I could have killed you for that before," he said. "That's one thing you and Dennis had in common. You both love dropping me in it."

"Your friend thought it was funny."

"He's not my friend. He's my colleague. And I'll never hear the end of it now. I'm a civil servant. Discretion is meant to be our watchword."

"Maybe you chose the wrong career."

"Maybe I'll need to look for a new job."

"He's not your boss?"

"No. He's senior to me, but he's not my boss. You were a big hit with him, by the way."

James grimaced.

"I thought you liked him," said Walter.

"He was quite funny, but that was all."

Walter felt suddenly calmer. He was already relaxed after two pints of lager, and the joint was working. Once again he found himself staring at James's nipples.

"Go on, then," said James softly.

Before the penny even dropped, Walter felt the back of his head pushed forward. Not resisting, he searched out the nipple with his mouth. He worked his hand round James's waist to clasp his buttocks and turned his face up for a kiss.

The pack around them scented action and moved in. Hands pried, were removed, and came back. Walter wondered about somewhere more private – his own bed. This was worth savouring. But he was nervous of proposing it. He was scared of ruining it. It was sweaty and blissful, and he didn't want it ever to end.

James was trying to talk to him.

"What?" he said, through poppers and grass.

"I need to take a break," James repeated.

"Oh, okay," said Walter. "See you later, then."

He re-arranged his jock-strap and watched James wander off in search of something better. He wondered if the naked boy was still performing his floorshow, and imagined the pair together. This was why it was better not to aim too high.

"Damn," he said, under cover of the music.

He made his way back to the brighter room and the bar. John was nowhere to be seen as he ordered another drink. Probably back in the scrum. No sign of Bomber Jacket either. The crowd was beginning to thin. He took his beer and ambled over to an arras of scaffolding at the far end, offering nooks for groping. He got a couple of looks from men he was not drunk enough to consider yet, and lingered in front of a muscular Chinese boy, who looked away.

He arrived back at the bar. Still no John to talk to. He looked at his watch. It was close to desperate hour, and time to cut his losses. He pushed through the double doors to the coat check. It was no shame to leave alone.

Decent in jeans, he stood on the pavement. The next taxi would be twenty minutes, he was told, but there was a minicab office just up the street if he didn't want to wait.

The cab firm was next to a kebab house where customers from the Eagle mixed with queens in lycra from the White Hart across the road. They all looked tired and shop-soiled under the strip-lighting. Walter steered clear.

He was second in the queue. The man beside him lit a cigarette. Walter suddenly realised it was Bomber Jacket, who noticed him too. "All right, mate?"

"All right," replied Walter. Perhaps the night was not over. He smiled, not too much, looked away, and back. Bomber Jacket was still looking at him.

"Had a good night?"

He was about Walter's age, and pale, with dark patches around the eyes. It added to the allure – as if he had better things to do than sleep. He was unshaven, and his mouth was too wide, obscene somehow. His teeth were gappy when he grinned, which made his leer dirtier. Chewing gum churned on his tongue.

"It was all right," said Walter, dropping consonants.

A cab pulled up.

"Who's first?" said the driver, an African, through the open window.

"Which way you headed?" said Bomber Jacket.

"Bloomsbury. You?"

"South. Streatham."

"Who's first?" said the driver again. "Make your minds up."

Walter made his mind up. "Come back to mine if you want."

Bomber Jacket grinned again. "Why not?" He held his hand out. "I'm Steve."

They barely talked in the cab. It maintained the fiction, for the driver anyway, that they were acquainted. Their knees touched in the dark. Walter stared out at the empty streets, feeling suddenly content in this odd companionship with a total stranger. All was right with the world; this was the life.

Steve did not offer a contribution to the fare when they arrived, which Walter tried not to notice. They squeezed into the lift. Steve was still chewing gum, and his jacket was zipped to the top. It was too late to worry about that.

They reached Walter's floor and he nudged his guest out of the lift with a hand on the buttock.

He unlocked his front door, and the plumped cushions winked congratulations.

"Make yourself at home," he said. "Let me take your coat."

He need not have worried. Steve was wearing an army vest that revealed big shoulders, a cartoon tattoo, and a bulging chest with a tangle of blond hair in the middle. His waist was thick, but not fat.

"Want something to drink?"

"Got any beer?"

"Only wine, I think." Walter could revert to class now. "I've got some whisky, though."

"Yeah, whisky. Cheers."

"Ice?"

"Nah."

He went into his tiny kitchen to fetch two glasses. When he returned, Steve had the *Telegraph* on his lap to make a joint. "Don't mind if I skin up, mate?" he asked, looking up. His eyes were as green as his jacket.

"Great," said Walter.

Steve crumbled grass into stuck-together papers. "Got a cigarette for it?"

"Sorry, I don't smoke. There's a garage though. We can go out and get some."

"Don't worry." Steve reached for his jacket and pulled cigarettes from the pocket. Walter remembered the cab fare, and again tried not to mind. Steve was providing the grass, and he didn't want to use all his cigarettes. He went back into the kitchen and dug out the ashtray he kept for visitors.

"Do you go to the Eagle much?" he asked, putting the ashtray by Steve's feet.

Steve looked surprised.

"You were in there earlier. I thought you saw me."

Steve lit the joint and stared into space as he inhaled. "Yeah, that's right," he said at length. "No, never been there before." He dragged on the joint again and passed it over.

"Where do you normally go?"

"I don't normally go to bars."

"So what made you go tonight?"

"Dunno. I was in the mood, I guess."

"I'm glad you were," said Walter. He smiled, and Steve looked back at him. There it was again, that dirty grin.

"Come here."

At last. Walter moved in, but Steve grabbed the back of his neck and pushed his head into his groin.

It turned out to be a one-sided business. But when they were both naked and in the bedroom, and Walter was high on poppers, he decided not to care that he was left to work his own erection, or that

Steve would not let him kiss. It was not often he found a man he wanted so much. The grass helped. He didn't care whether it was reciprocated; he knew he wanted Steve, and he was enjoying himself. Perhaps it was a turning point, and he was getting over his hang-up about self-esteem.

A finger probed him. He parted his legs, consenting. He pulled open his top drawer to show condoms. He heard a foil packet ripped, and the finger withdrew. He reached behind to check the condom was where it should be. More poppers. Then the first jolt of invasion, soothed as the rhythm built up, slowly giving way to a blissful warmth that, as ever, took him by surprise. So natural, why didn't everyone do this? Must do it – oh yes – more often.

Steve was flipping him over. Carefully, one leg and then the other, without slipping out, and onto his back. Legs in the air, not bothering to hold his stomach in. Another neurosis discarded. He could see those green eyes, and the grin. The thrusting jolted him back and forth. This was fu-u-u-un. Hands on his chest, his face, and now one around his neck. Yes. He had always liked that. Now there were two hands as the rhythm increased and hips ground, shuddering, into him. The green eyes closed, the head went back, and panting turned into a great, final grunt.

He stayed inside, and Walter was grateful. He didn't want to stop. He let his head fall back and closed his eyes. Don't pull out. Don't let go.

He was near his own climax when he realised. There was no need to will the hands not to let go – they were not going to. The grip was tightening, and when he looked up, the grin was gone. The green eyes were angry.

For a moment Walter considered panic, instinct telling him to struggle. But it hit him that he did not care. In an instant of clarity, he recognised he was content, and not in pain. This was what it meant to go out on a high – oxygen dwindling and blood rushing to his face. Would it be so bad? His parents were gone, and nobody else's life would be ruined. Dennis would find him. His finances were messy, but you couldn't have everything. Spontaneity was the thing, when you were feeling fucked and happy – before you changed your mind.

He looked up at the man – he suddenly couldn't remember his name. The eyes were wild with fury now. But still sexy. Was that pathetic? Hardly gay pride – but Walter had power over him. He was driving him to this.

And the bastard would be caught. John had seen him in the club, the cab driver would remember them, and his face would be on the security cameras – there was even one in the lift. Fingerprints all over the place too. For a murderer, the guy was pretty sloppy. He would be put away for years, and would never know he was doing Walter a favour. That was real justice.

He knew it wouldn't show on his face, but Walter was smiling inside as he teetered on the brink of unconsciousness. Serve the fucker right for not offering half the cab fare.

Breach

Joanne Elliot

Breach
Joanne Elliot

Its head lolled lazily above the frayed noose, features obliterated into an unrecognisable sticky pulp of gut-wrenching matter. Rapidly coagulating blood oozed slowly from frenzied gaping wounds, hacked the length of his naked body. The murder weapon – a serrated kitchen knife – was still embedded within the victim's pelvis, his genitals a separate sanguinary mass on the filthy cracked pavement of the deserted alleyway.

Morbidly transfixed, the plain-clothed police sergeant held the Polaroids with shaking hands. In the entirety of his time served on the force he had never before witnessed police images evidencing such foully brutal intensity. The violence that had been inflicted upon the most recent victim of the unidentified serial killer surmounted even the most belligerent of conjectures. The dire situation hit him with a force which took the air from his lungs; it was as though the world around him was moving in slow motion.

The chief inspector cleared his throat uncomfortably, abruptly interrupting Malcolm Limbic's disturbed thoughts.

"As you can see, Sergeant Limbic, the fifth victim has been mutilated in an almost identical manner to the previous fatalities. Note the presence of the noose, the serrated knife, and the complete physical castration of the genitals. An important aspect to note, however, is the increased severity of the stab wounds on the victim's body."

Sergent Limbic could do nothing but nod his head vehemently in agreement. His boss continued to read from the pages of the official report, "In keeping with the profile of the serial killers targets, the victim was aged approximately in his mid-twenties, with dark colouring, and is believed to have been a practicing homosexual. We are as yet uncertain of the victim's identity, but the coroner will be liasing with us later today reference a positive identification through the use of dental records.

"The victim was last seen leaving the Pink nightclub in Soho with another man at one-thirty a.m. on Thursday the tenth of September. From eye witness accounts it is believed that the men were strangers previous to their meeting on that night. The description of our key suspect is as follows; the male is between five-foot-eight to six-foot-two inches tall, with short dark hair, slim build, aged around twenty-five to thirty five years. The suspect has a distinctive tattoo of a viper coiled around a bleeding heart on his left upper arm.

"The body of the victim was discovered by a bin man at five-thirty a.m., Thursday the tenth of September. In keeping with the profile the lacerations on the victim's neck suggest that a choking noose was used as a restraining device, the victims neck has been confirmed as being broken *after* the repeated stabbings and dismemberment of the sexual organs. One positive development within the investigation is that the corpse was discovered in time to collect a semen sample. As you are aware, this is the first time where we have been able to retain any meaningful DNA evidence within this ongoing investigation."

Sergeant Limbic exhaled audibly, and rubbed the bridge of his nose tensely.

"Any positive identifications yet, chief?"

"Not as yet, sergeant, the DNA analysts are developing a profile as we speak. However, I am still concerned regarding the implications disclosed through the discovery of the most recent victim in this case. I have read a report by our criminal psychologist which indicates that the serial killer is likely to murder again; more fiercely, and most probably sooner than we think.

"We need to put an end to this dire situation, before it gets even more out of hand. The way I see it, we need an officer to infiltrate the nightclub as a customer, to act as bait.

"Sergeant Limbic, I want that officer to be you."

Sergeant Limbic walked away from the police station, hands rammed in pockets, a heavy feeling in his heart. He was furious. And threatened. He knew unremittingly that by agreeing to carry out the chief's wishes he had inadvertently placed himself in an inordinate degree of potential danger. In his eyes the magnitude of the situation had reached colossal proportions. The last thing he needed at this stage of his life was to increase the risks to his own self-preservation. But his hands were tied, there was nothing which he could do except to comply with his boss's orders.

"Bastard!" he shouted aloud, kicking a loose stone on the pavement, oblivious to the stares which his actions evoked from innocent passers by. The pebble skittered into the gutter, coming to rest amid a mushy assemblage of dead leaves and discarded paper. A soiled headline immediately caught the sergeant's attention, and his eyes narrowed.

"Gay Rights Demonstration Ends Amicably."

Limbic bitterly spat on the paper in disgust.

"Fucking puftas! I've so many more important things to do with my time!"

Sergeant Malcolm Limbic reluctantly stepped into the night club. He tried to ignore the nervous tension which bad crept into his shoulders, and the anger which burned with fury inside of him. Tacky neon lights blazed, burning his eyes, and the smell of smoke hit him like a blanket of tear gas. He felt out of place, he was much too old, he shouldn't be here.

Malcolm struggled to think straight as he moved further into the building. He uncomfortably navigated groups of inebriated revellers as the thumping music coursed through his today; he could feel it beating within his rib cage and vibrating painfully through his brains. The sergeant subtly shook his head in a failed attempt to clear the beginnings of a headache. The dull aching throb was beginning to creep about his temples. He knew that the migraine and its horrendous stabbing sensation was not far off.

Malcolm attempted to look casual as he strolled towards the bar. He took a seat on an uncomfortable minimalist silver stool, struggled to keep his balance, and once again wondered what in the name of Christ was he doing here. In his mind, it was above and beyond the call of duty. Limbic shouted to the transsexual barman, ordered a double scotch straight, thrust his money forwards, and didn't wait for the change. He knew that he had to get himself under control. Right now.

To distract himself Malcolm took a gulp of his drink. It burned on the way down, and at first he felt a reflexive gagging action. At heart, he was a quiet pint and packet of crisps kind of man in his local. Swallowing the remainder of the beverage decisively, Limbic immediately ordered another. Grasping his glass in hand, he struggled to climb down from the precarious bar stool. He walked towards the imposing set of stairs which dominated the rear of the night club. He wanted to move upstairs to get a better view of the dance floor. After all, Sergeant Limbic reasoned, he did have a job to do. Dull recognition. Perhaps the alcohol was helping; the room was starting to spin.

The undercover officer rested his forearms on the low balcony, nonchalantly leaning over to peer at the spectacle below. He watched them all as they rhythmically moved on the dance floor like a writhing mass. Like animals. The men in here sickened him. Fucking queers. A hand pressed suggestively against his buttock, and despite himself the sergeant jumped. Spinning around he glared down at a short fat old man with receding hairline and visible gut spewing over the belt where his armpit stained lime green polyester shirt ended. Malcolm almost felt sorry for him, but not that sorry. The fat little bastard revolted him. A few choice crushing words soon sent the unwanted admirer on his way, and Limbic returned to the job at hand. As the all consuming need to locate his target took over, the Sergeant searched with renewed vigour. His eyes darted to each and every young dark haired man, but it took time. There were so many men in the Pink tonight. And then he saw him. Malcolm was immediately sober. The blood drained from his face and his hands began to shake. With trembling knees Limbic adjusted his position to gain a more covert surveillance position. It was him all right. The target himself. Limbic was certain.

Malcolm gulped as he watched the dark-haired queen move beside the entrance of the dance floor. The target delicately sipped a long cocktail through a luminous straw, his eyes scouting around at the men. Limbic noticed how his eyes lingered on specific members of what he would assume to be "talent" in the room – Sergeant Limbic watched as the target confidently approached a slightly shorter man on the dance floor. The man had toned muscles, and he wriggled his pert arse seductively as the target moved towards him. "You'll have to be careful, shortarse," Limbic mumbled to himself, "or you're going to get an awful lot more than you bargained for!" Limbic's mouth was set in a grim line, watching the couples' every move, his teeth gritted together in anticipation of the chase. It was not long before the target began to move towards the cloakroom area. Limbic immediately sprung into action; he knew that he had to be quick if he was to complete his mission successfully.

From the yellowing illuminations of the broken street lights, it was just possible to make out the fluctuating silhouette of the couple ahead. Sergeant Limbic followed the target from a safe distance. He realised that the two men were moving towards the set of alleys where the third and fifth victims had been discovered. Limbic shook his head. Some people asked for trouble.

When the couple turned a corner, Limbic paused. In his anticipation he had nearly forgotten. Digging deep in his jacket pockets, Limbic pulled out leather gloves and a thick black balaclava. Just in case. The last thing that he wanted was to be identified. He pulled on the disguise, and hurried in the direction of the darkened alleyway. Sergeant Limbic crept around the corner silently. The sight which greeted him made his guts lurch.

The target had the shorter man pinned against the wall. They were passionately kissing, groping each other with vicious intensity. Limbic felt sick. He pulled his gun from the holster with surprisingly steady hands. As he cocked the weapon, the couples' heads suddenly jerked upwards. The sergeant wasted no time.

"Just go!" Limbic bellowed his order to the shorter man, who did just that.

Within seconds the target stood petrified, alone.

Limbic watched gleefully as horrified confusion registered upon the target's face.

"Stay still, you fucking queer, you sick bastard!" hissed Sergeant Limbic as he moved forwards towards the target.

"What the fuck are you doing? Who are you? What the...?" To Limbic's delight the man was panicking, backing away. "What the hell do you want with me?!"

"Shut the fuck up," Limbic replied coldly and calmly, advancing upon the target, trapping him in the greasy corner of the deserted alleyway.

The target's blood ran cold as he watched the sergeant pull out a strong, frayed piece of rope from his pocket. The evil look of deadly intent was etched upon the deviant's face as he bore down.

"I'm going to enjoy this, I've been watching you for far too long."

Despite himself, the sergeant felt his cock stiffen as he roughly undid the unconscious man's trousers and rapturously plunged the knife into his sixth victim's flesh.

Direst Cruelty
Nigel Fairs

Direct Cruelty
Nigel Fairs

She just sat there and watched me. Sat there in her stupid cut-off cardigan with a fag hanging out of her mouth and *watched* me, whilst her *own daughter*... It was like a public execution. Then she had the gall to say, "Oh, it wasn't as good as last year's. We thought you was gonna to do balloons. Don't you *do* balloons?"

I'm a rabbit. Rabbits don't do balloons.

The child's name is Kylie Butcher. Horribly apt. She's eleven. I said to her mother, "Isn't Kylie a bit old for it?" but she wouldn't have it. Said Kylie insisted on Geoffrey the Amazing Rabbit because *Cherise* had had Geoffrey the Amazing Rabbit at *her* party and anything *Cherise* has... which I can't say surprised me. Cherise was a right little madam. The sort of right little madam that could incite one to murder, or at the very least, grievous bodily harm. She decided that it would be fun to pull Geoffrey's tail off. And of course all the little buggers followed suit. How we laughed!

The thing is, they think they can hit, or kick, or pinch, and the rabbit doesn't feel anything, the rabbit's okay, it'll take it on the chin and still come up smiling. "Ha ha ha, Kylie, aren't we having fun with that cocktail stick – why not try poking out my other eye, then I'll be completely blind!" Geoffrey the amazingly blind rabbit, a major step forward in equal work opportunity for children's entertainers. It's what I call the *Tom and Jerry* mentality. Not that any of them would know who Tom and Jerry were. They probably get their kicks watching *The Texas Chainsaw Massacre!*

If she tries to charge me for that broken window I shall have her sued by Equity. It wasn't *my* arm that went through it.

He actually laughed in her face, you know. Wayne. The kid that broke it. So she swore at him a bit, he swore back – this little eight-year-old – and then she left it at that. Didn't even clear up the glass! Lit up another fag... A huge great shard fell right into my Magic Potato Pie – look at it! Could have killed me!! Christ, if *I'd* have done that when I was his age, I'd have run away from home with the shame of it! *Imagine* the hiding I'd have got for that! My dad would have kicked my arse from here to Sainsburys! Not like now. They daren't even *touch* the kids. They'd be had up for molestation or something. Either that or they really can't be bothered. They really don't care...

I hate children.

I refused to call myself a "children's entertainer" for a while. Kept trying to convince myself that I was a "jobbing actor", and that Geoffrey the Amazing Rabbit was "just another part". Even put "trained at Middlesex University" on my flier. Geoffrey the Amazing Rabbit, BA Honours in Theatre Arts. An amazingly educated rabbit. Gave that up when I heard the old story about Sybil Thorndike... was it Sybil Thorndike? Might have been Edith Evans. Anyway, whoever it was, she'd hit a bit of a dry spot, acting-wise, and she was doing some waitressing to bring the pennies in. As you do. And this woman recognised her in the restaurant, said, "Excuse me, you're an actress, aren't you?" and Dame Sybil turned round and said, "No, my dear, when I'm acting, I'm an actress. When I'm waiting, I'm a waitress. What can I get you?" That was the only way she could maintain her dignity. It kind of struck a chord. So when I'm doing this, I'm not an actor any more, I'm a rabbit. An amazing rabbit.

I was going to be a *star* when I was 12. I'd given my Nancy in the my local Gang Bang Show – or whatever it's called. You know, cubs. Nancy as in Oliver and Nancy, I mean. *"As long as 'e needs me..."* And afterwards these three butch old women – Akela, Baloo and someone else – Bagheera? Whoever – they were creaming their knickers over me, telling me I'd be the next Michael Crawford, or whoever it was back then. And that kind of got me into the habit... I was a Godsend to Mrs Tibbett at the boys' school. The only pupil not only *willing* to put on a dress for her but actively pursuing the female lead! Not that I ever *got* the female lead, but I was a damn good supporting actress. And it's funny, but whenever I was on stage, I'd get this really odd feeling. Almost indescribable. Like I was *meant* to be there... like when I *wasn't* there, the audience were simply waiting for me to come back on again... as if I was the only one they were really interested in. It's the best feeling in the world, you know, having the audience right there, in the palm of your hand. It's like holding your breath – or rather, like *they're* all holding their breath... A silence, a kind of *ecstasy*... and I felt it at the age of 12. Well, after that, nothing else could measure up to it. Not sex, not chocolate, nothing. So when it came to choosing a career, there really was only one choice. I was going to the RADA!

But then my mother said, "You're not *that* good at acting, are you, dear? You're nothing special. Why not do a degree instead? Then at least you can get a proper job at the end of it" And I *know* why she was saying it, I know she didn't want me to be disappointed, that she was maybe trying to protect me from all the unemployment and so on – and maybe she was right. I believed her. Well you do, don't you, at that age? But if you *start out* thinking you're nothing special, you're never going to end up on number one tours, popping in for a pre-show g'n't with Dame Judi or a post-show bitch with Sir Ian. You're going to end up here, *degrading yourself* in people's living rooms, sewing buttons onto sock puppets and singing stupid songs about Magic Potato Pies to kids who'd far rather be upstairs playing *doctors and nurses* with their Barbies and Kens... you're never going to get *anywhere*... Thanks, mother.

I invited her to see Geoffrey the Amazing Rabbit once but she had a beetle drive to organise for the WI. Just as well, really. I don't expect she would have enjoyed it much.

I have to admit that my talent, if I ever had any, wasn't greatly recognised at Middlesex University. Any bright ideas I'd had of being a star, already fading when I arrived, had just about been snuffed out by the time I left. I didn't even get to play the second female lead. No, they must have seen me shamble in on the first day and thought, "He's strictly chorus line, him." My greatest triumph was playing Rosencrantz *and* Guildenstern in *Hamlet*. On alternate nights. Guildenstern was my favourite – he had the better boots. I decided to play him as a bit of a fop – my Rosencrantz was far butcher, because in my humble opinion, he's the one who wears the trousers, if you get my meaning. Stoppard actually thought it was the other way round, but then, hey... Anyway, I could never have played Guildenstern butch in *those* boots. Anyway, one afternoon I'd been swanning around the campus feeling sorry for myself with a bottle of sherry, as you do, and I arrived at the performance completely rat-arsed. Awful. I got on stage, and honestly forgot which one I was supposed to be playing, so I played them *both*. Much to the irritation of the guy who was playing the other one, and to the fury of the flouncy little queen playing Hamlet. My God, you should have heard the language when we came off! It certainly wasn't Shakespearean. And I thought, well, this is it. Bye bye, BA Hons. Because Hamlet was shagging the head of drama, you see. And sure enough, I was hauled up to the Oracle's office, and I was ready to give an impassioned speech about how abused I felt as an artiste, having to play bloody walk-ons in my final assessment, and d'you know what he said?

"Benjamin, you wore the wrong boots. Horatio was supposed to be wearing those boots, not you. He had to go on in Polonius's leather uppers. It ruined the final scene."

I wore the wrong bloody boots. So I apologised and that was it. He died last month. Typical, that. Him dying before I get the chance to prove to him I'm more than *a pair of boots*.

Balloons! Bloody cheek! If she wanted balloons she should have hired a fucking magician! Or done the fucking balloons herself! And what kind of mother *smokes* in front of her kids? Stupid *bitch*...

People think it's such an easy life, you know, being an actor. "Ooh, I wish I had your job. Being on the telly, all that applause. Ooh yes, that'd suit me down to the ground" Yes, I'm sure it would. Try it.

The trouble is, you see, when you are working, it *is* actually a bloody good job, unless you're sharing a dressing room with an egomaniac or a manic depressive... and there's nothing more depressing than a depressed actor, because they *feel* it so. Because that's our job, you know? *Feeling. Being* something we're not. And the trouble is, unless you're a name, or you're sleeping with Cameron Macintosh, 99 per cent of the time you're *not* being someone else, you're being *yourself*. Which for an actor, is not good. Because most actors, contrary to popular belief, really don't like themselves very much. Hence the desire to be someone else. Because when you're someone else, you can be loved. Or despised. Or *whatever*. You can have an *effect,* make an impression, albeit fleetingly. Justify your existence...

Thou wouldst be great;
Art not without ambition...

When I was in *The Mousetrap*, I had a dressing room all to myself. I even had a fridge! And now look at me, perched on the Butchers' avocado bath suite with bog roll and a hand mirror!

Of course, *The Mousetrap* was just about all I ever *was* in. That and a whole lot of shite in pub theatres. A ground-breaking dissection of the plight of the radiographer entitled *The X Man Cometh*. All stethoscopes and broken bones. *Time Out* said it was like watching paint dry, only paint drying would have been infinitely more entertaining. Then there was the musical version of the *Titanic* story at the Old Red Lion, *On the Rocks!* I was the captain going down with the ship. I was also a lifeboat. And a shard of ice. It was all very experimental. There was talk of it going into the West End. The *Daily Mail* said it had "promise". They also said the director should sack the cast, who were, according to the reviewer, "dragging the whole thing down faster than the iceberg". What do they know? Critics...

When Kylie the Horrible's mother asked me if I did anything else, if I could maybe do a bit more than the hour-and-a-quarter, I said, well, sometimes I stay in character and join in with the games, you know, as the rabbit; the children like it sometimes. And she said, "Oh no, we ain't going to play no games, can't you do sumink else? Like another character or sumink?" And I know I should have just refused, but for some reason I said, "All right, I'll do another spot, that's fine." Of course, when I put the phone down, I thought, *you bloody idiot, what have you done that for? You didn't even ask for more money!* But anyway, a change is as good as a rest, as they say, and nobody will be expecting this, not at a children's party!

You see, I really am more than a pair of boots. The part I was born to play was Lady Macbeth...

Come, you spirits
That tend on mortal thoughts, unsex me here;
And fill me, from the crown to the toe, top-full
Of direst cruelty.

I've heard people say that she's the most underwritten part in Shakespeare, that he missed huge chunks out, but that doesn't bother me at all. I like filling in the gaps! And the journey is *fantastic* – her ambition, her rise to power, her disillusionment, her madness, her suicide – off stage of course, but hey, I could always do it in the dressing room...

I'm hardly going to become a household name playing a rabbit, you see. And you get sick of waiting. You get sick of the endless auditions, the endless rejections, you drive yourself mad trying to pick yourself up every time, tell yourself that particular job wasn't meant to be, "there's always the children's parties – they may not be number one tours, but at least you're still performing..." but it's not enough any more. It's not enough. Which is why I decided to bring things to a head... but how to go about it? How to be noticed?

It'd have to be something really spectacular. Something unexpected.

You know, she really ought to have cleared up that broken glass; it could do no end of damage.

Art thou afeard
To be the same in thine own act and valour
As thou art in desire?

I think I heard one of the mothers saying her husband worked for a local news programme. That'll do, for a start.

Canvas
Steve Ferris

Canvas
Steve Ferris

Lázaro Chevalier was in his studio.

The male model opposite him was beginning to feel a little pain because he was having to strain to keep the pose. His name was Jacinto. He was not a professional. Lázaro had picked him up in a bar at the bottom of a hill that led to one of the many shantytowns that almost circled the city. He had been laid off from the car repair shop he had been working at since migrating to the metropolis from the hinterland. Now he had no work and was determined to get absolutely slaughtered.

There was a blending of architecture from the permanent part of the city to that of the shanty, but there was no clear boundary. A cantina made of brick could stand next to an unpainted construction of breezeblock and corrugated asbestos. There were houses made of plywood and polyurethane, cardboard and crates, bin-liners and burlap, all of it recycled. It was an advantage to be nearer the top of a hill in the rainy season, but when the wind blew it was better to be nearer the bottom of the valley. When the floods flashed torrents down from on high, the occasional corpse would wash out of the mud, either scooped from its supposedly final resting place, or dumped opportunistically in the hope that it would be mistaken for a body buried some time before.

After a baker's dozen of lightning quick sketches, and a batch of polaroids in which the copper-coloured man looked more like a mummy, the naked model was placed in front of a wooden roof-support, facing away from the artist. He straddled a large box so that his legs were at the maximum spread without it being impossibly uncomfortable. Both arms were taut above his drooping head, hands secured in loops of rough rope. His buttocks thrust outwards because of the tension. His spine curved away from the viewer. The muscle blocks on his shoulders stood out like those on a medical teaching aid. His skin glowed slightly, from a thin coat of sweet sweat, transforming the metallic into oiled wood, polishing the hardened figure. No band of under-tanning marked him as a man more often found on the far away beach than working. Rather, he was a member of the people, reliable and strong.

Chevi had felt the bullet of his beauty when the craftsman minus his craft emerged from behind the screen set up as dressing-room in one corner of the space which was lit by a row of skylights. His manhood hung low, inflated a bit like a pumped tyre. The bristle of the brush's tip would caress the lines and the measure of it in due course, but from behind the reverie of the paint-smeared palette, it was easier to stifle his wishes. His fingers might move the willing slave into precise positions, but propriety ruled out the final touch.

Out in the city the murder and mayhem continued, by day as well as by night.

The series of ruling powers gave its blessing to disappearance. The vanishing of a trafficker, whether he was a dealer in arms, drugs, antiquities or some other unspecified obscenity, served their intentions either way. The streets swept themselves clean, and in the days of elections, the reactionary and the criminal could be railed against, and a promise could be given to rid the paradise of its pestilence. Motive was frequently irrelevant. The unclaimed dead, previously among the numberless, became another part of the numbered. They became one of the unsolved crimes, simply listed and filed.

The police force was riddled with nepotism and duplicity. The 'little bite' was king. That meant a payment to officialdom in its various forms so that it would turn a blind eye or seek out some other sap to fit up for the murder or whatever it was this time. Death took its little bite too, commissioning from government, officialdom and the man inn the street alike. Vigilantes eradicated piecemeal the kids that infested the place, both above and below the ground. These were orphan scavengers that deserved no other fate than extermination. The crooks and the hoodlums deserved the same thing. The communists, when the right was in power, and the fascists, when the liberals were in power, altered the make-up of the legislature for a while, but the opposition still came under constant fire whatever that opposition was. The pendulum swung. 'The devil and the deep blue sea' was the proverbial rule that applied to everything, everywhere. Assassins tangoed to the tune of provincial musicians, there in the capital of the dead to make a quick buck, to scrape a living, to survive, to do the dance of death.

Lázaro had a contact in the boys in blue, a detective who would smuggle him copies of photo records so that he could use them as source material. In the early days, up north, he had found sufficient pictures of horrors in papers and magazines. But there was a certain charm to depicting site-specific killings in his work, however disguised. The canvases were getting larger, the colours darker and more muted. The shadowiness of his style allowed suggestion rather than true reality to creep into the images. The richness of the colour-scheme, even when restricted, called to mind the Grand Tradition, the seventeenth century with its Inquisition implied, or the despairing dread of High Romanticism, with its the powerful autonomy of the artist as creator.

Certain postures occur again and again throughout art history, patterns resounding since the original discovery or excavation, old gods becoming secularised. Evidence, on the other hand, sometimes seems fabricated, when the shape of the victim's final second echoes a popular pose.

The other main wellspring of his paintings was very old-fashioned iconography, culled from fuzzy engravings in the tombs of outdated books. The lack of a verifiable spectrum allowed him to chose his own, to insist on deep purples, earthy and autumnal browns, combinations of hue that spoke of candlelit sacrifices, immolation, impalement, all in the darkness of others' souls. He lifted contortions from Leonardo and Michelangelo, but despised Raphael. Amazingly, the greatest number of poses came from the luxury of Delacroix and the other Salon favourites, cross-dressing Sardanapulus' virgins, harem girls becoming boys, making passive males in decadent beds, available in their throes, compliant in their *rigor mortis*, their posthumous lust for life lost.

He had ceased to show livid wounds, hinting at them in a spill, a slur of red wine glazes. A hole in the head was garish so he obliterated it, a neck shadowed by oxides quite sufficient unto itself. He wanted to clothe the corpse with late dignity, with stillness and tranquillity. It was all down to suggestion now.

Several months later, Lázaro's friend from Headquarters came round to share some purloined copies with him. They reeked of burning magnesium, flash, frozen, fossilised, immortal and barbaric.

One of them showed an execution of sorts, carried out on a courier for one of the cartels who had just grown careless or greedy or both. He had been siphoning off small – oh, so small – profits from both rivals, unlaundered, supplying information to the gangs as a way to ingratiate himself and rise up the little ladder. Or that is what he thought he was doing. But he was found out.

The man's privates were distorted beyond recognition in their leafy, secluded suburban square, made public property, a warning against unwise play with the bigger players who were always all-seeing. The flunkeys of the one side persuaded him to part with his trivial treasury of knowledge, and then toyed with him until he resembled a rag-doll, a guardian of some demon's palace. The symbol of masculinity had been transformed into a bunch of putrescent fruit dangling from an unholy bough, an inflated tropical parasite.

Had the violation taken place before or after the extraction? The policeman did not know, could not tell. He remained mute like the ex-informant. The latter's face was restructured by blows, blackened by crystallised fluids, which gummed his eyes, his mouth, his nostrils, depriving him of supplication, and ultimately, breath.

A month or two after that the name was supplied by the chatty supplier of real-life pornography. Jacinto Flores. The name meant nothing to Lázaro Chevalier. It did not ripple or register. No echo came. He assumed that his own little Vulcan had returned to the forge.

A visiting dealer from overseas asked casually one day why he had not produced a self-portrait?

It was tempting to come out with some bullshit about his not wanting to look at himself, but there was a nag nibbling at his brow that reminded him that each and every image was rooted deeply in an understanding of his inner being. It was a deep-seated, deep-felt understanding that the need was in fact already cancelled by the massive self-abuse of the artist in his overpowering, fixation on his own secret centre. The innocent and the guilty that appeared in his paintings were all exclusively himself. All his works were about his works. There was no room for doubt. He murdered himself on a daily basis, or at least placed his soul in compromising situations, apparently impaled upon his own desire. His paintbrush was his phallus and he fertilised each and every plain rectangle with the ejaculation of his spiritual outpouring. The fine weave, the primer, became impregnated with his linseed. It was an eternity of flinging himself into the lion's den, under the dragon's claw, onto the pyre of a lost beloved. Self-love fuelled him.

One day a limousine drew up outside the rambling mansion he had purchased and was in the process of renovating using the northern gold, reclaiming some of the state's terrible debt, bit by bit.

The big boss got out. He was notorious and untouchable, protected by the long arm of the unreliable law. Bespoke tailoring, imported silks, hand-made shoes, elegance incarnate, a car so exotic it seemed alien. Not a drop of blood or dirt clung to his gloved, manicured hands, not a suspicion of a suspicion, though the taint followed wherever he passed, the vague stink of authority without mercy, of violence uncontained, falsity, lack of merit, lack of reason and lack of justice. He personified the notion of massacre and butchery.

'I want you, Señor Chevalier, to do me a tiny little favour. I want an oil painting done of one of my rivals in a – what shall we call it? – an imaginary state of morbidity, a prediction of extinction if you will.'

The artist raised an eyebrow without making any comment. He needed to be fully apprised of the facts before taking on the commission, though he knew full well that once the boss had made his personal will known, no one dared stand against him, no one was able to refuse, no one was that foolish.

'Here is a picture of the son of one of my competitors,' he simpered. 'I would like you to incorporate his features into one of the dead in your famous paintings. Then I will have it delivered to the troublesome entrepreneur.' He paused. 'And perhaps any unpleasantness will mercifully be avoided thereby.'

How delicate, how refined it all was.

'I normally let the light bathe the body and not the face. I like to keep the image universal if I can. I cannot do specific portraits. Every political party round here would want pictures glorifying its martyrs.'

He dared speak that plainly.

'But if you could reclaim the canvas afterwards and remove all its distinguishing features. If you could have a rare chance to try something you haven't previously tried? If you could experiment, develop?'

The game was up. He could not refuse, especially after a ridiculous sum was mentioned to carry out the little joke! He could resell the stretcher, repaint completely if he liked, reduce it to a ghost of its former self. But already he thought of it as a winding sheet. His own.

The intimate details of the picture were worked out. The boss's henchman withdrew once the handshake had been shaken, so the two men could chat as though they were old friends.

The only son of the independent was to be shown naked, from above, arms open and legs spread as if either lying on a broad bed, or crashing from a steely sky ruffled with pubic cloudlets. His genitals were slashed off and a spatter of dark liquid randomly dribble across his torso.

He did the deed. He found a youthful model in the art school he intermittently taught at, a poverty-stricken guy from the outlying agricultural belt, a calabash-eater, a radish-head. His body was etiolated, ridiculously pale for a country lad, full of growing, lean to the point of cadaverousness. He had been ill frequently as a boy, it transpired in conversation, confined to the farm on numerous occasions. His body hair was sparse and his cock disproportionately small in comparison to his height, a juvenile in an adult frame almost. The intended recipient of the painting, or rather his son, was only sixteen. The body fit.

As though dowsed by moonlight, the falling angel was positioned on white sheets crumpled across a tilted mattress, head tipped back for a few quick sketches before the blood began to throb. The student was grateful for the cash and expressed the desire to become a permanent fixture. His wish was granted, or would have been except that the summer intervened and he didn't return to college after the harvest had been gathered in. He would not have been out in the fields, but assisting back at the ranch, looking after the children, feeding the pretty chickens.

The plan Lázaro had for the specious portrait was simple. Once it was returned he would drape a cloth over the face of another model to redraw it masked and spatter a grey stream into the background to hint at the spillage of something other than blood, perhaps repositioning one of the hands to guard the previously unguarded. It would be a sort of homage to Girodet's *Endymion*, the magnificent youth raked by moonbeams.

In due course the fortune-telling history was framed in gold and deposited in the hallway of the fool that was trying to challenge the omnipotence of the baron, embalmed in layers of paper and sacking, and even some reused foam-rubber perhaps. The delivery note did not announce the sender's identity, but the butler accepted it as just another piece of art to crowd the walls, fitting in well amongst all the other tasteless glitter.

Before dinner that evening a fatal shock staggered the family as they crowded around the unveiling before dinner. The boy stood stock-still and blushed at the mirror, offended that what he took as his penis had been shrivelled to a dwarf of its true self. His own legs were hairier by far, his nipples doubloons compared to the widow's mites that decorated the corpse-like waif. Only after further acquaintance did he become aware that the indistinct splurge of paint he had taken for a prick belonged to the grey scumble of the background and not the pewter of the torso, that the blackish splashes wetting his smoothness were spurtings from a wound of grave obscenity. He felt faint when the implication struck home. He felt his testes contract and his stomach begin to retch involuntarily.

His father knew who the perpetrator of this outrage was. He would fight rather than capitulate, challenge the supposition, bite his thumb at him.

The son was sent into hiding as a precaution. Shortly after, a set of bloodied wedding tackle was express-delivered to the house. And shortly after that the gruesome remains were found in the summerhouse up country. The bougainvillea and the jacaranda flared at the atrocity.

Meanwhile, what the dealer had suggested stayed in the artist's mind. He could approach the project casually. In the past the technique of grafting a nobleman's face onto a posed stand-in was common practice. He had effectively used the method to predict the horrific violence meted out to the big boss wannabe.

It took a while to find a man who matched his own body-type. He couldn't resist giving the preliminary drawings a more washboard stomach, tighter buttocks, better-developed pecs, but he would soften the flesh as he progressed, refraining from a full roundness, but layering delicacy.

He decided that a vaguely similar pose to the assassinated youth would be appropriate, but that he would return to his usual shadows. He would include the attributes of the artist, the palette, the brush, the knife, squidges of paint from the tube, oily rags, a mahlstick maybe, but the enigma would be increased not only by the invisibility or illegibility of the face, but by an alchemy that sprang unbidden to his inspiration.

He arranged the guy on all fours, elbows on the boards, arse in the air, one leg extended, the large ovoid with the thumb pushed through it as a penetrating metaphor, its unmistakable shape a halo displaced from the scalp, right in the centre on the lower edge of the huge testament. In sketches, on coarse brownish paper, he used charcoal and chalk to bulk out the plan, and on one could not resist the sudden temptation to scribble on the exposed back as if the skin were a living parchment on which to elaborate some idea, or else the schizophrenic scrawl of a piece of automatic writing.

On several black-and-white photos he took of the body before him, he succumbed to the pressure of his sub-conscious and squeezed miniscule slugs and snails of vivid acrylic onto the glossy surface, jewelling the dorsal flatness with a cape of rare jewels, a poncho of sapphire, ruby and topaz.

Alvaro Alameda, the officer that had brought him the records of other homicides, attended the scene. He looked on as the forensic team gathered their fluff. Explosions of light illuminated the studio and then dulled it to near-darkness as the eye first failed to cope and then readjusted.

The dead man had fallen over a chest that contained art materials. A hessian sack hung limply over that. It was the same colour as the raffia matting beneath it. The naked corpse had been splashed and slashed with a rainbow of dying pigment. Tubes had been emptied onto the spine, the neck, the backside, the upper thighs. It had then been blended with a stiff brush, streaking the cold skinny undercoat with an action painting splurge that could have graced the wall of any modern art museum. The murderer, or murderers, had undeniable talent as well as a morbid sense of humour.

It would take a while before the body could be turned and the weapon of choice discovered. A palette knife up under the ribs had entered the heart and allowed the life to escape. It was less blunt than a new one, constant use having worn the edge sharper, though considerable force would have had to have been used to ram it home. There was also lead white in his mouth, a large quantity of it, probably administered prior to the stabbing, seeing as a considerable amount had been swallowed along with some form of chemical thinner. The masterpiece had taken great care to execute.

Just another victim in the eternal warring in this country of the factional. No suspects, no criminal caught, no information despite offers of reward. Nothing.

The lawman noticed the correspondence between what was drying on the gigantic easel and the pattern made by the limbs and colours of the deceased. It was disturbingly similar.

He stood dead still a long while in the shadow-shrouded chamber, contemplating it once the hive of activity had halted, once the drones had gone home to their wives, to moan about the government, the insurgents, the neighbours, refusing to bring their work home with them. The final squad would be there in a minute, the coroner's assistants, to cart the man off to his autopsy.

There is a certain shape that reminds everyone of the notion of the fallen victim, a single outline that indicates an untimely death, a chalk circle indented and projecting that tells a tale of an unexpected end and the vain attempt to flee it: arms up, one perhaps straighter than the other, as though reaching for last minute salvation, a weapon to put off the inevitable; one leg rigid and the other crooked, as though in mid-crawl; a bubble where the head was, ready to burst, to cease to exist. That shape decorates many a crime-scene, on pavement, kitchen floor or bedroom sheets. And stains many a canvas with its shade.

Lázaro Chevalier, alone in his studio.

Soon he would be gone.

For ever.

L & I
Hugh Fleetwood

L & I
Hugh Fleetwood

"Strauss! Peter Strauss!"

Already when he had seen the car approaching he had shrunk back – like everyone else in the street. And when the great black vehicle with its tinted windows had started to slow down, he had felt his stomach lurch, his legs go weak. There again like all the other passers-by, he had continued walking and tried to stare straight ahead of him; at the same time he had kept an eye on the car and wondered why it was pulling up. Of course it couldn't be stopping for him, he had told himself. Nevertheless...

When he saw the rear window lowered, and heard his name called, not only his stomach and legs felt they had dissolved. Such was his panic he felt his whole body had turned to jelly. He thought he would faint. He told himself he was imagining things. It had to be a mistake. He looked around, wildly, and all those people who had shrunk away from the car, as their forebears might have from the plague-cart, now shrank away from him, the fear and pity in their faces mingled with relief.

He wondered whether he should run, but knew he couldn't – he couldn't move. He wondered whether he should deny he was Peter Strauss, but knew that that was useless, too. Oh God, he told himself, this cannot be happening. This happens to other people. And what compounded the nightmare, was that even as the driver's door opened and a massive bullet-headed chauffeur in a black uniform got out, stared straight at him and opened the rear door, it occurred to him that he recognised that voice that had called. He couldn't have; he *had* to be imaging things. And yet...

The chauffeur gestured with his chin.

Again Peter looked round, still more wildly than before, and saw now only pity on the faces of those passers-by, some of whom he recognised and some of who probably recognised him. Would they ever see him again? It seemed unlikely. Then, since there was nothing for it, and feeling as a passenger must on a plane that is crashing – knowing that even if he screams there is no way out – he managed to take one, and then another step towards that rear door.

He was nearly there. He looked up at the blue sky. He saw the clouds. Oh please, he wanted to cry. Oh please. Not me. What have I done? Oh please, *please*...

Making an effort not to lose control of his bowels, he ducked into the car and sat in the empty seat – next, he was aware, to an officer in uniform.

"Strauss! Peter Strauss!"

Again that voice – and now as he heard it, and a split second before the officer removed his peaked cap, he remembered.

"L?" he said, his voice hoarse. "I mean..." He felt sick with relief himself, and in a way still more terrified. "Should I – what should I call you?"

"L will do just fine," the officer said; as, with his cap off, he allowed Peter to see his face. Nearly twenty-five years had passed; but with his short brown wavy hair, small pale eyes, large nose and grinning dangerous mouth, the man was still quite recognisable. As the L who, at eighteen, and in his final year at college, had spotted a thirteen-year-old just starting at the school; and had taken it upon himself to make the boy's life a misery, both physically and emotionally.

The physical abuse that L had inflicted had taken various forms. He had tied his victim over scalding pipes in the shower room, sodomised him, and got his friends to sodomise him – or beat him if they preferred, or stick their penises in his mouth. He had made his victim do push-ups and other exercises, again and again, till all his muscles were screaming and eventually he collapsed onto the concrete floor of the shower room – over which L and his friends had urinated, or defecated. And he had made his victim accompany him on long runs in the winter, and had lashed him around the legs with twigs, or stinging nettles, whenever he had slowed down.

The emotional abuse he had inflicted, however, had taken just one form. Even while subjecting him to these tortures, L had contrived to make Peter Strauss fall in love with him.

It was not the tortures themselves that had prompted this response. Rather, the fact that as well as being a bully and a sadist – and a star athlete and boxer – L had revealed himself to be the best-read boy in the school, the most musically knowledgeable; and the first person ever to recognise that young Peter Strauss had talent – or even genius, it was once suggested. Sometimes this talent seemed to drive the older boy mad, as if he couldn't bear not to be possessed of it himself. Other times, more often, he felt proud that he was the only person who did so recognise it – and saw it as his task to nurture it. "You have to have steel put into you," he had shouted at Peter. "You have to have fire put into you. Otherwise your talent, as it matures – as you mature – may become... fluttery. Pretty. Whereas if I make you strong... Oh," the eighteen years old had said, longingly. "You can be great, Peter. You can be – extraordinary."

It was not only by inflicting pain on him and raping him that L sought to make his protégé strong. It was also by teaching him to box, and box well; by teaching him to shoot, in the school's military corps; and by getting him to make clear, somehow, to the members of "The Gang" – as L's side-kicks were called – that they were fawning stupid thugs who would never amount to anything in life. And to bear the further abuse to which, as a consequence, he was subjected.

"I can't *bear* fluttery things," Peter remembered L shouting one day – when they had gone off to the country together, and for the first time L had made him shoot something living. "The Spanish like killing bulls. But I like killing – no, not necessarily killing, *hurting*, fluttery things. I like ripping the wings off butterflies. I like breaking the fingers of semi-talented pianists and violinists –" he did, too; Peter had seen him do it, even while managing to make it look like an accident "– who refuse to explore the outer limits of their talent, but just – flutter around on the edge of it. I like – there Peter, look!" L yelled, as a pheasant, alarmed by his voice, flapped up from the undergrowth. "Fire! Fire"! He waited a second, and watched; and as Peter squeezed the trigger and the bird crashed out of the sky, he turned back with bright eyes to look at his creature, who felt giddy and sick, but dared not show it. "Good. Well done!" L continued to study the marksman, and did of course see his revulsion, however hard Peter tried to conceal it. But he pretended not to, and grinned. "It's great, isn't it?" he said. "Whenever I fire and hit something – it's like coming. Now, let's go get a rabbit."

"Why?" Peter said, quietly.

"Why what? Why do I hate fluttery things? I don't know," L said. And then: "because we're only here once, and it seems to me, while we're here – we should go to the very ends of the earth, so even if we die tomorrow, we know we've been there. Whereas people who just hover around the entrance, just stand at first floor windows and say 'oh what a pretty view' – I despise them. They're just tourists. And – all right, that's what most people are meant to be. Are happy – in a manner of speaking – to be. But when, once in a while, you find someone who could go further, who could even point out things to you you've never seen, take you places you've never been to yourself or even suspected existed – and that person refuses to do it – I see it as my mission to destroy him. To make him wish he had no ability, no talent at all. That's what I mean when I say I hate fluttery things. And that's what I won't..." Suddenly uncontrollably, insanely angry, the young man caught himself, and grinned. "Well that's the theory, anyway. In practice, I'm just a psychopath who enjoys inflicting pain and killing things. And..." The roller-coaster dipped again, and once more he was serious. "I shall, kill you, Peter Strauss, if you don't fulfil your – destiny, let's call it. One day, however long it takes... You are the first person, the only person I have ever met or am likely to meet who could, really – yes, go all the way. And if you don't, I swear to you – I shall be like a demon in your dreams. Haunting you. And even though ten, twenty years may pass, one day, when you're least suspecting it – when you're just walking down the street maybe, trying to look insignificant, normal... Look!" L shouted, as another pheasant rose into the air. "Shoot it, Peter! Kill it!"

Dutifully, and not feeling so sick now, Peter raised his gun, and shot.

At the end of Peter's first year at college, L left; to the relief not only of all the people whom he had tormented, but of his friends, such as they were, and the masters. Who had not known what to make of this young man who seemed to delight in out-bullying the bullies, out-arguing or out-shining the more intellectually brilliant boys, and in regarding both with a contempt that was as all-encompassing and all-consuming as a swarm of locusts.

Some said he would come to a bad end; others that he would go far. But both agreed that in the current uncertain political climate, he was likely to find an outlet for his peculiar gifts.

The only person who missed him was Peter Strauss; and he missed him with a passion that was almost as great as his sense of liberation – his joy that the horror had gone. Or perhaps, he sometimes thought, his passion was still greater than his joy...

Whatever he felt: L never really abandoned him. Peter completed his own five years at school. He went on to university. And he abruptly left university when, at the age of twenty-one, he at the same time published his first book, had the first exhibition of his paintings, and was hailed, almost overnight, as "the brightest hope of his generation". Yet for all that in the meantime he had not heard from the man again, the demon with which L had threatened him – the demon that *was* L – was always in his mind. Making him work, work, work, making him strive, strive, strive for always better, higher, more extreme things – and making him feel, by the age of thirty, that he had already exhausted his talent. Some of his friends called him the "Colonel", because tall, thin, and inclined to severity, he seemed to pursue his career with almost military zeal – and besides, "you *look* like a Colonel." Others called him the "Puritan" because fair of hair and grim – at times – of lip, he seemed to pursue his career with almost religious zeal – and besides, "you look like a Puritan. Some bleak, Protestant pastor." But neither the one group nor the other, Peter suspected, realised to what extent he tried to keep up that outward appearance so that no one – above all that invisible but ever present L – should suspect that inside him there was some soft, feeble, and yes, fluttery creature. A creature that was only too eager to lie back and rest; and might have done so had he not needed to earn a living, and not been scared that if he even attempted it, L would come to get him.

It was, he sometimes thought, as much to get away from L, as to distance himself from the political turmoil, that he had sold his flat in town and retreated to a small town on the banks of the River R-----. All right, as government after government fell, the extremists gained in power, the "Leader" took advantage of the confusion to advance his own cause, and with a combination of cunning and ruthlessness eventually got himself named head of state, wisdom dictated that people such as he – so-called intellectuals, and homosexuals – should keep as low a profile as possible. But fear – fear of L looking into his soul and seeing that what had once soared like an eagle now but weakly flapped its wings in its nest – was what made Peter listen to the voice of wisdom. To listen to it, and conclude that even should the Leader be killed and his regime overthrown – as sooner or later they must be – he might stay on where he was; coming in his middle and then old age to be taken for: a retired military man, who had never been "the marrying kind"; or a Protestant pastor who had lost his faith, and never ceased to regret it. For surely, Peter argued, even if that threat that L had made all those years ago had been real, he wouldn't come to seek him out here, would he? Not in this provincial backwater where, for the present at least, "P. Strauss, artist" was hoping to survive by living off his savings, and painting flower-paintings or portraits of local worthies and their families. Once the war was over he might think about getting back to serious work. But till then – surely, surely, he asked himself time after time when he woke at four in the morning and was unable to get back to sleep, L would stay away till then?

Surely, surely, Peter told himself now as he sat beside L, the real L, in his black armour-plated car, he should have realised that the answer to that question was "no". What was happening had been bound to happen, and he had been crazy to think he could get away. All right, maybe the real L wouldn't be quite so terrifying as his imaginary L, but –

Even that hope was absurd. Of course he would be! Still more so, probably. Imaginary demons were one thing; senior officers in an elite division of the state police were something altogether different. Not for nothing did people cringe at the sight of these huge black cars as they made their way through the narrow streets of the town. Not for nothing had he always cringed himself. One could fool oneself all one liked; not talk about "that place" that had been built some fifteen kilometres up river. But even if one pretended it didn't exist, still when there was a wind from the north-east, the smell that came to one was unmistakably the smell of death. Moreover, every now and then one of those black cars would be seen cruising the streets at night, and in the morning it was reported that Mr X or Miss Y had "gone away". "Probably just visiting a relative," people said – not daring to ask the family or neighbours of the missing person for confirmation of this fact. But they knew that having left, it was most improbable that Mr X or Miss Y would return.

As it was most improbable – Peter told himself for the second time in five minutes – that he would return; to his flat in Mozart Street; to his quiet life. Of course it was possible that L had just spotted him walking down the street and told his chauffeur to stop because he wanted a chat for old times sake. But the chances were...

He had left a window open at home, he remembered. Oh well, he guessed it didn't matter. Someone, eventually, would close it.

"So, how've you been?" L said, continuing to grin. "I heard you were living round here. To tell the truth, that was partly why I accepted this posting when they offered it to me. Though I would probably have accepted anyway, given the job... I was planning to look you up. I've only been here a few months. Got a lot to arrange, clear up. My predecessor killed himself! Stupid fool. But then, when I saw you walking along... You haven't changed much. Got a bit older, obviously, but – how old are you now?"

"Thirty-seven," Peter murmured.

"Yes, I suppose you would be if I'm forty-two... You still queer?"

Peter glanced at the driver.

"It's all right. We're in private here. Nothing you say will be taken down and used in evidence against you. Right, Otto?"

Otto, at the wheel, grunted.

"Yes," Peter murmured, his throat dry.

"Thought you probably were, from your books. Besides, people don't often change... I used to fuck him in the ass when we were at school," L said to the driver. "He used to scream and squawk, but – always give a boy what he wants, I say. Eh?"

Otto, glancing at Peter in his rear-view mirror, grunted.

"How long you been living out here?"

"Nearly – seven years, now."

"What you doing? Lying low till the war ends?"

Again Peter glanced at the driver.

"Stop looking at Otto every time I ask you a question! We're not fools. We know it's all over bar the shouting, as they say. Another six months, a year at most... We should never have got into a war. That's what really messed us up. And once America had become involved... If we'd just done it quietly, creeping up a little here, a little there... In twenty years the whole of Europe – the whole world, probably – would have come round to our way of thinking. Or recognised that in the final analysis they had always been of our way of thinking. But impatience, impatience, and what do you get? Defeat, ruin, and another century or two of dullness, worthiness and hypocrisy. Well I'm glad I shan't be around to see it. These past twelve years have been so exhilarating I don't think I could bear... Well?

"Well?" Peter echoed.

"Have you been lying low?"

"Yes," Peter murmured. "I suppose so."

L looked at him; looked, Peter felt, into him, as he used to, all those years ago.

"Or did you think that if you moved to a small town you'd be safe from me?"

Again Peter felt faint. It really was as if the man inhabited his head, could read his every thought.

"I always told him," L said to Otto, "that if he didn't fulfil his promise I would come back to get him. Fuck him – figuratively speaking now, of course! – like I used to. What's more," L continued, still to the driver, "he always believed me." He turned. "Didn't you?"

"Yes," Peter whispered.

"Well," L went on, "we'll talk about that later. But I have read all your books, you know. And I used to sneak off to see your exhibitions. You still painting?"

"Yes," Peter whispered. He cleared his throat, and went on, not much more loudly: "though in the present climate..."

"It's all right. You don't have to apologise. I quite understand. A man must make compromises to survive. As long as they're only temporary of course, and he doesn't deviate permanently from his allotted path... I must say, I think you've been quite clever in your books. But then you always were, weren't you? The knuckle-heads could see one thing – if they could read at all! – and the... sharper of eye, let's say, could pick out the real figure in the carpet. Do you know that story?"

Peter nodded.

"Thought you probably did... Anyway, it'll all be quite different once we're gone and the good guys have won, and – why did you never leave? You could have gone to America, couldn't you?"

"Yes. Probably. But... I wanted to watch, I suppose. See the whole thing at first hand... And even if I'd gone to America, I couldn't have got away from..."

"What?" L asked, with real intensity; he waited a beat, then went on to say, with an almost wistful smile rather than his usual grin: "Me?"

Peter too waited a beat, and met the man's eye before he nodded. "Yes," he murmured. He hesitated, and continued: "You meant it, didn't you?"

Just for a second L wondered what he was talking about; then he got there. "Yes," he said. "I did." Another pause. "And I still do."

The car was picking up speed; they had reached the outskirts of town and were driving beside the river.

L nodded in the direction they were heading. "You ever been out here?"

"No. Of course not. It's forbidden to go more than two kilometres along this road. And even if it wasn't..."

"Out of sight, out of mind, eh?"

"Something like that."

"Well, it'll be an experience for you. Something else you'll have seen."

Peter wondered if this implied that at some stage he would be coming back along this road. He realised that L hadn't quite said so, but – he relaxed very slightly.

"Not many of your colleagues have seen a fully functioning extermination camp, I'll be bound."

Peter stared.

"Not many would be interested, I suppose, but – no, that's not true. They'd all be interested. Just most wouldn't admit it. They'd be too frightened of their consciences. And of course of not getting out alive themselves! But that's not something you have to worry about, is it?"

The grin returned; Peter didn't reply.

What he said, after he had looked out of the window at the fields on the far side of the river, was: "And you? I mean what do you...?"

"I'm the commandant, of course! What did you think? That I'd be taking orders from someone? Come, Peter, you should know me better than that. I've never taken orders from anyone in my life, even when I seem to." He frowned, and said seriously: "I wouldn't take orders from God, if he existed."

"That," Peter said, "I can believe."

L's eyes narrowed slightly. He changed the subject. "I'm married. I have three young children. My wife used to be a barmaid." Did he say that with just a hint of defiance, of defensiveness? "She cries a lot," the man murmured, himself looking out of the window.

Peter glanced at him as if to say: I imagine you give her a lot to cry about; L, who had turned back and caught his look, nodded.

"Actually," he went on, "I've been coming into town myself most days. But in disguise, as it were. In civilian clothes. I've been bringing the children to school."

Again there was wistfulness in his voice; even love.

"And since no one ever sees my face when I'm in uniform, or can look into this car when I'm riding around selecting my next victim," he laughed, "as far as the other parents are concerned, I'm just a good papa doing his duty before going off to work. Somewhat reserved of course – in fact I never speak to anyone other than to say good morning – but oh, a real gentleman."

Peter considered him at length now, before asking, quietly, as he had asked many years before: "Why?"

"Why do I play the good papa?" L paused. "Or why *that*?" He lay back in his seat and appeared to be thinking. "I sometimes ask myself the same question. I suppose the short answer is the same as ever. I *am* a psychopath. One who gets pleasure in inflicting pain on and destroying his fellow human beings. I always have been. I've always *loathed* humanity. I think humans are the most repulsive of all animals, the cruellest, the most greedy, and the most, far and away the most, hypocritical. No other animal believes itself to be *good*. Or bad. Yet we, in our self-serving way... We pretend that Mozart and Beethoven, Shakespeare and Michelangelo can somehow justify the horror... and we also seem to think that if we weren't around to see them, sunsets, mountain ranges, spring flowers wouldn't be beautiful. Of course they would be! It's just our staggering egos that make us..." He stopped, looked down at his hands, then up again at Peter. "I suppose, given the choice, I would have been some sort of 'artist' myself. Part of the justification. Since I have no discernible talent... I've always had a longing to expose. To expose all the baseness, the stupidity, the foulness of..." He pointed, surreptitiously at Otto the driver. "Of the brutes, the blow-flies that buzz around those who stink of power. Especially those who give themselves airs and graces and think they're superior animals... But also to expose, as I say, the hypocrisy of the – of the hand-wringers, the intellectuals, the aesthetes, the – artists. The other flies that cluster on the bloated, disgusting body..."

A further examination of the hands, then: "When I left school... well, everything was descending into chaos, and I suppose I joined the Party because I thought I was going to have some fun. Like a small boy who gets to go round smashing everything up... At the same time, even while I was having fun, and was attracted to the whole – psychopathic streak in the Party, I think in the back of my mind I knew that it was doomed. It reeked of self-destruction. No movement, no religion, no – love, can be that powerful, that violent and nihilistic – even if it pretends to be the opposite – without having its end built into its beginning. It was going to be a blaze that lasted – well, rather less than it has lasted, I thought at the time. And its destructiveness has been on a far greater scale than any I ever dreamed of – hoped for. It's been *staggering*, hasn't it? All mankind's beastliness not just bubbling to the surface, but bubbling right over and flooding the earth. Oh it's been breathtaking, Peter, glorious, and – now it's almost over. We're just mopping up the last drops before... as I say, it's back to the same old show..."

Complete silence fell now, and L stared gloomily out of the window as if he could see, through that dark glass, the ruined earth.

Indeed, the only further words he spoke before they arrived at the camp were in reply to a question of Peter's.

They had just gone through the second of two check-points – at which the guards had saluted L – and in the distance watch-towers, a great expanse of low dark buildings, and five high chimneys could be made out.

As if there had been no lull in their conversation, Peter said, very quietly: "But you did, in your fashion, care about me, didn't you?

L turned back to him, and nodded. "Yes," he murmured, his voice distant. "In my fashion, I did think – I thought you had... promise." Looking straight ahead of him now, at those watch-towers and chimneys, he said: "It's the usual old cliché, isn't it? Hope springs eternal. Even in the hopeless..."

They drove, after L had lowered his window several times more to prove that it was really he in the car, right into the camp. Past three rows of barbed wire; past guards with their guns at the ready and their black dogs on leashes; past innumerable ghostly figures in grey rags shuffling around as if they had been given orders to do just that. Shuffle aimlessly in circles until... Here and there bodies lay on the ground, whether alive or dead it was impossible to tell; now that L's window was permanently down, the stench was appalling. A smell of urine and faeces, of rotten meat and burnt flesh, over which lay a thin and ineffective layer of disinfectant, that only served to make the underlying effluvia more revolting yet.

L breathed in deeply and grinned as the car came to a halt. "Ah the perfume, the perfume," he said. "Out you get, Peter. We're here."

Just half-an-hour ago Peter had been walking down a street on his way to buy some milk. Now – he had already forgotten the terror he had felt when he had heard his name called. It was as if there had been an earthquake, he had slipped through a crack, and plunged so far, so fast, that the world above was impossible to imagine, let alone recall. This was an entirely different world, and if he should not leave it alive – even that, from this perspective, was no tragedy. It would be just normal.

"I thought first we'd have a little tour. Then I'll take you home to meet my wife and children – they're on holiday at the moment. And, then, after we've had some lunch – we'll talk about your work." He grinned again at Peter. "I'll – pass judgement."

No, it would be no tragedy if he were killed here today; even so,

Peter felt a twinge in his bowels again.

He walked around the camp in a daze. Looking into huts where the prisoners slept, or lay all day if they were too weak to move, four to a bunk. Not quite daring to look at the guards, whose blank brutal faces reminded him of L's side-kicks, at school. Not daring to look at all at those thousand upon thousand of shuffling spectres; yet seeing them anyway, and registering the fact that it was impossible to tell what age they were, what sex they were, so emaciated were they, with their shaven heads and shrunken eyes.

"What," he heard himself whispering to L, "is the *point*? What are they doing here? Why, if you're going to kill them all, don't you just – kill them?"

"Logistics," L explained. "They're sent here from other camps when they're too weak to work any more. But the crematoria can only cope with so many a day. And now that other places are closing down or being evacuated, we're getting more and more – every night train loads arrive. We're working round the clock as it is. But eventually a back-log builds up, and as it's useless putting them to work here... Come, I'll show you what we do."

He marched off, leading Peter through more and more rows of low, stinking huts, across a marshalling yard from which a train had just pulled out, past a high wooden fence, and on towards the river; following at last a set of rails that ran down into the water, and over which, suspended on pylons, hung a thick steel cable.

On the other side of the river the great black chimneys of what were obviously the crematoria pumped dark smoke out into the fine October morning.

"We won't go over there," L said. "You might find it a bit much, with your delicate sensibility. But I just thought I would show you... I don't know if you can see, right under the main entrance, there are a series of cages on wheels?"

Peter narrowed his eyes and looked where L was pointing; he nodded.

"It's very simple. Quite beautifully simple. The prisoners are loaded into the cages on this side. The cages are hauled by that cable on those rails, that run right across the river on the bed. It takes about ten minutes for the crossing to be completed; for six or seven minutes the cages are completely submerged. By the time they emerge at the other side – the contents can be unloaded, and tipped straight into the furnaces."

The man spoke so casually, so flippantly even, that Peter more than ever felt he was dreaming.

"Don't they protest?" he heard himself whispering. "Before they're... loaded?"

"Some do. But the guards don't take very kindly to protestors, so – on the whole they go quietly. Also, that fence there hides what's going on from the main body of the camp. So they don't know exactly what's going to happen when they're put into the cages. Though obviously they have a pretty good idea. It's amazing, isn't it? When you see all those people, and think just a few months, or maybe a couple of years ago, they were – housewives, bank-clerks, lawyers, school-teachers, nurses, miners, shop-assistants, factory-workers – even artists! And now, reduced to..." He looked at his watch. "But enough of all that! It's lunch-time!"

They were driven in a jeep to L's house, that stood about a mile outside the perimeter fence, and was built on the side of a low hill; from its windows, it was impossible to see anything of the camp itself, but the smell was as pervasive as ever.

As they approached the front door, and Peter gazed down the hill across a wood stretching almost as far as the eye could see – the trees were changing colour in the autumn, and all was gold, and russet, and red – L said: "I've taken a small flat in town. I take the children there to change, before they go to school. Or my wife does. Otherwise I'm afraid their friends might complain of the odour clinging to them."

"Don't they say anything to their friends?" Peter said, still whispering.

"No. I've told them that I work in a top-secret establishment, so they can't know anything more, and – as far as they're concerned, it's true."

"Even so," Peter continued to whisper, "they must know."

"Must they?" L said. "Did you? Or any of your fellow citizens?"

"No. But – yes, of course we knew. But not – not that it was like that." He gestured towards the unseen camp.

"Bullshit," L muttered. "What did you think? That it was a rest home? Of course you knew, if you thought about it. Just as the children must have a pretty good idea, even if they're too young for their ideas to be clear. But – they prefer not to think about it, too. As their friends prefer not to think about it, and their teachers prefer not to think about it. It's easier if you tell yourself that this place is top-secret, and that, therefore – Marie!" L bellowed. "We have a guest!"

As L and Peter went into the hall of the house, a woman emerged from a room on the far side. She was blonde, and quite pretty in a washed-out way; but she looked tired, scared and unhappy. Her eyes were puffy.

"Hello," she said, in a voice as lacklustre as her complexion.

"This is Peter. An old friend of mine."

"Hello," Marie repeated, her tone unchanged.

"Do you think we can give him some lunch?"

"Yes. I expect so." The woman paused, and went on, a little petulant now: "It would have helped if I had known in advance."

"I didn't know myself in advance! I just saw Peter walking down the street and I called him over, and – Peter's a distinguished writer, you know. And painter."

Marie stared. "Oh," she said. Then, wearily: "It'll be ready in five minutes if you want to go and wash your hands."

"Marie's very particular about hands being clean," L said, with one of his grins. "I think she thinks soap is the solution to all the world's problems."

Marie gazed at her husband, then went back through the door she had emerged from.

Peter couldn't help glancing at L; L, as ever, knew what he was thinking.

"Why did I marry her? Because she was pretty. Because she was submissive. Because – she was lost." The man hesitated, and went on, striking for the first time since he had hailed Peter, a slightly false note. "I have an affinity with the lost." He caught that note himself, and pulled a face. "At least," he said, with a smile, "I like to think I have."

When the men went into the dining room they found the children already seated at the table. The two boys and a girl rose, instantly, to greet their father's guest.

Peter's first impression was that L was almost as severe and pitiless a father as he was a commandant. Hans, Brigitte and Peter seemed too perfect to be true. Their fair hair was neatly brushed and combed. Their clothes were spotless and without a crease. Their beautiful faces had not a blemish or an irregularity. They looked, all three of them, as their mother must have looked when she was young. It was only if one looked into their extraordinary blue eyes that one caught a glimpse of their father in them – a glimpse of spirit, of wildness. And if one then looked back at their father, one saw that though he appeared to be scanning them for any hint of a flaw – that he would no doubt pounce upon and use as an excuse to mete out punishment – in fact his severity was for the most part a mask to disguise how intensely proud he was of his off-spring. Proud and amazed, that such saplings should have grown from so unpromising a soil.

Indeed, Peter thought, having observed him further, the man could scarcely conceal his love...

The meal was stiff and formal. L's wife, who sounded as if she had learned "polite conversation" from a manual, asked Peter a number of questions.

"What made you move to this area, Mr Strauss?"

"Oh, the hills, the river – the quiet, I suppose," Peter replied.

"I bet you didn't know what they were planning to build when you bought your flat!" L said with a laugh. "I bet you hoped you would be moving some place where your conscience would be as out of sight as you were!"

"What kind of books do you write? I'm afraid I don't have much time for reading."

"Oh, you know, all sorts. Novels. Short stories. And I've written a couple of plays..."

"My husband said you were also a painter?"

"Yes. Though just at the moment I'm rather – I mean I've been doing landscapes, and flower-paintings, that I can sell."

"I like landscapes and flower-paintings."

"Flutter flutter," L growled, ominously. "Flutter flutter."

Then, intimidated by her husband, or having exhausted her supply of questions, Marie fell silent; and it was up to Peter to try to lighten the mood. He did so by talking to the children; asking them what their favourite subjects were at school, if they liked exploring the woods.

The answers he was given were – of course – immaculate. Polite complete sentences, even from the youngest; each one accompanied by a "sir". Yet, conscious of L's gaze on him, every time he addressed the angelic-looking creatures, Peter sounded to his own ear as fatuous as Marie; and felt that for all their faultless manners, the children were regarding him with contempt.

Oh, they had their father in them all right; and even if their parents had kept everything hidden from them, those sapphire blue eyes had already seen too much.

As soon as they had finished eating L, who had been growing steadily more impatient, got to his feet. "Let's go," he muttered to Peter. "I've got to get back to work. I'm sorry the food wasn't better. Cooking is not one of Marie's talents."

"No, no," Peter mumbled, flushing slightly. "It was delicious, thank you," he went on to his hostess, though in fact L was right.

"And I'm sorry the talk wasn't as brilliant as that to which you are accustomed."

"No, no," Peter again felt obliged to protest.

"No doubt in another few years the children will be able to contribute something. At the moment, they're a little small. Hans! Brigitte! Peter! Say goodbye to Mr Strauss."

"Goodbye, Mr Strauss," the children chorused, their unwavering stares sinister. They sounded as if they were bidding Mr Strauss farewell forever.

"And now," L said, opening the door of the dining room, "I suggest we adjourn to my office."

"Goodbye," Peter told the children. "Goodbye," he muttered to Marie, even as he was being herded out. The woman looked as if she were about to start crying. "And – thank you again."

As they walked towards the jeep that would take them back to the camp, L murmured, very reasonably: "It can't be easy being married to me. And having to put up with all this." He gestured towards the brow of the hill. "That's why I don't say more to her. Poor thing. But what can you do? We can't always choose those whom we love, can we?"

"No," Peter replied. "We can't."

L's office was a narrow, four storey house on the edge of the camp. L accompanied Peter to the top floor, and showed him into a study at the back. The room had a view of the river; into which, even as the two men went over to the window and L murmured "look," three cages were being towed by the now taut cable, that was attached to a winch on the far side. Each cage contained what must have been a hundred tightly packed people, half of whom were screaming, reaching out through the bars of the cages, trying to clamber on each other's shoulders, half of whom stood with heads bowed apparently resigned to their fate. It was a scene so horrifying it reminded Peter of some painting by Bosch; and for the third time that day he thought that he might faint. But L was holding his arm, holding him up; and despite himself he was unable not to keep watching, until all those cages, running smoothly on their rails, had disappeared beneath the surface of the river.

"We've built a system of locks and weirs a little way downstream," L murmured, "so even in summer the water level never falls below... what is required."

Those were the only words spoken by either man until, some minutes later, the cages re-appeared. Now all was still inside; the bodies piled in contorted heaps, arms outstretched between the bars.

As he finally allowed Peter to leave the window, and accompanied him out of the study, L said: "The rails go right into the crematoria; the cages are up-ended automatically. So no one has to touch anything..."

The front room of the office-building was furnished only with a long table and twenty or so wooden chairs; off it there was a large terrace, that over-looked the main body of the camp.

The first thing Peter noticed, as L opened the glass doors to the terrace, was a rifle propped up against the railings.

There was also a single stool, set right in the middle of the broad expanse of tiles.

It was to this stool that L led his prisoner, as Peter suddenly came to think of himself. "Sit," he barked; and as Peter did so, the man started to pace slowly up and down the terrace, his black boots clicking on the terra cotta.

"We were talking, earlier, about figures in the carpet," he started; then paused, and seemed to start again. "I suppose, even when you were thirteen and you seemed undecided whether to become a serious person or a fluttering, effeminate... butterfly, I detected a vague, as-yet ill-drawn... yes, let's call it figure in your carpet. That made me both want to fuck you, destroy you, and hope at the same time that I didn't – that I could make you stronger, make you – yes, choose your serious side. You seemed, as no one else at that school did, and as few people whom I have met since, to see... clearly. And when I looked at those paintings you were doing then, and read your first little stories – they were immature, of course. Careless. Unformed. Even so – I detected in them that same – hint of a vision I could share. There always seemed to be, somewhere within them – the stories, now, I'm talking about – some figure who saw civilisation as both an unceasing struggle for decency, justice, a degree of equality and a certain amount of freedom – plus a seed-bed for extraordinary inventions, amazing discoveries and great works of art – and, at the same time: a catalogue of crimes. Of unspeakable, appalling crimes, that fertilised the seed-bed, and without which those flowers – those trees – could never have grown.

"Maybe I was reading too much into them; seeing what I wanted to see rather than what was there. And I'm not saying that your vision was the only valid vision. It was just... one that appealed to me. One that I responded to. That was why I decided to take you under my wing. Though it may not have seemed like that to you.

"And then, after I left school and went into... politics, let's say, I always kept an eye out for you. I think I saw the first poems you published when you were – seventeen, you must have been."

Peter nodded.

"And then the first short story you wrote, and the first novel, and – I felt a tremendous sense of achievement. I felt you were my creation. Pure vanity, of course, you were your own creation. Nonetheless... And always, if your work could be seen as a carpet and there were a thousand different patterns in it, all wonderfully well arranged, I felt that I could detect one underlying pattern, the pattern that bound all those others together.

"For five, ten years – I was so proud of you I cannot tell you. So proud of myself, for having first spotted you, even if I had had no real hand in your creation.

"And then, as the political situation became more... fluid, and the world – our world – started to fall apart – I thought I detected a certain... paling of your imagination. A loss of energy that became more marked as the Party took over, and my own rise became more marked. Though I was always too crazy, even for the lunatics, to make it quite to the top; I disturbed even the profoundly disturbed."

L gave one of his slightly wistful smiles.

"It wasn't that that fundamental pattern that I had always found so attractive had disappeared. Rather the opposite. It was that all the other patterns had disappeared; all the colours, the variety, the vitality. Until, in you last few books, there was nothing left in the carpet apart from that one *ur*-figure. Again and again, however much you changed the story, however much you... changed the clothes, let's say, the hanger off which you suspended those clothes was the same. There, at the centre of the novel, or the novella, or whatever it was, was some artist-type – whether he was literally an artist or an artist in all but name – who, instinctively liberal in outlook, came to believe that he was living in an essentially corrupt society, and that to have any measure of success in that society – both material success and yes, 'artistic' success – he had to embrace the corruption. Or at least, acquiesce in it. He had to become an accomplice to murder, if not an actual murderer himself. He had to lie about what he saw, and at the same time draw strength from it. He had to – what is it you keep saying? 'Become a laughing, prancing joker in the court of a depraved monarch.' I think I've read that, or words to that effect, in about six of your last seven books.

"It was the truth, of course, to my way of thinking. But paradoxically, the more you told the truth, or the more baldly you told it and it did become the only figure in the carpet, the more contrived, schematic, somehow *less* truthful that figure became. Until I couldn't help feeling – this has just become theory for him. This is just some automatic response he is trotting out, that he no longer really believes in. It became as superficial, frivolous... fluttery, in its way, as your paintings had become. Oh, I realise you had to protect yourself, had to go on earning a living. And I have to say, the more schematic, arid you became, the more my fellow animals in the zoo were taken in by you, and *didn't* see what, by now, was the only thing left to see. They praised your breadth the narrower you became; they admired your palette when you had ceased to use all colours but grey, they took you to be wry and ironical and if not on their side at least indifferent, when I saw that over and over you were condemning them, damning them. If, there again, damning them constantly with the same words, in the same automatic fashion, until even your curses became meaningless. You retired to this place not so much because you wanted to keep a low profile, Peter, or even hide from me, as because – you wanted to get away from the world. You wanted to cease being what you were born to be. And you thought if you kept on trotting out the same line, you could keep your conscience clear. "You see, I was always denouncing the beasts, even if the beasts were too stupid to notice." But if you get away from the world, if you let everything become theory...

"Everything becomes dust, Peter. The jungle becomes the Sahara. And frankly – you might just as well be dead."

L stopped his pacing at last and stood staring at Peter. His eyes narrowed.

"You have disappointed me, Peter. In the final analysis... You were climbing, climbing the mountain, but then, when you got to within reach of the summit, you stopped. You didn't turn back. But you didn't go on. Whereas had you dared to go those last few metres... yes, you would have seen what you had come from. The dark valley, let's call it. But you would also have seen, on the other side – I don't know what, Peter. Maybe that's why I am disappointed in you. I feel you have given me only half the story. The half I already knew. Whereas if you had reached the top... Oh, maybe the view on the other side would have been identical. But at least it would have been the complete picture. Instead of just... I feel sometimes, Peter, that you have given me only The Beast. The Beast I know so well because I am he. What you never gave me – what you teased me with, but never entirely offered, was... Beauty. As I say, maybe it's wishful thinking. Maybe there *is* no such thing. Maybe there *is* only the corrupt court, and you so-called artists can only be jesters, licking the arses of the powerful and telling them their shit tastes sweet. But, whether it is your fault or my own, whether you are to blame or essentially I am disappointed in myself – in my own inability to haul myself out of the slime, the filth, the horror, that instead I revel in – you have, ultimately, failed me, Peter.

"I told you many years ago I should be your demon, and should come back to haunt you.

"So I have. And as soon as I got this job, and I found myself near you, I determined that before everything went up in flames and the new age of decency was ushered in, I would do what I had long ago threatened to do. To punish you – I suppose is what it amounts to – for not saving me...

"I was just trying to work out how to do it, when, amongst all the... rubbish sent here for disposal, I spotted someone who reminded me so much of you that when I first saw him I did a double take. I thought it *was* you. Same build, same colouring, same self-effacing manner, same... I hauled him in and asked him what he had done before he was arrested. In his clear, yet slightly soft voice, he told me he had been – wonder of wonders! – a writer and a painter... It really was you, I thought. A lightweight writer and painter, the poor fellow went on, plaintively. A writer and a painter who had never meant to give offence to anyone. Who had never meant to criticise the regime, let alone 'tell the truth'. He had just wanted to amuse... Yet, irony of ironies, one of our most noted and respected critics read his last book, and thought that the light – yes, *fluttery* – figure in the centre of that little rug was indeed a damning indictment of the powers that be. He had a word with a highly placed party official... it was discovered, horror of horrors, that our home-grown Dostoevsky was a homosexual – actually, I suspect the critic was too, and that's the real reason why... but that's another story. In any case, he was arrested, 'tried', and sent here.

"Poor thing. If it wasn't so funny, I think I should cry.

"On your feet, Peter," L said, summoning the writer to the parapet by which he was standing. He pointed down into the vast compound round which the prisoners were shuffling. "You see that figure in the blue shirt – that's rather like yours, come to think of it."

Peter nodded, and felt himself grow cold.

"And the blue jacket and the beige trousers... that are rather like yours, come to think of it."

Colder still, Peter nodded again.

"And the brown shoes... I had him specially dressed like that so you would be able to pick him out. That is he. Your frivolous alter-ego. The person whom you might have become had it not been for me. And the person who is now down there where, if my dear colleagues did but know it, you should be."

L went over to the rifle propped up against the railings, picked it up, pulled back the bolt, and handed it to Peter.

"Shoot him," he said. "You were always a good shot. Thanks to me. Oh, I dare say you have grown a bit rusty, but if you miss the first time you can always have a second go. Or a third or fourth, if needs be."

Peter stared.

"Don't look at me like that," L snapped. "I said shoot him. If you do not wish to, you may shoot yourself. And if you do not wish to do that either," he drew a pistol from the holster in his belt, "I shall shoot you.

"I hope it won't come to that. It would be so banal. But I assure you I shall if I have to, Peter, and I think you have known me long enough, and you have seen enough today, to know I mean what I say.

"Shoot him. Shoot yourself. Or be shot. You have a choice. But whatever it is, be quick about it. I have a meeting in five minutes. We have to decide how to close this place down. Destroy every piece of evidence that it ever existed, so that when the good times come again – oh, people will say this could never have been. It was just some – sick dream.

"A couple of months, I reckon it'll take us. To restore all this to nature."

Peter stared at the rifle he was holding; he could smell its particular smell. He contemplated shooting L, but knew that before he could even raise the rifle to his shoulder L would have shot him. He contemplated shooting himself, but knew he would never be able to bring himself actually to fire. So, feeling that his world had come to an end – no, that *the* world had come to an end – he shouldered the rifle – and oh, how it all came back to him, as clearly as the memories triggered by the sound of L's voice – took aim at the figure in the blue shirt, blue jacket, beige trousers and brown shoes, and shot him in the back.

A few of the shuffling figures lurched away from the man as he fell; Peter thought he heard one of them scream. Then they went on shuffling, shuffling.

"Bravo," L said – looking, for the first time that Peter could ever recall, quite stunned himself. "It's not just theory now, is it, Peter? You've actually – done it."

He cleared his throat, aware perhaps that he was shaken, that his face was pale. Then he pulled himself together.

"I'll have a car take you back into town."

Peter never saw L again.

Shortly after their meeting, it was reported that the promised dismantling of the camp had begun; and by the time the war ended, just five months later, not a trace of it remained. Every scrap of barbed wire, every brick from the crematoria, every plank and every rail had, apparently, vanished – though for a long while no one liked to go and check. And within weeks, as L had predicted, the townsfolk were either pretending that the place had never existed, or were careful never to mention it.

Still, in certain bars, late at night, when people had drunk a little too much, rumours circulated; and Peter gathered that one building – the commandant's house – had survived the general destruction. "Presumably because it didn't really form part of the camp itself," said a man who claimed to have "inside knowledge". Since, however – the man went on – in that house had been discovered the body of a blonde woman who had been strangled, the bodies of three children who had been shot in the head and, in an out-house, the charred remains of a middle-aged man, it was likely that that too would be demolished, before very long. So there would be nothing to remind people of what had been.

Peter, as he packed up his belongings and prepared to move back to the city, accepted without question that the woman found was L's wife, and the children, L's children. But whether the charred remains were of L himself, he sometimes wondered, and more often than not doubted. He couldn't help feeling that somewhere in the world, that man still existed; a demon, destined to haunt him for the rest of his days.

Alive or dead, L – or a fictional version of him – was the central character in the first book that Peter wrote after the war. A book in which there was not a single artist figure, nor even the suggestion of one. Rather, it was a novel that charted the rise and fall of a self-confessed monster; a man who was so much larger, and more frightening, than life, that he was taken – by critics and the public at large – to represent the regime that had so recently been swept away, leaving behind it a continent in ruins, and countless numbers of people dead.

It was, it was almost universally agreed, "a stupendous achievement", a "terrifying cataclysm of a book, that exposes with merciless accuracy the true face of evil"; and it was awarded so many literary prizes that its author soon grew quite used to being acclaimed as "the first great artist to have emerged from the rubble". "Nothing in Strauss's spare, austere previous works has prepared us for such a shattering, magnificent apotheosis", one commentator wrote; while the London *Times* headed its review with the single word: "Genius."

"Strauss! Peter Strauss!" was for a while the name on everyone's lips...

There was just one critic, in a small literary magazine that was published in Buenos Aires, who begged, a little apologetically, to differ from the general view. He signed himself, this dissenter, simply "I": and his complaint was the following.

That for all that Strauss's depiction of a monster was a masterpiece of sorts, and "reminds us why the author has a reputation as a painter as well as a writer"... and for all that "he does not spare us a single wart on the face of the beast... one ends the book with the uncomfortable feeling that despite everything Strauss, like Milton before him, is just a little in love with the Devil he has created.

"But then perhaps, in a sense, precisely because he has inspired a masterpiece, the Devil has created Strauss. So it could not be otherwise."

To this anonymous reviewer, Peter wrote a short note, c/o the magazine. "You have seen what no one else has."

He didn't receive a reply.

The Mirror's Kiss
C.J. Fortescue

The Mirror's Kiss
C.J. Fortesque

He is an army major, tall, blond, Nordic looking, more like a sea captain than a serviceman. I liked the way he walked despite the heavy suit and the hat that hides the fair hair and accentuates his straight nose. He is beautiful but wearing these things ugly and organised, conforming to a code.

I have driven my sister, a lieutenant back to her barracks. We've been shopping. She likes me to take her out of there. On the way through we stop at the officers' mess – she has to see someone who might be there, a man I suppose.

I pass him in the hall but he doesn't notice me, skinny, messy hair, my mouth slightly open, top lip pushed a little forward – the look. Flushed from the summer heat, I'm sweaty, sexy, dishevelled. He is perfectly groomed, uniformed and gift wrapped in authority.

When we leave I ask my sister about him. Major Sorrenson. She says his first name is Bryce but it should be Hans or Johann and he might be gay because she hasn't seen him go after any of the girls on the base. Why would he, they're scrubbers. She's tried it with him herself. My sister is pretty stunning.

We see him again outside and Claudia stops him, introduces me. He smiles and says it is obvious we are brother and sister. This always flatters me, it's nice to have my looks indirectly or maybe unintentionally admired.

I should have joined the army with Claudy when she asked me, purely for the men, but I didn't like the idea – I'm a nurse – of being posted somewhere I didn't want to go and instead took a job in the biggest hospital. Plenty of places to go there without leaving town or being shot at.

I have now fucked my fair share of doctors, being young and I have that look, that silent yes. There's money to be made too, selling the drugs I steal, mainly downers, morphine which has become for me like the earned glass of wine after a hard day's healing. I haven't fucked the right ones yet, the ones who have access to the pethidine stores, the horse pills. Straight unfortunately. I am an unethical slut.

Oh doctor, your *instruments* are so warm. *My*, that's a big thermometer you've got. This sort of thing goes on all the time. There is sex to be had if you have a spare minute, on the other hand, nothing like the sight of a half-dead invalid to eliminate an erection.

My boyfriend is a doctor in the same hospital. We fuck during the day in the old, closed-down wards, the Dickensian death cells, dangerous and off limits. We have recently begun living together, one month but it's not working out, like I told him it wouldn't. He has caught me twice so far, in our bed fucking other men. He objects to this and my argument is that he knew what I was like. I love him like I have loved all of them but I don't care, other men want to fuck me too and I don't say no.

In the heat outside her quarters my sister holds her cheek out for my goodbye kiss, putting her tongue into it as I do so, pretending it is a penis then teases me about being so obviously attracted to Major Sorrenson.

Simon, my boyfriend and I are at a party three weeks later. Bryce, one easy syllable to draw out in a sexual hiss, is there with another man. Together for five years someone informs me. So fucking what, doesn't mean they love each other. I say hello, mentioning my sister and he remembers. Shakes my hand authoritatively, an extension of the uniform, now not wearing.

Later on everyone is very drunk, everyone shows, there are penises out, ugly soft hairy things like baby birds pushed from a nest of denim. I rub on the outside of my jeans. Simon is half conscious on the sofa, giggling, looking trying to stay awake so he can drink more.

Major Bryce Sorrenson takes my wrist, he has been looking at me all night, it means that he did notice me the first time I saw him at the barracks. Of course, he pretended not to, has his career to consider. Simon was getting angry with him from a distance, likes me to look good for him and gets angry with strange men who stare. Bryce pulls me downstairs and outside into the black tissue paper air. Wears a blue shirt the colour of the national flag and looks about five years younger, more even, about twenty-five.

Every time I close my eyes, kissing, I see the army hat and the ugly serge. Is it serge? Do they still wear that these days? It's not 1915 any more, I assume they wear something cooler. He's six inches taller than me and in the dark beside the house I feel he is imposing, the walls of night either side of me are solid, his body a slab to which I press my face, shirt's silk. Tells me he knew I was gay. He's been talking to my sister. Says he thinks I'm cute. I hate that word. Sweet he says, sassy, like an American college boy, half-virgin. His hair is white blond. Mine is gold, straw-like, getting long enough to flick, brushes my jawline, sticks under my collar at the back of my neck. He is Thor, a David from the fiords, the big one from the German pornos who only says "*Ja, oh ja, oh ja*", over and over again. German, Swedish, Dutch, I don't care to know what his heritage is. Kisses savagely with a drunk confidence then pulls his shirt out of his jeans. I suck it. Pretend his over-exaggerated army cock smell is juniper or spruce. We arrange for him to come to my house for the fuck, the beginning of it all.

Dash back upstairs, to Simon. I return nonchalant and he makes me sit on his lap and uses his hands all the time when he talks, dropping them onto my thighs, my dick, making me flinch, and squeezing my waist between sentences. Sniffs at my neck because I have a scent that he can smell under the Eternity. A purer smell, different to my groin. He wants me in a bottle, in more ways than one. The magic trick. When I mumble later on at home that I don't think it's a good idea to fuck at work any more, we're pushing it too far, so we don't get caught, he's angry. How can I, the one, he says that half the doctors in the country have fucked, reject such an opportunity. In bed all of him is forced hard into me. Drunk. Not interested really in me. Still has to come so he can sleep despite being so lashed. We break the condom and he curses. "Shit. Oh, shit," because he has come clean into the hospital slut. Passes out, still wearing it, a red one, split and frayed like burnt flesh. Lights off, I press my thigh to his, hot with tequila and he curls up, nose against my bicep like a puppy. Now alone I don't feel so drunk. Stopped drinking after I sucked Bryce off. Had to remember it.

Compared to him, Simon looks like a soccer hooligan, a good-looking one. Cut all his hair off a week ago because he thought he was starting to look like a model from a second-rate menswear catalogue. I can't wait until it grows again. Wouldn't want anyone operating on me who looked like that.

Major Sorrenson pays his first house call one day later. He pulls my hair so it falls over my nose and cheeks, half hides my eyes so I can glare at him and it looks sexy. Fucks me so hard that the shock of it leaves me thinking I am where I used to live, before Simon's, the flat *everybody* knew. It taps me on the temple, we are in Simon's bed. Bryce has to leave. Your country needs you, I joke.

Changing my shift on purpose is easy so that Simon and I are working half the time apart. Day/night. He goes to work very early whereas my shift now starts at midday. Bryce comes over early, before he starts work, just after the boyfriend leaves. Both our boyfriends come to think of it.

Simon sees Bryce at the local shops one day and accuses me, of course he knows what I am, of fucking him. I deny this. I'm not sure why. He's certain I'm fucking others. I deny it because next to Bryce, Simon is ugly. Next to me Major Bryce Sorrenson is ugly. Big. Thuggish. Tanned skin's not that of a bronzed backpacker any more, now like wax which covers cheese. Lying beside me his muscles don't twist, the ones I pictured correctly under the serge. After sex he is diluted into Mr Average. I remain the same. The impenetrable beauty.

Simon again attacks, home early on a Saturday which is odd because the weekends are busiest at the hospital. Asks me again if I'm fucking Bryce. He can smell someone else on my neck, not the usual scum I screw, whose odours, therefore personas, are not worth detecting by the one who counts. We fight. Simon tries to grab my neck but as I dodge it is more like an uppercut and I bite my tongue, taste red, so spit it at him. He states the obvious, yells the obvious – I'm a nurse for Christ's sake. I should know better. Can't go spraying blood around the room. I get upset, crying over something Simon doesn't know about. Earlier Bryce bit my neck and I hit him. There must be no marks. He hit me back, why twice I don't understand, hard enough to make me hate him then kissed me, the lips, their membrane has poisoned my skin and Simon can taste it, the bitter liquid of deceit. If it happens, it happens, won't be the first time he's caught me.

With the offensive territorial mark of another man disintegrated with violence, Simon makes love to me, comes into me like a shot and whispers I love you. I reply with the same words, squeezing him so he believes me.

Then – there is when he catches me. In bed with Major Bryce. Shit brick, Simon calls him and kicks at the figure, a marble effigy hidden under the sheet. I stand naked between the man and the genuflected figure now groping for his trousers on the floor. I don't want Simon to see him naked. There must be no more to compare with. I compare my self to too many men already and don't want more to judge themselves by my comparisons. I may see things I don't like about myself.

After a few months of this roundabout, Bryce's boyfriend leaves the country for a job in London. Now I find him less attractive. Major Bryce Sorrenson asks me to move in with him and I do because he hasn't experienced what Simon has. I have broken Simon's heart and this causes problems at work. He makes a point, in front of me, of asking other male nurses to assist him with procedures. I tell him I don't care, it means less pus and shit that I have to deal with.

I can start afresh. Pretty soon though, Bryce knows about the men. I am the rotten whore, your slutty bunny. I continue to kick away the men who fall at my feet. But he stills knows, knows they have been there. Guesses that I fuck at work too.

I change my shift so that I am there for him when he gets home. A present in a box. Sometimes when he comes home he is rough with me. Always after we have wine or spirits. I say things I can't help and trigger him off until he hits me, a white headed fire. Because I am pretty I deserve to be treated this way. The awful things he screams at me – vicious little cunt. Tells me to go back to my fucked-up fairyland. These things are true. I am. I do live there. The aptness is so fitting I revel in it.

He is going away soon. six months to the Middle East. I picture Persian slaves, hairy camel drivers, terrorists screwing boys, the same boys the army officers will share, to hear the same faked groans dirty money pays for. He is leaving me. If he is no longer here I will love him for ever. I will have won. He can't stop me because he won't know what I am doing. I have to try not to withdraw obviously from him, have to keep giving my all as his whatever-it-is-I-am.

There are days when he comes home in a bad mood and he is horrible, so austere it's aging. He thinks he's dignified. I'm not sympathetic and fights ensue. He punches me in the shoulder and I fall back over a kitchen chair, which scrapes about, fragile steel, as I try to steady myself with it. I feel safer on the floor and swear up at him. Prick. Don't ever touch me again. I will kill you I snarl at him. What with, he dares, a 6'4" cunt leaning over me, skin flushed orange in anger through the tan.

Because he doesn't want anyone at the barracks to find out, we have to be discreet. The story goes, in case it comes close to people thinking, is that because he knows my sister and because I was looking for a place to live, he is letting me stay with him. It is a simple deception, one which no one will question. So no one will think past it. Gay Major. Game over.

He always comes away from the barracks. I refuse to go there. He wouldn't let me go there anyway, only just to see my sister, to go nowhere near him. Too risky. The words 'no one must find out' loop in my head. His ex, the one he cast off for me, sends obscene text messages to my mobile phone. All intermittent until one day I receive them continuously for an hour. It breaks me and I call him. It only serves to let him vent orally what has been written so far in liquid crystal. Parasitic whore. Nurse Fuckme. I text back bad puns. Major Bryce. Major orgasm. Major stroke me. I don't tell Bryce about it. Who knows what the ex would do. Out him at the base all the way from England. Ruin him. It would be the end of us. Major minor and head nurse. I love it when I have secrets from him.

At dinner, I eat, apologising for being skinny. I'm not sorry. Across from me he is a huge thing, at an angle a rock, chipped, only smooth when he wears his uniform. He is my bodyguard who will not leave my side. He chews his food as though his jaw is a piece of farm machinery, threshing, sorting. It's a production line which works to clear the plate before the food gets cold. Still tastes the same. Bastard flavour. Naked or in serge.

His cock's flopped out after we have more wine and proffered with demand. Suck it honey. I am drinking his blood. His come is formed of this and his money, blood, the alcohol we've drunk, how it contributed to the times he's hit me. I am drinking it again.

Deep is a word I want to use to describe us. Not forest deep, not ocean deep. Not fecund but like I was already at the bottom of us in the first place because there was nowhere else to go. Incomprehensible and inscrutable like the looks he gives me. There is a judgement in our relationship which has left the surface and incubates into what I must do to own him.

I pull away, go to see Simon and lie naked on his sofa to shed frustration. I don't talk to him because if I open my mouth I will cry, he will have to fuck me. I will hurt him again.

On the way home I buy wine and beer. Bryce is there before me and I immediately pour him a glass then go into the bathroom. I look at my face in the mirror, as I am pretty, he is ugly. The greater beauty, unlike him I am not standard. I will need his body to be unmarked. The way it's done must be with insulin. To reduce his blood sugar and him to nothing. An overdose will cause hypoglycaemia and he will tremor, sweat and fail.

When he is in a numb, liquored slumber I do it. I insert the needle so steadily with my trained hand where the access mark will not be seen. Many minutes later he sleeps differently, moving, murmuring, un-asleep. Presses against me and I feel his heart race. Quick thuds like someone running on concrete. I move away from the perspiring chest and he wakes. Grips me, agitated. Says he can't sleep, can't remember the nightmares. He is sweating more now and clenches his hands a lot, wet, he wipes them on the sheets. Lies back down. I know his head is spinning and the imbalance will make him want to vomit. Do you want me to take you to a doctor, I ask. I refuse to hypothesise on what is wrong. I'm only a nurse I tell him, I could be wrong. It could be anything. I tell him I'm scared. I know he is terrified and I am aroused. It hasn't been enough. Next time I will double the units and get him drunker. The injection will hurt more next time.

He sits up quickly again, slams his feet to the floor. Water, he demands. I'll get it I say and move slowly. He pushes past me, naked and primitive, running from the beast into the kitchen. Shaking and so afraid, he leans over the sink, head under the tap, swallowing then standing up, breathing hard before he goes to the refrigerator. The door light flashes into his face, spotlights his confusion. He drinks the first thing he sees, Soft drink from the bottle. Caffeine, I admonish, won't help the heart palpitations. He pulls out cheese, crackers, rips open a packet of dried fruit with crunching teeth. Eats so fast he retches as he swallows. More drink drowns food unchewed. He sits on the floor. Sighs up at me. Lives. I won't offer him morphine to help him sleep. Instead I give him Rohypnol and fold him back into bed like an old man, shrivelled and shaky. Next time it will be enough.

There is something in my hair, fluid which has dried and I pull it out to the end past my nose. It's Bryce's spit or sweat. I roll the hair in my fingers and the strands separate then I go back to sleep,

In the morning he goes to work earlier than usual to see the army doctor. Before he goes he wonders to me whether it was an asthma attack. No, I assure him, it wasn't that. Mild psychosis caused by a bad dream, I suggest is more likely, causing a sudden increase in adrenalins and body temperature. Panic attack. I throw him a medical term. Sympathoadrenal. You just freaked out, don't worry about it. I try to calm him. He leaves, brow creased, fists closed, not the smooth god who has control over himself. That has passed to me.

When he arrives home I wear practically nothing, coddle him and am flung away. Slash, he says and heads to the toilet. He had a series of meetings today and informs me he is embarrassed because he kept having to leave to pee. He is still nervous and edgy. I offer to make dinner. It will be about hour but he begins making, eating, two-minute noodles, fruit, tea and biscuits. In a temper I throw the vegetables I have already cut and the frying pan into the sink with the dirty dishes. I sulk in the lounge-room and when I creep back he has gone to bed. I go out. I find someone but it is an angry orgasm and still leaves me dark.

I am ready to try again. We are at a party, intoxicated. I push drink after drink into him. I distract him and say his name over and over again. As I do in private. It is something that annoys other people for instance when we are at a party and I begin each sentence to him with his name followed by an aposiopetic pause. I say his name in a particular way, with a particular tone of voice to show everybody that we are bound by sex and other things unspoken that lovers hide. I could show them the bruises too but it would only lead to more.

When we get home, the fight starts because I made it so clear that I had wanted to fuck half the men in the room. Can't control myself in front of him. He is too drunk, huge and frightening. Tries to initiate sex but I say no, you need to go to bed and I move away.

I am standing near the stereo on the other side of the room. Bryce turns, whirls, wild at me, swings a punch which I duck and fly to the front door but he grabs me by the hair in efficient jerks and pulls me back down. Drags me across the floor as I kick at him but he is too hard, too heavy. Away from the door. I reach out at nothing, the stereo speakers, coffee table. He lets my hair loose and holds me by the neck, bites my arm when I try to hit him and holds it in his mouth, drinking me as I bleed, snorting, his nose is pushed into my arm. The pain and pressure of the teeth is immense and I start to choke on my screams. My bottle of cola, dropped on the carpet nearby. He lets me go for a split second, a splinter of my life is given back to me, snatches the bottle, froth spills out, white it sprays across the room as he smashes the bottle against the wall. Back he's grabbed me, one huge arm my barricade, in the other hand the broken glass cold against my cheek. I can feel the edge ready to slice me. He puts it down, yanks me to my feet and throws me onto the sofa. Walks from the room as I sob, still on tenterhooks. He brings a steak knife from the kitchen and I reach as I scream no, for a cushion to protect my chest. It is only a ball of cotton wool he flicks away and stabs me in the breast plate, the middle as though to vivisect me and see who I am. As I struggle he aims for the exposed parts, into my upper back. The knife thrusts feel like punches, wind me as if I am not gasping for breath enough. Aims for my head and I raise my hands. It opens my palm and the blood gushes, escaped veins fleeing down my arm. My hands away from my body he stabs my side, my lower back in the soft part. Deep, hard then it's soft again when he retracts. Fast, it feels like an awl, like an accident happening over and over again, you have no time to get ready for it. This time he has broken the knife. Out of me the blade falls to the floor. He stops, sits on the carpet. Now, only now do I think about my fear and that I must overcome it to stop him killing me. I say, come to bed with me, fuck me, I want you, while he sits there, panting, like a gladiator. He leads me into the bedroom by the wrist, my shirt wet with all fluids except the only one that he has fed into me, the one that will not come out through my skin or veins. Lays me on the bed, puts his legs onto me, around me so that I can't move suddenly. My heart is racing, I am dizzy, bloody. I think the cut on my hand is deepest. I hold it against the mattress, hot and throbbing. He is inside me, loving me, fucking to my bleeding.

I faint, must have. He has let me sleep for a bit. Wakes me up and presses onto me. I can feel the blood now thick between the bed and the length of my back, soaking, clotted blackly into the sheets. My temples surge.

Cold I am, as he shudders into me.

Little Jimmy
Christopher Francis

Little Jimmy
Christopher Francis

I awake cold and shivering from what feels like the deepest sleep I have ever had. I am awake in body but not in mind. My mind is still several paces behind, still in a hazy, dazy, dream-like state. I look up and see stars against the black night sky. My brain is receiving a message about wet hands. I peer in the amber glow from the street lamp, they are covered in blood. My senses awaken with a mixture of confusion and surprise, or is it shock? I sit here trying to make head and tail of what is happening but I don't understand.

Two minutes later I am still sat on this cold, wet pavement, desperately trying to rid my hands of the colour red. Again and again I try but no matter how hard I will, I rub, each hand is still clad inside a velvet glove of the brightest, yet deepest crimson. Contrast colliding, merging to stain every inch of skin and cloth it comes into contact with. The blood is fresh but does not seem to seep from the inside. Confusion sets in, still I do not understand.

Suddenly something catches the corner of my left eye. I turn my head towards the object. Fuck... am I dreaming? I blink two, three, or is it four times? Each time hoping that when I look up 'it' would disappear but each time 'it' is still there, lying there. A body lying there. Motionless. My eyes are transfixed, staring at its form. Lying on its side, slumped over, face down. Something inside tells me 'He's dead'. Is 'it' a he? Of course it is, isn't it? Even though I am sat about three feet behind its back, 'it' seemed like a male. Dressed in jeans, bootleg Levis, the number I cannot remember but they are the exact ones I like to wear. A pretty shirt sparkling in the damp air. Hair dark, dyed, in an effeminate style. Boy's hair in a girl's style. Yes, definitely a male. I'm certain, I think?

I try to move but my body does not respond. It has shut down, shocked to shit. I know that I must go to him and check that he is actually dead. Confirm my suspicions, or should that be confirm the obvious? How can he still have a pulse, a heartbeat, a breath, a life, when he does not have any blood left inside his body. There he is lying with a deep pool of blood all around him. Surely he cannot have enough on the inside for his heart to pump the necessary oxygen to his organs, the most important being the brain. What does nine pints of blood, or any liquid come to that, look like anyway? How many pints of his own lifeline is this poor sod lying in? How long had it taken to pour from his body? Had he felt immense, intense pain? I sit here frightened, my mind doing overtime, my body rendered useless. Something inside snaps. I am moving towards it, him, he. My heart is beating twice as fast as usual but I am barely breathing. I am scared, so scared. Scared of what though? Scared of what I might find. Scared of what has happened to him and could happen to me, you, any of us. Scared of what I should not be. A dead body, however it has come to be in this state, a life no more. What is so scary about that? He does not pose a threat to me. No threat has been put in my direction at all. An inner voice tells me to 'Get a grip for fuck sake'. A second's pause, a deep intake of breath and my hands are tightly clasped on his body. I roll him over.

Oh my God. Oh fuck. Fuck me.

I look at his face. A red mask staining his skin, his eyes half closed, never to re-open. A deep laceration is running the length of his right cheek. His throat has been slashed. A long, deep gash from one side to the other. His lips are turned down at the corners but his throat is smiling a grisly smile carved in torn flesh. His shirt is ripped in two places. One above his left pec, the other in the centre of his stomach. Not only is he dead but he has been murdered.

I let go of him and vomit a mouthful of foul-tasting, textured liquid. I look back at the body, lying there torn and blood-soaked. Tears well in my eyes until each lower lid cannot contain them any longer. The salty droplets fall in overflowing streams, meandering through freckles, merging with a separate stream of snot. Looking at his face is making me feel more and more uneasy, queasy.

I turn away, not being able to look any longer. Something is niggling at the back of my mind and has been for the last five or ten minutes or so. Then it dawns on me. I know him, but who he is I cannot remember. I turn to glance at his face but cannot place a name or remember why he seems so familiar. It is all too much. I move back, away from his lifeless shell and the amber glow from the street lamp. I move back into the darkness, just a little away from the section of pavement I had earlier woken up on. As I move back I notice that the place where I had been sick is awash with blood and any signs of vomit have since disappeared under a bright crimson tidal wave that is submerging and staining everything in its path.

I sit alone in the darkness, cradling myself. Wishing to wake up from what is not a dream and never will be a dream, but is wished to be one. I sit for minutes, hours, I cannot tell.

The silence of the night air is eerily comforting. I sit shocked and shaken, listening to the sounds of my own breathing. Suddenly, laughter penetrates the airwaves. Fuck, someone is coming.

I see legs appearing around the corner from the street adjacent to the road where I sit. I move back, deeper into the shadows. A voice in my mind questions my retreat. Actually I have done nothing wrong. I have not committed a crime. Did I not find the body, not rip it to pieces in cold blood? I am no murderer. I would not, could not, do such a thing. Could I?

I peer out at them. A couple, one man, one woman. They are giggling like a couple of love struck teenagers even though they surely cannot be a day under thirty. Suddenly, the woman looks up. She stops laughing. Her mouth drops open. Simultaneously, she drops the bag of chips she was holding, they fall to the floor and she lets out an almighty scream. The man is taken aback and looks startled. He looks up, now they both stand there in silence. Their night is ruined in a matter of seconds. They are in shock, entering that dazed space between reality and dreaming. After a few moments he puts his hand inside his pocket and pulls out a mobile phone. I do not quite catch what he is saying but presume he has dialed 999. As he is doing this, the woman is vomiting. The pavement is now adorned with deep-fried potato. She looks up sobbing and falls into the man's arms. Crying big tears into his perfect chest.

I look on enviously, wishing it was me instead of her. I want someone to tell me, 'It is all going to be okay'. To feel his breath against my neck, my white knight holding me in his big, strong arms. To pick me up and carry me to his waiting car. He takes me back to his place which is far enough away from this place, the scene of this nightmare, but close enough not to spend too long travelling. After a twenty-minute journey he pulls up outside a swish loft-style apartment. He opens the car door and leads me into his modern abode. Inside he wipes away my tears and washes my hands, ridding them of the blood forever, before taking me into the master bedroom. He lies me down. My clothes are being pulled off as he smiles, always smiling. I get lost in that smile, lost in the moment. Every now and then he reassures me that 'everything will be alright'. I start to feel safe and forget about the body, the mutilation, the blood. As long as I am close to him I am safe, he will take all my fears away. Yes, he will protect me, wash away my pain. He lifts me up and pulls me closer to his warm body. My legs are put over his shoulders. He may be causing me pain but it's of the pleasurable variety. He smiles and I feel myself getting lost in a sweet sense of security. For the first time since I woke on that cold, wet pavement, I feel safe.

The sirens are getting louder and louder. Closer and closer. Reality sets in. I look around and see the body is there, the couple, the blood, my hands... oh my hands... covered in blood. I feel as if I am on another planet, floating in a weightless state of existence. My brain snaps back into first gear. I have to go. NOW.

Standing up I move in closer to a red brick wall. I move quickly but quietly. Suddenly I am falling to the ground. I let out a deep, loud moan upon impact with the pavement. Shit, the couple must have heard me. I get back up and run. Faster and faster I run, to where I do not know. As long as I keep running in the direction that makes those police sirens fade away then I know I will be safe. For now at least.

It feels as if I have run a marathon while strangely it seems as though I have only been running for seconds. Alone I sit on a green bank. A field lies down below. I do not remember getting here or running the length of the large field. What is happening to me? 'It must be shock,'

I tell myself. Yes, that's it, shock.

The moon is awake but seems to be in distress. Half her body is clouded in darkness, a black descent. The night, her one-time friend and companion on these cold and lonely times, is now waging a deep war on her. A veil of dark mist clouds her so only half her light can be seen. On the bank where I lie, I see stars across the bleak eternity, falling in all directions until they are no more. They are the moon's teardrops, falling from the depths of her very soul. Burning droplets of light. Emotions set in fire, not knowing where they will land once fallen.

Could the moon be crying for the lost soul of that poor slaughtered lamb? I try to think of his name again and again, how I knew him, but I cannot remember, even though I keep seeing his face at every turn.

Something is moving in the shadows. I sit up, startled, I am not on my own. Looking down I see it move again. As it comes closer I realise it is only a cat. A grey cat with a splodge of white on its tail. It carries on prancing in the moonlight across the field. Suddenly, it stops and turns its head and looks in my direction. 'Puss, puss, puss,' I whisper, trying to beckon it to me. I hear a hiss as it strikes the air with an outstretched clawed paw. A look of both terror and ferociousness adorns its once soft and gentle face. The fur on its arched back stands on end, tail poker-straight. It hisses again and strikes the air. Rearing up, one last hiss and it shoots into the darkness, out of sight.

I try to comprehend what has just happened. The cat seemed to fear me for some reason. It looked straight at me, through me even, then fear sets in. How could it think that I posed a threat? Maybe it knew about the murder and sensed that all was not what it seemed. That I was not all that I seemed to be. A feeling of unease and terrifying thoughts enter my heart, my mind, my body and soul. What if I did kill him? No! It couldn't have been me, could it? Me a murderer. No. Surely not.

As I sit confused, thinking, fearing, his face appears in and before my mind. This time it is intact. No laceration to the right cheek. He is smiling, cheeks sparkling with a fine film of glitter that adorns them, face free of blood. He winks at me, his eyes twinkling, like two stars before their fall from heaven and from grace. My mind turns to sex. Fuck... that's it, something to do with sex, that is how I know him. He must have been a one-night stand I had at some point. No, he seems too familiar for a night's fleeting sexual encounter. As much as I am trying, I cannot work this all out. Each time I think of him I know that we have had many sexual encounters but not actually had sexual intercourse together. It does not make any sense. I have another piece of my memory's jigsaw puzzle but the picture is far from finished. I need to find the other pieces.

The confusion is unbelievably frustrating and a single lonesome tear trickles down my face. As I look up a star shoots across the night sky. It seems that I am not the only one crying.

Looking into the distance I see his face again. He is pointing at me, laughing, shaking his head, but does not let me in on the joke. He is laughing at me for some reason. A mocking laugh but not out of cruelty, out of stupidity. He is trying to tell me something but I cannot work it out. I close my eyes, these games must stop. I open then and he is gone. I sit alone, under the watchful eye of the she-moon.

Why? Why in God's name did I run? It seems as if I have been sitting on this bank for an eternity. I look up to the moon but she has no answers to my questions. 'Please', I beg to no avail. I chastise myself again and again. How stupid am I to flee the scene of the crime in the first place. That couple were bound to have heard me, seen me. If (or should that be when?) the police catch up with me, how can I explain, well, anything? I do not know how I ended up on that cold, wet pavement, let alone next to... next to... him. I shouldn't have run away, but I did. I was confused, am confused. I was scared, am scared. And what about all the forensic evidence that is mounting up against me. I vomited on that pavement, my sick mixed with his blood. Also my handprints are on his body. They are going to throw the book at me, I know they are. I cannot go to jail, I will be killed. Me, a camp queer in prison, it doesn't bear thinking about. The inmates will definitely kill me. Rape me and kill me and when they do, will it be even worse for me than it had been for him? Self-pity and fear have engulfed my whole body. If I am a murderer and did kill him then where was the weapon? I don't remember seeing any weapon. Oh fuck me...I'm going insane.

Lying back, I whisper, 'Help me.' The moon hears my plea but is powerless to change the past and show me what the future has in store. She starts to sing the softest lullaby, the most perfect pitch to the sweetest of melodies, played with perfection on angels' harps. So beautiful it sounds to the human ear. I am starting to feel sleepy. I am drifting... drifting... drifting...

The bitter chill subsides and a warmth enters my body, which I have not felt for I don't know how long. I awake to find myself walking down a long, white corridor. The white is so brilliant it should be too bright for the naked eye to cope with, but I do not even blink or feel the slightest bit of pain. A comforting feeling enters my body. I do not understand where I am but this does not seem to distress me at all. The corridor seems to be never-ending as I walk on and on and on into an eternal blaze of the purest white light. A strange humming echoes all around, as if the walls are singing as I pass on by. It is the very same melody that accompanied the moon as she lulled me to sleep.

There seems to be no sense of time in this place of destitution. I cannot tell how long I have been walking but I never seem to slow down or get tired. I hear a note that is far higher in pitch than any sound that the human ear should be able to hear.

Suddenly, out of one of the walls that run along the great length of this corridor, steps a man. I stop dead in my tracks and look at this handsome stranger. He is dressed in a long, flowing cloak of the same brilliant white as the corridor. His face is exposed. It is the most beautiful face I have ever seen. It is hard yet soft, masculine yet feminine, wise yet full of the carefree abundance that only accompanies youth. His skin is almost black and in complete contrast to the surroundings. He is the closest I have ever seen to perfection. Maybe he is perfection?

He undoes his cloak and out spread a pair of glorious, golden wings. He smiles at me and I get lost in that dazzling, beautiful smile. I hardly breathe as he stands only three feet in front of me. He puts his hands out ready to take mine. As I extend my arms ready to feel his firm grasp, I notice the blood dripping from my hands. I cry out loud, tears falling in violent splashes down my cheeks.

Just in front of his feet, a bowl of pure light appears. He pulls out a small cloth from inside his cloak and places it into the bowl. He takes out the cloth and wrings out the excess light. Droplets of shining silver and gold fall through the air back into the bowl. He motions to my hands.

Behind me I hear a scream and as I look at the beautiful stranger's face, he shakes his head from side to side. I know he is telling me not to turn around. I hear another blood curdling scream. As I turn around, I see the body, the blood, the couple (and this time both are screaming, not just the woman). Each image comes one after the other in quick succession. Flashback after flashback, each one hitting my mind's eye like a sledgehammer to my brain.

I look away and turn my gaze to the handsome stranger, but the face that stares back at me is not his, but of the young man whose body I had found. He looks at me for a few seconds then screams. Blood flows from his chest and stomach. The cloak he wears is stained with a crimson tide. His cheek opens up and blood pours out thick and fast. Then a red smile appears on his neck. He grabs his throat trying to stop the inevitable. Blood spurts from his neck at an alarming rate. He is screaming but no sound comes from his mouth, only more and more blood. He looks at me expectantly, wanting me to help him somehow, but what can I do? So I do the worst thing and turn back around. 'Out of sight, out of mind', isn't that how the saying goes?

Suddenly, I am being pulled into blackness. I try to scream but no sound comes out. Now I am submerged in blackness. A feeling of cold shoots up and down my spine. Bitter winds bite harshly at my limbs which are rapidly becoming numb. I am falling through nothing into nothing, black into black. I close my eyes to try and blot out what is happening to me. I keep on falling into this black nothingness. Punishment for turning my back.

The harsh winds now seem little more than a gentle breeze, but even though they may have died down, my body is still bitterly cold, although the inner feeling of weightlessness has subsided. Opening my eyes I look down and see the ground. All around the sky is black but the nothingness has been filled with stars. 'I don't understand,' I whisper.

The moon is looking down on me, smiling sympathetically, 'You will, in time,' she whispers back.

In front of me stands a house. There is an acknowledgement of familiarity but I cannot think how I know this place. Half a foot in front of me there is a large window and just to my right stands a door. They are both double-glazed and on the other side of the glass is a dull wooden kitchen. I do not understand how I came to be here or why I am here, but I have all but given up trying to understand anything. Ever since I awoke next to that body, nothing seems to make sense, no matter how hard I try to work it all out.

Turning around I notice a shed, a lawn and a sad excuse for a rockery. As I turn to re-face the house, I hear a scream. Looking through the window into the kitchen, a silhouette of a person appears, hovering just above centre of the patterned lino. The silhouette moves closer to the window and with every forward motion, its image becomes clearer and clearer until it is detectable. It is 'he'.

'Why are you haunting me?' I shout, but he just looks at me without answering, his body drenched it its own blood. Or should that be its own form drenched in its own blood? He puts his hands to his throat but the bleeding won't stop. He looks at his blood-soaked hand and screams a silent yet deafening cry. Putting his arms in front of his body, he motions to me for help. I do not move. He points at me with one of his crimson-clad fingers and gives me a cold, harsh, deathly stare. I want to turn around, run away again, but fear of the nothingness which I am sure is ready and waiting behind me, to take myself wherever it decides, more than I fear what is in front of me. Namely the dying, tortured image of a young man who is already deceased.

I turn and reach for the door, open it and step inside into the kitchen. But there is no body or being, no blood either, just an ill-fitted wooden kitchen and an ugly, outdated, patterned lino floor. Nothing makes sense any more. Nothing adds up.

A light shines from another room beyond where I stand, silently, shaking. Voices can be heard. My heart jumps, skipping several beats. What will happen if these people catch me here in their home? How will I explain what I saw? And why am I seeing such images in the first place? As time ticks on by, I sense that it would be wrong to just run away, keep on running away. I have to stay put, face my fears, instead of running to where I do not know. Always taking confusion and fear with me wherever I go, or should that be, end up?

'Your time has come my child, your time has come.' I look out of the window at the moon, trustingly. What she means I do not fully know at present but I do not question her there is not use in that.

'It is my time,' I tell myself.

I stand and listen to the voices. Even though they are only coming from the next room, they sound in echoes, as if they are travelling though time, space and realms to reach my ears. The voices are of one man and one woman. Like this house I stand within, they seem familiar. I cannot hear every part of the conversation which is strange as the voices are raised. The woman is sobbing as she speaks, her tones mirror the pain she is feeling at what the man is saying. His voice is angry and directional. Every word that escapes his mouth has the sole purpose to hurt, to stick into the woman like a poison dart.

'… a dirty little faggot, that's what he was. Making out he was fucking God. And what does God think about faggots, aye? Go look in yer bloody precious Bible. He was never my son, not after… not after…'

'He told you he was gay,' the woman interrupts. 'May God forgive you for what comes outta your mouth. It says the devil comes in many disguises…'

'The devil now am I? You'll be telling I speak in forked tongues next.'

'To speak ill of the dead is one thing, but your own son. Don't you look at me like that. He was your son, our son. Have you no heart man? Don't you feel any emotion? Little Jimmy's dead. Mur… murdered. Our beautiful angel murdered, and you sit there and say… oh, can't you just let him rest in peace?'

The man barked back at the woman's angry sobbing, 'Aye, as long as you leave me in peace. Goin' on all the bleeding time. He's dead woman, dead. Maybe it's for the best.'

'I hope Jesus forgives you because for as long as I live, I will never, never. Do you hear me? Never.'

'Aye, I hear ya.'

The voices stop and laughter echoes through to where I stand. A television has been switched on, but all I can hear are her words. 'Little Jimmy's dead. Little Jimmy's dead.' Those three words spin around and around my mind, sending a series of freezing cold shivers to the very depths of my soul. I have never felt as cold as I do at this present moment in time. I feel nauseous, my stomach doing somersaults. 'Little Jimmy's dead.'

Something is taking me over. Before I can stop myself, my legs are moving towards the other room. I don't know why but I must see the two people to whom those voices belong. When that woman said those three words, 'Little Jimmy's dead', it was if she was calling to me to come to her, comfort her. I walk tentatively through the open doorway from the kitchen into the other room, the living room. Where lino ends, cream carpet beings. As I see the man, I stop dead in my tracks. He is sitting in an armchair, his fat, hairy body clothed in a grubby white vest and baggy, check boxer shorts. His hand is tightly clasped around a television remote control. As I look at him I feel an immediate, intense dislike. He reminds me of the past, my past. The more I look at him sitting there, slouched in that chair, the more I feel disgusted, nauseous. I cannot bear to look at him any more and my gaze falls to the floor.

Five minutes, ten minutes, how long I stand staring at the carpet, I cannot tell. My thoughts losing themselves in each and every cream-coloured fibre. As I look up to my left, I stop suddenly. I blink, not quite believing what I am seeing. It is 'him' again, haunting me. Forever fucking haunting me. I turn to face him head on.

I stand looking at his face, it is adorned with a morbid expression. His cold eyes are staring deep into my soul, stripping away layer upon layer. I refrain from shouting at him as I cannot let this man and this woman hear me, see me. He circles his hands around his face. Again the action is repeated. Taking a step back I notice a mirror of medium size and circular in shape. At its centre lies his image. His lips are down turned but his eyes are smiling. He points at me then red tears fall from his eyes, droplets of blood running down his gaunt features. As he puts his hands to his cheeks to wipe away the damp I feel my hands brushing my own cold, wet face. His image stops still just like when you press pause and it freeze-frames on whatever you may be watching on video tape. I stare at his image, a picture set in mirrored glass. As I stare, I hear the moon, 'My child, your time is now, your time is now'.

The pain is unbearable, both mentally and physically. I am seeing flashback after flashback. Everything that night, everything before I awoke on that cold, wet pavement. Every strike, every blow, every incision with the knife's blade is recalled in a series of images. Horrific mind pictures from the past.

I look into the mirror and this time the image, his image, is reflecting my every move. Or do I reflect his? As a red gash appears on his cheek, I feel a terrible burning sensation on my face. My right cheek is on fire and pouring with blood. I bend over, doubled in pain. Suddenly, I feel a great piercing force and my body leaps off the floor. The pain in my chest is excruciating. I look down and see that my shirt is ripped in two places. The fabric that covers my chest is sodden, as is the bottom of the shirt. I can feel my blood oozing, pouring in fact, down my stomach, flowing violently over my skin and into the well that is my belly button, only to flow onwards and downwards.

I stand up straight, trying to wipe the tears from my eyes. As I do so, I catch the mirror's reflecting image. A deep red angry line appears across his neck. I put my hand to my throat but cannot stop the blood, nor can he. Our hands are covered, it clings to every finger and thumb, staining every inch of skin.

As I turn, I see the woman sobbing on the stairs.

'Stop your blabbering woman. I canna hear the telly,' says the man in an angry, fed-up tone.

I turn to look at the man sitting there with his belly hanging over the top of his boxer shorts. Sitting in a brown leather armchair that has become moulded into the shape of his fat arse. I look at him chuckling to himself, caring more about that bloody programme than his poor, dear wife. Yes, they are married. I remember. I know exactly who they are.

Tears stream down my bloodstained face. With every tear that falls, anger rises inside until I cannot contain myself any longer.

'Why?' I shout. 'Daddy, why did you murder me? It's not my fault I'm gay.'

But he does not answer. I do not think he can hear me. The bastard, sitting there watching telly as if nothing has happened.

I want to comfort Mam, hug her pain away but I can do nothing. All I can do is stand and cry. Helpless. Powerless.

It feels like I have been standing here for an eternity, but in reality it may only have been seconds or minutes.

'Turn around my child. The end has come, all is understood. A new chapter has begun. Now dry your eyes for the journey ahead. Dry your eyes my child.' The moon's voice is but a whisper. A series of words dancing upon the gentle night's breeze.

I wipe away each teardrop and the blurred visions of yester moment. I turn my gaze from the cold-blooded killer who I have called 'Daddy' for the past eighteen years. Looking at Mam, I try to smile but my lips remain down turned. 'Please watch over her,' I say quietly, hoping the moon hears my plea.

As I turn around I look into the mirror, its rim is framed in the most dazzling white light. Each second that ticks by, the stronger the light appears. The stronger the light becomes, the larger it seems to get until an oval of light appears covering virtually the whole of the living room wall.

Something is moving far away inside the light. As it comes closer, its image becomes detectable. It is the angel from the corridor. My beautiful stranger. He seems to have become more beautiful, if that is at all possible. The skin on his face is much darker than before. Out of his cloak, two hands appear, arms outstretched, hands ready to receive mine. I put out my own hands to take his. As I look down at them, tears roll down my cheeks and over my lips. I start to smile and for the first time since I found myself in that corridor of pure light, I feel a warmth entering my whole body. My hands are clean, no longer wet with the crimson river that once flowed through my veins. As our fingertips touch, I feel my whole body come alive. It is a feeling that is indescribable. The most fantastic earth trembling electrifying orgasm does not even come close.

My heart is racing but I am barely breathing, too caught up in the moment. His hands let go of mine before bringing them to my face. Tenderly he wipes away my tears, soothing the ache inside. Even though his hands are so big and strong, they have the gentlest touch.

Like barbed wire wrapped in yards of the softest silk ribbon.

Each word skips merrily through the airwaves and into my ears, 'Goodbye, my child.' I think of the she-moon and her pretty face spreading her delicate rays through the dark of night.

'Thank you,' I reply softly.

The angel puts his arm around my shoulders and guides me into the light. I look at his beautiful face as we walk. He does not speak, only smiles. I get lost in that smile, that beautiful smile.

The Excursion
Patrick Gale

The Excursion
Patrick Gale

The idea was to make a full day of it rather than have the demonstration as the be all and end all. The minibus collected them from outside the church at ten-thirty. Gwen and Bernie bagged three seats at the back so she could sit with them.

They were like that, Eileen had realised. Forceful.

People who escaped from inside aeroplanes seconds before they turned to fireballs did so because for a few moments something in their genetic makeup enabled them to override all inculcated sense of decency to trample on the faces of other passengers in a single-minded rush for life. Afterwards they would say how guilty they felt and people assumed it was a becoming sense of unworthiness at being spared. Actually, it was uncomplicated guilt at their memories of elbowing an air steward in the face or punching a dithering child aside from the escape chute.

Gwen and Bernie were such people and she was not. They bagged her a seat because they wanted her with them but if the minibus were balanced on a cliff, they'd jump out without a backward glance at her.

They were big boned, wet-lipped, hot-palmed meat-eaters; more like brother and sister than husband and wife. She preferred not to imagine them naked.

It was not far. A forty minute run on the motorway then half that again dawdling in queues through the city's outskirts and system of roundabouts. Someone had a daughter-in-law in the police who had tipped them off so they knew exactly where to meet up and when. There were two hours to kill so they tried on shoes in Marks – Gwen was a martyr to corns, apparently – before enjoying a sort of package deal OAP lunch in the café at the top of Dingles.

She had not known them long. They had met through church. She had attended the same church most of her life. It was the one her mother had preferred, which embraced an undemonstrative, tasteful brand of Anglicanism, a church for women like herself who were happy enough to lend a hand at a fundraising bazaar but preferred their religion undiscussed and uninvolving.

At least she thought that was the sort of woman she was. Then Gwen and Bernie turned up in the congregation one Sunday – the numbers were never spectacular so one could always spot new faces – and sat beside her. It was one of the few churches in the diocese that persisted in holding out against doing the Peace but they startled her by clasping her hands in theirs at the moment in the service where other priests might have intoned *let us offer one another a sign of peace* and murmuring, "Peace be with you," with such urgency she spent the rest of the service worried that hers was not so tranquil a soul as she had thought.

They sought her out during coffee and biscuits afterwards and introduced themselves.

"We can tell you're not happy here," Gwen said. "Can't we, Bernie? I mean, it's not right. Not right for you. I'm sure he's a lovely man but you have to go back to first principles, sometimes."

"I'm sorry?" Eileen said, confused.

By way of explanation, Bernie nodded towards Reverend Girouard, who had not long been with them. "*Homosexual*," he hissed.

"Shame," said Gwen. "It's a lovely church otherwise. Old."

"He even wants to bless their unions," Bernie added. "He asked the bishop."

Eileen had already gathered from the flower arrangers that there was no likelihood of a Mrs Girouard and that Mr Clancy, who had been giving organ recitals for a while now, was rather more than a lodger at the vicarage. The two men were exceptionally polite and good looking and, after her initial surprise, she had begun to decide that their domestic arrangement made a pleasant change from the previous incumbent who had one of those resentful, difficult wives who seemed almost standard C of E issue these days. She had not analysed her response very deeply but a small part of her pleasure stemmed from the sense that she was not reacting as her parents would have done. Her unvoiced welcome of the two men was a timid rebellion against the norm. Now she found she lacked the courage to give it voice, however, and felt shamed into agreeing with Gwen and Bernie.

"I know," she heard herself sigh. "It isn't right but what can one do?"

"Vote with your feet," Gwen said. "Next week you're coming to us at St Mungo's."

She could have laid low, perhaps, pleaded sickness or lain out of sight on the kitchen floor when Gwen came tapping on the window with her wedding ring. She had gone with them, however, meek as a lamb.

St Mungo's was not at all the sort of church her mother would have liked, so there was a tacit satisfaction in changing allegiances. The hymns were happy and unfamiliar, their words projected onto a big screen so that everyone's hands were left unencumbered for waving in the air or clapping. The priest was a muscular, short-haired man – like a soldier or PE instructor – who wore a plain suit instead of robes and kept walking among them and making eye contact so that everything in the service felt tremendously personal. The Peace was no mere embarrassed handshake but a heartfelt festival of greeting in which people actually left their pews to meet strangers across the aisle. The priest tracked her down. There was no escaping him. Offset by his short silver hair, his eyes were hard chips of sapphire.

"I'm Paul," he said, offering a hand both large and warm.

"Eileen," she told him. "I'm Eileen Roberts."

"Peace be with you, Eileen," he said, bringing his other hand into play so that both of hers were trapped. "Welcome to St Mungo's. I really mean that."

And she felt so hot behind her eyes she thought she might faint.

His handshake was so firm and his welcome so compelling that she proved unswervingly disloyal and came back to St Mungo's week after week. Reverend Girouard was undoubtedly better bred but there was no denying that his twinkly charm was effete by comparison, weak even, and she reminded herself – and her mother's disapproving shade – that some of the Disciples had been rough-edged working men, men her father would have dismissed as *common*.

Gwen and Bernie did not come every week. She soon realised this was because they worked as covert missionaries, targeting churches where the priests were unmarried or unorthodox, to lure away to St

Mungo's discontented worshippers who might otherwise have left the church entirely.

"I suppose it's all the same God, though," Eileen let slip in a weak moment and Bernie corrected her,

"Yes but some vessels are unworthy, Eileen. You wouldn't feed your guest off unclean china."

She had since seen Reverend Girouard's good-looking friend, Mr Clancy on the High Street a couple of times and crossed the street quickly to avoid any awkwardness. Reverend Girouard himself had come round once and actually called her name through the letterbox when she did not answer the bell. She hid from him in the broom cupboard in case he peered through a window and saw her. She felt ill afterwards from the excitement and had to lie down.

There was already a small crowd outside the law courts but, tipped off by the policewoman daughter-in-law, they knew to stand in a less obvious position down a side street where the authorities thought the van could emerge unimpeded.

They had all enjoyed a glass of wine with lunch and, as they waited, Gwen expounded on the accused's crimes with something approaching relish. Eileen did not take a newspaper as a rule because the photographs upset and haunted her. She preferred the radio, whose rare horrors one could always switch off. But Gwen talked horrors now, how the victims had been young men, little more than boys really, how they had been drugged and sexually preyed upon, how there were signs for those who knew how to read them that his purposes had been Satanic. He had shown no remorse and had even laughed softly to himself as the judge read out the charges.

By the time the gate swung open and the unmarked van emerged, Eileen was fired up and ready for it. She ran out into the road with the others, head full of the poor boys, of lads she had known who might have been victims. She had a box of eggs and hurled them against the windows in a volley one after another with a speed and accuracy that astonished her. "Filth!" she screamed. "Filth! Murdering scum! Satan!"

Bernie and Gwen shouted and threw things too but she was louder and angrier. She really screamed. She caught them throwing glances at her.

The rear of the van was blanked out, of course, and she found she directed all her hate at the startled man who was driving, all but hidden by the grilles over the van's windows. She fancied there was fear in the look he gave her before the police came to his rescue and made the crowd stand back to let him pass.

It was over in seconds. She felt her cheeks on fire and found she was laughing, almost hysterical, by the time the van was rounding the corner. Bernie looked at her with respect.

"It's the Spirit," he said. "The Spirit is on you!"

But it wasn't, she knew. Gwen knew it too, glancing at her with a woman's sharper instinct. Eileen had tasted something more like ecstasy and her flesh was alight in a way that made her want to hide herself.

On the minibus home everyone was chattering and excited, as though they had been abseiling or done a bungee jump at an age when no one would have expected it of them. Eileen pretended to join in but she was thoughtful, disturbed at the almost sexual rage their messy little demonstration had unleashed in her.

By the time they were being dropped outside the church again, her old mute passivity had fallen on her however and she was easily persuaded back to Gwen and Bernie's for a restorative cup of tea.

It was an unremarkable house over-furnished with unremarkable things; a house in a gravy advertisement. She donated a box of fondant fancies she had bought in Marks and was saving for later. Gwen sliced up a Battenberg and past it round. The pieces were far bigger than Eileen would have allowed herself. She normally made a Battenberg feed eight, not three. She broke her slice into more manageable blocks of sponge and marzipan.

"Hey," Gwen said. "Show Eileen the tape."

"Are you sure?" Bernie asked.

"She's in the gang, now," Gwen said, dabbing a pink crumb from the corner of her lips. She had not finished her mouthful properly. Eileen saw mashed cake on her tongue. "After this afternoon's display," Gwen chuckled. "Eh, Eileen, who'd have thought you had it in you!"

So Eileen sat on in a vast Parker Knoll recliner like an imprisoning dentist's chair – Bernie had yanked up the footrest because they knew she had vein trouble – and watched a video with them.

It was a home-made affair, crudely shot by their son who worked in the Middle East as an engineer with an oil company. Because of the crowds, the passing cars, the glimpses of women, children, people on mobile phones, it took her a while to decipher what she was supposed to be focussing on. Then she saw the diminutive figures beyond the bustling foreground, figures in a clearing of bloodstained sand. It was, she realised as Gwen began her fascinated commentary, footage of punishments and executions, shot by the son with a hidden camera. It was not all shot on the same occasion or even in the same place. He was an ever-ready collector, like a trainspotter; a connoisseur of extreme justice.

She glanced away from the screen long enough to take in again the photograph on the mantelpiece her eyes had skated over earlier in a restless search for something beautiful. There he was. A mixture of Gwen and Bernie. Big boned. Cheerful. Smirking in his mortarboard. Her eyes were drawn back to the screen.

There were floggings for adultery and lechery and removal of hands for theft. There were stonings and, astonishingly, beheadings. The shootings were shockingly banale by comparison, because they were so familiar from films yet quieter and less dramatic than anything faked. (Gwen and Bernie afforded these their slightest respect and talked across them, ordinary talk about food plans, neighbours, fish food pellets.) Then there was a scene so specific yet so odd that she could not quite believe what she was seeing and, reading her mind, Bernie rewound the tape to show her again.

Two men were pushed to their knees then tied to a stake. Then everyone backed away to allow a bulldozer to cause a sizeable wall to topple onto them, hiding them from view in dust and rubble. There was a cheer from the crowd on the video and an answering murmur of assent from Bernie.

"Homosexuals," Gwen said. "They used to stone them apparently until someone decided that was spiritually unclean for the executioners."

"Splashes," Bernie explained.

"So they topple a wall," Gwen said. "Go on, Bernie. Show her again."

Somehow Eileen found the lever to lower the footrest and made it out of the chair and onto her feet. Somehow she found excuses and even thanks to stammer before finding her way out without actually seeming to flee.

Back at her house she locked the front door behind her, ran to the bathroom and brought up everything, OAP lunch, fondant fancies, Battenberg. She rid herself of everything of the afternoon but the stains in her memory, the fear in the driver's eyes, the admiration of ingenuity in Gwen's voice. She heard the woman's placid suburban tone, that would have been no different if she had been explaining a cunning technique for building a rockery or installing a water feature.

The spasms were so violent she had to wrap her arms about the lavatory bowl and left her so weak that she rested her cheek against its cold porcelain for minutes afterwards, still hearing Gwen and seeing atrocities.

"We missed you," Reverend Girouard said as he shook her hand after the next Sunday's service. His grasp was so coolly reassuring she found herself imagining how it might feel to hold his hand across her face. "Daniel – Mr Clancy – thought you might have forsaken us for St Mungo's."

Mr Clancy passed them, dunking a custard cream in his coffee. "The dark side," he murmured flirtatiously.

"I tried it out," she admitted. "Because they asked. But it wasn't for me. They do the Peace, you know and it's all a bit much."

"Well, welcome back," he said and she saw how it was possible to feel at once judged and forgiven by a smile.

The Pitch
Drew Gummerson

The Pitch
Drew Gummerson

It was the last house on a long day. It was my last chance. My feet were sore and I was hot. It was past seven but the sun was still beating down. Sweat ran down my back and my shirt was sticking to me. I thought of that morning's motivational meeting. The talker's easy phrases.

"Go for it," I said under my breath. "Sell."

The house had a wall around it. Eight feet high, white stucco. It was the kind of wall that knights in shining armour ride up to in medieval stories and then ride away again. It said go away, keep out, do not disturb. Not me. I was desperate.

I found the silvered square of the intercom and pushed it's button. I kept my finger on for a full three seconds just as they had taught me. Then I released. Then I stood back. Then nothing.

"Shit," I said. "Shit."

I was one sale away from ten. Ten was the magic number. Hit ten and your bonus doubled. I needed the double money or I was washed up, beat, screwed. Big time. I owed money to the kind of people who when they threatened you they meant it. They had threatened me. They meant it.

I wiped the damp palms of my hands against the coarse material of my trousers and then pushed the button again. I counted to three. Three was just right. Four was cocky. Four would blow it. It was all about numbers. Statistics. Keeping to the method. The method that got sales. I released my finger. I waited.

Still nothing.

"Shit."

I pulled a tissue from my pocket. I wiped stinging sweat from my eyes. I looked up, looked down the road. There was the sea. In Australia there was always the sea. A whole nation perched on the edge of one huge continent. And me. Ready to fall off. I needed that money.

In this situation the rule was clear. "If after two attempts there is no answer. Leave." There was no room for interpretation. None.

"What the hell," I said quietly. "What the hell."

I pushed a third time.

There was no crackle of an answer. No buzz to enter. Instead the gate swung slowly open.

Standing there was a man. He was tall, hairy, sunburnt. I guessed he was in his forties. He was naked except for a pair of shorts whose elastic waist had seen better days, seen a better waist. In his left hand he was holding a large cocktail glass. I guessed he had once been handsome. Once. Now it would have been polite to say that he was past his prime. But still, there was something about him. He was meaty, sweaty. I had known his type many times late at night in the backroom of the Pleasure Chest bookshop. Married man. Opportunity.

"Lost your way?" he said.

Instinctively, I checked my tie, pushed it up a notch. "Not lost," I said. "No."

"Then you're selling something?" His words weren't aggressive, more amused. Amused was good. Ninety-five per cent of all sales are sealed with a smile.

"Not selling," I said. "More of an investment." I fixed a grin on my face. In the business it's called a shit-eating grin. I went for the kill. "Are you under-insured?"

"You better come in," said the man. He took a swig from the cocktail glass, swivelled on his naked heel and stepped inside. I followed.

The house was impressive. It was three stories, white stucco like the wall. One side was all glass and the front looked out over a pool, a private beach, the sea.

"Call me Gary," said the guy. "Can I get you a drink?"

We were in a large downstairs area. You couldn't call it a room, it was too big. It was definitely an area. There was furniture everywhere. Too much of it, shucking up to walls that were a short jog away. Everything about the place said money, lots of it.

"No drink," I said. Then I felt more sweat run down my back. "Unless you've got water."

"Water on the rocks it is," said Gary and he laughed.

I watched as he produced another cocktail glass like his own. He filled them both to the top with whiskey. To the one that was mine he added a dash of water from a soda bottle.

"Well," he said, raising his eyebrows as he passed me the glass, "it is the cocktail hour."

"What kind of cocktail is that?" I asked.

"It's not," said Gary. "Now about this insurance."

I sat down in a huge leather armchair. That was the rule. Never stand during a pitch, always sit. Gary sat opposite me. Sitting didn't do him any favours. His huge belly overhung the waistband of his shorts. He didn't look like he cared. He was big and he didn't care and he was rich. That was all that mattered.

"Well," I said. I clicked open the clasps on my case. I pulled out a sheaf of papers. I had ten different policies. Ten different spiels. But life was the big one. I wondered whether I should go straight to the life. Life was worth double bonus in itself.

"You haven't touched your drink," said Gary.

"Sorry," I said. I leant forward and took a swig. I had seen Gary make it. I knew it was strong. But still the burning sensation was a surprise. Like fire. Fire on an already hot day.

I took a deep breath and then started to talk. I had to get this right. I gave Gary the general guff about Mercantile Insurance, about how we were underwritten by Lloyds of London. I fired out some figures, glamorous ones, what we in the trade call the "come fuck me figures". I stressed what a good deal we could offer, how by taking out his insurance in one package he could save himself a packet. I told him how he could put his life in our hands. We were a safe bet, a sure fire winner. We were team players but gave individual service. I was good and I kept up my grin, the shit-eating one. I knew Gary's type and I knew I had him hooked. Married men of a certain age were my forte. As a rule, they were all the same.

"Actually," said Gary as I finally came to a halt, "it's normally my wife who deals with the insurance kind of things."

"Oh," I said. I picked a speck of dust off the end of my tie. Then I took another sip of my drink, a large one. "Do you think we should wait for your wife?"

Gary laughed. "Are you sure you want to? She's a real ball-breaker my wife."

"A ball-breaker?" I said.

"Yeah," said Gary, "a real ball-breaker."

I had never heard anyone say ball-breaker before. At least, not in real life. I wasn't sure I knew how to answer. But then, I didn't have to. Out of nowhere, Gary started to cry. Silently and into his hands.

Crying wasn't good. Crying didn't scream at me, 'I'm going to buy your insurance.' In fact, it said the opposite. I didn't know what to do. I guess it would have been polite to make my excuses and leave. However, I needed that sale. I wasn't going anywhere. So I just waited and hoped he'd stop. Eventually he did.

"You okay?" I said. It was a foolish thing to say, but it is the kind of thing you do say. I was unsure of myself now. We were off the script.

"Sure," said Gary. "I'm great. Super. You want another drink?"

I looked down. I was surprised to see I had finished the one in front of me. "Sure," I said. "Sure. Another drink."

Gary got up, scooped up the glasses and then padded across to the bar. I watched as he went through the same routine with the whiskey and the dash of soda. It looked well practised. I noticed that now.

"Is it about your wife?" I said as Gary handed me the drink. I was trying to be a mate. Kid the client that you are their new best friend, they said. "Is she leaving you?" I said.

"I wish," said Gary. "That bitch will never leave. She's on to too good a thing here."

"Oh," I said.

"Would you leave all this?"

I looked around. "Guess not," I said.

"No," said Gary. "Exactly. Guess not." He took a long swig of his drink. He put the glass down. The liquid left in the bottom looked lonely, all there by itself. Drink me, it seemed to be saying. It wouldn't have to say it very loudly, Gary seemed to be on a roll.

"You wouldn't leave me, would you?" said Gary. "You'd want to stay with me, wouldn't you?"

They weren't questions that I cared to answer. I looked down. I noticed that I'd spilt drops of whiskey onto the facing sheet of the first policy. Ink had started to run, bleeding the words into one another.

"How about your wife," I said finally, "is she fully insured?" It was the wrong thing to say. It was partly the nerves, partly the whiskey. And it was hot. The heat went on and on and I wondered if it would ever end.

"What?" said Gary. "What do you want to talk about her for? I don't want to talk about her. I know, do you want to go for a swim?"

"A swim?" I said but Gary was already up and out the glass patio doors that opened from the front of the room. By the way that he swayed I could see that he was about two drinks away from oblivion. I knew. I'd been there myself.

I picked up my glass and followed him out. That was another rule. Don't let the client out of your sight. Wear them down. Don't give them time to think. I just needed him to sign one of my policies and I was home and dry. The magic ten. Double bonus.

Outside somehow it had got dark and nobody had told me. It was still hot, humid hot and sticky. Gary was nowhere to be seen and then some lights came on and he was there. He was standing next to the pool and he was naked. His cock was brown and thick like the rest of his body.

"Come in," he said. "The temperature will be just right."

"I've got nothing to wear," I shouted but Gary had already knifed into the water.

"Come on," he said, reappearing at another side of the pool, laughing now. "It's lovely. I'll buy your bloody insurance if that's what you want."

Famous last words, I thought. Then I was taking off my clothes. Then I was diving into the water. Then I was next to him.

"If you're quiet," said Gary, "you can hear the sea." He put his fingers to his lips and made a shushing sound. And then we were quiet. Gary was right. Near there was the lapping of the water on the sides of the pool. But further off was a deeper, more cogent lapping. Eternal. Powerful. The sea. In Australia, there is always the sea.

It was dark. The sky was clear. And above us, round, was the moon.

"How badly do you want your sale?" said Gary finally.

"What do you mean?" I said.

"You know what I mean."

I laughed because this wasn't happening and then Gary was hauling himself up over the side. "I'll get us some more drinks," he said.

I trod water and waited. I liked the way the water enveloped me, liked the way I was naked inside it. I was happy, sure of my sale now. I didn't care that I had to have sex to get it. Morals were for other people. You've either got them or not. Me, not.

I watched as Gary came back. His black hair was matted to his body. He was hairy all over and he looked good like that. Wet. Slick. He sat down on the side of the pool with just his feet in the water and I scooted over to him. His cock was hard.

"I haven't done anything yet," I said.

"Yet," said Gary.

"I thought you were all upset about your wife," I said.

"I told you," said Gary, "she's a real ball-breaker."

"Really?" I said and then I took one of his balls in my mouth. It tasted of chlorine. Of childhood summers and other children's fathers.

Gary put his hands on either side of him and arched his back, pushing himself towards me. He put his head back and groaned softly. I released his ball, then worked my way up his shaft and then down further. After a while Gary took my hand and said he wanted to take me to bed.

"Okay," I said. "But first you have to sign."

"You are like my wife," said Gary.

"I know," I said. I laughed. "A real ball-breaker."

I hadn't read the rulebook on this issue but I was pretty sure what it would say. Get the signature before climax. In my experience with married men, after came regrets. I didn't want regrets. I couldn't afford them.

Back in the lounge I made Gary dry his hands before he touched my policies.

"So what am I signing?" he said.

"Life," I said.

"I'd better put my wife's name on it," said Gary, "and then we can both pray."

"You're joking, right?"

"You haven't met my wife."

"Life insurance doesn't count if you kill her," I said.

"I'll be careful," said Gary. "They won't suspect a thing. Honestly."

"Not funny," I said but I watched silently as Gary carefully wrote the name of his wife in each of the marked boxes. After all, it was his decision.

"Okay?" he said after he had signed in triplicate.

"Okay," I said. "And now you can fuck me."

The bedroom was hot. The windows were closed and the day's heat was trapped inside, heavy on the air. Gary made to open the window but I told him to stop, it was alright as it was. He paused for a moment and then smiled. He nodded okay.

Gary wanted to be on top. That was fine. I liked his weight on me. The coarseness of his hair. The smell of his breath. Outside through the window I could see the moon and somewhere distant was the sound of the sea.

Gary lifted up my legs, leant his body against me, and then he entered me. The sweat was running down my back again and down the inside of my legs, pooling onto the sheets. I groaned and Gary groaned and when he asked if he could come inside me I didn't say anything but reached forward for the cheeks of his arse and pulled him deeper inside. Gary shuddered, held his breath, then breathed out, then laughed.

After a bit of post-coital banter, Gary pulled his cock out. He lay down next to me and squeezed me tight. He said he wanted to stay with me for ever, like this, for ever.

Then I fell asleep.

Then I woke up.

Gary was shaking me. He had his fingers to his lips again. But this time it wasn't playful like in the pool. His eyes said it all.

"Shit," he said. "It's my wife. I heard the gate."

"Shit," I said, "I must have fallen asleep. What time is it?"

"Hide," said Gary. "Don't worry about the fucking time."

"What?" I said.

"Shit," said Gary, "she's not supposed to be home. Hide."

I frowned my eyes. I was angry with tiredness. And after all, I had his signatures. I had got what I wanted. "Let her find me. Perhaps then she'll leave you."

"You don't understand," said Gary. He was breathless, speaking staccato. "All this. Everything. Is hers. Everything."

"Shit," I said. I was thinking of my life-insurance policy, those triple signatures, and whether they were worth anything at all.

"Come on." said Gary, "in the cupboard. Just get into the cupboard."

Gary pulled me up. He pushed me across the room, bundled me into a cupboard. Then he went out. Moments later he was back. He was carrying my clothes. He threw them on top of me and closed the door.

It was dark. My head was heavy from the alcohol. I was naked and in a cupboard. And more important than anything I was back to where I had started. I had needed that sale and now it was slipping away. I was an idiot. I put my head in my hands as I felt Gary's come begin to drip out of my arse. Then the shouting started.

I recognised Gary's voice. And there was another. A woman's. His wife. They were both screaming. They were loud. Loud enough to wake the neighbours. Except there were none. We were all alone here. In this exclusive area, with the same old problems. I tried to make out what was being said, but it was all pitch, no substance.

Downstairs things started to be thrown. There were crashes and I imagined flowers over the floor, hanging limply off the side of heavy furniture. Then there were footsteps on the stairs. Loud. Fast. Running. And someone was in the room. I heard more footsteps. There was the sound of a runner on a drawer. There was breathing, out of breath breathing, loud enough for me to hear. Then a voice. The wife. Close.

"You wouldn't," she said. "You don't have the balls."

"Bitch," said Gary. "I'd be better off without you."

She laughed. "Back to where you came from? You were nothing. My father was right."

"You always were your daddy's girl," said Gary.

"Yes," said the wife, "and you were your daddy's boy. You've blubbered about it enough times. Oh, the horror, the horror. Believe me, if I thought electric shock treatment would work I would have plugged you in years ago."

There was a crash. Something breaking.

"Where is he this time then?" said the wife. "In the cupboard? How very original."

"Don't," said Gary.

"Or what?"

"Don't open the door." Gary. Louder.

"Or what? Come on. Let's see your dirty little secret. Get him out. Perhaps he can entertain us both. You know Gary, I am always partial to a bit of fun. God knows, I never see any with you."

Footsteps came towards the door. Then more behind them. I hugged my knees to my chest. I held my breath. Like it would make a difference. There was the sound of fingers against the wooden frame. Then suddenly. Crunch of body hitting body. A scream. I heard Gary grunt like when we were having sex. Only different. Then a shot. A gunshot.

The gunshot changed everything. They always do. In that they are like children. Only often, more final.

I couldn't move.

Slowly the come that now flowed more freely from my arse dripped down the back of my arse. Released by fear. And then it came to me. The sound. Out of nowhere we were back to where we had started. The sound of the sea. Waves crashing on the beach. Shingle sucked down to the heart of the ocean. Distant yet near. Beautiful yet deadly.

She was dead. I knew she was dead. Yet I couldn't open the door. How could I? What would I say to Gary? What would he say to me?

I pulled my knees tighter up to my chest. I started to cry. Silently. Almost without tears. I was crying for myself, because of the day's tension and because I had lost the sale, the sale I had needed so badly. And then the door opened.

Light. Flooding in from the bedroom, bathing me in brightness. I looked up, squinting.

I couldn't see. And then I could.

It wasn't Gary. It was her. The wife. The ball-breaker. Just as Gary had said.

She was dressed in red and her hair was aflame. It was like Mount Vesuvius on a bad day. She was all curves and cleavage.

"Well, well," she said brushing down an invisible crease on her flawless dress. "What have we here?"

I wiped my face with the back of my hand.

"Get up," she said.

I did as I was told, struggling to push myself upright. My limbs were stiff from their cramped enclosure.

The first thing I saw was Gary on the bed. He was dead. Obviously. My first dead body. He didn't look that attractive dead. In retrospect, he hadn't been that attractive alive.

"You killed him," I said. Again it was one of those things which it was pointless to say but which the situation required. I didn't know how to play it.

The wife, she didn't say anything. She looked cool, like she was off for cocktails at the club. She didn't look like she had just shot someone.

"We'll say it was an accident," I said. "I heard you arguing. The gun went off. I know you didn't mean to do it. It was definitely an accident."

"Accident?" she said as if the waiter had given her prawns when she had definitely ordered oysters. Then she looked at me and then at the body. She folded her arms. Her next words were very clear.

"How could you have done it?"

"What?" I said. "I didn't do it."

She laughed. "Oh, believe me. Yes you did."

On the floor by the bed was a widening stain of red. Gary's head was back, his mouth open. Just above his heart was a hole, wide and messy. I couldn't move. I was still naked.

"I didn't do it," I said. "It wasn't me."

The wife brushed down another one of those invisible creases. I guessed it was a studied mannerism, something other men would find attractive. "You were having an affair," she said. "He wanted to finish it. You were distraught. You killed him."

"No," I said. "That's not what happened."

"No." She shook her head. "You're right. Affairs need evidence. People who have seen you together. Hotel receipts." She stopped a second, looked me up and down. "I take it you weren't having an affair?"

"No!" I said.

"No," she said. "Let's see. You come to the house. You're selling something. He does his old my wife's a ball-breaker routine."

"What?" I said. "You had a fight. You killed him."

"Yes, that's it. You look like the type. You let him fuck you. Then you find out he hasn't got any money. Whatever he's promised to buy from you he can't afford. You've got debts you have to pay. You get angry. You have a fight. There's a gun in the side drawer. Gary showed it to you. Boasted he was going to kill me and then he left it out. You didn't mean to do it. You grabbed it and it just went off. Then I come home and discover the body and you standing over it. You see me and you run, you start to run."

"No," I said. "That's not what happens. You know that's not what happened."

"Oh but my darling, it is. That's exactly what happens. Now why don't you run along and be a good boy."

"I won't," I said. "I won't go anywhere. We're calling the police. We'll tell them what happened. It was an accident." I started shouting. "It was just an accident."

And then I noticed the gun. It was in her hand. It was pointing at me. It was pointing at me and she was smiling.

"Go," she said. "Just get out of here. You know I can't stand hysterics. I can stand anything but hysterics. They really piss me off. Ask Gary."

"But..."

"Now. I mean it."

And so I went because I could see in her eyes that she did. I didn't even stop to get my clothes. I ran out of the house, straight past the pool and then down to the beach. The private beach that was part of the house. The sand was cold under my feet, having finally given up on the heat of the day.

I knew the evidence was shaky. For a start my fingerprints weren't on the gun but she would think of a reason why. She would make up a story. She would think of something. I knew she would.

Every morning at work we had sales experts come in to train us in the art of getting a sale. It was all about making a pitch. Executing it with confidence and self-belief. And in Gary's wife I had seen straight away that she was a professional. If it was me and her in court I wouldn't stand a chance. Not a chance. Next to her I was a bum, a drifter, someone who was down on their luck and after money. In my past were petty misdemeanours, minor sex offences. They would all count against me. Drag me down.

The sand firmed up as I approached the shore. I stopped with the sea lapping at my feet. I turned and looked back at the house. It was stucco white, three stories high. Impressive against the black of the night. It had been my last house of the day. My last chance. And I had blown it. It was all about statistics. Doing the right thing, following the rules. Smile, eye contact, enthusiasm. It was about making the sale and then getting out. No mess. Easy.

I turned back to the water, turned my back to the house. I took a deep breath and said quietly under my breath that I was sorry. Not sorry for Gary and whatever troubles had plagued him during his life. Sorry for myself, for being a fool, for ending up as just another gay sex scandal headline when the truth was so very different.

The sea was cold as I hit it.

A whole nation perched on the edge of a continent.

And I had just fallen off.

Britain's Fattest Killer Tells All
Michael Hootman

Britain's Fattest Killer Tells All
Michael Hootman

At sixteen I was diagnosed morbidly obese, which, to my adolescent ears, sounded less like a medical term meaning 'overweight to the point of endangering life' than a direct insult. The consultant may as well have flicked through his notes and pronounced me 'grotesquely' or even 'repulsively' obese. Mother contrived to looked shocked as if official confirmation of my immense bulk came as a complete surprise to her. If dad had been alive he would have demanded a recount, insisted the scales were faulty, at any rate there would have been some kind of scene.

We drove home in silence. Mother was presumably lost in a castigating loop of maternal self-doubt. Where did she go wrong? Should she have breast fed? Did she give me too much food as infant? Or perhaps too little? Was I started on solids too early? Or too late?

This was all of no concern to me as I had other, loftier thoughts on my mind: for I was in love. Curtis Smith (the first name a slight over-compensation for its companion's lack of distinction, but hardly his fault) had joined the sixth form halfway through the year. He had moved from somewhere called Pompey, which was evidently on the south coast, for reasons connected with his father's work. He was a blue-eyed blond so blandly handsome that, even then, it was impossible to recall his features without them instantly dissolving into nothingness. How on earth did his parents manage to recognise him? Yet he was handsome and I loved him.

Is it worth stating whether or not this love was reciprocated? Whether he saw through vast undulating layers of adipose tissue to the beautiful person that dwelt within. Well, dear reader, it wasn't and he didn't. In fact our paths hardly ever crossed. He was taking A levels in arts subjects whereas I favoured the sciences. We were also in different forms and, apart from the occasional break he would spend in the sixth form common room, I would go literally days without seeing him. Of course I did not see him outside of school for, as my mother would have said, we 'ran with different crowds'. An unfortunate point of comparison considering that my crowd didn't – couldn't – run at all.

My crowd. Could me and Peter Truman be classified as a crowd? If the definition rested on weight alone then yes for, ever respectful of centuries-old school tradition, the two fattest children had, in way that was almost magical to behold, sought each other out and had become each other's best and only friend.

It was not a close relationship. Although we affected a bemused tolerance of our callow and immature fellow students, when alone our conversation would have put many nine-year-olds to shame. We seemed to discuss little else except masturbation and although we covered this topic exhaustively we still did not feel able to share any emotional intimacies. The mechanics were a fit subject for analysis but there was no room to confess that when fantasising about Curtis, at the exact moment of release, I would plaintively cry out his name.

From what I understand first love is given its savour by a pleasant undertow of melancholy: in likelihood it will not be consummated but instead will serve as a template, an ideal, for future relationships and thus a romantic continuity will thread itself through, and help bind and make sense of, a person's life. For those in my position, however, the diminished probability of ever finding a partner threatens to sabotage the whole enterprise. Somehow I managed to push such drear thoughts from my consciousness and instead concentrated on a rich, fulfilling, yet wholly imaginary present.

There existed a panoply of varied romantic scenarios which ran almost continuously in my head for five months, a rolling mantra of my desire: I bring in a tape of a Bach concerto to play in the common room. Curtis finds himself moved and, when no one else is around, asks me who composed such sublime music. He then seeks out my advice on further listening and soon a deep friendship blossoms from our mutual passion for baroque masterpieces. Another favourite involved him switching to Maths and my offering to coach him at home. In order to speed up his progress he decides to institute a curious system of rewards weighted to the difficulty of each problem. The only one I remember was that if he managed to solve a fourth-power differential equation I had to lick ejaculate off his still-sodden shorts. I should stress that this fantasy was the exception with sunlit picnics, autumnal walks and winter nights in secluded log cabins making up by far the majority of these mental tableaux.

Thus school life would have progressed for the next eighteen months until I took up a place at Oxford and Curtis went to somewhere like Sussex to engage in Media Studies. At college I would no doubt have found another Curtis, albeit one who possessed slightly more intelligence, and then would have embarked upon another imaginary affair.

If I hadn't come across that singular piece of information then we would no doubt both be in our respective universities instead of where we are now: me in gaol and Curtis (how it pains me to write this) very much dead.

It was one of those unexpectedly warm March afternoons, a brief foretaste of summer which would have to see us through the next three months of relative gloom. Me and Peter were in the common room getting on each other's nerves (we were engaged in some absurd argument about whether a certain elementary logic puzzle was elucidated in *The Pyramids of Mars* or *Genesis of the Daleks*). To our left a group of fellow lower-sixth formers, perhaps still a little boisterous from the football they had just played, were winding down with cups of coffee laced with whisky passed round from a sports bag.

Maybe half an hour passed. There was then a noticeable lowering of volume as they discussed something of an evidently sensitive nature but still I managed to hear Curtis's name mentioned, then some laughter whose tone, filthy and somewhat scornful, I did not care for and finally the words that heralded my downfall: 'The size of it!'

In theory those words could have referred to any object in the universe. Even as I pretended to listen to Peter, every ounce of concentration focussed a few feet away to my left, I had already narrowed down the statement's subject from an infinity of possibilities to its one, true, inevitable form.

One judged it as ten inches, another said it was easily eleven, perhaps twelve. Still another pointed out how it came down to just above his knee. Curtis Smith, my Curtis Smith, so handsome, so beautiful, so desirable, so everything-I-was-not had instantly put himself beyond my reach, my love, my compassion even my hate by possessing a penis of truly gargantuan, even freakish, proportions. I could have wept at the injustice of it all.

It's a tired old saw but nevertheless true: nature abhors a vacuum. My soul, emptied of its vast store of love, instantly replenished itself with a desire just as strong. Stronger, for it was realisable and did not involve the willing participation of its object: I promised myself in the most solemn terms that even if it killed me I would see Smith naked, see *it* in all its monstrous glory and having seen it would be able to walk away, sated, triumphant, and that would be an end to it.

My plan was a simple one (though plan is perhaps too grand a word implying as it does some degree of forethought whereas the idea presented itself to my consciousness simultaneously with the problem it was supposed to solve): I would engage in some sporting activity and then, in the showers afterwards, my eyes – my very soul – would feast upon Curtis's unclothed body until sated.

The theory was simple, the practice presented insurmountable difficulties. My health – no, I must forego the euphemism – my excessive weight forbade any physical exertion much beyond the lightest of strolls. Before my sporting career could commence I would have to go on a diet.

I would certainly not eat for the next two days, I decided, and afterwards would consume only the most meagre portions of rice and vegetables. Almost as soon as I arrived home mother had an absurdly fat- and carbohydrate-laden meal on the table which prompted me to finally utter those three words she'd waited most of her adult life to hear: 'I'm not hungry.'

Upstairs I tidied my room and by placing my bed in its centre managed to construct a circuit which I could walk round. I then devised a timetable mapping out both food intake and exercise for that Friday evening and the rest of the weekend.

Those three days were spent in a truly pitiable state: I had an almost constant headache from not eating coupled with dizziness caused by circling my bed for hours at a time. The hunger itself was a capricious adversary: one moment it would claw at my vitals until I felt I would cry out and then, in an instant, it would disappear. Each time this happened my heart would soar believing that through sheer willpower I had conquered this most basic form of human frailty. But no. Hours later, without warning, it would be back wreaking its predictable havoc. At such times all I could do was focus my mind on Curtis and the preternaturally magnificent sight he would soon afford me.

Come Sunday evening, and in a state of some excitement, I ventured to the bathroom to weigh myself and then luxuriate in the extent of my loss. Which proved, give or take a pound, to be nothing at all. Or at least no more than you would expect as part of my normal weight fluctuation due to water loss or perhaps even a particularly severe haircut.

It had all been in vain, I thought. In my precarious mental state I had expected instantaneous and miraculous results. I briefly entertained thoughts of continuing this diet for some months but realised that I would not be able to keep to such a regime even for an organ twice the size of that possessed by Curtis.

I sat down on the toilet and cried. But they were not mild tears such as those shed by the sad, lonely and defeated; rather they were tears of frustration, anger and determination. Thus feeling cleansed and strangely elated, I devised my second plan.

In its favour was simplicity, but its inability to allow a thorough and relatively lengthy examination of my quarry counted very much against it. There is no dignified way of putting it: I would sneak a look at Curtis's cock as he used the urinal in the boys' toilets.

Three hundred and thirty-seven boys shared three sets of toilets. By timing myself on various occasions I calculated that to urinate – from unzipping to zipping up – took an average of one-and-a-half minutes. A seven-hour school day thus provides two hundred and eighty distinct opportunities to witness a full urination. Taking into account the one in three likelihood of choosing the correct toilet meant that if

I innocently needed to void the contents of my bladder the probability of encountering Curtis's dick by chance alone was one in eight hundred and forty. If both Curtis and myself peed once a day it would take over four school years before this happy accident occurred.

In order to shrink the odds I would merely have to increase my visits to the toilets. From the next day I ensured that I went before school, in between lessons, at break times and twice at lunch. Even after a month of such assiduous toilet visitation I was still no nearer to seeing *it*; there had not even been the near miss of our paths crossing at the toilet's threshold – Curtis leaving as I entered or vice versa.

My school work, which I had already started to neglect through lack of home study, now began to suffer as I realised I had no option but to make these journeys in the middle of lessons.

Barely two weeks after I had stepped up my campaign to this new level I found myself following Curtis down a corridor which led to a T Junction where one could either turn right to the classrooms in the east wing or (surely he could hear my heart pounding in my chest!) left to the school's central block of toilets.

The gods were smiling upon me, or so I thought, as I watched Curtis veer off towards the latter. Breaking into something approaching a brisk walk I entered the toilets a few seconds later only to find them apparently deserted. The click of a cubicle door being bolted alerted me to the fact that, unfortunately, Curtis was here to empty his bowels.

It was of no consequence; there would be other times. The very fact that I had come this near to achieving my objective was cause enough for celebration. At least it was until I heard the sound of urine splashing against porcelain, the flush of an emptying cistern and the unbolting and slamming of a door.

How could I have been so foolish? Of course, someone in Curtis's position would never use a urinal lest he attract the unwanted attention of an opportunistic sightseer like myself. I could not help but reflect on how his prodigious organ must constrain and affect all aspects of his life from the places he felt able to relieve himself to the very clothes he wore. (Curtis naturally dressed in nothing but the baggiest of trousers – they could hardly let him leave the house in anything less for fear of causing a riot.)

Still, things were not progressing well. There was only one thing for it: I would have to seek professional help.

There were only three private investigators listed in the yellow pages. Two of them had efficient receptionists whereas my third call was answered by a rather common-sounding man whose brief conversation with me was punctuated by the most fearsome display of coughing, wheezing and hacking. I was further cheered to learn that he didn't have an office and that he intended to conduct our first interview in his car. I imagined, quite correctly as it turned out, that a man possessing such a comically seedy attitude to working practices would be more interested in money than legal niceties.

I also learned that his fee would run into many hundreds of pounds – a sum that was, despite my reassurances to the contrary, totally beyond my means. I could have earned the money but felt I had not the mental fortitude to handle the further delay this would entail. Instead I visited Uncle Dougie whose attempts to paw me during my early teens had resulted, on my part, only in an amused bafflement. From the occasional pat on my rump, on which his hand may have lingered a fraction of a second longer than was strictly necessary, I managed to concoct a harrowing tale of self-hatred, eating disorders and suicide attempts which had the poor man simultaneously incredulous, guilt ridden and deeply, deeply terrified. Blackmail may be an ugly word but paedophile is generally adjudged the uglier. Five days after this interview Uncle Dougie's cheque had cleared so I met my private eye with some confidence having three hundred pounds in cash and over double that in the bank.

Ricky – he did not furnish me with a surname – was perhaps the most physically repellent human being I have ever seen. Like most people he could lay claim to owning a nose, a mouth, a pair of eyes and two ears but their individual construction and the spatial relationship they bore each other in consort produced a countenance of singular repulsiveness. As far removed as I was from Curtis in the beauty stakes Ricky was thus far beneath me. This did not, however, give me any crumb of comfort for it was impossible not to imagine the sense of horror I would feel were I to learn that such a creature as Ricky had feelings towards me and then, by symmetry, to deduce that this self-same horror would be Curtis's were he to know the inner workings of my heart.

Even though I was paying him a substantial amount of money and was in many ways beyond all forms of shame, still I found myself unable to give an unvarnished account of the service I wanted Ricky to perform. It was a farcically inept story I spun, one whose sense of logic, motivation and elementary genetics would have aroused suspicions in all but the clinically insane. In short I purported to fear that Curtis was my illegitimate half-brother – the result of a union between my father and his secretary – and the only way I could confirm my suspicion was by seeing whether he bore the family birthmark on the upper portion of his left thigh. There were some minor elaborations involving a contested will and an aunt wrongfully confined to a lunatic asylum but as no one was actually supposed to believe the story I thought it would do no harm.

For a fee of five hundred pounds Ricky would endeavour to provide me with full-frontal photographic evidence of Curtis and his suspected lineage. He candidly told me that in the guise of a workman unblocking drains it should be quite simple to install micro-cameras in the school showers. He could then present me with pictures of various boys until by luck we happened across the correct one. This was the perfect solution for, apart from Curtis, there were at least one or two other boys whose naked form I had taken to imagining in some of my more idle moments.

After a week I phoned Ricky to inquire of his progress in the investigation. There was a long pause and he replied that things were going as well as could be expected. Had he taken any photographs? No. Had he installed a camera? No. In what way were things progressing well? He couldn't tell me in case the phone line was bugged.

Two weeks later a similar call elicited a similarly evasive response. A month later I demanded either some proof that he'd been working on the case or my money back. At this he laughed a rasping, wheezy laugh and asked me exactly what would happen if he said he'd do neither. I was more than welcome to phone up Trading Standards or even the Old Bill – as long as I didn't mind explaining exactly what kind of job I had wanted doing. "If anyone needs locking up it's you, you filthy pervert," he said and hung up.

I had been an easy touch. Ricky was right, I could hardly complain to anyone or any organisation without exposing my own criminal vices to the world. I had tried and failed: every avenue was now exhausted. My most solemn promise to myself had, in the final analysis, counted for nothing.

It would be not much of an exaggeration to say that for the next two months I thought of little else except my own failure. The fact that I had not seen Curtis unclothed was of almost minor consequence; that I had been unable to have any impact on even this small part of the world and its inhabitants highlighted an already growing sense of impotence.

This feeling of worthlessness was the dominant theme of my thoughts over the next eight weeks; eventually it would subside to be replaced by any of a number of other fears, desires, and fantasies which took as their focus Curtis and his giant cock.

Tenaciously my mind explored every avenue of its restricted environment though I was not looking for solutions but simply following blindly where I was led. Thus I dreamt of cloning a new Curtis from saliva left on a coffee cup; tried to imagine what it would be like waking every morning with that enormity between my legs; believed through concentration I would travel back in time and kidnap the infant Curtis, bring him up as my son and – shameful paedophilic fantasy – bathe him well into his teens; wondered whether or not it was possible for him to penetrate himself. Who was the first person he fucked? Who would be the last? And when he died and his flesh decomposed would archaeologists, many thousands of years later, be able to deduce the size of his cock – perhaps correlating it to some aspect of his pelvic construction – or would that information disappear with the organ itself.

During one of these leisurely mental perambulations I found myself speculating on the surprise the undertaker would experience on preparing the naked corpse for burial. At the time I noted, quite dispassionately, that a dead body presents an ideal medium for detailed examination. Much in the spirit of my cogitations on time travel or cloning I further imagined killing Curtis for this express purpose but naturally did not subject this notion to any further scrutiny.

But once something has been thought it cannot be unthought. There was no one moment when it crossed the divide between obscene fantasy and intriguing conjecture. But once it did it was only a short distance to distinct possibility and then a shorter distance still to plan of action.

For practical, aesthetic and (though few will believe it) moral reasons I rejected poisoning, stabbing, shooting, strangling, drowning, starving, garrotting, disemboweling and pushing down a flight of stairs. Such methods would either be impossible for me to carry out, would leave the body in an undesirable or even quite horrendous state, would lead to certain capture by the authorities or would simply inflict more suffering on Curtis than was tolerable. After much deliberation I settled on running him over in mother's Honda Civic. Once this had been avowed how did I cope with the knowledge of what I was about to do? How did I prevent it eating away at me until I abandoned the folly I was about to commit? In truth it was the simplest part of the whole enterprise: I decided that this course of action was the only one open to me. I took away the choice to not act and once this was accomplished I had no need to worry or even think about future actions or consequences. Thus, somewhat paradoxically, free will excised free will.

The very next day I took mother's car to school. As if compelled by some outside agency – so remote did I feel from my own actions – I followed Curtis home and when he was but a few steps down the road where he lived I accelerated, mounted the curb, struck him and, unfortunately, a six-year-old girl who had chosen that moment to visit her next door neighbour.

My lasting memory of that evening is the silence which suffused the scene an instant after I slammed on the car's brakes. For a few seconds it was as if the very world had ceased to turn on its axis. Nevertheless, I soon calculated that one death more made no difference to my plan so I stepped out of the car intending to put Curtis's body in the back and then transport him to a place I could examine him at my leisure.

I had managed to get most of Curtis into the car and now only had to go round the other side and pull the rest of him in by his feet. It was then I heard the truly blood-curdling scream of the girl's mother who was not only shouting at me but physically preventing me from going about my quite terrible business. I tried to explain that there had been an accident and that I was trying to take one of the victims to the hospital. I then advised her that she should phone for an ambulance for her daughter. This provoked her into unleashing a torrent of obscenities as she tried to ascertain, not unreasonably, why I couldn't take the child as well.

Unfortunately, the woman's shrieking had attracted the attention of the neighbours, one of whom must have phoned the emergency services for within a few minutes I could hear the wail of approaching sirens.

I had only a matter of seconds. Ignoring the woman I strode over to the car, opened the rear doors, and, kneeling on Curtis's legs, started to undo his belt. I have since learned, from many disparate sources, that untying someone else's belt can be difficult in the most relaxed of circumstances – the fact that the buckle's operation is effectively reversed makes the whole procedure as complex as some parlour game in which a task has to be accomplished whilst looking in a mirror. No matter how hard I tried to pull on the loose part of the belt it would not come free.

I then moved my attention to the fly: although obviously not a zip – as if fate would have been that accommodating! – its buttons presented less of a challenge that the belt.

The sirens were now loud in my ears and I could see the blue flashing lights reflected in the car's windscreen but I had just unfastened three out of the five buttons. There was now no time for the rest – surely the gap was sufficient to allow egress of the most mammoth appendage; as I heard the abrupt braking of police cars and ambulances I tried to force my hand into the parting I had made in the denim. Large as it was it was still not capacious enough to accommodate the massive bulk of my hand and, as I was being forcibly dragged off him by a police constable, two of my fingertips brushed against Curtis's manhood, running down its length as I was pulled out of the car and then lowered to the ground and handcuffed.

After so many months of toil my sole reward was to be this

tantalising taste a thousand times worse than mere abject failure. At night I try to imbue my fingertips with memory for surely an estimate of their length of contact with Curtis coupled with knowledge of the velocity with which they were pulled back would provide the raw data needed to produce a measure of his organ's vital dimension. But even an accurate estimate would be no substitute for direct experience of the thing itself.

A few years ago I learned that they had cremated Curtis's body so my one last hope – that after being released I would disinter his corpse to find it miraculously preserved like some saint – can no longer give me comfort. In twenty years' time I will be released and I can only pray that advances in genetic engineering will produce a race of boys who would have made Curtis feel inadequate. If this happens, I feel sure I will be able to die a happy man.

Love and Hate and the Scent of Almonds
Randall Kent Ivey

Love and Hate and the Scent of Almonds
Randall Kent Ivey

When I agreed to poison my brother Eric, I did it, ostensibly, because I loved him, when, in fact, I did it because I hated him.

Eric had asked me to do it weeks before I finally agreed, and of course I laughed off the request as some macabre joke. When Eric didn't laugh, and when he gave all clear signs of being perfectly serious, I fumed about his perverse and exaggerated romanticism and walked away, leaving him standing alone. When he persisted, I stopped and stared at him and saw in the blank depths of his eyes that he was not joking and not acting on some false impulse to appear tragically resigned to an awful fate: he meant it. He wanted to die. And this stark confirmation, summed up by a reading of his sad eyes, reminded me that I wanted him to die.

Let me deal first, though, with the reasons for Eric's request.

For what seemed like the umpteenth time in the last twenty years, Eric had fallen in love with a handsome and unattainable heterosexual youth. Oh how many there had been before this one! I still remember many of their names: Eugene, Aaron, Derrick, Logan, Trevor, Rob, Craig, Isaac, Jonathan, Brad, Andy etc., *ad infinitum, ad nauseum*: all handsome, all athletic, all completely out of Eric's reach.

"Why don't you," I asked him once after he had cried on my shoulder about one such lamentable fixation, "take up with your own kind? Someone your own age with the same interests as you?" It was one of the common denominators linking these young men together, a distinct lack of intellectual curiosity and interest in high art. "Then you can be happy. Maybe. Oh, Eric, you're always making the wrong choice!"

Eric's eyebrows rose sharply at that last statement. "Choice? Did you just say 'choice'? God, Eddie, please don't tell me you buy into all that religious right malarkey that it is all a matter of choice!"

I assured him I did not and told him that he knew exactly what I meant. There was no need to deflect me.

"The next thing you'll be advising me to do is date a woman!"

"It's just that I hate seeing you so unhappy," I replied. Perhaps I should have added, "And I hate for you to try to make *me* unhappy with *your* unhappiness," but I didn't.

He went on to explain to me, again, that he was seeking an Ideal, not an actual person, and that his Ideal was the strong youth. The non-intellectual. Someone engaged vitally in life, in all its raw vicissitudes. And this could not be achieved, he went on in irritated pedagogical fervor, with someone like himself – fat, balding, and nearly forty. "Oh, well," he finished, exasperated. "I shouldn't have expected you to understand, Eddie. It's an *artistic* thing."

That's right. I wasn't an artist. He was. I owned a stationary store and a small printing press in town. Eric wrote fiction and book reviews and of late had come to refer to himself more and more as a "man of letters". He wrote novels too but had published none so far. He wrote unproduced plays and screenplays. His stories and reviews appeared in university journals and small magazines, nothing like *The New Yorker* or *The Atlantic*. He had a couple of book reviews featured in a magazine right outside of Chicago with a respectably middle-range circulation. He published a chapbook of poems with my help and gave copies away to family and friends and students. He had a minor reputation at best, but that did not insulate him, at least in his own mind, from the 'slings and arrows' which accompany the pursuit of Serious Art.

His latest young-male fixation was Ricky Fore, an ex-Marine and student of Eric's at the small college in upstate South Carolina where Eric taught writing and literature. Blond, of course, as were so many of the others, Ricky was otherwise an anomaly in the pantheon of Eric's erotic heroes. For one thing he was brighter than usual, although hardly an intellectual, and he wrote fairly well, with just a minimum of misspelled words and no subject-verb disagreement to speak of. Even more shocking, he was hairy, which certainly defied Eric's usual criteria. According to Eric, Ricky often wore shorts to class and revealed strong, tanned legs darkened further by thick, silky hair, and once in class he got warm and went to remove the pull-over sweater he was wearing, and in one motion he pulled up the sweater and the T-shirt underneath it. His belly, Eric said, was a patch of brown-gold hair which threatened to crawl up his midriff and cover his chest.

When I remarked on these deviations, Eric smiled wanly, wisely. "It's all the sign I need that I really love him. If he can be so different from the others and still be so powerfully attractive, well, it's all the sign I need."

And he had gotten closer to this one than he had all the others. Many of the others had been aloof figures in Eric's life – young men he had had classes with in high school or college or men he had taught himself but who had formed no relationship with him outside the classroom. Ricky Fore was different. Ricky Fore was not only handsome and moderately intelligent, he had sought Eric out for his advice and practical help – reviewing a resume, help with writing a letter of application etc. Eric had offered his help freely, knowing he could never have the kind of relationship with Ricky that he wanted. Ricky was, like all the others (as far as Eric knew), irredeemably heterosexual. In fact one of the problems Ricky had consulted Eric about was his turbulent relationship with a girl in Columbia, South Carolina, a young woman who was pressuring Ricky into going to college and was upset that Ricky didn't take his studies more seriously. Ricky assumed Eric, being older, would, naturally, know all about these matters and so much else, and Eric did the best he could to advise under the circumstances.

And then Ricky up and left town. He sent Eric an email saying he could no longer stand the slow pace of a small town. He had been stationed for three years in San Diego, California, and had gotten used to a faster, bigger style of living. He hated school. He hated other people trying to live his life for him, and he hated trying to live up to their expectations of him. He had broken up with his lady friend on account of her constant meddling. In his email rage he even accused Eric of such coercion. He was going to Atlanta, Georgia, and try to make a life for himself there. To hell with everybody else and what they thought.

It was the last Eric heard from Ricky Fore, despite his own flurry of emails to the boy asking him to reconsider things, and it was shortly after that when Eric fell completely apart.

"I feel like somebody's died," he told me over the phone. I ignored him and talked about something else. He ignored me.

"If I could just see him again... just... see him. Speak to him. Say hello. Hear him laugh. He has such a sweet laugh, Eddie. A quiet laugh. Almost shy. Almost like he is embarrassed to laugh, to show his pleasure. He put his hand over his mouth when he laughed And his eyes. The glitter of those blue eyes."

"Oh, Eddie. Let go of it. Just let go."

"Let go. Sure. Like my feelings are a light switch that can be turned on and off. Let go." His lips curled contemptuously over the words.

"Take a vacation, Eric. Take a sabbatical next semester. Go to Atlanta and hire the services of a call boy. Go to New York and hire the services of several call boys. Go to Europe and have an affair."

"It's too late for all that," he said and hung up without another word.

"I want to die," he told me the next time I saw him. I had gone to his house because I had not heard from him in days. Apparently, he had kept out of class all week with the excuse of an intestinal virus. He looked like a wreck. He was unshaven and sallow and sunken, garbed only in a terry robe. He looked up at me with red-rimmed eyes. Had he been crying? A grown man? Over a flighty ex-Marine?

"Oh Eric" was all I could say as I took the chair across from him.

"Nothing's any good since he left. Everything's lost its flavor, its color, its music. All I want is to see him. Just to lay eyes on him. Talk to him. Ask him how he is. Hear him laugh. Just a minute. Five minutes. *Anything!*"

"Email him. Haven't the two of you been corresponding?"

"He hasn't answered me in weeks. He's cut himself off from everything and everybody."

"How do you know?"

"I phoned his mother. She says he hardly calls her any more."

I swallowed quietly. "You better be careful there. Sounds like you're verging on stalker territory. Phoning a student's house."

His weak eyes flared some. "I'm his teacher. I have a right to be concerned."

"You *were* his teacher. Be careful. Don't cross any lines."

A silence built between us before I broke it. "Well, you certainly won't run into him sitting here in your bathrobe."

"I won't run into him anyway," he replied wanly. "I'm here, he's in Atlanta."

"Go to Atlanta then."

He sighed. "Oh Eddie," he said, as though really meaning: "What a callous, unthinking fool you are." He stood and circled his small den slowly, restless to find something not there, then came back to the couch and unfolded himself upon it like a painter's model limning luxuriant despair, his legs tucked beneath him, his arms spread across the couch's back.

"This is a cycle I'm in, one I'll always be in. I can see that now. I'm doomed for life."

"It's what you get for playing around in the sandbox with the kiddies."

"I tried someone my own age once. Don't you remember? And he was a bigger child than any of my freshmen."

"Well, the least you could do is stick to the gay side of the field. That would help."

He sighed again and eyed me wearily.

"If I could die, I would. If I could kill myself I would do it... but I can't. Too afraid to live... too afraid to die. That's me."

His voice irritated me. His self-pity irritated me. I stood up and walked away from him and looked back at him and hurled invective at him: "You gay men and your melodrama. Don't you ever get tired of being so... so... operatic?" I looked away from him again.

He snickered then laughed loudly, but when I looked back at him there was no humor in his face: his mouth was pursed and his eyes narrowed.

"You straight men and your *lack* of melodrama," he said, quietly. His face relaxed, and he even smiled as he went on. "So tell me, Eddie. How does it feel to be comatose? To be the living dead? Because that's what you are, you know. A dead man walking around. You would have never let this happen to you, would you, brother? Being consumed so much by a romantic passion you're willing to die on account of it. That's too messy, isn't it? Too *unseemly*. Not a thing a reasonable man would do. So you protected yourself against all that by marrying Laura right out of high school and having your children as soon as possible. You insulated yourself against any embarrassing entanglements or embarrassing episodes. Even when you were a boy, you did that. I was the one who made a fool of himself. Me." His eyes bulged at me with new life. "And I tell you what. I would do it all again, all the same way. Because I would rather be a fool than a zombie."

"Someone had to be sensible," was all I could say, and I said it as though rehearsing a line from a script.

"Oh yes. Sensible. Safe and sensible. You have always been the one to come in behind me and clean up my messes. You stood up to the schoolyard boys who taunted me for my lack of 'manly' interests. You intercepted the love letter I sent to the high school quarterback. I owe you a lot, dear brother. A lot. And it's especially incumbent upon me to tell you that you have missed out on life. You have guarded yourself against it and guarded yourself well, because it has passed you by. Never, ever to come back. That's why you have kept yourself so attached to me. You could have abandoned me. You could ignore me, even living in this small town. But you haven't. I entertain you with my antics, don't I? I fascinate you. A man who puts himself on the line, risking his heart, his reputation, his very sanity, when you have done no such thing and wouldn't dare."

I turned red but managed to control my voice and my temper. "If life as you call it means making a fool out of myself over the affections of unattainable boys, then, by God, I am glad it has passed me by."

Eric laughed too loud and kept on laughing for some couple minutes. When he regained himself, he said, "Oh, Eddie, I want to be dead as you are. Deader even, if such is possible."

He had said all these hateful things out of his peculiar form of grief, I knew that, but, the bastard!, he had unleashed something unwelcome. Maybe he had wanted me to kill him right then – to get so angry and irrational I would bludgeon him or strangle him on the spot, acting from a rage I had never known before. I didn't give him the satisfaction, of course. I left him shortly after our exchange and didn't see him in the flesh for another couple weeks. I went home, pursued by his words, gnawed at, for the first time I was conscious of, by the thought that I had lived my life completely without the sort of extravagant passion that makes life so worthwhile for so many (or so they say and write). Still I would not apologize for the mathematical neatness of my own life. Not everyone could give in to his emotional caprices. Someone had to strike a balance in the world between excess and order. That was me: I was order, Eric was excess.

I went home that afternoon and found my wife in the kitchen preparing a delicious-smelling roast. We spoke shortly about the events of the day, which had been few. The children were in the den watching television. I spoke to them a few minutes then went to my library to listen to music – the last two, great Beethoven string quartets. My wife brought me a vodka martini. I sat and sipped my drink and listened to music and re-read the Overture to *Swann's Way*. An hour later my wife called us for dinner. We ate. Afterwards, I went back to my study to listen to more music and to read. Around midnight I laid down beside my wife for the night. I slept steadily for a couple of hours then woke up to this overwhelming sense of something I couldn't name: it wasn't an oncoming illness, it wasn't fear, it wasn't anxiety. It was nothing. An emptiness. An absence of something important, and I couldn't name what. I tried for two hours to get back to sleep, tossing and turning and watching the ceiling as though one lighted spot of it might hypnotize me back to sleep. And beside me my wife gently snored. I couldn't do it. Eventually, I got up and went back to my library and read until dawn. Then I went to the kitchen and made coffee and began the day properly.

I fell into a pattern that continued for the next couple weeks. I would sleep two hours then wake with this awful feeling of being perched above this awful, gaping chasm, this black nothingness. I became afraid after awhile. I woke up in a sweat with the certainty that I had lost something which I perhaps had never had in the first place. It left me confused, frustrated, even near tears.

I had never been afraid of anything before.

At the end of this period of insomnia, Eric called. He spoke barely above a whisper and asked me, please, to come see him. *Please.*

He had grown a beard since I last saw him and put on weight. He looked like a stranger to me, the more so when he smiled this strained smile and walked over to me to give me an uncharacteristic hug. We never showed that kind of affection to each other.

When we sat and talked, Eric's face resumed the sallowness of the last time I'd seen him, except this time it was worse because his face was thinner. The beard made him look so old. He looked up at me with red, steady eyes and said, "Eddie, I've decided to die, and I want you to help me."

I let out a long sigh and rolled my eyes to the ceiling. "Eric," I started then stopped. I stood up.

"I'm not being melodramatic!" he said in as even a voice as I had ever heard from him. "I don't want to live any more. Not like this. Not in this irreversible cycle, this pattern –" He broke off and covered his face with both hands and cried quietly for a few minutes. I watched him without saying anything until he stopped. He looked at me through splayed fingers, his eyes red and wet, and told me that he had heard from Ricky Fore a few days before.

"That's a good thing, isn't it?" I said without emotion. "You should be happy."

He went on, though, and told me how Ricky had gotten a job with Federal Express in Atlanta and that he had reconciled with his woman friend and she had moved in with him and they were engaged to be married. Eric slumped in his seat at the end of the account.

"Well, the boy's stabilizing. Getting his life in order. And he thinks enough of you to tell you about it. Mark it down as a success story."

Eric gave me a cold stare. He pressed a fist to his mouth and said, "You don't have a clue, do you?"

"About what?" I asked, suddenly perplexed and strangely embarrassed.

"About what it means to love somebody so much... that..." He couldn't finish. His eyes teared up.

I shifted my feet, exasperated, and sighed shortly. "No, Eric. I don't. I don't have a clue, and I don't know what you want me to do. I've given you all the advice I know to give. I'll be at the house if you need to call me later." I turned to go.

"I wrote him back," Eric continued as though he hadn't seen me move toward the door. "And I confessed everything to him. The way I feel. I didn't hold anything back. I told him I love him. I thought telling him would relieve something, lift the burden some, perhaps even spark some sympathy in him." He paused. "He answered me."

After a moment I asked, "And what did he say?"

Eric's eyes flashed with tears. "He said he was disgusted. Sickened that he could have been responsible for such a thing. He was sorry he had ever trusted me. He said it was best if we didn't communicate any more and for me please not to write him again."

"Did you expect anything else from him, Eric?"

"I want to die!" he hollered at me in a strangled voice than bore no resemblance to his own. I watched him sitting there, a pathetic wreck, his face wrinkled with his heaving cries.

"Then go ahead and die," I said quietly. "If that's what you want, then go ahead and do it."

He rose with surprising quickness and came to me and gripped my arms.

"I can't do it alone. I'm not brave enough. *You* have the courage to do what's right. You always have. You've always looked out for me." He stopped when he saw that he was not affecting me and tried a new tact. "It's the *logical* thing to do, Eddie. Oh, if you only knew what it was like –"

"Stop saying that, please."

"– to know someone out there who is so beautiful, so *perfect*, and you can't be with him... there's no chance in the world of being with him... God, there's no worse loneliness than that –"

"I beg you, Eric, to get psychiatric help. This has gone too far, much further than the other ones. At least get on Prozac. Something."

"Can you imagine me – at fifty, at sixty, at seventy years old snared in this same kind of trap? It'll *kill* me."

"There you go then. There's your solution. Just wait it out." I tried to smile. Then I laughed, hoping Eric would relent and reveal this whole business for the joke it must surely be.

But he didn't. His eyes did not waver one bit in their seriousness as he said, "What use am I like this? Who will miss me? I have no children dependent on me. I have nothing to live for. I don't give a damn any more about teaching or writing or anything else. Oh Eddie, help me." He burst into tears again.

I pushed him away from me, disgusted, and left him to his misery.

Eric had infected me with something – an emotion I hadn't felt much of in my life: hatred. That night I experienced the same interruption of sleep I had a few weeks before, except this time I did not wake up to a feeling of emptiness. I woke up hating my brother, which seemed odd and irrational and exciting too but more bothersome than anything else. I didn't try to suppress it or reason it away. Instead I got up from my bed and went to my study and sat and listed the reasons I hated Eric. There were two main ones. I hated him for his pretense and theatricality – not his homosexuality, let me be clear about that. I have always been tolerant of "alternative sexuality". I am no homophobe by any means. But I must say my tolerance does have its limits, as when gay men see their lives as some great Elizabethan drama in which the rest of us are bit players or mere onlookers. At some point I guess I must have found Eric's tendency to such amusing, but now, as he approached early middle age, it became simply grotesque and tiresome.

Secondly, I hated him for his adventurousness, which had led him into this current mess – his willingness to risk his heart, something I had certainly never done. And a sense of the vacuity of my own life overcame me like a pall and distressed me. It never had before. I tried to reason with myself that it was the nature of nearly all gay men to be risk-takers, unlike we heterosexuals, who can be more free in our pursuits and courtships and therefore not as clandestine or dangerous. The explanation didn't satisfy me. After all Eric was a risk-taker in other ways as well: his writing, for example. Each time he sent a story or a poem or a book to an editor or agent, he was opening himself to rejection and criticism. When he stood in front of his students each day, he risked the possibility of their ridicule. I had done no such thing. I had played it safe. But instead of admiring Eric for his audacity, I hated him. He had reminded me of the austerity of my own life. He no doubt would again.

I left my study and checked in on my sleeping wife and children. I stood over them and tried to force upon myself more than mere satisfaction at being their husband and father. I tried for a grander emotion than that, whatever it might be. But it didn't work. I loved them well enough. My wife was a good woman, but she was no female counterpart to Ricky Fore or any of Eric's other fated paramours. I would not have compromised my reputation or livelihood in pursuing her. The same went for my children. They were enough, or so I thought. At any rate forty-five years old seemed a little late to be embarking upon the career of a Hopeless Romantic.

The next morning, as my wife and children got up to start their day, filing past me in the kitchen and chattering cheerily with each other, I didn't have much to say to them. Indeed I felt a kind of petulance towards them, a resentment even, which startled me with its freshness and newness. Their voices irritated me. What they said bothered me, although it never had before. Their hands on me made me shudder, and a curious sentence threaded through my head with the clarity of lightning: Here's my death, circling me with smiling faces and talking to me in familiar voices. Where had it come from? Not from me. Its appearance upset me so I snapped at my son for asking me a question. I apologized quickly then left the kitchen to shower and change.

At the store I couldn't concentrate on work. I'd be reading off stock numbers to Jennifer, my assistant manager, for example, and I would stop in the middle of an entry and feel my whole body tense up with anger, with hatred. It persisted all morning. Finally, I told Jennifer that I had a throbbing headache and was going home for the rest of the day, that she could reach me there. I did no such thing. I wound up at the public park, strolling around the duck pond, thinking of Eric and hating him. It was as though he had introduced some germ into me, a virus, an offshoot of his own devouring unhappiness, and it had metastasized into this malignancy that had only one cure.

I left the park and drove out of town to a wooded spot in the northwest part of the county where our father used to take us deer hunting. Eric hated going. Such a pursuit wasn't in his nature. He was sensitive even then, especially about inanimate and inarticulate things which might be in danger. Our father insisted. He saw it as a rite of manhood. On one such outing, a deer came into view. My father whispered to Eric to take aim and fire. Eric wouldn't do it. His rifle trembled in his grip before he threw it to the ground and turned away crying. I knew I had to save the moment somehow, so I aimed and fired and got the deer in the neck. My father was so impressed with the cleanness of the kill he did not castigate Eric for his "cowardice". Years later, I stood on the outskirts of those same woods and thought about

Eric with contempt and embarrassment and wondered why I had spared him the humiliation.

I got home after dark and ate a cold supper by myself in the kitchen, which was what I preferred. I was not sure how I might have reacted to my wife and children – what I might have said to them or how I might have said it – I was still seething with an anger that boiled right at the surface and which I could hardly control. My wife drifted in now and then with questions, which I answered monosyllabically. After a while, she gave up and left me alone. I went into my study and sat with a scotch and water and stared ahead at nothing, and after awhile I noted the appearance of another emotion that had never much vexed me in the past: sadness. Depression. Melancholy. I have always been one to look on the bright side of things. Life presents problems; it is inevitable. So the best thing is not to stew and fret about those problems but to face them head-on and defeat them if possible. Now, however, I felt paralyzed by sadness – again as though Eric had passed along some of his own lugubriousness to me during one of our recent encounters. Depressed about what? An unnamed loss. The disappearance of a thing I had never had in the first place and probably never would have. I stood and rummaged through my music collection, found a Mozart wind concerto, and put it on. It did not work its usual lightening magic. I finished my drink and went to bed around midnight. I did not sleep and got up early, filled with quiet rage.

The next night I did sleep and wished that I hadn't because I dreamed the whole night long of how I would kill Eric if I were to do such a thing: a grisly tableaux of images succeeded themselves of Eric dying at my hands all accompanied by what sounded like a bastardization of some Mozart tune. *Eine Kleine Nacht Musik*? Maybe an eerie distortion of it. Something cheerfully macabre played, at any rate, as I garroted my brother and slit his throat and drew and quartered him and fed him to rats and tied him to rampaging horses and locked him into an iron maiden and shoved a nickel plated against his temple and pulled the trigger. I was never fully present in these murderous acts. Only my hands. But there was no doubt I was the perpetrator. And I had an audience. Surrounding me in stands, as though we were at some gladiatorial event, were rows of handsome, semi-naked youths, the great majority of them fair-skinned, muscular blonds, who cheered me on in violence against my brother and welcomed the appearance of his blood with great acclaim. They were, I came to understand, all of Eric's love interests, gathered to watch him suffer one last time and to take their own kind of vengeance against his senseless obsessions. I awoke and sat on the side of the bed. Part of me felt some pleasure at the experience of the dream; another part of me felt great, inexpressive sadness. But I wasn't morning my brother and his many, awful imaginary deaths. I was mourning myself.

Eric greeted me at the door sullenly and didn't speak even after I entered his den. He turned and stared at me. There was hope in his eyes. "Well?" he said finally.

I paused before I spoke and started to say something irrational like "What sort of curse have you put on me? Why do you want me to be as unhappy as you are?" Instead I said, "I came to see how you were."

He bit his lip and batted his eyes several times. "Oh really? I think you know how I am. You could have called to ask about that. There's something else bothering you, isn't there?"

"No," I said quietly but emphatically.

He smiled. "What is it, Eddie? Oh this is a turnabout. Me asking about *you*. Wow. Nothing ever bothers you."

"Nothing is bothering me."

He smiled again and kept smiling and kept staring at me as though he could look at me forever and never blink.

I shifted a bit and cleared my throat. "I came to tell you that you have taken this thing too far."

He laughed. "My goodness. How behind the times you are, Eddie! It bothers you, doesn't it? My talk of death."

"Well, of course. You are my brother."

"I mean it really, really bothers you, doesn't it? Because you would like to kill me. I can tell it."

"Eric –"

"I can see it. You are just holding yourself back, aren't you? I can see it. That tremor in your jaw. The red coming into your face. I've never seen that before in you, and you've never felt it. I know you as well as you know me. You never let anything get to you. But this has.

This is something new for you. It scares you. Oh come on, Eddie. Don't hold back. Give into it once. Just once act on your feelings. You won't believe how liberated you'll feel. Hit me as hard as you can. Hit me many times. Put your hands around my neck. Find something here. There's bound to be something. Find it and use it on me. Again and again until I'm gone. You'll feel so much better. Come on, Eddie! I'd do it for you. Oh, if you only knew what it felt like –"

I left him in mid-sentence.

A week later I called Eric and told him, "I will help you. But you must do everything I tell you do, and you must not ask any questions."

He exhaled deeply on the line, and I could hear the sound of relief and gratitude in his heavy breath. "Yes. Thank you," he whispered.

Before I hung up I told him to prepare a hand-written note detailing his recent distress and to leave it in a conspicuous place and not move it.

I had always done the right thing. I was a keeper of order. Order had been disrupted. I couldn't think of any other way to restore it but this.

I chose arsenic. It seemed like such an elegant vehicle for such a distasteful operation. Arsenic is said to leave behind the scent of almonds as it works upon its victims. We had arsenic locked away in an outside storage house for our infrequent gardening purposes. I filled a flask with arsenic, dropped it into my coat pocket, and went over to see Eric, my brother, whom I loved and hated at the same time but presently hated more than loved.

Ever the Anglophile, even to the end, he fixed us tea. We sat and talked. Ricky Fore never entered our talk. We spoke of old times, when we were boys and I watched out for Eric. When conversation lulled, Eric sat and looked at me with utter gratitude. He didn't need to thank me with words. His eyes gave thanks.

This process could not be rushed, this termination of my brother. I would not let it be rushed. For what peace of mind I had left, it had to be careful and methodical, as most everything else I had done in my life had been. Otherwise it would have been a failure. I went back to Eric's house every other afternoon for two weeks, when he made us tea and we talked of days gone by in the calmest of voices, even with some humor and some fondness which we had never expressed as boys or young men. At some point during each visit I sent Eric into the kitchen for something and brought out the flask. When he came back he took a deep swallow of his tea and we resumed talking as though there had been no interruption.

We had never been closer in our lives than we were in those last couple of weeks.

Bala the Woodworker

Alan James

Bala the Woodworker
Alan James

It was very hot at the island flea-market: the stretch of rough tarmac – actually an overflow car park for the racetrack, on the edge of town – was only partially shaded by the sparse planting of scruffy, scrubby trees, which frequently had their branches ripped off by cooks, looking for firewood. Some stalls, the ones selling CDs, and playing the latest western sounds, or pulsating, wailing Hindi disco, had their own square sunshades, covered in primary-coloured segments of shiny PVC, and standing on splayed, cross-shaped iron feet, which tripped people up, and could be painful to the flip-flop wearers. Other stalls, the more interesting , simply pieces of cardboard or old sarongs spread on the ground, and piled with the detritus of ages, found what shade they could, or lay in the full morning sun.

Bala, out of uniform, but smartly dressed in a clean pale pink poly-cotton shirt, worn carefully tucked into neat, navy-blue trousers, was poking about amongst the old magazine stalls when he saw the white man, wearing a baseball cap against the sun, his hair emerging shoulder-length at the back in a golden, wavy ponytail. The man was wearing typical tourist gear – a local tie-dye T-shirt and khaki shorts – and his exposed arms and legs, covered with blond down, were in their first pinky-brown stages of a tan; he was slim, and quite tall. Bala, of medium height himself, thought the man looked friendly and approachable.

During the everyday course of his work, at one of the big beach hotels, he saw plenty of white men, and usually knew whether they could be talked to or not; could sense when his dark skin frightened them a little, or when, come to that, it excited them. In his early forties, no longer a pretty, long-eyelashed boy, Bala had nevertheless a personable face, and always a sharp, modem haircut, clipped at the back and sides, and flat on top. Bala could see that, like himself, the white man was interested in the old books.

Tim was, in fact, flicking through a dog-eared family album, feeling strangely nostalgic over the old wedding pictures; on several pages, framed by deckle edges, Chinese brides, in the full-skirted lace gowns of the fifties, held huge bouquets to their tiny waists, their grooms standing stiff beside them, moon-faced in white duck. Tim would like to have asked the price, but was shy to do so, and didn't quite know how, as nobody seemed to be speaking English; in any case, the stall was unshaded, and rivulets of sweat were running down the sides of his face, meeting at his chin, and dripping onto the photographs. Tim was not yet, a couple of days into his trip, in the habit of carrying a bottle of water around with him, and he could feel himself dehydrating; when he tried to wipe his face, the cheap hotel toilet paper he had stuffed into his back pocket came to wispy pieces on his light stubble.

Unaware of his human shadow, Tim wandered from stall to stall, until he reached the fruit section, and gazed at the huge piles of rust-red hairy rambutans, and the mangosteens, like small round aubergines, oozing droplets of yellow from their purple skins. The stall-holders were breaking things open, for the housewives to try, and some of the white-fleshed fruits looked juicy and refreshing, but trying to buy here was even more daunting, as Tim had no idea of the weights, and some of the cheekier stall-holders were laughing at him and saying things to him they must know he couldn't possibly understand, which of course caused some of the customers to turn round and smile at him, too, although it all seemed to be just about on the right side of good-natured; Tim didn't even dare try any of the opened fruits that were being offered to him, in case he somehow ended up buying a great sack of over-ripe stuff at a funny price.

Across the road stretched a long, straggling line of food stalls, very crowded, noisy and smoky, with a lot of crashing and sizzling going on, but Tim thought, whatever the odds, he must go over and find a drink. First, he went into the little tiled public toilet, paying twenty cents for the privilege of peeing into a filthy trough, noticing with alarm how thick and marmalade-coloured his urine had become since he had left the hotel. Someone sidled in next to him, and Tim glanced over; a smart-looking Indian was smiling up at him. Aware of the other man's steady gaze at his penis, Tim looked ahead at the cracked green tiles, up which a line of ants followed the blackened grouting in a giant zig-zag of right-angles; shaking slightly too early, in order to make his exit, Tim shot a few dark drops over his shorts and feet. Bala was still standing, legs apart, smiling, a strong steady stream hitting the metal splashback; Tim had caught a glimpse of brown fingers and pink palms, slowly fondling.

Tim was lost at the food stalls; nothing was familiar, except for a few soft drinks, but he didn't want anything sweet or fizzy, The tea, he knew from experience, was undrinkably sweet, and thick with condensed milk. He sighed, feeling very self-conscious: for one thing, he realised that, despite the heat, he was the only one wearing shorts, which suddenly felt silly; all the males, if not in checked cotton sarongs, were in long trousers, mostly colourful tracksuity things. A few groups of youths, settled cross-legged on small zinc stools, were glancing at him, joking and click-clacking to one another in their staccato dialect, sipping bright pink drinks through straws, and puffing on Dunhills.

"You from where?" Tim heard the English words, and realised that the smart, trim little Indian was standing by his side. "What?"

"You, from where, which country?" repeated Bala, patiently.

"Oh, London, England."

"Ah. London, very good." Bala spoke the words thoughtfully.

"Very expensive," Tim replied.

"Hrnmm. You took your breakfast?"

"My – oh. Well, actually, no."

"Come. Eat with me can. I know where is good, my cousin place."

"Oh, it's okay..."

"No problem, I hungry, you also hungry, we eat together can. My cousin make good roti."

"Roti?"

"Yes, good roti, because using very plenty of ghee, top quality one. Your name?"

"Timothy. Tim."

"Oh, Teem. My name, Bala." Bala held out his hand, and Tim shook it, rather reluctantly, but there didn't seem to be a courteous escape route.

"Come." Tim followed on, thinking, Well, he looks quite smart, it's in the middle of the morning, and there are plenty of people about. And I don't have to eat whatever it is.

His guide trotted through the food stalls, stopping at an open place in front of a large, decrepit old house, half hidden behind broad-leafed trees. From its first floor, tall, shuttered windows, with broken fanlights, gave down into the courtyard, which was roughly paved with gravel, and fragments of tile; a mess of corrugated iron sheets supported by blue-painted wooden shafts formed a kitchen to one side, in which three or four thick-set Indians, wearing green aprons over colourful short-sleeved shirts, were sweating over huge aluminium cauldrons of simmering red and yellow curries, pouring drinks, or pummelling soft doughy balls on a large, circular black griddle. Scattered in patches of tree-shade, over the rough ground, were small square metal tables, surrounded by low red plastic stools, occupied mostly by male customers, who were shouting out their orders, demanding more little dishes of this or that, sending the boy-waiters on a continuous trail of fetching and carrying, harrying them all over the yard.

"My cousin," announced Bala, indicating a large, very shiny, very dark man with a good head of hair styled into a luxuriant quiff, who was thwacking some sort of thick pancake about on a griddle.

"Hey, Raja!" The man looked up, and smiled. In Tamil, Bala said, "Look what I found, a genuine blondie, get all that yellow hair, man! From London, some more."

"So, you up-to-no-good cousin of mine, what d'you want with him? As if I didn't know."

"A nice bit of pink. Want to join us?"

"You may have an easy job, but some of us have to work. Anyway, join you where?"

"Don't know. Working on it. Find out and tell you later. Meanwhile, two roti for me, one for him, dahl and curry sauce, and fresh, man, no old bits of leather from the bottom of that pile."

"Ha! For him the old leather is okay!"

"No, man, I told him you make good roti, and I want to keep this one sweet for a while."

"Oh, sweet, is it, with your brown sugar?"

The next few roti seemed to be spoken for, and as Bala wasn't having any off the pile, to fill in time he went to the kitchen and selected two thinner, green-coloured, rolled-up pancakes, taking them back to the table which he had had a boy move into a shady corner, and where he had parked Tim. "Here, pandan cake, sweet one."

"Oh. They're very bright, aren't they? Bright green, I mean."

"Green colour, good. Pandan leaf, fragrant one."

"You mean it's all natural?" Tim asked, doubtfully.

"Yes, of course, natural. Natural to eating good things."

"Yes, but..."

"Be tasting. Inside, coconut." And, indeed, the sweet, slightly spiced filling was intriguing, and very tasty. Bala had ordered two tumblers of strong local coffee, again very sweet, but very good; Tim would never have drunk such sweetened stuff at home. The roti arrived: succulent filo-thin pancake layers, ripped apart and fluffed up in the kitchen; small green plastic dishes of dahl and hot-looking red curry sauce also came. "Sugar you want?" Bala asked. "Sugar can also be having."

"N-no, I don't think I want anything else sweet." Tim chose the dahl, because it looked milder, and with it the roti was delicious.

When they had finished eating, Bala took a cigarette from a gold packet of Benson and Hedges, and handed it over to Tim, asking, "You smoking, or is it not to smoke?" Tim smiled, reminded ridiculously of the airport check-in.

"Er... not for a long time."

"Come, can enjoy!" Bala waggled the cigarette under Tim's nose until he took it. Lighting his own, he passed the lighter to Tim, who thought, Hmnmi, this place needs willpower. The full-strength cigarette went to his head.

"Nother drinks?" asked Bala.

"Please, could I have another coffee, but black, and without sugar?"

"Without sugar?... Is it?... Yes..." Without sugar didn't sound quite right to Bala, so for Tim he ordered a black coffee with a little bit less sugar than before.

"Is okay, without sugar?"

"It's... yes, yes, it's fine... thank you."

Bala blew smoke across the table into Tim's face and smiled at him. "So, where you stay?"

"In Chinatown." But Bala was not to be evaded, and said, patiently, "Yes, of course, Chinatown, and which is it hotel?"

"Oh, the Windsor." Tim gave in; the Indian had an attraction, a kind of prepossession, perhaps.

"You come one person?"

"Come, one person? Me? Oh I see, one person, yes, I came on my own."

"You have family, in London?"

"Well, yes, my parents."

"No, no, family! Wife, wife, children!" Bala spoke a little louder, thinking. Hey, these white men, supposed to be so clever-clever, even his own language this one isn't understanding. Tim was saying, "Oh, that sort of family, no, I'm not married; are you?" Bala took from his wallet a cracked picture of a family group, the colour faded; Tim peered at four or five very similar-looking dark faces, lined up in a row. "Now, boys having two, one of girl; first boy, years twenty-five," explained Bala, jabbing at the photograph. "I, marry eighteen, very young," he added, offering Tim another cigarette. ("No, thanks.")

"So," Bala, eyeing Tim's rucksack, asked, "Now buying what, is it?"

"Oh, nothing."

"Then why coming?"

"Well, I like flea-markets, and it was in the guidebook."

"In-the-guide-book, yes. Are many things of interesting here, also not in the guide-book. I can take you. Bala is also not in the guide-book. Haha." With the laugh, quite a lot of smoke came out. Tim coughed. Bala continued, "I, magazines buying." He laid on the table a grubby plastic carrier bag, and pulled out three old magazines, one on American wrestling, and two *House and Garden* types, but glitzier, from Singapore. "This one, nice. Inside good furniture." "Are you interested in furniture?" Tim asked, somewhat surprised. "Yes, of course interested, I am woodworker man, always interesting to see furnitures ideas. Maybe you can send to me?"

"Urn, I suppose so. I mean, yes, of course I will; you'll have to give me your address. So, do you actually make furniture?"

"Ak-choo-alley, yes, akchooalley I do, in my spares hobby time. My job is, Woodworker for Pearl Beach Hotel."

"Oh, the big posh one."

"Posh."

"The very expensive one."

"Ah, posh. Yes. Pearl Beach very poshly and expense. Many rooms having things to be repairing. Also carvings."

"Oh, can you do carving?"

"Yes, yes, carvings also can. But idea for carvings also I need. New magazine from UK, here very expense."

"Well, the best ones at home are quite expensive, too."

"How much?"

"Around three or four pounds, I suppose, that's, let's see, perhaps twenty-five local dollars."

"Oh. Very expense."

"Yes. But it's okay, I can still send you some. I work in a bookshop."

"But so good, a bookshop!"

"Yes, well, it's my father's, so I'm really a partner; I hope to be carrying it on. I'm an only child."

"Only a child?" Bala asked, surprised.

"No, an only child, I mean, there's just one of me, no brothers or sisters. We specialise in art books."

"Arts books, yes. What it is, arts books?"

"All sorts of big, glossy books; architecture, design, travel."

"So, travelling books, is also why you like to come here?"

"This is my first big trip."

Bala came to the end of his current cigarette, tossed the butt onto the ground, and, calling out to one of the scurrying boys, pulled his wallet from his shirt pocket. "Oh, no, let me."

Tim started to fumble about in his rucksack, but Bala had already put a small-looking note and some change on the table. "This time, I pay, my cousin place. Next time, you."

"Oh. Next time. Yes, of course."

"Now I take you, Windsors Hotel."

"Oh. No, really..."

"How you come here?"

"Actually, I walked."

"Akchooalley, from Windsor, is long walking."

"Yes, but for me, it was quite interesting."

"But now also interest, we go back on my bike one."

"Oh."

Bala led the way to the wire mesh fence which ran round the market, and to one of a long line of identical-looking Hondas, parked jam-packed next to each other. "Wait, I take out." Bala manoeuvred his bike out backwards onto the road. He handed Tim an old, scarred white helmet, the inside lining almost gone from the foam padding, the remains of two straps hanging frayed and unfastenable. "My wife one," Bala explained.

"Oh, won't she..." Tim was looking hesitantly into the grubby interior, but by this time Bala was up, and revving. Tim hurriedly thrust his head into the dingy helmet, and climbed on, his long pink-flushed legs sticking out at each side as he tried to keep a respectful distance behind the trim little bottom in front. Bala half turned his red-helmetted head, and threw out a few helpful instructions.

"Must move to forward, balancing not good. Island road very bad, holding tightly must, modern young boy drive like bat from Hell region." Tim wriggled forward, until the baggy crutch of his shorts touched the seat of Bala's tightly stretched navy trousers. Bala called, "Come, hold," and Tim put his arms around the pink-shirted waist, feeling a slight midriff bulge beneath. With embarrassment, he felt his penis start to harden inside his loose cotton boxers. Bala, if anything, relaxed back slightly, and they rode through the town cosily packed together.

The ride through town was exciting, as Bala drove hardly less erratically than the young kids, swerving in and out between huge, fume-belching lorries, and shooting right up to the front of the queues at traffic lights. Tim soon learnt to keep his legs in, tucking them close under Bala's. Eventually, they bumped to a halt halfway down a long street in Chinatown, at the bottom of the steep, narrow staircase which led up to the Windsor Hotel, between two shops selling black, white and blue funeral clothes. Tim was glad to take off Bala's wife's helmet, and handed it back to him, thanking him for the ride home.

"Is okay," Bala threw over his shoulder, already heading up the stairs; mounting in Indian file, Tim panting behind Bala, they reached the small lobby at the top, where Tim asked for his key. The old Chinese man on duty looked neither surprised, amused, disapproving or welcoming; he pulled open a compartmented wooden drawer, silently selected Tim's key, and handed it to him. "Numbers?" Asked Bala.

"Urn, eighteen," Tim replied, glancing needlessly at the large brass tag, "and thank you once again for breakfast, and the ride back."

"Yes. And now we go to your room can. This rooms I didn't see before."

"I see."

"And eighteens, lucky numbering, is good." Is it, Tim wondered. For whom, in particular, as he resignedly turned the key in its suddenly propitious keyhole.

The Windsor, named by the Anglophile grandfather of the present owner, still retained much pre-war charm; the simple rooms opened onto small balconies over the busy street below, and were kept very clean. Bala was running his finger around the top of the dark-stained wooden dressing-table.

"Hmm, this one very olds."

"Yes, all the furniture came in with the hotel in the nineteen-thirties," Tim told him, "I asked the owner. It's very atmospheric."

"Yes," agreed Bala, looking up at the slowly-turning cream-painted ceiling fan. "Very atmosphere. Air-con don't have. All room in my hotel, air-con got."

"I know, but this place is so charming, and I wanted to be in the centre of town. I don't really know what I'd do at those beach resorts." Tim stood gazing out at the sagging green shutters drawn over the windows of the building opposite, the paint flaking, the colour bleached by the midday sun. His T-shirt felt like the heaviest garment ever made, and he itched to take it off. Hearing a movement behind him, he turned: Bala had taken off his crisp pink shirt, and placed it neatly over the back of the upright wooden chair by the small writing-table, and as Tim looked round, was dropping the catch on the Yale lock; he came to the window, and drew the faded blue rep curtains, which Tim had never done, even at night, preferring the air, and the sounds and lights of the streets. The room was dimmed into a stifling, aquarium-like gloom.

Bala went to the switch by the door, and turned the fan to a faster setting. He took off his polished tan slip-on shoes, and lay on the bed, loosening his belt buckle; his socks were rather off-putting, thin nylonish stripes of brown and beige. "Can relax," he said, cupping his hands behind his head. Tim looked down at Bala's umber-brown torso, purple-dark under the arms and around the large, flat nipples; the arm-pits were shaved, and bore traces of white powder, as did the navel, and there was a dusty-dry patch between the high breasts. Bala didn't look like the Indians in the new, lavish book on Varanasi they had just ordered, which Tim had flicked through, thinking. Maybe India next year; he had kept turning back to a page showing two wrestlers, their loins tightly draped in yellow, standing on a sanded floor in some simple kind of gym, with another man wielding clubs in the background. Their bodies, compared with the one lying before him on his bed, had been lighter in colour, leaner and hairier, perhaps more muscular; but then Bala, though thickening around the waist, had good strong-looking arms. "Can offing your shirt," he suggested, helpfully. Tim took off his T-shirt, rather self-consciously; there was a big damp mark on the back, where it had been under his rucksack.

Bala looked over the thin, gangly white torso with interest; at the wide, bony shoulders, the dust of light blond hair scattered on the chest, all so pale against the sunburned arms and neck. He eased down his shiny, smartly-pressed navy-blue trousers, under which he was wearing the kind of briefs sometimes thought to be alluring; a central grey pouch attached to a wide band of black elastic, which bore a large oblong Homme label.

"Would you mind taking off your socks, too?"

Bala looked surprised, asking, "Is it my socks don't like?"

"Well, I just thought it might be better," said Tim rather lamely.

"More of sexy?" Tried Bala. Tim agreed. "Yes, sexier, maybe." Bala complied, revealing small, squat feet with a garter-mark around each ankle. He smiled up at Tim. "Come."

Tim lay down beside him, and took off his shorts; Bala leaned over, and pulled the white penis through the slit in Tim's blue-checked boxers, and examined it carefully, turning it this way and that. "Mmm.

Very big. How many inches?"

"Inches? Good grief. Heaven knows. I haven't measured it since I was at school."

"Nice, long, big." Bala seemed quite satisfied. He played with the foreskin, and then gently pulled it back to inspect the pink, shiny glans, which was still sticky from the bike ride.

"Coming out already?"

"No, just... lubrication."

"Loo-bree-kay-shun, yes." Bala tested it with the tip of his tongue. "Good. Me, not so big. Five inches, one threes-quarter."

"Oh." Bala pushed down his pouch, showing a neatly rounded, very dark scrotum, and a short, thick shaft, all shaved around, leaving a tidy triangle of black stubble.

Pulling down Tim's boxers, Bala ran his short-nailed stubby fingers through the long, fair pubic hair. "So much." He put his mouth over Tim's erect penis, and sucked up and down on it five or six times; "Now, we go to the bathroom." Tim, relaxed on the bed, asked, "Do we have to?" But Bala had already trotted out of the bedroom. Following him, Tim found him facing the wall, braced, with his hands spread out on the pink tiles, legs apart.

"Ah. Let me find a condom." Tim went back to rummage in a dressing-table drawer, glad that he had packed them, having felt self-conscious at the time. Bala called from the bathroom, "Can try without."

"N-no, I really don't think so." Tim fiddled with the circle of rubber, finally fitting it the right way round and rolling it down, then returned to the bathroom; over his shoulder, Bala said, "Cream."

"Oh, shit. Wait a minute." Tim didn't have any special cream, but standing on the dressing-table was a plastic bottle of Boots' Soltan, so he went back and squeezed some of that over the taut Durex. Bala winced as it went in.

"Sorry."

"Is okay. Slowly can." Tim found it slightly awkward, positioning himself at the right angle, keeping himself in; whenever it slipped out, he could see Bala's mustard-coloured faeces smeared over the end of the condom, and he was surprised that they weren't darker, somehow, since Bala was.

He didn't ejaculate, but, before long, Bala did, sending a little creamy spurt onto the multi-coloured mosaic floor: relieved that his hostly duty seemed to have been done, Tim carefully drew off the condom and threw it into the toilet pan, and flushed, but the thing floated, so eventually he had to poke it round the bend with the lavatory brush. Bala, meanwhile, was vigorously washing himself under the shower, the sudsy water swilling all over the floor, until it gurgled down the drainage hole in one corner, taking with it the splodge of semen; the pink smell of hotel soap was in the air.

Quickly dressed, Bala sat smoking in the low, cane-seated armchair; Tim drew back the curtains, and perched on the bed. From a stall in the street rose the appetising smell of wok-fried noodles.

"So, now to workings, tomorrow also working; day after, free, evenings. So day after, I come, we go eating dinner can. Seafood can take?"

"Yes, I suppose so. So today's Tuesday, you mean Thursday evening?"

"Yes. You are free?"

"Uh, yes, I suppose so."

"Yes, you holiday enjoying, so of course free," pursued Bala, with logic. Tim asked, "What time will you come?"

"Eight something."

"Eight-thirty?"

"Yes. Eight something. You have paper, I write address for magazine."

"Oh." Tim scrabbled around, and found the cardboard folder his travellers' cheques had come in; opening it out to expose the blank reverse, he gave it to Bala, who, using a mixture of lower-case and capital letters, wrote out his full, long name, and his address. Tim underwrote in his own hand any words he knew he wouldn't be able to decipher later.

Bala rose, put on his helmet, and gathered up his wife's. Tim had wrapped one of the hotel towels around his waist; as they stood together, Bala, with his free hand, reached out and gave Tim's balls a squeeze through the thin, grey-white cotton. "Ouch."

"Tee hee. Then, until soon again."

Tim found himself, on the Thursday, rather looking forward to the evening. After all, what had he left Reeves and Son for? A little foreign adventure, instead of just looking at photographs of other people's. He was very much enjoying his trip, gradually finding a few places where he knew what food and drink to ask for, going back at the same time each day for more or less the same delicious, light little snacky meals, wandering around the old town, even daring to bargain for some old photographs at the flea-market; he had been back once to Bala's cousin's stall, and had been leered at from beneath the quiff.

At eight o'clock he was ready, and at eight-thirty still ready. Probably, he thought, Bala wouldn't really come. At five minutes to nine, there was a knock at his door; he opened it. Bala was standing there in a smart, long-sleeved, fly-fronted shirt of bright peach, with a large, self-coloured embroidered motif on the breast pocket. "Room servicing."

"Oh, Bala, hi."

"Yes. Ha ha. You see, isn't it, already can joking together. Olds friend. Come." Tim had drawn back his long fair hair, and arranged it in a tidy single plait, fastened with a rubber band, the better to fit it under Bala's wife's helmet. "Where are we going?"

"To the beach, my place. Hotel Pearls Beach."

"The Pearl Beach? Are we eating there?"

"Yes. Champagnes cocktail, importing beefsteak coming Oss-tray-leer."

"Oh."

"Ha ha. Jokes again only. We go next doors my place. My friend place."

The drive up the coast was cool and refreshing; Tim wondered, Am I mad to let myself be driven miles away like this? But the solid neatness of Bala, and the approaching lights of the package holiday strip, reassured him. The Pearl Beach was the grandest place, and stood apart at the end of the strip of white concrete high-rise blocks which lined the shore. By its side, on a long strip of land running down from the road to the sea, was a busy seafood place, painted red and hung with fairy lights; really just a wide spread of tin roof on metal supports, but undoubtedly a restaurant, as the large circular tables, spread with thin scarlet cotton cloths, announced.

They sat at one of the empty tables near the sea. A very jolly-looking fat Chinaman came over; "My friend," said Bala, to Tim, and to the Chinese, "Also my friend," pointing at Tim with his cigarette. The Chinaman stood, pudgy hands resting on substantial hips, which were wrapped in a grimy red apron, beaming and nodding at Tim. A brief conversation in another language ensued, which seemed mostly to comprise the café-owner suggesting things, and Bala saying Yes. At one point he turned to Tim and asked, in English, "You like chicken leg?"

"Drumsticks? Yes, I guess."

"I order," said Bala, as the Chinaman waddled away, "Chicken, crab, prawn, big fish one. This place," he added, "can buy beer." Tim took his cue.

"Tiger?" He liked the old orange Tiger logo, and had sometimes picked up discarded bottle-tops.

"Carlsberg maybe."

"Ah, of course, Carlsberg." Bala called out to a Chinese waitress who came over to their table; she had a rather large, hard face, apricot make-up and bright red lips, and wore a very tight white shirt with an embroidered "Carlsberg" across the back yoke, and a possibly even tighter, seam-straining black skirt. Tim asked for two Carlsberg.

"_____," added Bala.

"What?"

"Nothing only." The waitress returned, carrying a tray on which were two extremely large bottles of beer, and two glass tumblers, printed with "Guinness" in English, and in Chinese characters. The woman seemed to have trouble walking on the uneven, sandy ground: glancing down, Tim noticed that she was wearing tight black ankle boots with high clumpy heels, and that her bandy jockey's legs were encased in thick snagged tights; Tim felt hot at the sight of so much nylon.

Large oval red plastic platters loaded with food started to arrive, and Tim soon realised that Bala had given him only the sketchiest outline of the courses ordered; crabs and prawns, in huge pink and orange piles, certainly came, as did a big, rosy-scaled fish, swimming, or perhaps, as it was dead, lying, in watery-looking juice. Rice arrived, in small bowls; then fried baby chickens, resembling large glossy brown frogs, more fish, in pieces, sweet and sour, and duck, sliced into a thick black sauce. Two very mysterious dishes appeared. "What's that, and that?"

"That one, jelly fish, other one, cuttlefish, sweet one.

"Cuttle... I see. Any vegetables?" Tim was not such a great meat eater.

"There!" Bala pointed at a plate of chopped grey lung, out of which poked one or two spring onions. Finally came a deep bowl of clams on the shell, and a shallow tray filled by a dark glutinous pond, out of which reached two dozen chicken feet, clawing at the night air.

"Chicken leg," explained Bala, helpfully,

"Oh, I see. Actually, those are chickens' feet."

"Feets, yes, ha ha, I always mistake. You can take?"

"Well..."

Bala was looking over Tim's shoulder. "Ha! My cousin." Tim turned: bearing down on him was an immense grin under a crash helmet covered with stickers; and a dozen gentler smiles radiated from the repeated face of the Mona Lisa, which patterned cousin's voluminous Hawaiian shirt. Another bowl of rice, and, at a sign from Bala, another huge bottle of Carlsberg arrived. As the waitress hobbled away, Tim noticed a shiny gold ankle-chain trapped at a curious angle inside one leg of her tights, above the cuff of her boot.

Conversation abated for a while, in favour of a great deal of crunching, as the table (and the ground around Bala's and cousin's feet) became piled high with shells, claws, and bones; more rice came, and more beer. Occasionally, cousin would ask something of Bala, in Tamil, a long gobbley-sounding string; and he would often look, beaming, at Tim, his teeth and gums jammed with rice and crabmeat, red chili sauce running down his chin, then dripping onto his shirt, to add the odd spot of colour to various of La Giaconda's cheeks. Once he reached out, giggling, and drew a heart-shape on Tim's forearm with a crab pincer dipped in soy, leaving a slight scratch, and a faint dark trace.

Tim found the initially least promising parts of the meal the most intriguing; the watery fish-juice could easily have been the most delicious sauce he had ever tasted, leaving an exciting hint of ginger; and the scaly chickens' feet, sucked from their tendons as samphire from its stem, melted in the mouth. At last, the cousins went to wash the hands with which they had been eating; then Bala lit a cigarette, and produced a small plastic carrier bag, which had been lying on a spare chair, under his helmet.

"This one I make for you."

"Oh, thank you." Inside the bag was a ladle, the bowl made from a piece of polished coconut shell, showing its beautiful dark grain; such a thing could be bought for a dollar or two from any hardware shop, or for slightly more dollars from a tourist place. But the flat wooden handle of this piece had been finely carved to represent a stylised fish, with every fin and scale sharply defined, then buffed to a glowing sheen.

"Wow. It's lovely."

"Luv-er-lee, yes. In my spares time I make for you."

"Oh Bala, thank you."

"Is okay. Maybe you can send magazine for me, I can ideas. For more hobbies carvings."

"Yes. of course I will."

"Hey, this one also my friend." Bala nodded to a man at neighbouring table, another Indian, maybe even darker than Bala, with well-brushed wavy black hair, large spectacles and a gleaming white shirt. The man grinned back at them.

"I think I'll get the bill now," Tim said, glad that he had thought, at the last moment, mooching about in his room waiting for Bala, to put an extra fifty-dollar note into his pocket. But when the bill came, it wasn't that expensive; the cost of a few sandwiches, say, at Cranks.

"I am supposing this ignorance bloody fellow has upfilling your head with some lot damn' fool bullshitting nonsense." The Indian from the other table stood by them; Tim took in large, ivory-white teeth, and tinted glasses framed by plastic tortoiseshell, with flashing metal sidepieces. The eyes were hidden, but not still; a reflected pair of tiny revolving ceiling fans twirled on the surface of the dark lenses.

"This my friend," Bala repeated, to Tim, generously overlooking the man's conversational opener.

"If we waiting bloody introduction, are awaiting next Christmas yet to coming, so, if I can be allowing to inform, to meeting Doctor Lancet Dass, of New General Clinic, Lancet being, isn't it, a unique t'inking by the late Dada, inspiring of renown medicals journal." From behind him came a squeak of reprimand. "Ah! But to forgetting, Mannerings are Maketh Man, isn't it. My esteeming wife." The doctor stepped aside to disclose the many folds of a citric-yellow sari, pleated over an ample form; he swiftly stepped back. Tim had registered a glitter of sequins, and a piled-up hair-do, stuck with a browning garland of jasmine.

The doctor was bubbling to Bala in Tamil, but smiling, and, as far as it was possible to tell, gazing, at Tim. On either side of him could be seen the occasional flutter of gold-spangled polyester chiffon, caught in the breeze from the fans. At length, he said to Bala in English, "So what is to make you t'inking this respecting old chappie is want to wasting his damn' bloody valuables time at consortation with you sorts of ignoramus?" Turning fully to Tim, he enquired, "So at whom do I having the pleasures?" He spoke very rapidly, and placed emphasis in curious places.

"Oh. Tim. Timothy Reeves."

"Ah, Mister Reeve. Coming from?"

"England."

"Ah! Merrie Old-ee England-ee! Old roasting beefs of, Henley and Dickens, Marshall and Snellgroves, Changing at the damn' Guards, Christopher bloody Robin going down with Alice, (always sounding so much like contaging disease, but then of course one is medicals man, so very much to minds). On holiday is it, pleasure bending, yes indeedy. Perhaps you would be so very much of honouring to poor humbling self (squeak squeaky squeak) and, yes, of course, beloving wife, trouble and strifing, has not very so really, my poppet-moppet, figuring of speeches only, isn't it, by to drop off somes-time for refreshable bloody cuppa. I would also able to saying how my treasuring one is, amongst other manifolding domesticated talents, extremely adaptable to baking some sort like your very bloody fruitful English cake. (Squeak squeaky squeak squeak.) Oh yes you are, my ducky duckie, so no use to denying. Also to inspecting my very damn fine new clinic. Shall we be speaking of Sunday afternoons bloody teatime, but not, ha ha, on the lawns, the heat being so very very."

"Oh, thank you, that's very kind, but actually I'm leaving Port George tomorrow."

"Tomorrow," said Bala, "very disappoint."

"So is it that our workadays – ergo perhaps not so very damn' glamourising – PG, is not to be so very at your likings?"

"Peegee?"

"Port George."

"Oh I see. No, I've enjoyed myself here very much, but I have such a short time in the country, and I have other places to visit. Tomorrow I'm taking the train on the mainland, to Arthur's Hill."

"Ah! Our so very blood-cooling bloody hill station, where all that is needful for relaxings can be finding. But maybe, isn't it, you will be calling by this damn' way sometimes to later again, so I must be to giving you my names-card." The doctor took from his trouser pocket a wallet, and from the wallet a getting-grubby white card, onto which had been pasted a piece of paper of not quite the same size; he gave the card to Tim. The lines of photocopied print were blurred, and not exactly parallel to the edge of the card; Tim read,

> Dr. L. Dass, Md., Bsc., (Pending), Etc., (Bombay),
> New General Clinic, Sepoy Lines,
> Cook's Head, Regent's Island.
> All Medicals Problem can be treat to Termination,
> And charge Attractive Rates. Don't die. Call by!

Followed by a jumble of numbers, quite difficult to decipher. "As you will reading, I am to sticking of olden-days favourites British namings, which all are using in any case, new bloody government names so lengthenings and not so damn' popularising."

"Thank you. I'm afraid I don't have a card on me, but I'm sure I'll be back."

"Ah well bloody yes. Mister Reed, but to be make it soon not far away, and to be t'inking of us in your homestown, London, is it?"

"Actually, yes, London."

"Ah! Then most certains, isn't it, Christopher Robin goes down on Alice, the clonkings of Bow Street Bells, Lambeth bloody Walkings. I was my-very'self hopeful one times to studying in Londons."

"Oh really, which parts? Sorry, which part, I mean?"

"The Oxbridge part."

"Ah... that part... but you didn't manage to, exactly, get there?"

"A slightly financing problems on the bloody behalf my lately lamentable Daddykins. But whom is not to be at knowing maybe one fine days, one of these fine damn' day. So, I be seeing you, or

Abyssinia, ha ha, is it, as the Pearlised Kings and Queenies like to saying, Mister Rees, and not to be let this damn' bloody fellow of lower, is it native classing isn't it, to be speak at you any more further damn' bullshit nonsense, of course misfortune no doubting mine, being not very so damn' distancing at close neighbourhoodings, although he of course reside a hovelling, and me clicky-switchy partially air-con." The doctor departed, followed by his wife, who displayed from behind a generous, mobile brown layer, between short blouse and sari, like chocolate cream about to ooze from the middle of a highly coloured sponge cake.

The ride back to town was hair-raising; the cousins on their Hondas seemed to be having some sort of a race along the hilly, twisting coastal road, often riding abreast and screaming apparently massively abusive taunts at each other. Coming towards them, heading out of town for the trendy discotheques in the basements of the big coastal hotels, came the yuppies, tearing along in their flashy glitter-finish local cars, seemingly convinced that the narrow roadway was not only one-way in their favour, but for their exclusive use only, as they screeched around the tourist shuffle coaches and burst through the black, smoke-screen belchings of the bulbous old town buses. Tim kept his long legs clamped to the bike, no longer embarrassed by the gentle hardening in his shorts. The two bikes roared neck and neck down Tim's hotel street, and screeched to a bumpy halt, with Bala possibly winning by very short head.

"Good," announced the victor, in a satisfied manner, as he dismounted, "very good and cooling ride. Come."

"Is your cousin," began Tim, looking uncertainly at the beaming cook, who was starting to take off his helmet.

"It's okay, he come, can, too."

"Well, two visitors in the room, so late. I'm really not sure..." But Bala was saying, over his shoulder, as he climbed the stairs, followed by cousin, "Nice. Three friend also enjoy togethers can."

This time, there were two elderly Chinese men sitting behind the reception counter, although not exactly receiving, as they were engrossed in the obituary section of a Chinese newspaper, which was spread open before them on the counter; from the newsprint gazed up repeated images of bespectacled expressionless aged faces, each surrounded by a heavy black rectangular border. When Tim asked for his key, the old men looked up, and stared at the three standing before them; one said something to the other, who laughed, and spat on the floor; or maybe there was a spittoon down there.

Bala had number eighteen secured behind blue rep in a trice, and switched off the fluorescent tube which was fixed to the ceiling; there was a fair amount of light filtering through the thin old curtains from the street lamps, and the coloured flashing advertising neons. Bala, neat and efficient, soon had his crisp peach shirt hanging over the back of the upright chair, and his shiny black trousers folded on the table; he had on his black-and-grey "alluring" briefs, and white towelling socks, slightly threadbare at the ankle.

"Socks, isn't it, don't like."

"Well." Bala took them off, and carefully rolled them until they resembled in-flight towelettes, finally inserting one into each of his polished black shoes. Cousin's socks were not an issue, as he wore none; simply large, cracked, dusty-looking feet, slopped into large, cracked, dustier-looking plastic sandals. Cousin was playing rather coy, at the mirror, combing up the quiff after helmet-flatten. At length, he unbuttoned his shirt, and sat on the bed; the Mona Lisa faces on the floppy viscose fell away from a blotchy, wobbling stomach. "For goodness' sake take off that sarong. Whatever possessed you to come out to eat in that old village thing anyway?" Bala poked one of his short fingers through a hole in the green-checked cotton.

"Hey! I always wear a sarong, they're comfortable; anyway, all my trousers are too tight."

"Well, I've got my reputation; I'm embarrassed. Take you out and about, and coming like that. Take it off. And what state are your pants in? You'd better take those off, too."

"What about yours?"

"In a minute."

"It's all right for you, you've done it with him already; I've never even really spoken to a white man before."

Tim sat in the armchair, looking from one to the other, as the enormously long-sounding incomprehensible sentences bubbled out, like air being pumped swiftly through a thick liquid. Cousin let the shirt drop from his rounded, mottled shoulders; the swags and sags of flesh over his bulky torso gave him the appearance, Tim thought, of one of the brightly-painted plaster gods he had seen, seated in lines in the shop window of an image-seller in Little India the day before. Except that cousin would have had, say, a blue elephant's head, and some extra arms. As it was, he more resembled Elvis in later life, blacked up with inferior make-up for a fancy-dress party; thick black hair stuck out from under his arms, and made a T-shape over his heavy breasts, with extra long stiff fringes round the darker, wrinkled nipples. The hairs grew in an intriguing, haphazard fashion, as if thrown on later, rather than growing out.

Grinning broadly, cousin removed his sarong, standing to release the front pleat, then letting the garment fall to the floor, and kicking it to one side; he sat down again. Tim stared at the thin yellow cotton briefs, scattered with holes, at the patchy-brown flesh bulging out above and below them, and at the great tufts of hair which thrust out from behind their stretched elastic edges; more higgledy-piggledy black hair was scattered over cousin's varicose-ridged, swelling calves.

"Pick up that shirt, and the sarong; the shirt will be all creased, otherwise, cheap stuff, hang it with mine over the chair. You're such a great clumse; no wonder you can't get anyone."

"Scold, scold, scold, is all you do. Leave me alone, I can't help being big."

"Too many roti, cousin dear."

"No, just big bones. Can't help my bones." Cousin hung the shirt, and roughly folded the sarong: Tim was surprised to see that it was sewn into a tube; he had never seen anyone getting in or out of a sarong before, and had rather expected a single swathe, Dorothy Lamour-style. Watching cousin move around, Tim wondered what size his briefs could be; at the back, they were very stretched indeed, and ladders running down from the waist made dark, irregular stripes where his skin showed through.

As cousin had flapped the folded sarong down onto the dressing-table, he had knocked Tim's sunglasses to the floor; a dark lens popped out, and rolled around on the floorboards. "There, see, clumsy." Bala picked up the black plastic frames, commenting, in English, "Ray-ban. Is expensive."

"Well, yes, but I expect it'll be okay. I can probably fix it back in. Don't worry about it. Please." But Bala fiddled about with the lens and the frames, eventually pressing too firmly, and snapping them across the bridge. "Tt, tt, tt."

"Oh."

"See, who's clumsy now!" cousin laughed. Tim, rather crossly, asked, "What?"

"Oh, nothing what, he all-times talking nonsense," and to cousin, "Take off those disgusting briefs."

"Only if you do."

"Come back and lay on the bed, and we'll do it together."

"What?" Asked Tim again, frustratedly, wondering how he'd managed to end up with these two, when the town seemed to be alive with attractive, slender youths.

"Can take out your shirt."

"Take out?... Oh, take off my shirt." Tim did as Bala had suggested, with cousin's rapt gaze upon him.

"He's so beautiful. Pale, pale. But maybe too thin. Is he big?"

"Not so bad, I guess, but wait, and you'll see." To Tim, Bala said, "Can take out your shorts, also."

Tim did so; he was wearing Next cotton boxers, with a grey check. There was already a damp, dark patch, following the ride home, when he had leaked a little, rubbed up against Bala's warm, comfortable bottom.

Led by Bala, the pair took off their underpants, like a synchronised double act from some seedy review. Bala was matter-of-fact, and, having tidily placed his pouch on the floor, lay back, slowly fondling his penis, cousin, grinning, with sweat heading out on his forehead, eased his briefs down, caught them with one foot, and kicked them away.

Cousin had a large, thick, untidy black mat of tough-looking pubic hair, the hairs again growing in all directions, like the bristles on an old, battered and flattened house-broom. From it, his purple-black penis grew, resembling an exotic species of mushroom; the shaft, veined into ribs, supported a high dome, spotted with pink birthmarks; it was a mushroom from an old-fashioned children's book, the kind often depicted with a pixie sitting on it. Tim watched it rise and strengthen, as it filled with blood; cousin lay back on his elbows, grinning down at it, with sweat running down the sides of his face from his wavy black greased sideburns, as, without help, it became hugely and fully erect. Bala leaned over to run his fingers over the taught, shiny dome, from the deep cavity near its centre, a large, cloudy pearl appeared, which Bala smeared around with his thumb, leaving a glossy, glutinous film. Another large drop arose; Bala lowered his head, and licked it off.

Cousin, grinning up at Tim, slapped an empty patch of bedcover beside him, and said, invitingly, "Here can sit." Tim wedged himself rather awkwardly across a corner of the bed; cousin reached over, and pawed at the waistband of his boxers with a large, meaty hand; Tim slid them down. Breathing heavily, with mouth open, cousin pulled back Tim's foreskin, roughly enough to make him flinch away.

"Gently, you great goat."

"Okay, okay." Cousin riffled his banana fingers through the soft, fair hair around Tim's balls. "Will he let me take him?"

"Ask him."

"You ask him for me."

"He want at romance with you. "

"I – want – at – romance – with – you." Deeper, slowly, cousin repeated the phrase, grinning the while; his face and chest were moist and glistening.

"He want at romancing, backside."

"Oh, I see, well no."

"Why cannot?"

"Well, he's – anyway, I don't, but in any case he's too big."

"He said no."

"So, what to do?"

"Well, I suppose you'll have to give it to me. Come on." Bala left the bed, and went into the bathroom. Cousin leered at Tim, leant over and slopped a drooly kiss on his cheek; then, pulling Tim by the hand, he lumbered after Bala.

Bala was leaning as before, braced against the wall, but this time with one leg up on the toilet bowl; Tim didn't see how anyone could take cousin's, and it obviously wasn't going to be easy. After cousin had made a first crude, lunging attempt, Bala called out, "Cream, cream." Tim went back for the Soltan, and handed it to cousin, who squeezed a vast amount over his penis, and then thwacked another generous handful up between Bala's cheeks; Tim hoped there would be enough for the rest of the trip.

There was a lot of gasping from Bala, and cousin started to grunt as he swung into rhythm; "Ah, ah, oh, ah."

"Unk, unk, unk, unk." A rivulet of perspiration ran down the centre of cousin's back: momentarily fascinated, Tim rested his hand against cousin's spine, to interrupt the flow; the sweat ran over his fingertips, which, when Tim sniffed at them, smelt acrid; he rinsed them, and the Soltan bottle, under the tap. There didn't seem to be much else for him to do, so, returning to the bedroom, he started to pack.

Tim had a good few piles of magazines hoarded, some standing on his bedroom floor, neatly stacked against the wall, and others stashed away in odd corners of landing cupboards. One Sunday evening, soon after his return to London, his mother passed him in the hallway, her arms full of bed linen.

"Tim, do you really need all those magazines? It's getting so there's hardly any room for blankets."

"Okay, Mum." Tim had, in any case, intended to select a couple to send out to Bala, perhaps some copies of the *Architectural Digest*; surely they would be of interest to someone looking for ideas for furniture? Each issue seemed to feature something on the lines of an antique-filled Miami mansion, and there were endless advertisements for swishy modem things, too. Although he liked to flick through them, it was all a bit too Liberace Beverly Hills for Tim's taste; in the end, he selected a couple almost at random, and slid them into a large padded envelope, which he sent off through the shop's post, carefully copying out Bala's long full name, and unfamiliar address.

About six months later, the Singapore Book Fair cropped up. Tim or his father regularly visited the English or Continental fairs, but that was about it, this time, however, Tim said he wanted to go, which his father was happy about, telling him that he was on his own, and had he seen the prices of the hotels on the recommended list? But Tim was more than willing to stay in a youth hostel, as long as he had the fare, plus a few days' extension for a return trip to Regent's Island, which was only a short flight away. He looked through the Singapore guidebooks in the shop's travel section, where he was spending more and more time, in the end he sent a fax to the Palmer Road YMCA, and posted a card to the Windsor, which didn't seem to be quite faxed up yet.

A few days before he set off, he received a letter from Bala; he found it quite thrilling, having read the sender's name and address on the back, to carefully slit open the thin, pale pink envelope with its border of red and blue chevrons. Inside were some folded, lined pages which had been taken from a small spiral-bound notebook, filled with neat writing in bright blue biro.

Dear Sir and Friend,
and Thanking for Magazine, very Beauty and very cost. Looking, Fall Decorator Issue, on cover very POSH is it room for Swimmings Pool inside paint Gold color, and page 326 Left: In the elegant Upper East Side town House of Mrs Reuben Shwartz, atop an Empire table with original Gilding sits a collection of rare and Important English regency tea-Caddies in the Shape of various Fruit, crafted from PearWood. Notes society Decorator 'Bobbies' Klinger 3rd and more on other page.
This is Boxes for keep Tea can see place for Key and so think not common thing ow is box Important? So I make one fruits Box maybe is also important, now is finish and Sell my Friend Doc Dass you meet already and put inside his House one. My Box not U.K. Fruits shape and Pair Wood cannot. Make like Mangosteen you know what is mangosteen, use piece of wood can with glue and also can open Inside can put, but locking also cannot. Is very Polish and Green paint top leaf also carve. Make often Box but not so like this one very Special one. Next time when coming, Doc in his House and can be meet with You very Happy and also Wife (Big Size meeting already) I think I miss a friend. Loving from Bala, Sincere.

Tim bought from Rymans an airmail pad and a packet of envelopes; he sent Bala a one-page letter, giving him his expected arrival date on the island, and telling him he would be staying at the Windsor again, finally signing it Fond Regards. He wondered what Bala's box could possibly look like; he had often seen, in classy antique shops, the Regency tea-caddies made to resemble pears and apples, with their dainty diamond-shaped ivory key-plates, and he did now know what a mangosteen was, as he had eventually plucked up courage one day in the market and bought a kilo, from one of the few stalls displaying names and prices. At first he had imagined it to be some kind of small mango, but it was nothing like, being tomato-sized but aubergine-coloured, with a thick skin enclosing sweet white juicy segments. Based on that, what could Bala have made? Tim looked at Bala's spoon, which he had put on the bits-and-pieces shelves in his bedroom, along with the few old hand-tinted Chinese wedding photographs he had bought from the flea-market, arranging them amongst some Staffordshire pink lustre saucers from Portobello, and some rather nutty knitted toys his grandmother had once made for him.

Tim was walking back to the Windsor on his first night back on the island, having gone for something to eat. Across the street from his hotel, after dark, a coffee stall set itself up each night in front of an early-closing incense shop; a familiar figure sat there alone, smoking, and raised his arm as Tim glanced over.

"Come, sit." Bala handed Tim a cigarette, and a boy put before him a tumbler of hot coffee, swirling with condensed milk.

"See, can remember. I ordering you not sweet one." Tim sipped. "Oh, it's... yes, thank you."

Bala beamed; he was looking his usual neat self. "You're looking very smart tonight, Bala."

"Smarts, yes; shirt, new one, liking, is it?" The crisply pressed bright lemon poplin set off his dark skin well. "Yes, it looks very good, against your skin."

"Of course, shirts always against skin, isn't it,"

"Against... yes." It was very relaxing to sit sipping the syrupy coffee and smoking, watching the bustle of the night, even when a rat shot from a storm-drain and zig-zagged across the road, after the hard, glittering streets of Singapore.

"So, how many days you come?"

"How many... oh. Well, I arrived this afternoon, and I'm staying for one week."

"Then, Sunday going to doctor house, can."

"I suppose so, yes."

"Okay. Finish at drinkings? Come."

Up in his room, Tim gave Bala another four copies of the *Architectural Digest*, which he had added to his luggage after receiving Bala's letter; the carpenter was obviously very pleased, and sat quietly smoking, stroking the glossy covers.

"Inside later I look." He rose, crossed the room, and drew the curtains; unbuttoned his short-sleeved yellow shirt, and went over to where Tim was sitting on the edge of the bed. He put his hands on Tim's shoulders, and looked down at him. Tim felt up under the opened shirt, slowly running his hands up and down under Bala's arms, from the slight roughness at the shaved armpits to the waistband of his dark trousers; he let his hands wander over Bala's smooth, rounding stomach, and over his chest, gently rubbing his thumbs on the dark nipples.

Bala lowered his face to Tim's, and kissed him softly on the forehead, and on each closed eyelid, before running his tongue down Tim's nose, and around his nostrils; then, slightly to Tim's surprise, Bala kissed him on the mouth, pushing in his warm, firm tongue; it tasted of nicotine, and Tim was interested to find that he wasn't repulsed.

"So sorry."

"About the tobacco? I don't mind."

"Tobacco what. Sorry I cannot be better friend."

"But, Bala."

"No, Bala is no good friend. Tonight I stay."

They lay naked together under the single thin cover; Bala fell asleep, nestled with his back to Tim's chest, and snored lightly every so often. Tim lay awake, luxuriating in the feel of the smooth, warm, dry body next to his; he was loosely embracing Bala with his right arm, his hand gently clasped in one ofBala's, and listening to the faint, rhythmic phlap, phlap, phlap of the ceiling fan. Stretching out a leg to relieve cramp, he realised that Bala was still wearing his socks.

Riding along the coast road with the strip of high-rise beach hotels on their right, Bala suddenly turned his bike inland down a sandy track through a grove of feathery causarina trees; these gave way to a sizeable plantation of coconut palms, in which lay a straggling one-street village of picturesque little wooden houses raised on stilts, their single upper stories all shutters. The doctor's house lay somewhat apart from the other dwellings, a solitary shop-house, the start of a development that never was. The upper story had three long windows with arched tops: ochre-painted shutters stood closed under fanlights whose segments were filled with coloured glass, and decorative plaster-work filled the spandrels; Tim thought he could make out moulded bats, flitting amongst the stylised blossom.

Downstairs, however, the entire facade had been replaced by a wide pair of multi-folding, screen-like metal doors, which, when they were pleated back against the side walls, would open up the whole of the ground floor. Above them, a sign stretching the width of the building proclaimed New General Clinic in red block capitals on white, rendered dynamic with black shadowing, and underneath presumably the same, in Chinese characters. Today, the metal doors were pushed back only a little, leaving a narrow central space between them, through which Bala disappeared whilst Tim was removing his helmet. After a few moments, the doctor's head poked out through the gap.

"Ah! So he is leaving you outsides, the bloody ignoramus." The doctor pushed the doors a little further apart. "So, to be come, come, and welcoming to my damn' humbling abode and New General Clinic." Tim stepped inside.

The doctor stood for a few moments, gazing out at the palms, the empty, dusty road, and the shuttered houses along the street.

"Ah! All so peace in this our vales of bloody tranquil, don't you know, mate, how these locals are like to be sleeping, now being the hours of fiesta."

"Fee... oh, yes."

"Post-prandials nappings. So! Honouring, you to braving the damn' pollutingly coast road, so heating very very. Now for our bloody cuppa." He clanged the doors to, engaging the catch, and clicked a large padlock through the two projecting loops. "So naughtybloodynaughty these villaging boy, specimen of the lower rurals, isn't it, working classes such as like that bull shifting one there –" Bala gave the doctor a pleasant smile "– leaving tiny-tots damn' chinks in your armourings and in they are like to coming, isn't it, fingerings light and triggerings bloody happy."

The room, behind the metal shutters, was dim and hot; the doctor clicked a couple of switches, and above them a fluorescent light flickered on, while a large electric fan mounted on the wall began to whirr, sweeping slowly from side to side. They seemed to be in some sort of waiting-room reception area: shiny red plastic chairs on metal rod legs stood against the available wall space, and above them hung various framed certificates, together with a representation of the clock tower of Big Ben, made from old watch innards mounted on black velvet, displaying, in the appropriate place, a working dial.

The doctor gave an impression of slim elegance: he was fairly tall, and dressed in a fresh white long-sleeved shirt tucked into dark pleat-front trousers; his several gold teeth gave him a truly flashing smile, which he turned on Tim, often. This time, Tim could see his eyes, slightly magnified behind the thick, tinted lenses of his spectacles; the pupils were a deep, brownish-black, set in rust-tinged whites, and flickered continuously over Tim's face, torso and limbs, following his arms to his fingertips, and his legs to the tips of his toes.

"The Englishmans, toggings-up in less-heating-very tropicals kits, ha ha, the Navels and Army Stores, isn't it, so very damn' cooling, but in this days no sola topee to be distinguishing from the bloody low-life native type, such as he." Bala, scratching his crutch, smiled at the doctor again.

"I suppose not. But I do have a baseball cap."

"Hal So very transatlantical, but of course, you young and priming of life will not be wanting to dressing like your bloody grandaddy, isn't it. But from caps, can moving to cups, ha ha, Cockney slangs in rhymings, and times for tea-times. I like a nice cuppa tea in the morning-times, tra la, I like a nice cuppa teas with me tea-times, me old hearties, shiverings timber. I'm a bloody little tea-pot, short and stout, to be lift me up and pour me out. So, please to my inner sanctums I am inviting, even the bull shifting, he shall come, (the doctor nodded towards Bala), and excusing not to be taking up the wooden hills-top to meeting the bloody missus, she in every case being outs and aboutings her good enough damn' works, not so availables for meeting, in fact chairings a meetings, ha ha, (Chairing bloody Cross, She Riding a White Horse, remindful of), these modem dollies now they are have the, what, flapper's vote, isn't it, but before, my little Cookie, Lookie Lookie Lookie, also was putting her bun in the oven, a nutritional plums-cake, he put in his thumb, and then pulled out."

The doctor ushered them into a small office, partitioned off from the waiting-room. "Sitting, sitting." On a battered wooden desk stood a large fruit-cake, resting on an orange plastic plate, with some generous slices already cut, a floral china tea-service, and a cardboard box which, according to the label, had originally contained Deodorant Sticks, 40 Pieces, Two Sisters Brand, Let Your Arm-Pits Be Your Charm-Pits, Shanghai, China. The doctor was busy with a kettle and tea-pot, which stood on a filing cabinet; Bala opened the box, and lifted from it a dark spherical object, which he placed on the desk, directly in front of Tim.

"Oh Bala, your box?" In front of Tim was a glossy wooden mangosteen, about the size of a small pumpkin, bearing a high polish which beautifully emphasised the purplish-dark grain of whichever exotic Bala had found to work with; the wood had been cut into vertical sections, in the style of a beach-ball, and seamlessly joined together. The top of the box, which also comprised the lift-off lid, was subtly dimpled, to replicate the fruit, with the short stalk and four sepals carved from a lighter wood, delicately stained a deep green.

"Bala. It's beautiful."

"Yes," agreed Bala, proudly. "Very beauty. No metals fixing, all woods. Now making one pineapples box, very carving."

"Oh. I'd really like to see that. Maybe I could commission you to make me one."

"Com-ish-un, yes. But no time to finish for you."

"Well, of course it wouldn't have to be for this trip. I mean, I hope I can come back again, maybe next year."

"Or stay!" cried the doctor, turning from the tea-pot, and throwing up his pink-palmed hands in a gesture of gay abandon, long, gold-ringed fingers outstretched. "So many peoples, like to coming at my clinic from bloody big hotels, (So shocking damn' systems, no singling damn' doctor between one from the other, so who can it being they are on the telephoning from the receptions, but no bloody doubt New General Clinic, Hello hello yes Doctor Dass), and they are saying. So very-very beautifulling your island, Oh to stay sojoyfuls, isn't it! So, doctor can replying, Stay! And Do-You-Know (tap-tap-tap on Tim's shoulder), sometimes, I am t'inking, they do!"

"I see."

"Yes! Because, anyt'ing we are damn' want in this wide-wide worldly so sadly and wearyings, which as the Immoral Bard himself, the greatful Winston Shakespeares, was telling us with those oldy lip from long-times age ago, is justly a stagings, you can have if you. are so very really bloody wanting to achieving! Correct or not very so?"

"Well."

"Milks or lemon, ha ha, no lemon in this bloody barbarising country of ours, so cannot be expecting, A lemon tree, My Dear Watson, ha ha, the old joking from Baking Street, so milking is it?"

The doctor had carried over from the filing cabinet a dented tin tray, printed with a view of Eastbourne Floral Clock (By Night), bearing a battered aluminium teapot, a tin of Nestles condensed milk, with a teaspoon sticking out of it, and some restaurant-type individual packets of sugar.

"No, thanks, just black, but very weak, please."

"Oh. Blacks-but-is-it-very-very-weaks, yes." The doctor poured out a cupful of murky liquid, the colour of deep red mahogany. "So! Weak enough is it, and sugar? One lumps or is it to be two, no lumping of course, but instead having bloody portion-controllings packet from this ne'er-do-well, from hotel purloining, so that one is it we'll be having, or to lump it, ha ha."

"No, thank you, I don't take sugar." Tim sipped the strong, bitter brew. "But perhaps just one packet." He helped himself to a sachet displaying the name and logo of the Pearl Beach Hotel.

"And fruit-and-nutty cake! Please to tell what you will be t'inking, me old sport, the little lady, me old Dutch treat, will being mostly bloody anxiety with baiting on breath, as resting on her cakes a greatly damn' reputation." The doctor selected a large slice, and daintily whisked it onto a rose-pattemed plate, little finger upraised. Tim took a bite; it was delectable, sweet and moist, and rich with fruit and nuts, but also with overtones of cardamom, and other spices. Tim had never tasted a cake quite like it.

"It's extremely delicious." He had some more.

"Ah! She, my little turtle-necking dove, will be so happy to be hearing. From an Old-ee English-ee recipe, passing through my wifely auntie residing bloody Colombo, where they are adding the spiceful accenting."

The enclosed room was becoming rather stuffy; true, the cake was heavy and sweet, perhaps not the best thing for the climate, but so good. Tim took another bite. Surely he wasn't coming down with a stomach bug? A sip of the hot, sweetened tea made him feel better again.

"Bala, may I... open your box, and... look inside?" Neither of them seemed to reply, or could he have dropped off for a few seconds.

Then he heard someone saying, "Open the box you never should, maybe insides not so good."

"I'm... sorry?"

"Open the box and see unfurled, all the naughty in the world."

"Wait a... minute... that sounds like..."

"Ah! Already, you are remember that damn' story of old, all that glister cannot gold, often you having heard this told... open of box to seeing inside, maybe, isn't it, the knotting of paradise can to coming untied."

Who was saying all this? "I... don't..."

"The mirror is crack-crack from side to side, bloody Frankenstein, is it, will be your bride."

"... What?" There seemed to be several voices, but not Bala's? Things were becoming very confusing.

"Is it, did this one taking you for rides? The dentist he say, opens wide, but not this one Bala box! Is it that you were open the box. Mister Tirnofy? ("Open the box." "Take the honey!") Did you opening the box of Bala? I am t'inking you opening... this one, damn' bloody bullshitter such like he is being, I am liking to be the only one to be opening his box of treasurings."

"Please... I... didn't..."

"Ah! Boxes, yes, you should be see the other bloody boxes this one is making. From one of these we lift the lids, and put inside what must be hid."

"Eh...?"

"Box and cox, orange pippings, boxing his damn' ears is what this bloody old cockney sparrer is needing, on Boxing Day in the morning, tra la. With boxing gloves."

It was difficult to concentrate, but Tim thought he might be alright if he had another drink of tea. He tried to reach out his hand for the cup, but it seemed much too difficult to locate, and his fingers had become strangely heavy. In any case, he was delightfully tired, and the red plastic chair was so very comfortable.

Bala stood, smoking, leaning against the white-tiled wall of the small operating theatre at the back of the clinic. Over his neat clothes he wore a green surgical gown, lightly spattered with dried blood; he had lowered his white face-mask, which now fitted round his chin like a beard guard. On the stainless-steel operating table lay a long shape, covered by a white plastic sheet.

The doctor, maskless, gowned as Bala, was standing facing a wall lined with shiny metal glass-fronted cabinets, some of whose doors were standing open. The room was cool, and there was a fridge-like humming; placed on the floor were several portable ice-boxes, similar to those often seen at picnics. The doctor was checking through a number of metal and plastic containers of different shapes and sizes, occasionally stooping to lift a cool-box lid, and to peer inside.

"Yes, so to be counting, is that the damn' lot, heart, bloody kidneys, liver, lungs; All of me. Why not take all of me, tra la. Oh the playing, ha! paying, is it, sounding of merry organs music, sweetly singings in the choir, tiddly-urn, etceteras, and the bloody blood. Who would have been tanking that the old man would be to having so muchly bloody blood in him, though young and primings, of course, not so damn' bloody oldie; ten green bottling, hangings on the wall, though of course not to be having ten, shamely, and then again not so particular is it green but being bloody bloody blood-colour, and then standing on shelf, so of course not so like hanging. Always to having such like demanding, these damn' localling clinics, so under-resourcing, isn't it; you, me old chappie bullshitter, better to getting that bloody useless layabouting son of your loinings drive the van, just let me to making some phoning..." The doctor left the room, and shortly could be heard from a slight distance, conducting a one-sided bargaining: Bala lit another cigarette; soon, the doctor returned, to resume his checking.

"... Oh yes, these pairing oh-so-pretty blue eyes, so difficult to placing of course in this our regions, giving them let's to hoping some sort like kudos is it, or rarity valuing maybe... perhaps to finding some other white matey with pretty-pretty blues-bird eyes, then to poke-poke-pokings with the satay stick, can or not? Can call it, to creating the demand, market forces, must be resources, isn't it... When Irish eyes can be smiling."

"Not Ireland man, England man."

"Yes yes yes, a damn' figuring of speech is all, a quotating, gross ignoramussing. Jeepers Creepers, where did you obtaining those Peepers, ha! Well, we are knowing from where... but next time you are to rolling the white mans, you, the bloody white man burden, taking care of the eyes, isn't it! Bloody gracious! Too many blue eyes we're not wanting, who can go around, one of blue, one of brown, looking up, looking down? Two bloody lovely black eyes is what we want, Oh what a surprise, indeedy meedy. Five foots two, eyes of blue, no good for me, no goods for you! So, to be taking off that damn gown, not that green isn't suiting." Stepping behind Bala, the doctor gave him a playful little pat on the seat of his trousers, where the gown gapped at the back.

"We'll be making, isn't it, the bloody surgeon of you before we are knowing which times yet, lowly-born but neatly-does-it; at least this times can passing of scalpel, no droppings. But how to stop that damn' puff-puff-puffing, always to be lightings-up between snip-snips... Ah! So disgust! Ashes in the damn' kidney-dish, not wanting, bloody goodness."

"But you tell me, cannot stamp cigarette on floor."

"Ach! Mister litter-louting, of course cannot, my so beauty

floradora, the tiling, so bloody expense, this not to being one of your so filth toddy-shops for the labouring or native classes... but ashes to ashes, dusty to dust, ifthe cough isn't getting you, the doctor must; but, being mindful, ash being isn't it of sterility, but flicky-dicky in the patient, normally so bloody naughty-naughty, cannot be so harming for this jolly old chumster." The doctor tweaked back the plastic sheet to expose the head of a cadaver, the greyish-white skin covering the face was stretched tightly, and an uneven golden stubble covered the scalp. "Ah! Where is it you are putting the oh-so-golden flows and flows of this one whitey-whitey angel's hair?"

"Inside bag one, floor side."

"Ah." The doctor picked up a red-and-yellow McDonalds bag, and peeked inside at a mass of blond hair; lying on top were the remains of a plait, gradually unravelling, the end still held by a blue rubber band.

"What for wanting hair?"

"My sister one, Cheshires Home sadly residing, always for making little bloody dolly hobbies time, so changeful from weave-weave basket, (who can be needing so many basketings), more so change and refresh, to be having the golden trestle of Rapunzel, so much changing from common-black local types of wiggy-hairs, can now the cutesy-cutes blondie angel-dollies be making, isn't it? Dolly Varden, in the garden... You are checking the damn' choppers?" The doctor pulled back his lips, and clacked his flashing teeth together several times.

"Did, but that one not having."

"Is it. Only to checking, just." Resting under the chin of the corpse was a small, rolled-up towel, which the doctor flicked away, causing the jaw to drop; one sunken eyelid flipped open, exposing a pinkish-grey cavity beneath. Taking a slim torch, the doctor thrust it into the open mouth, and poked around with a pair of forceps. "Hmmm. The age of gold has fled the fold, no shiny yellows in this fellow. But, to working! I, to finishing phoning those oh so lucky-luckies on the waitings-list, waiting, ha! cash in bloody hands, for nice new bloody glands, your damn' lazy, but not to say entire unhandsome but total lacksadaisical boy, to delivering the goody-goods, and not to be so damn' heilraising with the driving, precious cargoes on boarding... then, lasting, you, woodworking bullshitter, to be fetching one of those others kind bloody shoddy-toddy boxings you are so fondly of making these day, and to be choosing big long sizing, isn't it, after to be hurry-scurry back to New General Clinic –" the doctor came very close to Bala, and, unfastening the white surgical mask which Bala hadn't yet removed, chucked him gently under the chin with the blood-spotted forceps which he still held in his hand "– because Doctor Dass, after having long day at, ha! cuttings-edge of medicals, is wanting some relax."

Bala hiked home, and went to the ramshackle accretion of rusty corrugated iron lean-to sheds which he was gradually adding to his small wooden house. Set up outside was a timber gallows, copied from an old Boris Karloff film, and hanging from it, swinging gently, a life-size skeleton, made by Bala from oddments of driftwood and old lumber, strung together with zinc wire, the bones smoothly curved with plane and spokeshave, the whole painstakingly based on an actual skeleton which he and the doctor had liberated from within the body of an old beach-beggar, as an experimental business venture, for sale to an overseas medical college; held between the whittled hand-bones was a wooden signboard, bearing, in carefully-incised lettering, the message,

BALAKRISHNAN, COFFINS MAKER. (Part Times.)

Inside, lined up against a wall, was a row of basic lidded oblong wooden boxes, between five and six feet tall, put together from lengths of salvaged planking, but neatly finished; Bala's work for the doctor was turning into a nice little sideline. He selected the longest coffin, and removed its lid, which he laid, with its inner side facing upwards, on his workbench. Bala deliberated for a while, drawing and scribbling in a small spiral-bound notebook of lined paper in bright blue biro, before taking a thick carpenter's pencil, and, paying attention to the spacing of his letters and words, wrote, on the inside of the coffin lid,

I find a friend,

I lose a friend.

May sweetful memories

Never end.

Under the lines, Bala drew, with the wide, black lead, the outline of a voluptuous heart, not in the shape of the bulbous, wobbling, tube-stuck, oozing thing he had briefly held in his latex-gloved hands that afternoon, but a symmetrical, curvaceous, Valentine's heart, rounding out from a deep cleft, and tapering to a gentle point.

Bala gazed at his handiwork for a while; it was, he thought, elegant, but needed a little colour. Looking around his workshop, he saw a pot of gamboge, which he had mixed himself by collecting, and then grinding to a smooth paste, the yellow gobbets secreted onto the purple skin of the mangosteen; Tim had, after all, liked the colour, for only a few days ago he had, had he not, admired Bala's new yellow shirt? Not to mention the mangosteen box, and here was Tim's own box, which he was, after all, so very recently asking Bala to make for him... in a way... so, very much fitting. Bala took, and dipped into the jar, a brush, watching as its bristles immediately became suffused with intense canary brightness; slowly, he applied the glowing pigment to the heart which he had outlined on the unprimed wood, taking great care to guide the brush up to, but not over, the strongly pencilled edge.

The Sitting Tenant
Francis King

The Sitting Tenant
Francis King

Mark and Howard were an upwardly mobile couple in increasingly obsessive search of an upwardly mobile neighbourhood.

At first Dalston appealed to them. There were all those ethnic shops, restaurants and cafés, and, yes, all those Turks, with the sort of bristly moustaches that made Mark gasp with delight, even if they also made Howard groan with horror. Prices could only go up. During their prospecting, they were particularly taken with a straggly street of semi-detached Thirties houses. But then they noticed the black teenagers sprawled across a cracked rise of front-steps, while passing around a joint with indolent furtiveness. And, more serious, there was no underground, to take Mark to the council office at which he worked or Howard to his dental surgery.

Acton? Acton was whizzing up. But there was something depressing about the quiet, even sombre streets, with so few people in them. Balham? A chum of theirs – well, more an acquaintance than a chum – had been mugged there when merely going out to buy some bananas in mid-afternoon. So, after a lot of discussion, they had decided, reluctantly, to rule Balham out.

Eventually, they opted for Stepney. It was a first view of Tredegar Square that clinched it. Oh, if only, if only! Mark, the older of the couple, who knew about such things, having once lived briefly and unhappily with a morose architect, was particularly enraptured. 'I love those giant recessed columns,' he sighed.

'Way beyond us.' Howard was always the practical one, apt to be tight when Mark was wanting to be generous.

'Yes, I know, sweetie, I know, don't I know! But one day ... That's what we're going to aim for.' Once again he gazed up at an elegant façade. 'You bet all the people living here are *very* grand. No council tenants.' His elderly parents still lived in a high-rise, much vandalised council block.

What clinched the matter was their finding of an estate agent who at once, as Mark put it, came up with the goods. 'Just call me Thelma – I hate formalities,' she told them at their first meeting. At that meeting she was already referring to them, flatteringly, as 'You boys'. Black and buxom, with a wide space between her front teeth and extremely long red fingernails, she at once adopted them as her friends. They reciprocated.

'I'm not sure how much this is going to appeal,' she told them at a second meeting after that first one had yielded 'nothing quite right'. 'It's just come in. You'll be the first people to view it.' It was a house unusually capacious for what, she had to admit, was still a neighbourhood largely occupied by Bangladeshis. Period. Well, Edwardian. The owner, an old lady, had had to go into a home, poor dear, after a stroke. The price was amazingly low for a property of that size, but that was because there were – 'I have to come clean to you boys' – two drawbacks that might put people off. Firstly, the old lady had let the house become a perfect tip. Secondly, there was a sitting tenant.

'A sitting tenant?' Mark pulled a face. He was good at faces.

'I'm not sure that I'm encouraged by that,' Howard said.

'Oh, he's a perfectly harmless old boy. A retired Army man – captain, major, I can't remember. I don't think you boys will have any trouble with him.'

'Well, let's take a dekko.'

'That's the spirit!' Thelma exclaimed, plunging downwards, arm outstretched, for her vast, red handbag and then lurching to her feet. 'It's a terrific bargain. And I don't think that the old chap is going to last all that long. You've only to look at him to realise that. On his last legs.'

Thelma panted up the uncarpeted stairs ahead of them. 'He has the attic area,' she explained superfluously between gasps. 'I'm afraid the higher and higher you climb, the worse and worse it gets.'

Mark did the face, expressing revulsion, that involved wrinkling his nose and pulling his upper lip upward and to one side. 'There's a distinct pong,' he said.

As they reached the final landing, both Mark and Howard were dismayed to discover that the tenant's quarters were not self-contained. There was a door open on to a lavatory, its linoleum worn here and there to holes. An ancient washbasin reared up in a corner. One pane of the dusty, cobwebbed window had been clumsily patched with cardboard now coming adrift at the edges.

Thelma rapped on a closed door beyond the open one. Silence. She rapped again. 'Major! Major Pomfrey.'

'Yes, yes. Come in. Come in!' The voice was high-pitched and nasal.

The major was seated on the edge of a narrow, unmade bed, with a half-smoked cigarette held at a jaunty angle between a forefinger and a middle finger amber from kippering with nicotine over many years. He was in striped flannel pyjamas, his feet, with their talon-like toenails, bare. 'Ah, Mrs Lucy. Good to see you. Forgive my *dishabille*. I overslept. A case of my alarm clock failing – not for the first time – to be alarming. Do sit.' There was one straight-backed chair, with a chamber pot, almost full to the brim, under it, and one armchair, over which some clothes were scattered.

The three intruders remained standing. 'We don't want to take up your time,' Thelma said. 'But, as I explained on the blower, these are the two possible purchasers of the house. They just wanted to say a hello to you.'

'They'll be fools to buy this place. Falling down. Rising damp in the basement and ground floor. Cockroaches. Mice. Even rats.'

'Now come on, Major, it's not as bad as all that,' Thelma chided, not attempting to conceal her annoyance that he should at once start to run down a property that she had had every hope of selling. 'Well, let me introduce...'

The major extended a shaky hand but did not get up. As Howard took the hand, he noticed, with distaste, the orange urine stain in the crotch of the major's pyjamas. He, not Mark, was the one who noticed such things.

'Have you been here long?' Mark asked.

'Thirty-two years. Moved here when I lost some money through a daft investment – and my wife died. Two disasters together. Within a month of each other.' He stared fixedly up at Mark with pale blue eyes that suddenly had a glitter of malevolence in them. 'Sitting tenant. Can't be put out. Controlled rent.'

'Yes, we know that,' Howard said. 'I don't see why that should be a difficulty.'

'The old girl tried to get me out. Many times. At one point even cut off the electricity. Never had any luck!' He laughed. 'You won't either.'

After the brief meeting, Mark and Howard invited Thelma to a cup of coffee at the Starbucks opposite to her office.

'I don't think he'll really pose any problem,' Thelma said.

'I noticed that he didn't have a television set,' Howard said. 'Or a hi-fi. So there'd be no arguments over noise.'

'We hate noise,' Mark said. 'Unless we ourselves are making it,' he added with a laugh.

'The house definitely has possibilities.' Howard raised his cup of *latte* and sipped daintily.

'It's an absolute snip,' Mark said. 'I can already see in my mind's eye what we could do with it.'

Thelma wondered whether to mention that, although the sitting tenant had his own lavatory and washbasin, he had no bathroom and was entitled, by a long-standing agreement, to use the downstairs one. She decided not to. After all, it didn't look as if the old boy took a bath all that often.

'Well, you boys must have a good think. I don't want to rush you. But I must tell you, I'm showing round two other interested parties tomorrow.'

'Then we'll have to get our skates on,' Howard said.

'But don't let's rush things,' Mark warned. Howard was so impulsive.

Howard was often kept late at the surgery. Much of the decorating therefore fell to Mark, even though, as he was the first to acknowledge, he was not the practical one of the two and in any case had a bad back. There were, of course, things that even Howard could not do, and so, though constantly anxious about the rising costs of repairs on top of monthly payments on a substantial mortgage, the couple from time to time had to call in two jolly black builders recommended by Thelma, whose cousins they were.

From the start, the major was all too obviously fascinated by the work going on below him. Usually wearing nothing more than those striped, flannel pyjamas and slippers, he would slowly descend the creaking stairs, crab-wise, a hand clutching the banisters, and then position himself in a corner of whatever room in which work was in progress. Leaning against the wall, emaciated arms akimbo, he would stare fixedly for a long time before finally making some suggestion or criticism, more often the latter – 'You've got some of that paint smeared on the wainscot', 'That nail's not straight', 'Here, here! Hold on! Hold on! You've forgotten that spot over there.' These interventions unnerved Mark and Howard, who then became even clumsier. They infuriated the builders, who eventually gave an ultimatum – 'That geezer's got to leave us alone or we quit.'

It was Howard, the more diplomatic of the two, to whom devolved the task of telling the major that work would proceed more smoothly if he did not interfere.

'Oh, dear! Oh-dear-oh-dear! Well, now isn't that sad? So-o-o sad!' The high, pinched voice was sarcastic. 'I'd hate to put you off your stroke. What a sensitive couple you are, aren't you?'

'It's the builders too.'

'The *builders*? Oh, you mean the cowboys. Did I tell you that I saw one of them pinching a packet of your biscuits? Chocolate Bourbons. I glimpsed him opening the top drawer of that cupboard in your kitchen, when he didn't know I could see him from the hall.' He chuckled. 'It's amazing how dark-skinned people are so often light-fingered.'

At first Mark and Howard, who were genuinely kind and tolerant, did their best to accommodate 'Pomme Frite' (as they had soon nicknamed Major Pomfrey). They told each other that, with his innumerable prejudices, he was a figure from the past; that, with wife long since dead and his estranged daughter, the only child of the marriage, far away in New Zealand, the poor creature was desperately lonely; that one had to remember that he was suffering from a host of ailments, ranging from the bronchial cough that reverberated through the house at daybreak every morning with all the regularity of a rooster, to the diabetes for which he had to give himself a daily injection. One could not really be unfriendly, much less hostile, to someone so pathetic.

But over the ensuing months Pomme Frite's intrusions became less and less supportable. Soon after they had moved in, he had asked them whether – since his television set had broken down and he was 'too old to go to all the bother and expense of getting another so late in the day' – they would mind if he watched the cricket on theirs when they were out at work. Reluctantly, they had acceded. Entering the sitting-room that evening, after a day of hard work, they sniffed angrily at an unpleasant combination of cigarette smoke and urine, before one of them rushed to fling up the windows and the other frantically busied himself with emptying the overflowing ashtray.

Then something even more appalling happened. They were seated before the television set one evening, watching *Who Wants to be a Millionaire?*, when Pomme Frite's head appeared around the door. 'Would you mind awfully if I joined you?' Without waiting for a response, he began to nudge a chair forward with a bony knee. Eventually, unable to stand the alien presence any longer, Mark exclaimed: 'Oh, this is a bore!', jumped up and switched off the set. 'Yes, we ought to be thinking about our supper,' Howard chimed in. But a few evenings later, Pomme Frite once again joined them, clutching a packet of cigarettes and a lighter against his narrow, bony chest, even though they had by then made it amply clear that they could not abide smoking.

Pomme Frite had a way of usurping the bathroom just when they themselves wished to use it before rushing out to work or a party. Eventually, exasperated beyond endurance by the sound of water constantly running at their expense with a counterpoint of coughing and violent expectoration, they suggested that it might be more convenient for all three of them if they agreed on fixed hours when the bathroom would be at his sole disposal. To that Pomme Frite responded: 'Oh, lordy, lordy! You two spend *hours* there, while yours truly waits around, sponge-bag and shaving kit at the ready. One might be living with two members of the fairer sex from the time that you take. No, no, I don't think it would be a good idea to fix definite times. I'll just go on slipping in whenever you give me the chance.'

Soon the intrusions extended to the kitchen. 'I hope you won't take it amiss. I suddenly found that I had run out of bread and so, transgressing on your good natures, I helped myself to two of those ciabatta rolls that I found in your bread bin. Rather past their sell-by date, but any port in a storm.' Seeing the look of indignation on the two faces opposite, he replied huffily: 'Of course I'll replace them. Though not perhaps with products quite so *recherché*.' He never did replace them. A short while later, when, having for once returned early from work, Howard went into the kitchen to make himself some coffee, he was exasperated to find a saucepan tilted sideways on the range, its sides clogged with a dark-grey deposit, so obstinate that he had to take a Brillo pad to it. He decided that it was the remains of a custard left over from the previous night. Pomme Frite must have succeeded in burning while heating it up for his own consumption.

At first, Mark and Howard had been concerned about the diabetes. One day, returning from one of his rare forays to the local Wop shop (as he called it), Pomme Frite had staggered through the front door, leaving it wide open, and had then collapsed on to the bottom of the staircase. Fortunately, Howard returned home a few minutes later. 'My syringe, syringe. Medicine cupboard. In the WC.' Howard raced upstairs, opened the rusty, dusty medicine cupboard, and found a disposable syringe and a phial of insulin. Later, Pomme Frite croaked, 'You saved my bloody life. Not that it was worth saving,' he added. 'You're a good chap. Basically.' Laughter caused his bony shoulders to shake up and down. 'Even if you're a queer one.'

Did that last sentence mean what Howard and Mark thought that it meant? At that stage in the relationship they could not be sure.

Later, they were. The two of them were having one of their intermittent spats in the hall, over an invitation that each of them thought that the other had agreed to answer, when from above them they heard that disgustingly phlegmy cough and then the high-pitched, nasal voice: 'Girls! Girls! Please! Why not give each other a nice kiss and make up?' Pomme Frite was leaning over the banister, his face a grey disk in the gloom of the attic landing.

When they next had a party, it was clear that Pomme Frite had similarly been surveying the arrivals – and perhaps also the departures – of the guests from above. 'What an interesting crowd,' he commented to Mark the next morning, at the end of a breathless struggle to pick up some letters off the doormat. None of the letters was for him. Having carefully scrutinised each in turn, he held out the pile. 'I was hoping to see some popsies, but all I saw ... Well, one lives and learns. This has become an odd old world. You two have certainly brought me up to date with a bump.'

A few days later, the old man and Mark coincided outside the bathroom. Mark was wearing a polo-necked cashmere sweater just bought at the Harrod's sale. Mockingly, Pomme Frite looked him up and down. 'Well, you look very saucy in that little number, I must say,' he announced in what sounded like a feeble imitation of Graham Norton. Certainly, Mark had wondered if that pale blue shade was quite right for him, but to be told, at the age of forty-seven and in line for promotion to the head of refuse collection, that he looked 'saucy' was bloody cheek.

Somehow these oblique aspersions on their sexuality exasperated Mark and Howard more acutely than any of the more flagrant outrages. It was, in fact, those aspersions that finally persuaded them to try to bribe Pomme Frite to leave – ill though they could afford to do so after all the money that they had had to spend on the house.

As so often, it was Howard who was the spokesman. He entered the low-ceilinged attic room, his tall, thin body leaning slightly forward, as so often when he wished to ingratiate himself. 'Am I disturbing you?'

'No, no! Liberty hall. Take a pew.'

Without taking a pew, Howard produced the spiel that he and Mark and prepared together. They were worried that their tenant was isolated up so many stairs. They were also worried that he might fall ill while they were both out at work. Had he thought that it might be better if he applied to the Council for sheltered housing?

'I can't say that I have. No. I'm perfectly happy here. You two do so much to look after me.'

'If you did decide to go, we'd be only too happy to – to – well, make a contribution.'

'A contribution? What sort of contribution?'

'Well, five thousand or so.'

'*Five thousand?*'

Useless.

'He's like those cockroaches,' Mark said. 'Quite disgusting. And amazingly persistent.'

'If only we could stamp him out of existence, as we did them.'

'It wasn't the stamping that finally got rid of them. It was that pest control officer.'

'I don't suppose that the Council employs a human pest control officer. That gas was awfully effective.'

Looking back later, each of them decided that that was the moment when the idea first began to germinate. But neither ever confessed that to the other.

Howard came home early with a feverish cold and, having made himself a pot of tea, got into his pyjamas and prepared to clamber into his bed. It was then that he noticed that the bedside radio had vanished. It was not the first time that Pomme Frite had borrowed it, his own ancient Roberts set having expired two or three weeks previously. Howard pulled on his dressing gown, thrust his feet into his slippers, and strode out into the hall. From above he could hear the blare, imperfectly tuned in, of a Sousa march. Taking them in twos and threes, he raced up the stairs.

He banged on the attic door and eventually, getting no answer, flung it open. 'You really have a cheek –' he began. Then he saw the emaciated body, naked except for some underpants, lying sideways across the bed. It was like a gigantic, grey grub, he often used to recall in horror in later days. Pomme Frite's mouth was open. Without the false teeth, it contained only two jagged, orange-black fangs. There was a whistling sound of air being drawn in and then expelled. The prominent Adam's apple bobbed up and down.

Howard began to dash to the lavatory medicine cupboard. As a dentist, he was used to giving injections. No sweat. But then he hesitated, turned back and re-entered the room. He stared down at the grub. He could leave Pomme Frite there, in the hope that the diabetic coma would be a fatal one. Or else...? He picked up the pillow in its soiled case, from where it had tumbled to the floor. He cradled it for a moment, like a baby, in the crook of an arm. Then, with a decisive movement, he put it over Pomme Frite's face. The grey body stirred, frantically twitched from side to side. The tassel penis dribbled some urine. With sudden ferocity – better to be safe than sorry – Howard jumped on to the pillow and bounced upside down on it. After that, everything was over quickly. He went downstairs, put on the clothes so recently taken off, and let himself out into the street. His feverish cold seemed miraculously to have cured itself. He decided to go to the gym, where on his last visit he had got into conversation with a muscular Bangladeshi attendant. Promising, very promising.

Pomme Frite's death brought with it three surprises.

Firstly, there was the surprise of the size of his estate: £626,000. 'And to think that we thought that the old brute was on the verge of destitution!' was Howard's comment.

Secondly, there was the surprise of what he wrote in his will about his bequest to Mark and Howard: *I had expected an increasingly lonely and unhappy old age. But the purchase of the house by these two gentlemen has totally changed my life. Since they took over the house, I have felt that I once more belong to a family. They have been like two sons to me.*

Thirdly, there was the surprise that the bequest to Mark and Howard consisted of the whole of Pomme Frite's estate.

Mark and Howard, their Renault loaded with the few possessions not taken by the removers the day before, drove towards Tredegar Square. They had sold the horrid old house to a young, spruce, Vietnamese couple, owners of a successful restaurant, with a large brood of children, for a sum almost twice what they had paid for it. They had haggled over the house in Tredegar Square with its ancient, upper-crusty owners, all but been gazumped, and then emerged victorious.

'I think this is the happiest day of my life,' Howard said.

'Happier than the one on which we first met?' That had been on Hampstead Heath.

'Well, no, not quite,' Howard remarked untruthfully. 'But almost.'

'Tredegar Square – here we come!'

Mark looked across the Square, to those giant recessed columns, with proprietary love. Then he gasped, pointed. 'Who – who is that?'

Howard craned his neck, gripping the steering wheel. A hand was raising the net curtain of one of the two attic rooms. Then, with horror and incredulity, both of them made out the figure in the striped pyjamas.

The sitting tenant had arrived ahead of them.

Poison Pen
Simon Lovat

Poison Pen
Simon Lovat

Dear Paul Jackson,

I hope you don't mind a complete stranger writing to you like this, but I have something of yours that I want to return to you: your diary, which I found yesterday when I was out.

Of course, I didn't realise it was a diary at first, not until I picked it up and began to read it. It's cheeky, I know, and I hope you won't be upset, but I couldn't help myself. I have a nosey streak. It's not the kind of thing I usually do, let me say, reading other people's private thoughts, but the entries were months (or even years) old, so it didn't seem like an intrusion.

That's partly why I'm writing to you now. Having read your thoughts, as it were, I feel that I know you. What a cliché. But at the same time, I don't know why I'm bothering. To begin with, the address on the front cover will almost certainly be incorrect, judging from the date of your last entry and its inference that you may be leaving...

Anyway, I'm sending it back in the hope that it will reach you (although I can't help wondering why anyone would carry such an old diary about with them). I also wonder if you will ever read this letter.

Regards,

David Walsh.

Dear David,

Thank you very much for sending me my diary.

By the way, you were right.

It did take a long time to get to me.

It means a lot to have it back.

I'm sure most people wouldn't have bothered.

You must be a very kind person.

I wonder what made you do it.

I know I would have kept it for myself if it had been me.

There I go again – baring myself to the page.

>   With thanks,

>   Paul Jackson.

Dear Paul,

So you received my letter after all! What a surprise. It's been quite a while since I wrote to you. I must confess that I had all but forgotten the whole thing when I found your letter waiting for me this morning. But no, I'm not being entirely honest if I say that. I've often wondered about you and your diary.

I see from your letter that you are hinting, intimating, that I had some dark motive for returning it, rather than slinging it into an open street bin, to nestle amongst the stinking trash and the dead rats. Or I could have kept it, as you yourself claim you would have done. Very well then, yes, there <u>was</u> a reason, or more accurately two reasons why I chose to play the Good Samaritan. (By the way you should check that story out in the Bible, it's a good one. A story that lots of people I can think of, not a million miles away from here, should read.)

First of all, it was the photograph that you glued into the frontis of the dairy (probably with Pritt, I'd say). I presume the photo is of you? What a handsome photograph it is, and how photogenic you are, considering the ghoulish, undead quality that Photo-Me pictures usually evoke in the subject. I congratulate you. If I can be frank, I've always been a sucker for a handsome face. So there you are, that was my first motive for sending you back the diary, even if I did take the liberty of keeping the photograph: <u>I sent it back because I was attracted to you</u>. (Touché, I've revealed myself to you now, so that evens the score.)

And the second reason? Far be it for me to point fingers, I am well aware that we are none of us perfect, (only God is perfect,) but the tenor of your last entry was… strained. Troubled. Needy, even. Do I go too far? In any event, I felt you needed the diary more than I. But how perceptive of you to infer that I might have kept it. It did indeed cross my mind to do just that.

Regards,

David.

Dear Paul,

I can't explain it, and I know you're going to think it's crazy, but this diary business has sparked me off. I can feel a correspondence growing here. As I think I mentioned before, I really feel as if I know you, despite the brevity of your last (and, let us face it, only)letter.

I'll be honest now, and tell you that you intrigue me enormously. Your diary (I'm reluctant to mention the confusion, the pain, that I felt rising from those scrawled private pages) strikes a chord in me. I really think that we could be friends. Pen Friends, Pals of the Page, Biro Buddies. I'm sure you agree. Can't you just feel it?

I await your reply with anticipation.

Yours,

David.

Dear Paul,

Have I offended you? I sincerely hope not. I have read back over my previous correspondence (I always keep copies, I'm a meticulous man) and have found nothing which I could construe as offensive... No, there is nothing in those three letters (That's three – count them. Three letters of mine to your one. That's a bad ratio by any standards: you owe me letters, Paul,) which could possibly account for your silence. If I were not a balanced person, I might consider that rude.

Think of it from my perspective. I'm wandering around minding my own business, feeling fragile, (I get headaches, bad headaches,) when I see this thing at my feet. What is it? A book. Suddenly it's just there, in front of me, lying open on its back like a murdered concertina, with its pages fluttering. So I pick it up, and I find it's your diary. I go to a bar, I sit and read through it, then I write to you and send it back. Now I think that's worth a little more than the monosyllabic, jumped up Haiku you sent me by way of reply, don't you? Think about it.

I'm going to stop now. I have a headache.
David.

Dear David,
I've just read your last three letters. Thanks.
Of course I'm not upset with you.
I didn't write before because I was... away.
By the way, what's Haiku?
I know I can't write like you, I find it very hard to do.
I didn't get on at school, because I was ill a lot and missed whole terms at a time.
I was only ever good at maths.
You sound like you went to a posh school.
I bet you are really clever.
I've been looking up some of your words in the dictionary.
My favourite is 'construe'.
It's funny what you said about feeling that you know me.
I think our hand writing looks almost the same, don't you?
Perhaps we should be pen friends, but I'm a bit boring I'm afraid.
I don't have a job or anything, and I haven't got any hobbies, except I like computers and stuff like that.
What do you think?
    Paul.
    PS. I get headaches as well. Sometimes they last for days.

Dear Paul,
    I feel so awful about how rude I was to you in my last letter. I run on a short fuse sometimes. I blame it on my headache – sometimes it just gets <u>so insistent</u>. But it sounds as if you know what I'm talking about there.
    And Paul, never apologise for your schooling, it's nothing more than a fluke of circumstance. I, for example, was inculcated by Jesuits, buggered and beaten in the name of education, and excelled in the arts. If you did not, then no matter. Sadly, mathematics is my failing. It passed me by completely. So let us be friends.

But Paul, no, I don't think our writing is even remotely similar. Yours is angular, sharp as a wicked, slicing knife, whereas mine is rounded and slopes forward. I have the writing of a Building Society clerk, where you possess the scrawl of an impatient doctor.

And for your information, Haiku is a kind of Japanese poetry, consisting of three lines, and containing a total of seventeen syllables. As you can see, three into seventeen does not go evenly, but then you, Mr Mathematics, would know more about that than my humble self.

Yours,

David.

PS. I don't want to sound censorious (oh, I can just see you reaching for the dictionary there) but <u>why</u> don't you have a job? What do you do with yourself?

Dear David,

I've just realised that I never told you about the photo you kept.

It is not me. It's ... someone ... else.

I'd never wear my hair that long.

I like to use clippers on my hair so that it's really short at the sides.

It might not seem like it, but it's to do with why I haven't got a job.

I'd like one, I suppose, but I can't get one, because I was in prison.

People don't hire you if you've been there.

They think you are a bad person, but I'm not.

Anyway, that's when I started cutting my hair short. In prison.

I was there for... six... years.

Here's a picture of me.

It's not photogenic I'm afraid, but it's what I look like.

I hope you will still want to be my friend.

Regards,

Paul.

Dear David,

Did you get my last letter?

I expect you have gone off me.

It is a shock to think of me as a criminal.

I will understand if you don't want to write to me any more.

People who go to prison are frightening to people who have never been inside.

If you want me to stop writing, send me an empty envelope and I will know.

Paul.

Dear Paul,

A photograph cannot be photogenic. It's the <u>subject</u> who either is, or is not, photogenic, and I must say that you are not. Unless this picture is not you either. <u>But I will let that pass</u>. (And incidentally, Paul, I have neither 'gone off' you, as you so quaintly put it, nor am I shocked by your news.)

So all this time I've been imagining you wrongly! I wish you'd told me before. Perhaps this is an indication of why you went to jail? Were you a fraudster?

Actually, I must confess to a certain middle-class fantasy when it comes to prisons. Is it true that they all administer drugs to one another, and bugger each other at the slightest opportunity? Are there beatings, in-house murders, and hangings? Are there ever days when an unsuspecting warder is set upon by a hardened gang of unshaven lifers, stripped of his uniform, and unzipped up the middle by a hacksaw blade stolen from the woodwork shop, leaving his steaming blue-black intestines to coagulate on the corridor floor? Are there ever days when the cells stink of piss, vomit, and excrement?

Paul, I think it's petty for people not to hire you just because you've been to prison. I would. I would hire you without hesitation. But then I suppose it all hinges on that vital question, a question that most potential employers would hesitate to ask. I have to admit to a rising excitement even as I formulate it in my own mind, and write it down here...

What did you <u>do</u>?

Ah Paul, don't worry for a moment. I shall not be inconstant. I just <u>know</u> this is the start of a beautiful friendship.

Love, David.

Dear David,

Don't be upset, but I am not a gay.

I only say that because you said 'love' at the end of your last letter.

Perhaps you are not gay either.

But if you are, it's okay.

I don't mind.

There were lots of the gays in prison, but they got picked on.

I didn't pick on them because they were nice to me.

You want to know why I was there?

I suppose you expect me to say I killed a person or something. Ha Ha Ha.

I WOULD NOT DO A THING LIKE THAT. THAT IS WHAT BAD PEOPLE DO.

It was ... just maths ... again.

I'm good at maths and I've got a computer.

If you know how, you can move money about.

That's why it's okay that nobody will give me a job.

Well, not okay, but I can manage.

I'm being cleverer this time. I won't be found out.

    Regards,

    Paul.

Dear David,

I think you are disappointed that I am not a big crook.

By the way, prison is not like you said in your letter, but you can get drugs everywhere.

Mostly the ones for bodybuilders.

I don't know how they get inside, though.

Nothing much is happening to me at the moment.

I've been out walking quite a lot.

Have you noticed how the days are getting longer?

    Regards,

    Paul.

Dear Paul,

Thank you so much for the good natured restraint with which you contain your bile. So it's <u>okay</u> that I am a homosexual? OKAY! And wonder of wonders – you don't mind! How fortunate of me to have such an understanding correspondent.

But listen up, Paul dear, I've got your number. Mr Multiplication. Dr fucking Division. You really are a stupid <u>fuck</u>, aren't you? Not only do I have your name and address, but you've also confessed, on paper, to a <u>serious crime</u>. I've been talking to the others about you, and they're concerned. Of course, they're all wet liberals, charitable types, so I'm the lone voice calling in the wilderness. (That's Walt Whitman. He's got a lot to say about your situation.) Yes, it's only me who is calling for radical action.

Because, Paul, sweetheart, I have options. I could ruin your life by turning up one day at the wrong moment, which would be very messy, believe me. Or I could phone the police and turn you in.

What's it worth, Mr Einstein?

And please don't flatter yourself that I fancy you. Your friend (and who exactly is he?) was cute, I admit, but I'm here to tell you that frankly <u>you are not my type</u>.

David.

Dear David,
I thought you were my friend.
Your letter has made me frightened and I didn't like it at all.
Please stop it.
I can tell that you are angry but I don't know why.
Also, there were bits in your letter that I didn't understand.
Who are the 'others', and how do you know them?

Paul.

Dear David,
You are scaring me now.
I didn't like your letter, but I don't like this silence either.

It's been a long time since you wrote.

Are you okay?

If you need help, just ask me. I will help.

    Paul.

    PS. I made lots of money on some share deals today. If it's money you want, just ask.

Dear David,

Why won't you answer my letters?

I think you are testing me.

    Paul.

Dear David,

Is this photo from you?

Is it you? Is this what you look like?

I don't like the picture at all.

I can't look at it without feeling sick.

It gives me a bad headache, like someone sawing at my skull.

I think it's the shirt.

That shirt.

The black one with the numbers on it.

The one that I...

That you...

Dear Paul,

    Please don't tell me that my unworthy countenance has made you sick! I have never, <u>never</u>, been so insulted.

    I'm sorry you don't like the picture. I thought it rather good myself. Especially the shirt. Yes, Paul, especially the shirt. <u>The one you wouldn't buy, so I had to buy it for you!</u>

    Is it coming back to you now, Paul? You weakling. You stupid, cretinous, sloppy <u>FUCK</u>.

    I can't believe you don't know who I am! What a fucking laugh.

The number of times I've got you out of the shit. Oh yes. Or if not me, then one of the others. Why are you so fucking useless, Paul? Why can't you do <u>anything</u> except add up numbers?

You know what you deserve, you piece of shit? You deserve death. Oh yes indeed, I've a good mind to take a blade right now, a good blunt blade – one that will <u>tear</u> as much as cut – and slice your pretty <u>heterosexual</u> throat... and then I'll slowly carve you up, dividing you piece by piece, subdividing you infinitely.

Did you know that you can do that indefinitely? As long as matter exists, you can always halve it. Now there's a mathematical principal that you can appreciate.

David.

Dear Paul,

I just <u>don't</u> understand why you haven't answered my last letter! It was convivial, cheery, and above all humorous.

Listen, Paul. I'm your man.

Let me apologise unreservedly for that letter. Pretend it didn't happen. (I hope you ripped it up.) Most importantly, I hope I haven't given you the wrong impression. It was a joke. Ha ha – the whole bit.

And Paul, please don't judge me. (Judge not, lest ye be judged. Amen.)

David.

Dear Paul,

I said I was sorry, and I meant it. I realise that I may have frightened you, you seem easily frightened. Please don't hold it against me, I simply have a... different... sense of humour from most people.

Can't we kiss and make up?

David.

Dear Paul,

This silence thing is getting just a lit-tle tedious. Its been four months, yes you heard me, four months since your last letter. Now I'm not going to grovel, but just you remember one thing: I KNOW WHERE YOU LIVE.

David.

PAUL I'M WARNING YOU YOU MORON IF YOU DON'T REPLY TO THIS SOON YOU ARE DEAD MEAT AM I SCARING YOU I FUCKING WELL HOPE SO YOU SOCIALLY CRIPPLED DYSFUNCTIONAL NERD AFTER ALL I'VE DONE FOR YOU YOU REPAY ME LIKE THIS CAN YOU HEAR ME PAUL CAN YOU HEAR ME I'M INSIDE YOUR FUCKING HEAD AND I'M NEVER GOING TO GO AWAY I DON'T WANT TO LIVE THINK ABOUT THAT IT'S SO GOOD IT MAKES ME WANT TO COME RIGHT NOW OH GOD

Dear David,

Paul isn't here at the moment, he's ... gone ... away, so I'm writing this letter for him.

First of all, I'm very angry with you for upsetting him like that. You must have known what that picture would do. Of course you did – that's why you sent it. You're very clever. But it's not going to work, because I am always here. I know I don't say much, but I'm always watching. I'm one of the ones you don't know, along with Daniel and Robin. We couldn't let you kill him.

I know you won't be reading this for a long while, because we are stronger than you, but when you do, I hope that you will behave more reasonably.

Michael.

London Evening Standard, 17th August 2004

Yesterday police discovered the body of thirty-six-year-old Paul David Jackson at his home in West London, after neighbours complained of an unusual smell coming from the property. The badly decomposing body had been dead for some weeks. The Coroner reported that Mr Jackson had slit his own throat with a rusty hacksaw blade. Police are not treating the case as suspicious.

Into the Cold
Anthony McDonald

Into the Cold
Anthony McDonald

Suddenly, it was raspberries. For nearly a fortnight it had been carrots but now, just after two o'clock this Friday afternoon, raspberries. The luscious scent of them filling the packing room promised a glorious release from the tedium of those orange discs. Matthew looked out of the window and smiled. In the yard there was snow and beyond, bare wintry trees were outlined above the rooftops against a grey sky. Raspberries. In a few days everyone would be heartily sick of them and an occasional plaintive voice might be heard extolling the virtues of carrots (one thing was, they didn't stain your hands) but today the raspberries were the heralds of change and bore the illusory promises of things new and exciting.

Slowly the last pallet-load of thirty-six-pound boxes of fluted frozen carrot rings toiled up the sloping corridor, Matthew pulling and all the women pushing. They negotiated the narrow doorway into the top room where Tom and the others were racing to get one more load of mushrooms processed before tea-break, then out across the concrete, through the slush, to the New Freezer, which was by now practically full of boxed carrot. There was just one space left. Matthew squirmed the pallet into it, let the wheels down with a bump and pulled them out at a run. The freezer was filled with a dense fog in which tiny ice crystals sparked as the light caught them. Air blew fast and freezing from the fans. It was too cold to linger.

Matthew shut the heavy door behind him, then, as he turned round, there was Stuart, standing silently at his side, making him jump. Stuart was the boss, the owner of the freeze and packing plant, and he had a disconcerting habit of materialising right next to you when you least expected him. There was another disconcerting thing about him. He was rumoured to be gay. And the disconcerting thing about that was that Matthew, who was just turned seventeen, suspected that he himself might be, too.

"And how's young Maths today?" Stuart asked. Friendly enough, but with a familiarity that Matthew didn't exactly welcome. His friends at school had called him Maths. He didn't know where Stuart had got the nickname from and he didn't like it when Stuart used it. But, since Stuart was the boss, Matthew could hardly tell him so.

"Farting fit," said Matthew. It was a way of getting back at Stuart, who might or might not have misheard, and could hardly ask, *what did you say?* "And it's nearly the weekend."

Stuart smiled, choosing to ignore what he thought he had heard Matthew say first. "Well, keep up the good work then." Then he walked briskly off towards the top room, to Matthew's relief. He didn't like the way Stuart stood so close to him. He didn't stand that close to the women, or to Tom, and, since Tom was sixty and the women were women, Matthew could see only one reason why he got singled out in this way.

Being gay, Matthew thought, might be okay as long as you looked like Matthew, or like Kevin, the friend he experimented with sexually, cautiously, at the weekends and in the evenings. But it wouldn't be okay if you ended up looking like Stuart: going bald, not noticing that your body had got bigger than your clothes, creeping around with that stupid apologetic grin on your face... being forty.

He trundled the pallet-loader, "the wheels", towards the Old Freezer, where the raspberries were stacked, Dutch tray upon Dutch tray, in the same punnets into which they had been picked more than six months before. They stuck to his fingers as he loaded a few trays onto his pallet. You couldn't take too many at a time. For one thing, they tended to thaw out rather quickly. For another, if they were piled too high you were liable to upset the whole lot on the way back across the uneven concrete of the yard. Especially if you were Matthew.

By the time Matthew had trundled his wobbling load down to the packing room the women were ready and waiting. The room had been rearranged to meet the requirements of the different product. Equipment had been hosed down and wiped clean. Customers didn't like to find even small pieces of fluted carrot in their twelve-ounce bags of frozen raspberries and you couldn't really blame them. Ellen and Ethel waited at the aluminium-sided table-top, rubber gloves on hands, mallets upraised. Plastic bags were attached to the chutes. Beside the scales stood Mary, holding the jug she would make adjustments with, Diana waited by the sealing machine and, at the far end of the little production line, Peg was making up the cardboard boxes in which she would soon be packing the sealed bags of fruit.

Matthew tipped the first tray of punnets into the table-top and gently squeezed the frozen blocks of fruit out of them. With a little persuasion they usually crumbled neatly apart into individual berries, but occasionally a smart tap with one of the mallets was needed to make them yield. Sometimes the mallet was applied by one person before someone else had quite given up hope of success with bare fingers... Matthew placed a raspberry on his tongue and let it melt there, the taste of June preserved for him till January and served fresh and cold as the snow outside. He tipped another tray and then moved over to the scales to help Mary with the weighing and adjusting, for the bulging bags were piling up. "Ellen, you're putting too many in." Mary disgorged an over-full bag. "They weigh heavier than carrots."

This was the start of one of the regular free-for-alls which Matthew was getting used to, in which Ellen would criticise Mary for her slowness in weighing, Mary would belittle Diana's skill as a sealer of boxes, Matthew's capabilities as a stacker of pallets would be called into question, until... "Ooh, look at that!" said Ethel.

"Ooh-urgh!" said Ellen.

Everybody stopped bickering and came over to the table-top to have a look. "That" was a caterpillar, frozen solid in the act of walking along the edge of one of the raspberry punnets some time last June. There he had remained ever since, his translucent green body hard as jade, lightly frosted as an ice-lolly: a study in arrested motion. Matthew reached over and lifted him carefully off his perch. He wasn't stuck to the punnet at all and he came away quite easily without breaking. Matthew transferred him gently to the windowsill. "He can stay there," he said, "until he wakes up."

It was teatime soon after that. The frozen trays and part-filled boxes were shunted into the nearest freezer to stop them thawing, and then Matthew made a dash for the rest-room before Tom could finish his mushroom-freezing in the top room and make the tea first. But he was too late. Tom had beaten him to it and made the tea already. He was now ensconced on an upturned crate watching it keep warm – the old iron teapot sitting on the red-hot electric ring with steam pouring from the spout, and the lid going up and down with an energy that would have delighted James Watt. Not the kettle, notice, but the teapot. That was how Tom liked his tea – and how Matthew didn't.

When tea was done, and fruitcake eaten, and the *Sun* peered into and discussed, all went back to work. Matthew tipped the first tray of punnets and paused, peering absently at the window and the snowy sky beyond. Then a tiny movement in the foreground caused his gaze to refocus on the windowsill. There he saw the caterpillar, exactly where he had placed it half an hour ago. No longer frosted like an ice-lolly, it had thawed out completely. By rights it should have collapsed completely into a flaccid tube of pulp. Frozen caterpillars usually did. But this one had not collapsed. It was standing there on its own six real and ten false feet. It looked dry, and as pristine as it must have looked that fateful day last summer when it took its last, unlucky, stroll among the raspberries.

Matthew peered more closely at it and as he did so, a ripple ran down its long back. Matthew refused to believe his eyes. But the spasm was repeated. It must have been a similar movement that had caught his attention a moment earlier. Matthew watched, spellbound. For perhaps half a minute nothing more happened, and he tore himself away to tip two more trays of fruit into the table-top. And then the caterpillar raised its head and waved it slowly from side to side, the only expressive gesture which its kind have at their disposal. It seemed to say, quite simply, "here I am".

After a certain amount of limbering up in this way the caterpillar began to walk, very slowly, like someone convalescing after a long illness, along the windowsill. Matthew's mind began to race. A frozen caterpillar restored to life after six months in an ice-box. Was this a scientific discovery? And was the discovery his? He would be famous. He would be...

"Matthew! What are you doing over there? We're running out of fruit."

"Come here," he called, excited. "Look at this."

They came. They crowded. They gasped. And Tom, who came into the room at just that moment, joined the little group at the windowsill. "Oh," he said. "You don't want that in here." And before anyone could explain, or thought to stop him, he had picked up Ethel's mallet and squashed it flat.

"You must have been gutted," Kevin said. They were in the pub later that evening. But not just any pub. They were in the only pub in town that had pretensions to being a gay venue. Not that, looking around them, they could see much sign of it. Perhaps it was too early. Still, it was exciting to be here, in a gay pub for the first time, still slightly under age. They were excited too by each other's presence, and by thoughts of what they would do together later when emboldened by a little beer. It showed in the way they talked, looked, occasionally touched each other. Still...

"Yes, I was gutted. There I was, on the brink of... and all my evidence just destroyed before my eyes."

"I call it vandalism," said Kevin. "Sheer bloody vandalism. When you think of the money you could have..." He took a mouthful of beer.

"Of course all the women turned on Tom. Poor bloke. Didn't know what had hit him."

"And then?"

"Well it all calmed down in the end, of course, and we got talking of other things." As now, so did Matthew, who didn't want to hear Kevin reminding him any more times about all the money he might have made. "You know I told you about my boss, Stuart, and that he's supposed to be gay. Well, apparently it's true. So Ellen was saying, anyway. And that there used to be two of them running the place. Stuart and this bloke called Andy. Only Andy pissed off and left him."

"Oh wow," said Kevin, who was still rather new to the idea that two men might choose to live together in the first place and had not yet got his head round the concept of marital breakdown between two people of the same sex.

Then Matthew, who would normally have nudged Kevin in the ribs, only because this was a gay pub he didn't, but pulled his head towards him and whispered in his ear: "Don't turn round but he's just come in."

Stuart hadn't just come in. He had been watching the two boys for some time, not knowing what they were talking about but realising, from their body language and the sexual energy-field that radiated around them, that the youth he had employed to stack pallets and load lorries had the same sexual orientation (though perhaps not the same tastes) as himself. Now he walked up to them with something like confidence and said hallo and he hadn't seen them in here before.

"It's our first time," said Kevin unselfconsciously. And then, when Matthew had introduced them, blurted out: "Did you know about the caterpillar?"

No, Stuart had heard nothing about it. Matthew was obliged to go through the story all over again, from the beginning.

"And just think of the money he might have made," Kevin said, when Matthew had finished. But Matthew was aware of a look on Stuart's face that suggested a reaction out of all proportion to the story he had just been told. Matthew wasn't sure enough of the meaning of the word *apoplectic* ever to use it in public, but that was the word that came into his mind. He looks apoplectic, he thought. But not with rage. It looked more like… elation, jubilation, exultation. Not that he would have used those words either, at least not with Kevin. But could you be apoplectic with… joy?

"Quite extraordinary," said Stuart, "quite … quite wonderful really. If you should find another one, well …"

"I'll make bloody sure no one squashes it, that's for certain," said Matthew.

Then Stuart bought both the young men a pint and Matthew began to think that he wasn't such an unpleasant, creepy person after all. Perhaps he just wasn't very happy, his boyfriend having left him. They talked, and Matthew found that Stuart was quite entertaining once they had got him away from the subjects of frozen broccoli and equipment-leasing. Eventually, Stuart took his leave of them, sensibly realising that if a little of his company could be welcome, too much of it would not be, and he didn't want the boys to have the awkwardness of wondering if they should buy him a return pint.

By this time Kevin's tongue, at least, was much loosened by drink, and wanting only to be friendly he said by way of parting words: "I'm sorry Andy left you. It must be lonely being on your own."

Matthew was horror-struck, silent and as suddenly red-faced as if the *faux pas* had been his. Stuart looked startled too. He stood very still for a moment and silent. Then he said to Kevin, quietly: "How do you know about Andy?"

"I told him," said Matthew, almost too loudly. "I had no business to, I know. Someone at work told me and... I'm sorry. I shouldn't have."

Surprisingly, Stuart smiled. "Don't be sorry. Everybody likes to gossip sometimes. We can none of us help it. Only I can't let you go on thinking that Andy left me. He didn't. And he will be coming back. Goodnight. Enjoy yourselves." He raised his eyebrows almost too expressively, Matthew thought. "And have a good weekend." He turned and went.

Monday mornings were always the same. The freezers, having been shut up all weekend, were perishing cold. It was dangerous to enter them without gloves. If your fingers accidentally brushed against any metal fixture you were stuck there until someone rescued you with warm water or else you tore the skin from your flesh. And this morning of all times Stuart collared Matthew the moment he arrived. "Job for you, Maths," he said. "You're helping me this morning. There's stock to rearrange in the Old Freezer. Boxes of apples need pulling to the front, they're going out later today, and some of that carrot can go to the back. It won't be wanted for another month at least." Normally, Stuart would have done this on his own. Now he wanted Matthew to do it with him. Was this some kind of promotion, resulting from their social encounter on Friday night? Funny way to show you were pleased with someone, Matthew thought: to give them a morning in the coldest place on earth. Still, Stuart was the boss and Matthew had to do as he was asked.

Together they heaved and hauled the huge boxes around with two sets of wheels, their breath coming in white sparkling clouds. At one moment it went through Matthew's mind that Stuart planned to seduce him in this most private of hideaways among the boxes, but he dismissed the idea as absurd. The temperature was quite unconducive to sex. The thought of even the preliminaries in such a climate made his blood run cold.

"You must find another caterpillar, Maths," Stuart suddenly said. "And bring it alive for me." Now this did sound creepy, baldly stated in this dark ice-cavern of a freezer-store. "Because then I've got another job for you. A harder one. And secret too. You mustn't fail me, Maths." Stuart said this with a sudden intensity that made Matthew look towards the door. They were almost at the back of the freezer now, having worked through rank upon rank of palleted containers, their exit practically blocked by a solid phalanx of them, ten deep and ceiling high. Then, to Matthew's horror, Stuart reached forward, pulled him towards him by the lapels of his thermal coat, and kissed him on the lips. It felt like being kissed by a piece of ice. "Don't fail me, Maths," he said again, his voice a whisper. Then he let him go, raised his set of wheels under the container at his side and pulled it out from the back wall. There was something in the shadow behind it, something crumpled and on the floor. It looked like nothing more than a bundle of clothes. But Matthew did not need to lean in closer to look, didn't need Stuart to take his hand and drag him – "Come and see. Nothing's going to hurt you." – didn't need Stuart to remind him once again that it was secret, and that he, Matthew, must not fail him. He knew already that he was being introduced to Andy.

Still There
Joseph Mills

Still There
Joseph Mills

Everybody said they were like brothers; not just physically – Victor with the blonde crew-cut, Roy and his Sinead O'Connor crop-top – but in the way they behaved together.

In particular, they were like very young siblings, the kind who spend every moment of their time together. They were together at home, in the nightmare high rise they shared in Glasgow's East End, and at work, in the cinema where they had first met. Victor was an usher, Roy a cleaner. And they were together every other place: in the park, the pub, the disco; they were together dancing, drinking, walking, talking, playing games against the world.

They were more than sibling, some people said, they were like twins: one of those odd sets of twins that dressed as one and finished each other's sentences. And they were even odd within that idiosyncrasy. They didn't wear *exactly* the same clothes, but complementary outfits. If Roy had a furry black jumper on, Victor bad a big white chunky sweater. If V wore his cap forwards R wore his backwards.

At work Roy would be in Cinema One, picking up Quality Street wrappers, staring through them at the light, marvelling at the colours and sighing. And V would be marvelling in Cinema Five, Big Purple torch light arcing through the crowd as middle-aged women tried to flirt with the handsome blonde in the silky bow tie and crisp white shirt.

The last thing anybody expected was that they would let anyone else into their oh-so private universe, any more than anyone could climb inside the screen and get into Oz.

They first saw little Azad in the street, happily walking home from an after-school trip to town, Virgin bag of goodies swinging away – a *Phoenix Nights* DVD and the latest *Best Ever In The Universe Three* part 2 (olume IV) CD they later discovered.

They had been engrossed in conversation. About suicide. They had both been philosophy students before they met – Victor at Glasgow, Roy at Strathclyde – and had been left with a crushing sense of worthlessness after studying one after another of the Great Thinkers.

Each had independently, the night before meeting Azad, slipped the phrase 'suicide pact' into the conversation.

'I'm so terrified the way that the idea just came into my head,' Roy was saying, scuffing off-white trainers along the wet road.

'I know,' said Victor, 'it's almost like the notion of suicide is this thing hanging in the air like a virus, trying to infect somebody in a weak moment. I'm almost afraid I'll –'

'– do it without even thinking, like it'll just happen to you – us.'

Victor pulled his old uni scarf tighter and smiled. 'Yes, but then such a pact can only happen if both parties are vulnerable at the same time.'

Roy laughed and imitated a nineteen forties British movie heroine: 'Well then darling, we'll both just have to be strong for each other.'

It was then they spotted Azad, whose youthful innocence and cheerfulness brought them from cynical laughter to a true joy, acknowledged in the most fleeting of telepathic glances which said yes: there is still reason to hope for humanity.

They stared across the road at the little brown face topped with slick jet black hair, which was gleaming Quality Street colours as chip shop neon strobed off it. A pack of schoolboys was approaching from the direction he was headed. They were only nine or ten years old. Azad looked five years older but he stiffened as they approached and walked through them, head down. Roy and Victor sighed with relief as Azad and the crowd increased their distance from one another but then, like something out of the jungle, a fat little skinhead broke off from the pack and went after Azad, shouting when his prey looked back and increased his speed: 'Am no gonny dae anything.'

Azad slowed down and stopped.

A car passed in front of Victor and Roy.

The next thing they saw was Azad walking away from his Virgin bag, which was going in the other direction now. He was crying and rubbing his jaw. The fat schoolboy, who had been walking away satisfied with his swag, turned and ran back when be was derided as a bully by the crowd and kicked Azad to the ground in a rage of shame.

Victor and Roy danced like lightning through the traffic. Roy helped Azad up, Victor caught the thief, held him against a wall and slapped him across the face over and over, cheek to cheeky until Roy pulled him off.

'Ye want tae get us fuckin' killed!'

On a vibrantly cold October morning six months later Victor suddenly brought up that evening again.

'It was that night that showed me how it's all an illusion – innocence, happiness, the good of mankind. It showed how the world is always waiting to crash down on you.

'Your sudden change of subject being a case in point,' Roy said. They had been talking about getting married in Scandinavia. Roy was annoyed. They had been luxuriating in their favourite weather: an early, icicle-crisp but still sunny morning in a deserted park. Azad was playing keepy uppy with a ball a few feet away, the tear in his trousers that Roy had darned coming apart again, he noticed. Another thing, he thought. As well as:

'How did *I* become the mother?'

Azad booted the ball into some other boy's lap making him fall over. Victor took the ball from him and chastised him. Azad booted the ball at Victor.

'How did *I* become the father ?'

The past six months had been a strain for all of them. There was the threat of being laid off as Victor and Roy found they were employed by the one cinema in Britain that wasn't booming; and there were the constant unbelievable battles with benefit agencies. Fuck the underclass – they get free morphine and counsellors; if your head is just above water there is a legion of petty (local government) officers waiting to pick you off.

And there was the long-running feud with the fat schoolboy's brothers and cousins, who had waged a war of terror on them ever since the day they intervened on Azad's behalf and continued to look out for him, his alcoholic father only too happy to have him off his hands most of the time.

'He's fucking damaged goods,' the father told them when they said they would try for adoption – 'as weird as his mother wiz! If she hudny uv jumped a'd hiv push'd her.'

As Victor went over to play with the boy, Roy thought how, despite the consequences, they were so lucky he came along. Victor and he had been finally feeling the claustrophobia everyone said they must. And neither of them could manufacture or fake the sort of joy for life that came naturally to Azad, who announced one day:

'A'm gon' tae merry a guy as well – jeest like youz!'

'He doesn't miss a thing, does he?' Victor said.

The strangest thing was that no one objected to two twenty-something guys having a fourteen-year-old staying with them. Not only that, in all the time both of them had stayed in the high-rise not one single gay insult had been hurled at them. True, they weren't, despite the blond, seen as camp in any way, but both Roy and Victor had been the subject of the usual taunts at school, where they had each been out, after a fashion. They were used to it, expecting it. But everyone knew them at school. Perhaps that was it. Here nobody, except drug cliques, communicated. Not even a nod in the lift. Nods in the lift were positively discouraged. Here also, the nuclear family was virtually extinct. On their level there were six flats. Four were empty, one occupied by a single alky. And their two-guy set-up was not unusual. In fact the frequency with which tenants came and went was so high that nobody was really sure who stayed where: almost no tenants put their names on the door – for fear of retribution from enemies, authorities – or just because they knew they wouldn't be there for long. And the setups were fluid even when there was a long-term tenant. The asylum seekers' flats often started off with one tenant then quickly mushroomed into pairs then gangs. Often a couple of junkies would move in a younger brother to deal with whatever they couldn't in the real world – in return for the gameboys or whatever else the junkies had stolen and not sold yet.

It was so strange that people were trying to hound them out purely for revenge. It wasn't even racism – half the gang that regularly abused Azad were from his own country. So, they thought, even when we wipe out homophobia, racism, misogyny – there'll still be a reason for anger to be mis-directed.

That morning there had been more graffiti painted on the door overnight, warning them to get out or else.

'I'm still fucking here!' Victor shouted out the window at six in the morning. 'I'm still here!'

That night they parted in the cinema. Victor would be home first, Roy was on late-night cleaning. Before parting they found an empty corridor and did their little private superstitious thing that nobody else knew about. They took off each other's caps, rubbed each other's scratchy blonde heads, turned the caps around and put them back on again, like they'd seen done to the doomed mentally deficient youth in *The Last Picture Show*, which was the first picture show they'd watched together, sat on the floor in the dark at the back of the cinema, insiders.

When Roy got home that night Victor wasn't in. And it was freezing. The window was open. And there was a blue flashing hubbub below that he'd ignored when he passed it. There was a blue flashing hubbub every night there.

Eventually he couldn't ignore it any more and suddenly he was down there.

Victor was smiling. But definitely dead. A big crowd of flashing blue faces was telling Roy all sorts: that he was seen jumping / he was seen being pushed / those fucking darkies / the wee bastards – they're getting younger every day.

Roy stared at Victor's white shirt, no longer pristine, but soaked through and through. Blushing, he stared at the hard pink body visible beneath thin white and was amazed and ashamed that all be could think of was that he wished they could do it again just one last time.

He stared at Victor's dead smile: he seemed to be remembering some Great Thinker's words about the link between sex and death.

Roy picked up Victor's cap, put it on, and was suddenly in the lift then suddenly back home. Then suddenly Azad was there.

Azad walked up to Roy, took off Victor's cap, scratched Roy's blonde head then replaced the cap, turning it around on Roy's head.

'Don't cry,' he said, taking Victor's cap and putting it on his head, glancing at the window. 'I'm still here.'

The Murdered Child
Patrick Roscoe

The Murdered Child
Patrick Roscoe

Once more something in the winter night, when the cold, dark lake leaks beyond the window, urges me to telephone my sister. Lily continues to live in the same square of stucco, one hundred miles from here, where we were once children. In those otherwise abandoned rooms, the only one left, she guards old secrets which refuse decent burial, meticulously tends souvenirs of skeleton, flicks dust from bone. Apparently, she can't or won't release information concerning what more than a decade of widening distance has failed to illuminate for me: nagging questions not hushed by the silencing Sahara; an image not choked from view by even Guatemala jungle.

That unseemly sprawl upon the surface of memory.

That obscenity in the snow.

Yet my reasons for being drawn to this cabin on this shore, almost counter to will, seemed less than specific upon arriving here from Lisbon at the end of summer. You must go back in order to move forward, I explained vaguely to myself, as if nothing more than that were wrong, as if survival were as simple as a mumbled mantra. If I were now within earshot of the past – near enough to squint at the source of its tug and pull, far enough to remain beyond reach of its dangers – no single question immediately clamoured more loudly than others to be answered. And there were several questions: What finally happened to my parents and my brother? To Lily? And to myself? While summer people shut up cabins and retreated into town, leaving the lake to just a scattering of souls, allowing it to reassert its indifferent self, the aloof essence of a place not created primarily for pleasure, I delayed letting Lily know I was – am – this close. For the moment, my proximity seemed sufficient; it dissolved haste. I could thumb a ride or catch the bus to Brale any autumn afternoon. Instead, I scuffed fallen leaves in Lovers' Lane and rowed to the cliffs at

Christmas Bay and learned a landscape almost familiar, nearly known, from before. I could imagine it was enough to understand that the evening train whistles along the opposite shore just after eight o'clock. I could believe that the wisdom whose lack I suffer was contained in comprehending that wind sweeps down the valley always from the west. I could convince myself, during darkening days, that I was here to learn the shape created by a group of Canada geese against the mountains, the sky.

Only after the arrival of cold that after my southern years seemed unusually harsh, only at a first sight of snow in all this time, did I begin to shiver from some sense of a child wandering in such weather. He is nine or ten or a stunted twelve. A second mouth has been slashed, beyond healing, into his throat. In bare feet and scarcely more than rags, accustomed to the elements after extended existence outside, long separated from home and school and other children, he steps lightly through snow to pause at the end of the beach, near the ferry landing, where he skips three stones across the water; before disappearing into the pines that cluster upon Greene's Point, face indistinct in dusk, made visible only by my memory, he turns to look through the uncurtained windows into these rooms where I am illuminated, as upon a stage, and where it is surely warmer, as in another climate of another country.

It became urgent that I see Lily. To feel out the possibility of a visit, whether or not my sister's condition would permit it, I telephoned our aunts in Brale. (I still knew that if you call one, you have to call all three; these women take offence easily, like to nurse slights like tall teetotal drinks.) Each sounded unsurprised to hear I was back in the area; anyone who goes away becomes unaccountable, expected of nothing less than the outlandish. "There's no work around here, you know," Dorothy informed me, briskly puncturing what could be the single sensible reason for turning up anywhere. "A cabin on the lake," echoed Madeleine flatly. "At this time of year." Just hippies and crackpots and people who don't curl would make such a choice, then pretend it was the superior option. "Sure she'd love to see you," Kay decided doubtfully, giving me Lily's number.

That was November. Now it's January. I've been to Brale and I've seen Lily and nothing has been uncovered by the experience. Or has it? There is this: at morning now a child's footprints, sometimes confused by tracks of deer and bear, lead to and from the cabin windows. There is a handful of pumpkin seeds, twisted within a scrap of silver paper, in my mailbox beside the road at noon. There is something in the bitter night, when the ferry becomes a glide of lights across black water, that every week or so insists, despite what did or did not recently occur between us, that I call my sister.

This is never a simple matter. Often Lily allows her telephone to ring unanswered, I suspect; or she disconnects the cord, forgets for days it is not plugged in. Maybe a recorded voice informs me that her number is not in service. For reasons I can' t guess, Lily frequently changes or temporarily cancels or unlists her number. Worried, I will consider then decide against calling the Brale aunts; though the town they inhabit with my sister is small, they would not necessarily know if she is all right. By her choice, and to the aunt's injured puzzlement, they don't see Lily often. I am left to check periodically with directory assistance until a new number appears under – and this always startles me – our shared last name.

It has never been easy to reach my sister.

If she does happen to lift the receiver tonight, Lily won't speak first. Like a secret agent trained never to reveal herself to a possible enemy, she waits silently for the caller to identify himself. Learning this is only me doesn't ease her suspicion; nothing like a conversation follows. She is well, the house is fine, the weather is not unusual for this time of year. No, she hasn't been away. Yes, her number has changed. She won't ask how I am or what I am doing. She won't refer to November's meeting. She does not call me herself.

My sister has grown even more guarded than the child who concealed herself behind impassive features and covert movement and silence. I spent my first sixteen years living with Lily without fathoming how she felt or what she thought. I wasn't alone in ignorance; my older brother, MJ, and my parents, Ardis and Mitch, were also uncertain why Lily's bed yawned on summer dawns, who she met on the mountain in spring, where she went on winter nights as cold and dark as this night that conceals the answer to a question, the identity of a corpse.

*

Lily finds him on the mountain when the November world is frozen and stiff, still unsoftened by snow, five months before we will search for pussy willows and dam trickles of April thaw. "Come," she says, materializing in the doorway of the furnace room, wearing a grey felt coat, several sizes too large, that looks unfamiliar. Lily has stolen it from a house on the other side of Brale or from the change room at the skating rink. In my dim cave carved out of discarded furniture and abused boxes, and of hockey sticks that belonged to an uncle from whom I inherited my first name and sharp features and fear of smoke, I look up from the letter I am composing to Jesus. The furnace switches on; the pilot light hisses blue. The house suspends itself in uneasy Saturday quiet: Ardis engages in a series of naps in the big bedroom upstairs; Mitch shuts himself in his study across the basement; and MJ always spends the weekends with television and treats at Aunt Madeleine's, by the river. "Come," my sister repeats, in neither command nor invitation. Lily's speech is generally uninflected; little emphasis lies behind her words to lend them shade or nuance. Her communication is blunt and flat as that of cardboard Indians in the westerns Mitch drags us to see at the Royal Theatre, where from the front row he watches John Wayne, another simple man, with wide, admiring eyes.

"Hurry," says Lily, beckoning with one reddened hand. She always loses the mittens our concerned aunts bestow on her; it would surprise Lily to have this pointed out. She doesn't seem to feel the cold, and in winter roams unfettered by hats or scarfs. Lily has been outside all morning, I can tell: waves of dark chill pulse from her direction. She knows a way of leaving the house unnoticed; only half way through a weekend afternoon, or long after the streetlamps blink on, does her absence cause remark. Where does she go? Mitch and Ardis don't ask; it's better not to. They accept that Lily lies as lightly as she breathes. "She's different," our aunts describe my sister, using the catch-all adjective applied in Brale to harmless eccentrics and non-practising homosexuals and tentative pedophiles, and to a thin girl of twelve who goes where she wishes, takes what she needs.

Unsettled by Lily's rare summons, I emerge from the back of the furnace room. I believed my hiding place, amid the asphyxia of oil and dust, to be a secret shared only with my buried uncle; but Lily always knows where to find me. Even after my sister stops looking for me, even during all the years when across the globe I cover myself beneath heavy blankets of time and distance, Lily knows where I am.

*

On a late November afternoon I walk down Aster Drive, toward my fist meeting with Lily in fifteen years. During my two brief visits to Brale in the early eighties, while she was enclosed in the hospital on the hill, Lily would not see me. The lingering power of those refusals, and the weight of all the years since then, made me nervous dialling her number from the cabin. When I stated my name, a long silence ensued. "Donald," I repeated. Fumbling with words that received little response, I tried to believe that the awkwardness of the call came from our not having spoken for so long. "If you want," Lily met my suggestion that I visit for several days.

My single small light suitcase that brims with questions concerning what happened to my parents and brother while I was embracing distance. My knowledge of their fates has been gleaned from what lay behind and between the lines of several letters from the aunts: there is much I don't know, much that perhaps only Lily can tell me. Did she ever hear from Mitch and MJ, anything at all, after they disappeared from Brale? Was Ardis's death easier than her life? And how has Lily managed to hang on?

Approaching the house, I wonder if I'll learn anything inside it after all. It looks small, old, worn. A modest single-storey structure, similar to others on the block, with a bare front yard and a vacant driveway. Though dusk has not fallen, the curtains are closed. I ring the doorbell, then touch it again when no one answers. Has Lily forgotten about my visit? As I am about to test the door, it opens.

She wears a grey skirt, white blouse and dark sweater. The clothes are cut simply, like a uniform, and look home-made. No jewellery adorns them. Though she is only thirty-three, two years older than myself, Lily's dark hair has turned mostly grey. The neat bun folds above a pale face that, once sharp, appears puffy, perhaps from medication. The lines and angles of her body have also blurred, but with no concession to softness. She would feel stiff and cold in my arms, I suspect. Her grey eyes loom unusually pale behind thick glasses; they don't blink when I say hello. Glancing at my suitcase, she turns and retreats down the dim hall. It strikes me that each of her steps is measured to cover precisely the same distance.

Taken aback by her lack of greeting, then recalling her distaste for words, I follow my sister inside. She pauses, partly turns. "You can sleep in your old room," she says in a voice as toneless as ever, though pitched lower now. "There are sheets on the bed. Supper is at six."

Perhaps because she didn't initiate this visit, Lily continues with the housework it has interrupted, as though she doesn't have a guest. The living room she dusts appears painfully tidy and clean already. I notice that old furniture retains its old arrangement. The room that belonged to our parents is shut, like Lily's across the hall. Curtains from my childhood have faded in swaths, paths betray where the carpet has been paced. If the walls were ever repainted, it was with the same colour as before. Turning on the back left burner of the stove, I place my hand above it. The element still doesn't work.

"Yes," says Lily, not looking up from her work when I mention that the house appears the same. "No," she says when I ask if I can help with supper. I linger nearby for a moment. I don't know how to give Lily the present in my suitcase. It's a book about what I imagined happened to us all.

Descending to the basement, I place my luggage on one of the twin beds in the room I shared with MJ, then glance into the furnace room. It is still crowded with broken tools and rusted skates, and with empty jars that hold breath beneath a film of dust. The scent of oil twines around my head, shuts my eyes. As if a finger of bone traces my spine, I shudder. Across in Mitch's study, out-dated history texts weigh the shelves and the manual Olivetti squats on the wide desk. Avoiding a sharp, exposed spring in its corner, I curl up on the rumpus room couch that reigned upstairs until a new one replaced it. At card-table islands, MJ, Lily and I bent over homework in this sunken space, while

Ardis lurched through hours above and in his study Mitch toiled at his memoirs. Although their title was A Simple Man, my father was not blessed with a sense of irony.

"It's time to eat," Lily calls down the stairs.

The kitchen table is set with two plates, two forks and two glasses of water. Lily serves a casserole made with macaroni and tuna; soft and bland, a child would enjoy it. Her eyes focused on the wall behind me, Lily eats steadily. She pauses only to sip water and to respond briefly to my tentative remarks. The neighbours to the left have moved; she doesn't know who lives there now. Yes, downtown Brale has changed. No thank you, she prefers to clear the kitchen herself; she knows where everything belongs. Her movements before the counter appear carefully considered and executed; each hints of an obscure ritual, an invisible significance. I realize how difficult it will be to ask the questions that have brought me here. Her back still turned to me, her hands plunged into scalding water, Lily lets her shoulders loosen, then sag. Steam appears to rise from her body, drift from her skin; it lingers around her head. Lily stands before the sink as if she has forgotten what she is doing or where she is. The tap drips a persistent reminder. Abruptly, Lily's back stiffens again. She pulls the plug, shakes her hands, dries them on a tea towel. "I expect you're tired from your trip," she says, her back still facing me. "Good night."

She turns the corner of the hall toward her bedroom. Or does she sleep in our parents' room now? Water runs in the adjacent bathroom. A door opens, then closes. It is seven o'clock.

What have I expected? What do I deserve? To be eagerly welcomed as the long-lost brother? To be greeted with open arms? Yes, Lily, I am tired from my trip. My trip has been longer than a hundred miles from a cabin on a lake, I hadn't realized how long my trip has been until circling back to where it began, it's been too goddamned long and it isn't over yet, not by a long shot, not by half. I grimace at my reflection floating on the kitchen window. Though I can't see through my image, I know a maple tree, bare at this time of year, rises half way across the back yard. Beyond the fence runs another row of single-storey houses; past that, the highway. Then the mountain looms jagged and forbidding, scantily clad even during summer, splintering the chemical sky. Sometimes we tried to reach the top to discover what lay on the further side. But we never could conquer the peak; the slope was too treacherous, too steep. "I'll reach it without you," Lily said, after the last time she allowed me to attempt the ascent with her; before she began, at twelve, to scramble alone upon the mountain, along the cold, swift river.

No. Not quite the last time. There was at least one more time. Yes. A November Saturday.

Something like a scrap of paper stirs in a dark room in my mind.

The house stands silent. Has Lily already gone to sleep or does her light still burn? She lies on her narrow mattress and looks upward through the dark? Or tosses in the wide bed where Ardis sweated pills, where Mitch planned escape. I am tempted to steal down the hall and look for a stripe of light beneath a door, then remember that several floorboards creak.

All I know is that, after the age of nineteen, Lily passed in and out of the psychiatric unit of the Brale Regional Hospital earlier haunted by our mother. I know only that, five years ago, she was permanently released. From what I understand, Lily doesn't have a job or own a car or visit our nearby aunts. Though everyone in Brale knows everyone, she is without friends. There has never been a lover. Solitude and the quiet of this house may be essential for her stability. She may be unable, rather than unwilling, to answer questions. It may be wrong to remind her of the past. It may be necessary for her to forget.

Downstairs, I sift Mitch's study for his memoirs, without hope. Failing to discover the manuscript during my pair of Brale visits, a dozen years ago, I was convinced that Mitch had destroyed or taken with him his story upon vanishing in 1978. I inspect the basement bedroom for evidence of MJ's childhood: baseball mitts, model planes, unblinking eyes of marbles. Though his transformation into thin air was apparently less carefully planned than my father's, nothing telling remains behind of MJ, either. Yet I recall that on my previous returns at least some souvenirs of my brother had survived.

The house is the same, yes, but with a difference. Every significant artifact, all momentos of the presences which abandoned it, have been scrupulously removed. Hidden away or destroyed. Closing my eyes, I envision Lily methodically clearing out closets and drawers, carefully wiping fingerprints from surfaces, stripping space of evidence until only the intangible secrets remain. In the back yard, she stands before a bonfire, unflinching when flames leap at her face, inhaling smoke while wisps of ash snow upon her head. With a stick she stirs the coals, prods their hiss, makes the red eyes blink sparks.

I lift my opened eyes to the narrow window set high in the wall, above MJ's bed, at the level of the ground.

It lies out there, in the cold, dark night, the question I need answered.

It's not a question concerning Ardis, Mitch or MJ, after all.

Hours later, finally sliding into sleep, I'm disturbed by a known sound from above. The click of the front door. My watch glows three o'clock. I push away sleep and wait for Lily to return. Didn't she always come home eventually, when we were children, when we saw the truth?

*

The child stands above my bed of frozen earth and jabs a stick. "He can't feel anything," she informs the presence that hovers behind her. The point of the stick presses against my bared belly, seeks to pierce the skin, gain entry to entrails. The child pokes harder with her tool, she wants to see inside. The grey felt coat flaps from her effort; the sharp face frowns. She is angry that I don't cry, moan, plead for her to stop. My eyes refuse to close against the intent face above. My gashed throat grimaces. A bubble bursts from my blue lips, escapes into the sky. "His name is Billy," she says, dropping the stick and turning away. The pulsing shadow leaves her, nears me, bends low. Its warm hand, the same size and shape as mine, strokes my stone cheek. Scented breath urges me to speak.

*

At the kitchen table, Lily bows her head before a cup of coffee.

"Good morning," I say, foggily filling a mug. My hands wrap around its heat. I'm cold, despite the groaning furnace. Though it is early, I feel I've slept too long, too deeply. I can't remember hearing

Lily return last night. She wears the same neat skirt, blouse and sweater as yesterday. Has she been to bed at all?

"Did you sleep well?" I stare at the scars. The one on her right wrist is thicker than the other. She did it in the back of the furnace room, Aunt Dorothy wrote me at the time. Ardis found her; the rest of us had left Brale by then. Come, my uncle summoned Lily in the blue basement light. Dig deeper, he urged. See what's inside.

"Yes," replies Lily, rising from the table and leaving the kitchen. After a moment, the front door opens then closes. I move to the living room and part the curtains. Without a coat, Lily passes slowly beneath a slate sky, between the frosted yards.

The house has to tell me something that Lily can't or won't. I open the door to our parents' room. Obviously, Lily hasn't made it her own; the wide mattress below the spread lacks linen. Nothing litters the dressing table; the closets and bureau prove bare. The adjacent bathroom contains toothbrush and paste, soap and towel. The medicine chest holds several full vials of pills, with a prescription made out to Lily several years ago. Chlorpromazine. Across the hall, Lily's old room is uncluttered as a nun's; even during her childhood, it lacked girlish touches. The narrow bed is neatly made. A Bible rests on the night table. One drawer contains underwear; like the closets, the rest are empty. Not even a small, white valise, locked tight, lurks anywhere.

Wandering back to the living room, I realize with fresh force that it has no television or music system, no framed photographs or magazines or books. A small radio perches on the mantel. Turning the switch, I find it tuned to static. The buzzing seems to rise in volume inside me. It says that these curtains upon the street are never opened. The telephone and doorbell rarely ring. My sister wears the same clothes and eats the same bland food each day, and late at night walks to the same dark place.

She lives simply, that's all. Not everyone hoards old photographs and love letters, torn ticket stubs and tattered maps. Lily exists on a monthly government cheque that is probably not enough. She can't afford sleek machines and the latest gadgets and an extra pair of shoes. Apparently, she no longer takes what she needs. Or no longer needs.

I move toward the old-fashioned rotary telephone. Aunt Madeleine expects me to visit today. In her house by the river, we will sip tea and nibble cake and skim lightly over the past and present. Lily will be mentioned cautiously, if at all. We will visit Ardis's grave in the cemetery where my uncle also shivers. We will drop in on Dorothy and Kay, end up playing dice and cards for change. (When I went out into the world at sixteen, the single piece of advice offered me, by Dorothy, was to bring a deck of cards along: everyone likes to play; it's the best way to meet people; you'll never be lonely.) I'll catch my aunts peering at me sideways for clues to how their younger brother would have looked as an adult. I won't ask them if they remember the murder of a child more than twenty years ago. I know their resentful answer already. Children have never been murdered in Brale, BC.

*

"This way," she says over her shoulder, walking quickly. Where are we going, Lily? She won't wait for me, I know. I hurry to follow her across the highway and through brush on the mountain's base. Lily threads her way surely up the lower slope. Her breath puffs signals that vanish before I can read them.

My sister stops in a narrow gully and bows her head toward the ground.

What is it?

I don't want to see, don't want to know.

"Look," says Lily.

A boy. There's something wrong with him. He's wearing only running shoes and socks. The left shoe is torn at the toe; green peeks out. It's cold, he should be dressed, why didn't we bring him a shirt and pants? My drawers are filled with clothes that would fit him, he's the same size and shape as me, nine or ten or a stunted twelve.

Something else is wrong. His throat shouldn't look like that.

A second, messy mouth. Torn lips caked with rust.

"Who is he?" I ask Lily. I don't recognize him. I haven't seen him among the boys who yelp like wild dogs across the schoolyard. Maybe he goes to the Catholic school with the Italians, lives up in the Gulch or down in one of the shacks on the river flats.

"His name is Billy," says my sister, poking his stomach with a stick.

His hands curl around something that isn't there. His legs twist at odd angles and dirt sticks to his white chest. He stares at Lily as she jabs the stick. He won't close his eyes, he won't cry. His lips are blue. He must have been eating berries, no, that's not right, berries don't grow on the mountain in November, we slather their juice in July.

"He doesn't feel anything." Lily drops the stick. She turns and faces me.

"He's mine," she says.

I bend over the boy and touch his face. Cold skin tingles my hand.

"It's going to snow," Lily says behind me. "It's going to get dark."

"Billy," I breathe. "It's time to go home."

*

After my walk from Aunt Madeleine's, the house seems very warm. It feels empty, though something is baking in the oven.

A muffled thud sounds from below. Steps ascend the stairs. Lily walks past me and opens the oven. "Greetings from the aunts," I say, attempting lightness. Silent, Lily peers into the dark cave barred with glowing light.

Downstairs, I throw my coat onto MJ's bed, where the few contents of my suitcase are strewn. I start to leave the room, turn back. Is something different about the things on the bed? In their appearance? Arrangement? The book I brought Lily is gone. I search the space, even kneel to look beneath the bed, without success.

"It's time to eat," Lily calls down the stairs.

We have the same supper as the night before. I suggest we see the movie at the Royal Theatre. "We'll sit in the front row," I propose. "It wouldn't surprise me if John Wayne still exterminates Indians on that screen. My treat."

Lily declines. "It's going to snow," she says. As she clears the kitchen, again refusing help, I feel as if I have sat in this room every evening of my life, as if I have never gone away. There ha been only a single supper and a single evening. Long ago, time stopped, stiffened, froze.

Before Lily can finish at the sink, I move to the living room and turn the radio on. I fiddle with the dial until I find the CBC. Voices cant about Quebec. Perhaps Lily will settle on the opposite couch; even if we don't talk, that would be something, a start. Water runs in the bathroom down the hall. Lily enters the living room, walks to the radio, turns it off. Before I can speak, she has left the room. Her bedroom door closes.

I can't remain in this silent house. I slip on my coat and step outside. Cold jabs me awake. Lily's window is dark and the empty street is quiet. I move past curtained squares which glow with yellow light, leak cancer from television screens. Lily, is it going to snow?

*

"Yes," she says in 1972, parting the curtains and looking into the dark street. Snow is late this year. Though Brale stores preen with Christmas decorations, the ground remains naked. "He's still there."

I haven't been back to the gully since Lily showed me what it holds. "Stay away," she has warned, sidling up beside me. In the schoolyard I study the shouting boys, puzzle whether one is missing after all. Maybe Billy was here all along, maybe I didn't notice him before. His parents must be looking for him, they must know he is lost. His toys must wait for his hands to curl around them. He must shiver where he lies. I still want to bring him clothes, but I'm afraid. There was something the matter with him, something more than blue berries and a second throat, I can't remember.

"Don't tell," says Lily, dropping the curtain.

When she slips from the house, I know where she is going now. She sits on a flat rock near Billy and tells him things she won't tell me, describes what is locked in the white valise at the back of her closet. He will never betray her secrets; my uncle won't reveal mine.

Down in the furnace room, at the warmest part of the house, I curl in my hiding place. My uncle swallowed too much smoke when he was twelve. The Christmas tree caught fire, there was something wrong with the wires of its lights. The boy tried to crawl through the smoke, it was thick and white, he couldn't get out. His can of marble sighs from the corner; his hockey sticks stir the shadows. My pencil presses against the pad of paper I have taken from Mitch's study. Dear Jesus, I print. Dig deeper, my uncle whispers. There is something different about his voice. My uncle sounds like Billy now. Dig harder, he pleads. I press the pencil until there is only a hole where Jesus was.

*

I can't find the gully in the dark. Dear Jesus, it's cold. Stumbling across loose rock, I wonder if the features of this slope have changed since my childhood, altered as though a million years of weather have done their work. Or has sly memory played another of its tricks? "It was just a game," Lily told me in January that year. "He was just pretending. Billy lives up on Shaver's Bench. He goes to the park there all the time. He's probably there right now. We just wanted to see how your face would look." His face looked pale and thin; a smudge of dirt clung to his risen ribs. I saw the shoe with the hole in the toe and a clue of green sock so I wouldn't see something else. As winter passed, my memory of Billy froze into a picture of my uncle in my mind. The same face. Speaking shadows in the furnace room turned muffled, then mute. Only the deep freeze hummed. He was silenced so he would never tell.

*

Lily walks quickly toward the mountain through the snow that finally falls. I don't think she knows I am behind her, at a quiet distance, until she stops and turns. "Don't follow," she calls, standing still, becoming white. The snow will bury Billy until spring. It's too heavy and thick, he can't dig himself out from the hole where Jesus was. I retrace a dozen steps; my trail has already been covered. I stop to look where Lily stood a moment ago. A shape of darkness moves through falling flakes. The white curtain closes, the white valise snaps shut. Billy's heart beats against my chest, hammers the cage of bone. Let me out, let me out.

*

Falling, no longer a nimble child, I grunt. A small, sharp stone presses into my spine. I can feel it, Lily. My hands curl as the sky begins to shred white scraps of a letter from Jesus. Something like glass glints over the earth; a shape of darkness breathes nearby. I try and fail to close my eyes against the intent face above me. The puffy features. A white blanket covers me with warm weight. I'll never tell, Lily. My blue lips will never ask why.

*

Snow won't stop falling through the past. It fills the hole as quickly as I can dig, forbids me to find the face. I can't reach Billy. Dig harder, he calls up to me. Dig faster. Dig.

*

The house on Aster Drive hovers in darkness amid descending snow, though I left the living room lit. My iced feet feel their way quietly down the hall and stairs. This way, Billy. In the black hole, I fumble for the edge of a bed. Objects fall to the floor as I pull back covers. We've climbed into MJ's abandoned bed instead of mine. It feels the same. Billy's skin feels as cold as mine. We shiver in synchronization, chatter teeth in tune until dawn.

*

At morning, silver light gleans the kitchen. The snow has stopped. Six white inches conceal the features of the landscape. The blanched bones of the maple rise from the back yard, foreground to black and white mountain. A cup of coffee rests on the table. My dipped finger discovers cold, dark liquid.

"Lily?" I call. My unanswered voice sounds thin and frightened as a child's.

Let's go, he says. Hurry, he urges.

My suitcase is packed. Should I leave a note? Dear Jesus... Fresh footprints lead from the front door, bend in the direction of the mountain. Shivering, I stall. My feet start to follow my sister's trail, then turn the other way. Toward downtown Brale and the bus that will carry me back to the cabin on the lake.

*

The fire in my stove has gone out and the cabin is cold. Beyond my wall of windows, the small ferry still floats across a black hole yawning between white shores. Still pursues the endless back and forth. On the further side, lights from scattered cabins peer down into liquid darkness, seek the contents of its depths. Steam rises through the falling snow, from the lake, as someone down there sighs.

The receiver in my hand is warm. How many days have passed since my telephone has rung? Since my voice has spoken? My lips kissed? I glance around the cabin. After four months, it still looks unknown. There is no television or music system. No framed photographs or sleek machines or glossy magazines. Only a few pieces of shabby furniture left behind by previous tenants. I don't hold a job or own a car. My clothes are washed in the sink, hung to dry on a string above the stove. Taking what I need for warmth, I steal wood from distant neighbours. There is no money to buy a cord of larch for the stove, curtains for the windows. I am exposed in this cabin hugged from behind by brush and cottonwoods and ponderosa pine but in front perched boldly upon the shore. Anyone driving on or off the ferry can see inside. "He's different," people have begun to mutter.

How and why have I ended up in this flimsy structure, this unlikely location? I sense I am experiencing someone else's life. My own existence has ended; this is afterlife, though the empty shell of self still sings. In some indeterminate season, the source of my ghost wanders the clearing above Lover' Lane, hand in hand with my uncle among berries and thistles and weeds, up where the cold wind blows.

I dial Lily's number. A measured sound fills my ear. He was raped and killed and left upon a mountain. Once, searching the slope for pussy willows during the following spring, I found myself by accident in that narrow gully. Not even a pair of running shoes remained there after the April thaw. "You lied. He doesn't play on Shaver's Bench. Where did he go?" I asked Lily, who had turned more silent that season. Inside a locked, white valise, she was already storing razor blades and pills, with other secret things. My sister didn't answer me, or even turn her face toward my question, as if its sound had failed to reach her.

Is it possible? In a small town, children are apt to hear disturbing news that adults might try to keep secret. The sexual murder of a boy would have filled *The Brale Daily Times*. The town would have bristled with panic, shivered with fear. Doors would have been locked at night. The park and other places where children play would have been deserted after dark. Uniformed men would have combed the mountain and dragged the river until they found a body. They would have knocked on every door on Aster Drive, seen the white valise at the back of Lily's closet, discovered the green sock inside.

A sound like nails of fingers scrapes against the window at the back of the cabin. Or it's just a branch. I've been here too long already. It's time to leave. I can no longer share the cold with you. Donald. Billy. Whoever you are. My shell of self must seek warm climate again.

Snow shakes steadily through the dark; the cabin roof groans beneath its weight. The buzzing in my ear persists, swells in volume. I glance at my watch. Is it too late, Lily? Ringing violates the house on Aster Drive. It won't stop until I put the receiver to rest or until my sister disconnects the cord. I never told, Lily. I never asked who, I never asked why.

Death by Eros
Steven Saylor

Death by Eros
Steven Saylor

"The Neapolitans are different from us Romans," I remarked to Eco as we strolled across the central forum of Neapolis. "A man can almost feel that he's left Italy altogether and been magically transported to a seaport in Greece. Greek colonists founded the city hundreds of years ago, taking advantage of the extraordinary bay, which they called the *Krater*, or Cup. The locals still have Greek names, eat Greek food, follow Greek customs. Many of them don't even speak Latin."

Eco pointed to his lips and made a self-deprecating gesture to say, *Neither do I!* At fifteen, he tended to make a joke of everything, including his muteness.

"Ah, but you can *hear* Latin," I said, flicking a finger against one of his ears just hard enough to sting, "and sometimes even understand it."

We had arrived in Neapolis on our way back to Rome, after doing a bit of business for Cicero down in Sicily. Rather than stay at an inn, I was hoping to find accommodations with a wealthy Greek trader named Sosistrides. "The fellow owes me a favor," Cicero had told me. "Look him up and mention my name, and I'm sure he'll put us up for the night."

With a few directions from the locals (who were polite enough not to laugh at my Greek) we found the trader's house. The columns and lintels and decorative details of the façade were stained in various shades of pale red, blue and yellow that seemed to glow under the warm sunlight. Incongruous amid the play of colors was a black wreath on the door.

"What do you think, Eco? Can we ask a friend of a friend, a total stranger really, to put us up when the household is in mourning? It seems presumptuous."

Eco nodded thoughtfully, then gestured to the wreath and expressed curiosity with a flourish of his wrist. I nodded. "I see your point. If it's Sosistrides who's died, or a member of the family, Cicero would want us to deliver his condolences, wouldn't he? And we must learn the details, so that we can inform him in a letter. I think we must at least rouse the doorkeeper, to see what's happened."

I walked to the door and politely knocked with the side of my foot. There was no answer. I knocked again and waited. I was about to rap on the door with my knuckles, rudely or not, when it swung open.

The man who stared back at us was dressed in mourning black. He was not a slave; I glanced at his hand and saw a citizen's iron ring. His graying hair was disheveled and his face distressed. His eyes were red from weeping.

"What do you want?" he said, in a voice more wary than unkind.

"Forgive me, citizen. My name is Gordianus. This is my son, Eco. Eco hears but is mute, so I shall speak for him. We're travelers, on our way home to Rome. I'm a friend of Marcus Tullius Cicero. It was he who –"

"Cicero? Ah, yes, the Roman administrator down in Sicily, the one who can actually read and write, for a change." The man wrinkled his brow. "Has he sent a message, or...?"

"Nothing urgent; Cicero asked me only to remind you of his friendship. You are, I take it, the master of the house, Sosistrides?"

"Yes. And you? I'm sorry, did you already introduce yourself? My mind wanders..." He looked over his shoulder. Beyond him, in the vestibule, I glimpsed a funeral bier strewn with freshly cut flowers and laurel leaves.

"My name is Gordianus. And this is my son –"

"Gordianus, did you say?"

"Yes."

"Cicero mentioned you once. Something about a murder trial up in Rome. You helped him. They call you the Finder."

"Yes."

He looked at me intently for a long moment. "Come in, Finder. I want you to see him."

The bier in the vestibule was propped up and tilted at an angle so that its occupant could be clearly seen. The corpse was that of a youth probably not much older than Eco. His arms were crossed over his chest and he was clothed in a long white gown, so that only his face and hands were exposed. His hair was boyishly long and as yellow as a field of millet in summer, crowned with a laurel wreath of the sort awarded to athletic champions. The flesh of his delicately molded features was waxy and pale, but even in death his beauty was remarkable.

"His eyes were blue," said Sosistrides in a low voice. "They're closed now, you can't see them, but they were blue, like his dear, dead mother's; he got his looks from her. The purest blue you ever saw, like the color of the Cup on a clear day. When we pulled him from the pool, they were all bloodshot..."

"This is your son, Sosistrides?"

He stifled a sob. "My only son, Cleon."

"A terrible loss."

He nodded, unable to speak. Eco shifted nervously from foot to foot, studying the dead boy with furtive glances, almost shyly.

"They call you Finder," Sosistrides finally said, in a hoarse voice. "Help me find the monster who killed my son."

I looked at the dead youth and felt a deep empathy for Sosistrides' suffering, and not merely because I myself had a son of similar age. (Eco may be adopted, but I love him as my own flesh.) I was stirred also by the loss of such beauty. Why does the death of a beautiful stranger affect us more deeply than the loss of someone plain? Why should it be so, that if a vase of exquisite workmanship but little practical value should break, we feel the loss more sharply than if we break an ugly vessel we use every day? The gods made men to love beauty above all else, perhaps because they themselves are beautiful, and wish for us to love them, even when they do us harm.

"How did he die, Sosistrides?"

"It was at the gymnasium, yesterday. There was a city-wide contest among the boys – discus throwing, wrestling, racing. I couldn't attend. I was away in Pompeii on business all day..." Sosistrides again fought back tears. He reached out and touched the wreath on his son's brow. "Cleon took the laurel crown. He was a splendid athlete. He always won at everything, but they say he outdid himself yesterday. If only I had been there to see it! Afterwards, while the other boys retired to the baths inside, Cleon took a swim in the long pool, alone. There was no one else in the courtyard. No one saw it happen..."

"The boy drowned, Sosistrides?" It seemed unlikely, if the boy had been as good at swimming as he was at everything else.

Sosistrides shook his head and shut his eyes tight, squeezing tears from them. "The gymnasiarchus is an old wrestler named Caputorus. It was he who found Cleon. He heard a splash, he said, but thought nothing of it. Later he went into the courtyard and discovered Cleon. The water was red with blood. Cleon was at the bottom of the pool. Beside him was a broken statue. It must have struck the back of his head; it left a terrible gash."

"A statue?"

"Of Eros – the god you Romans call Cupid. A cherub with bow and arrows, a decoration at the edge of the pool. Not large statue, but heavy, made of solid marble. It somehow fell from its pedestal as Cleon was passing below..." He gazed at the boy's bloodless face, lost in misery.

I sensed the presence of another in the room, and turned to see a young woman in a black gown with a black mantle over her head. She walked to Sosistrides' side. "Who are these visitors, father?"

"Friends of the provincial administrator down in Sicily – Gordianus of Rome, and his son, Eco. This is my daughter, Cleio. Daughter! Cover yourself!" Sosistrides' sudden embarrassment was caused by the fact that Cleio had pushed the mantle from her head, revealing that her dark hair was crudely shorn, cut so short so that it didn't reach her shoulders. No longer shadowed by the mantle, her face, too, showed signs of unbridled mourning. Long scratches ran down her cheeks, and there were bruises where she appeared to have struck herself, marring a beauty that rivaled her brother's.

"I mourn for the loss of the one I loved best in all the world," she said in a hollow voice. "I feel no shame to show it." She cast an icy stare at me and then at Eco, then swept from the room.

Extreme displays of grief are disdained in Rome, where excessive public mourning is banned by law, but we were in Neapolis. Sosistrides seemed to read my thoughts. "Cleio has always been more Greek than Roman. She lets her emotions run wild. Just the opposite of her brother. Cleon was always so cool, so detached." He shook his head. "She's taken her brother's death very hard. When I came home from Pompeii yesterday I found his body here in the vestibule; his slaves had carried him home from the gymnasium. Cleio was in her room, crying uncontrollably. She'd already cut her hair. She wept and wailed all night long."

He gazed at his dead son's face and reached out to touch it, his hand looking warm and ruddy against the unnatural pallor of the boy's cold cheek. "Someone murdered my son. You must help me find out who did it, Gordianus – to put the shade of my son to rest, and for my grieving daughter's sake."

*

"That's right, I heard the splash. I was here behind my counter in the changing room, and the door to the courtyard was standing wide open, just like it is now."

Caputorus the gymnasiarchus was a grizzled old wrestler with enormous shoulders, a perfectly bald head and a protruding belly. His eyes kept darting past me to follow the comings and goings of the naked youths, and every so often he interrupted me in mid-sentence to yell out a greeting which usually included some jocular insult or obscenity. The fourth time he reached out to tousle Eco's hair, Eco deftly moved out of range and stayed there.

"And when you heard the splash, did you immediately go and have a look?" I asked.

"Not right away. To tell you the truth, I didn't think much of it. I figured Cleon was out there jumping in and out of the pool, which is against the rules, mind you! It's a long, shallow pool meant for swimming only, and no jumping allowed. But he was always breaking the rules. Thought he could get away with anything."

"So why didn't you go out and tell him to stop? You are the gymnasiarchus, aren't you?"

"Do you think that counted for anything with that spoiled brat? Master of the gym I may be, but nobody was his master. You know what he'd have done? Quoted some fancy lines from some famous play, most likely about old wrestlers with big bellies, flashed his naked behind at me, and then jumped back in the pool! I don't need the grief, thank you very much. Hey, Manius!" Caputorus shouted at a youth behind me. "I saw you and your sweetheart out there wrestling this morning. You been studying your old man's dirty vases to learn those positions? Ha!"

Over my shoulder I saw a redheaded youth flash a lascivious grin and make an obscene gesture using both hands.

"Back to yesterday," I said. "You heard the splash and didn't think much of it, but eventually you went out to the courtyard."

"Just to get some fresh air. I noticed right away that Cleon wasn't swimming any more. I figured he'd headed inside to the baths."

"But wouldn't he have passed you on the way?"

"Not necessarily. There are two passageways into the courtyard. The one most people take goes past my counter here. The other is through a little hallway that connects to the outer vestibule. It's a more roundabout route to get inside to the baths, but he could have gone in that way."

"And could someone have gotten into the courtyard the same way?"

"Yes."

"Then you can't say for certain that Cleon was alone out there."

"You are a sharp one, aren't you!" Caputorus said sarcastically. "But you're right. Cleon was out there by himself to start with, of that I'm sure. And after that, nobody walked by me, coming or going. But somebody could have come and gone by the other passageway. Anyway, when I stepped out there, I could tell right away that something was wrong, seriously wrong, though I couldn't quite say what. Only later, I realized what it was: the statue was missing, that little statue of Eros that's been there since before I took over running this place. You know how you can see a thing every day and take it for granted, and when all of a sudden it's not there, you can't even say what's missing, but you *sense* that something's off? That's how it was. Then I saw the color of the water. All pinkish in one spot, and darker toward the bottom. I stepped closer and then I saw him, lying on the bottom, not moving and no air bubbles coming up, and the statue around him in pieces. It was obvious right away what must have happened. Here, I'll show you the spot."

As we were passing out the doorway a muscular wrestler wearing only a leather headband and wrist-wraps squeezed by on his way in.

Caputorus twisted a towel between his fists and snapped it against the youth's bare backside. "Your mother!" yelled the stung athlete.

"No, your shiny red bottom!" said Caputorus, who threw back his head and laughed.

The pool had been drained and scrubbed, leaving no trace of Cleon's blood amid the puddles. The pieces of the statue of Eros had been gathered up and deposited next to the empty pedestal. One of the cherub's tiny feet had broken off, as had the top of Eros' bow, the point of his notched arrow, and the feathery tip of one wing.

"The statue had been here for years, you say?"

"That's right."

"Sitting here on this pedestal?"

"Yes. Never budged, even when we'd get a bit of a rumble from Vesuvius."

"Strange, then, that it should have fallen yesterday, when no one felt any tremors. Even stranger, that it should fall directly onto a swimmer..."

"It's a mystery, all right."

"I think the word is murder."

Caputorus looked at me shrewdly. "Not necessarily."

"What do you mean?"

"Ask some of the boys. See what they tell you."

"I intend to ask everyone who was here what they saw or heard."

"Then you might start with this little fellow." He indicated the broken Eros.

"Speak plainly, Caputorus."

"Others know more than I do. All I can tell you is what I've picked up from the boys."

"And what's that?"

"Cleon was a heartbreaker. You've only seen him laid out for his funeral. You have no idea how good-looking he was, both above the neck and below. A body like a statue by Phidias, a regular Apollo – he took your breath away! Smart, too, and the best athlete on the Cup. Strutting around here naked every day, challenging all the boys to wrestle him, celebrating his wins by quoting Homer. He had half the boys in this place trailing after him, all wanting to be his special friend.

They were awestruck by him."

"And yet, yesterday, after he won the laurel crown, he swam alone."

"Maybe because they'd all finally had enough of him. Maybe they got tired of his bragging. Maybe they realized he wasn't the sort to ever return a shred of love or affection to anybody."

"You sound bitter, Caputorus."

"Do I?"

"Are you sure you're talking just about the boys?"

His face reddened. He worked his jaw back and forth and flexed his massive shoulders. I tried not to flinch.

"I'm no fool, Finder," he finally said, lowering his voice. "I've been around long enough to learn a few things. Lesson one: a boy like Cleon is nothing but trouble. Look, but don't touch." His jaw relaxed into a faint smile. "I've got a tough hide. I tease and joke with the best, but none of these boys gets under my skin."

"Not even Cleon?"

His face hardened, then broke into a grin as he looked beyond me. "Calpurnius!" he yelled at a boy across the courtyard. "If you handle the javelin between your legs the way you handle that one, I'm surprised you haven't pulled it off by now! Merciful Zeus, let me show you how!"

Caputorus pushed past me, tousling Eco's hair on his way, leaving us to ponder the broken Eros and the empty pool where Cleon had died.

*

I managed that day to speak to every boy in the gymnasium. Most of them had been there the previous day, either to take part in the athletic games or to watch. Most of them were cooperative, but only to a point. I had the feeling that they had already talked among themselves and decided as a group to say as little as possible concerning Cleon's death to outsiders like myself, no matter that I came as the representative of Cleon's father.

Nevertheless, from uncomfortable looks, wistful sighs and unfinished sentences I gathered that what Caputorus had told me was true: Cleon had broken hearts all over the gymnasium, and in the process had made more than a few enemies. He was by universal consensus the brightest and most beautiful boy in the group, and yesterday's games had proven conclusively that he was the best athlete as well. He was also vain, arrogant, selfish and aloof; easy to fall in love with and incapable of loving in return. The boys who had not fallen under his personal spell at one time or another disliked him out of pure envy.

All this I managed to learn as much from what was left unsaid as from what each boy said, but when it came to obtaining more concrete details I struck a wall of silence. Had anyone ever been heard uttering a serious threat to Cleon? Had anyone ever said anything, even in jest, about the potentially hazardous placement of the statue of Eros beside the pool? Were any of the boys especially upset about Cleon's victories that day? Had any of them slipped away from the baths at the time Cleon was killed? And what of the gymnasiarchus? Had Caputorus' behavior toward Cleon always been above reproach, as he claimed?

To these questions, no matter how directly or indirectly I posed them, I received no clear answers, only a series of equivocations and evasions.

I was beginning to despair of uncovering anything significant, when finally I interviewed Hippolytus, the wrestler whose backside Caputorus had playfully snapped with his towel. He was preparing for a plunge in the hot pool when I came to him. He untied his leather headband, letting a shock of jet-black hair fall into his eyes, and began to unwrap his wrists. Eco seemed a bit awed by the fellow's brawniness; to me, with his babyish face and apple-red cheeks, Hippolytus seemed a hugely overgrown child.

I had gathered from the others that Hippolytus was close, or as close an anyone, to Cleon. I began the conversation by saying as much, hoping to catch him off his guard. He looked at me, unfazed, and nodded.

"I suppose that's right. I liked him. He wasn't as bad as some made out."

"What do you mean?"

"Wasn't Cleon's fault if everybody swooned over him. Wasn't his fault if he didn't swoon back. I don't think he had it in him to feel that way about another boy." He frowned and wrinkled his brow. "Some say that's not natural, but there you are. The gods make us all different."

"I'm told he was arrogant and vain."

"Wasn't his fault he was better than everybody else at wrestling and running and throwing. Wasn't his fault he was smarter than his tutors. But he shouldn't have crowed so much, I suppose. Hubris – you know what that is?"

"Vanity that offends the gods," I said.

"Right, like in the plays. Acquiring a swollen head, becoming too cocksure, until a fellow's just begging to be struck down by a lightning bolt or swallowed by an earthquake. What the gods give they can take away. They gave Cleon everything. Then they took it all away."

"The gods?"

Hippolytus sighed. "Cleon deserved to be brought down a notch, but he didn't deserve that punishment."

"Punishment? From whom? For what?"

I watched his eyes and saw the to and fro of some internal debate. If I prodded too hard, he might shut up tight; if I prodded not at all, he might keep answering in pious generalities. I started to speak, then saw something settle inside him, and held my tongue.

"You've seen the statue that fell on him?" Hippolytus said.

"Yes. Eros with his bow and arrows.

"Do you think that was just a coincidence?"

"I don't understand."

"You've talked to everyone in the gymnasium, and nobody's told you? They're all thinking it; they're just too superstitious to say it aloud. It was Eros that killed Cleon, for spurning him."

"You think the god himself did it? Using his own statue."

"Love flowed to Cleon from all directions, like rivers to the sea – but he turned back the rivers and lived in his own rocky desert. Eros chose Cleon to be his favorite, but Cleon refused him. He laughed in the god's face once too often."

"How? What had Cleon done to finally push the god too far?"

Again I saw the internal debate behind his eyes. Clearly, he wanted to tell me everything. I had only to be patient. At last he sighed and spoke. "Lately, some of us thought that Cleon might finally be softening. He had a new tutor, a young philosopher named Mulciber who came from Alexandria about six months ago. Cleon and his sister Cleio went to Mulciber's little house off the forum every morning to talk about Plato and read poetry."

"Cleio as well?"

"Sosistrides believed in educating both his children, no matter that Cleio's a girl. Anyway, pretty soon word got around that Mulciber was courting Cleon. Why not? He was smitten, like everybody else. The surprise was that Cleon seemed to respond to his advances. Mulciber would send him chaste little love poems, and Cleon would send poems back to him. Cleon actually showed me some of Mulciber's poems, and asked me to read the ones he was sending back. They were beautiful! He was good at that, too, of course." Hippolytus shook his head ruefully.

"But it was all a cruel hoax. Cleon was just leading Mulciber on, making a fool of him. Only the day before yesterday, right in front of some of Mulciber's other students, Cleon made a public show of returning all the poems Mulciber had sent him, and asking for his own poems back. He said he'd written them merely as exercises, to teach his own tutor the proper way to write a love poem. Mulciber was dumbstruck! Everyone in the gymnasium heard about it. People said Cleon had finally gone too far. To have spurned his tutor's advances was one thing, but to do so in such a cruel, deliberately humiliating manner – that was hubris, people said, and the gods would take vengeance. And now they have."

I nodded. "But quite often the gods use human vessels to achieve their ends. Do you really think the statue tumbled into the pool of its own accord, without a hand to push it?"

Hippolytus frowned, and seemed to debate revealing yet another secret. "Yesterday, not long before Cleon drowned, some of us saw a stranger in the gymnasium."

At last, I thought, a concrete bit of evidence, something solid to grapple with! I took a deep breath. "No one else mentioned seeing a stranger."

"I told you, they're all too superstitious. If the boy we saw was some emissary of the god, they don't want to speak of it."

"A boy?"

"Perhaps it was Eros himself, in human form – though you'd think a god would be better groomed and wear clothes that fit!"

"You saw this stranger clearly?"

"Not that clearly; neither did anybody else, as far as I can tell. I only caught a glimpse of him loitering in the outer vestibule, but I could tell he wasn't one of the regular boys."

"How so?"

"By the fact that he was dressed at all. This was just after the games, and everyone was still naked. And most of the gymnasium crowd are pretty well off; this fellow had a wretched haircut and his tunic looked like a patched hand-me-down from a big brother. I figured he was some stranger who wandered in off the street, or maybe a messenger slave too shy to come into the changing room."

"And his face?"

Hippolytus shook his head. "I didn't see his face. He had dark hair, though."

"Did you speak to him, or hear him speak?"

"No. I headed for the hot plunge and forgot all about him. Then Caputorus found Cleon's body, and everything was crazy after that. I didn't make any connection to the stranger until this morning, when I found out that some of the others had seen him, too."

"Did anybody see this young stranger pass through the baths and the changing room?"

"I don't think so. But there's another way to get from the outer vestibule to the inner courtyard, though a little passageway at the far end of the building."

"So Caputorus told me. It seems possible, then, that this stranger could have entered the outer vestibule, sneaked through the empty passage, come upon Cleon alone in the pool, pushed the statue onto him, then fled the way he had come, all without being clearly seen by anyone."

Hippolytus took a deep breath. "That's how I figure it. So you see, it must have been the god, or some agent of the god. Who else could have had such perfect timing, to carry out such an awful deed?"

I shook my head. "I can see you know a bit about poetry and more than a bit about wrestling holds, young man, but has no one tutored you in logic? We may have answered the question of *how*, but that hasn't answered the question of *who*. I respect your religious conviction that the god Eros may have had the motive and the will to kill Cleon in such a cold-blooded fashion – but it seems there were plenty of mortals with abundant motive as well. In my line of work I prefer to suspect the most likely mortal first, and presume divine causation only as a last resort. Chief among such suspects must be this tutor, Mulciber. Could he have been the stranger you saw lurking in the vestibule? Philosophers are notorious for having bad haircuts and shabby clothes."

"No. The stranger was shorter and had darker hair."

"Still, I should like to have a talk with this lovesick tutor."

"You can't," said Hippolytus. "Mulciber hanged himself yesterday."

*

"No wonder such a superstitious dread surrounds Cleon's death," I remarked to Eco, as we made our way to the house of Mulciber. "The golden boy of the Cup, killed by a statue of Eros; his spurned tutor, hanging himself the same day. This is the dark side of Eros. It casts a shadow that frightens everyone into silence."

Except me, Eco gestured, and let out the stifled, inchoate grunt he sometimes emits simply to declare his existence. I smiled at his self-deprecating humor, but it seemed to me that the things we had learned that morning had disturbed and unsettled Eco. He was at an age to be acutely aware of his place in the scheme of things, and to begin wondering who might ever love him, especially in spite of his handicap. It seemed unfair that a boy like Cleon, who had only scorn for his suitors, should have inspired so much unrequited infatuation and desire, when others faced lives of loneliness. Did the gods engineer the paradox of love's unfairness to amuse themselves, or was it one of the evils that escaped from Pandora's box to plague mankind?

The door of the philosopher's house, like that of Sosistrides, was adorned with a black wreath. Following my knock, an elderly slave opened it to admit us to a little foyer, where a body was laid out upon a bier much less elaborate than that of Cleon. I saw at once why Hippolytus had been certain that the short, dark-haired stranger at the gymnasium had not been the Alexandrian tutor, for Mulciber was quite tall and had fair hair. He had been a reasonably handsome man of thirty-five or so, about my own age. Eco gestured to the scarf that had been clumsily gathered about the dead man's throat, and then clutched his own neck with a strangler's grip: *to hide the rope marks*, he seemed to say.

"Did you know my master?" asked the slave who had shown us in.

"Only by reputation," I said. "We're visitors to Neapolis, but I've heard of your master's devotion to poetry and philosophy. I was shocked to learn of his sudden death." I spoke only the truth, after all.

The slave nodded. "He was a man of learning and talent. Still, few have come to pay their respects. He had no family here. And of course there are many who won't set foot inside the house of a suicide, for fear of bad luck."

"It's certain that he killed himself, then?"

"It was I who found him, hanging from a rope. He tied it to that beam, just above the boy's head." Eco rolled his eyes up. "Then he stood on a chair, put the noose around his neck, and kicked the chair out of the way. His neck snapped. I like to think he died quickly." The slave regarded his master's face affectionately. "Such a waste! And all for the love of that worthless boy!"

"You're certain that's why he killed himself?"

"Why else? He was making a good living here in Neapolis, enough to send a bit back to his brother in Alexandria every now and again, and even to think of purchasing a second slave. I'm not sure how I'd have taken to that; I've been with him since he was a boy. I used to carry his wax tablets and scrolls for him when was little and had his own tutor. No, his life was going well in every way, except for that horrible boy!"

"You know that Cleon died yesterday."

"Oh, yes. That's why the master killed himself."

"He hung himself *after* hearing of Cleon's death?"

"Of course! Only..." The old man looked puzzled, as if he had not previously considered any other possibility. "Now let me think. Yesterday was strange all around, you see. The master sent me out early in the morning, before daybreak, with specific instructions not to return until evening. That was very odd, because usually I spend all day here, admitting his pupils and seeing to his meals. But yesterday he sent me out and I stayed away until dusk. I heard about Cleon's death on my way home. When I came in, there was the master, hanging from that rope."

"Then you don't know for certain when he died – only that it must have been between daybreak and nightfall."

"I suppose you're right."

"Who might have seen him during the day?"

"Usually pupils come and go all day, but not so yesterday, on account of the games at the gymnasium. All his regular students took part, you see, or else went to watch. The master had planned to be a spectator himself. So he had cancelled all his regular classes, you see, except for his very first of the day – and that he'd never cancel, of course, because it was with that wretched boy!"

"Cleon, you mean."

"Yes, Cleon and his sister Cleio. They always came for the first hour of the day. This month they were reading Plato on the death of Socrates."

"Suicide was on Mulciber's mind, then. And yesterday, did Cleon and his sister arrive for their class?"

"I can't say. I suppose they did. I was out of the house by then."

"I shall have to ask Cleio, but for now we'll assume they did. Perhaps Mulciber was hoping to patch things up with Cleon." The slave gave me a curious look. "I know about the humiliating episode of the returned poems the day before," I explained.

The slave regarded me warily. "You seem to know a great deal for a man who's not from Neapolis. What are you doing here?"

"Only trying to discover the truth. Now, then: we'll assume that Cleon and Cleio came for their class, early in the morning. Perhaps Mulciber was braced for another humiliation, and even then planning suicide – or was he wildly hoping, with a lover's blind faith, for some impossible reconciliation? Perhaps that's why he dismissed you for the day, because he didn't care to have his old slave witness either outcome. But it must have gone badly, or at least not as Mulciber hoped, for he never showed up to watch the games at the gymnasium that day. Everyone seems to assume that it was news of Cleon's death that drove him to suicide, but it seems to me just as likely that Mulciber hung himself right after Cleon and Cleio left, unable to bear yet another rejection."

Eco, greatly agitated, mimed an athlete throwing a discus, then a man fitting a noose around his neck, then an archer notching an arrow in a bow.

I nodded. "Yes, bitter irony: even as Cleon was enjoying his greatest triumph at the gymnasium, poor Mulciber may have been snuffing out his own existence. And then, Cleon's death in the pool. No wonder everyone thinks that Eros himself brought Cleon down." I studied the face of the dead man. "Your master was a poet, wasn't he?"

"Yes," said the slave. "He wrote at least a few lines every day of his life."

"Did he leave a farewell poem?"

The slave shook his head. "You'd think he might have, if only to say good-bye to me after all these years."

"But there was nothing? Not even a note?"

"Not a line. And that's another strange thing, because the night before he was up long after midnight, writing and writing. I thought perhaps he'd put the boy behind him and thrown himself into composing some epic poem, seized by the muse! But I can't find any trace of it. Whatever he was writing so frantically, it seems to have vanished. Perhaps, when he made up his mind to hang himself, he thought better of what he'd written, and burned it. He seems to have gotten rid of some other papers, as well."

"What papers?"

"The love poems he'd written to Cleon, the ones Cleon returned to him – they've vanished. I suppose the master was embarrassed at the thought of anyone reading them after he was gone, and so he got rid of them. So perhaps it's not so strange after all that he left no farewell note."

I nodded vaguely, but it still seemed odd to me. From what I knew of poets, suicides, and unrequited lovers, Mulciber would almost certainly have left some words behind – to chastise Cleon, to elicit pity, to vindicate himself. But the silent corpse of the tutor offered no explanation.

*

As the day was waning, I at last returned to the house of Sosistrides, footsore and soul-weary. A slave admitted us. I paused to gaze for a long moment at the lifeless face of Cleon. Nothing had changed, and yet he did not look as beautiful to my eyes as he had before.

Sosistrides called us into his study. "How did it go, Finder?"

"I've had a productive day, if not a pleasant one. I talked to everyone I could find at the gymnasium. I also went to the house of your children's tutor. You do know that Mulciber hanged himself yesterday?"

"Yes. I found out only today, after I spoke to you. I knew he was a bit infatuated with Cleon, wrote poems to him and such, but I had no idea he was so passionately in love with him. Another tragedy, like ripples in a pond." Sosistrides, too, seemed to assume without question that the tutor's suicide followed upon news of Cleon's death. "And what did you find? Did you discover anything... significant?"

I nodded. "I think I know who killed your son."

His face assumed an expression of strangely mingled relief and dismay. "Tell me, then!"

"Would you send for your daughter first? Before I can be certain, there are a few questions I need to ask her. And when I think of the depth of her grief, it seems to me that she, too, should hear what I have to say."

He called for a slave to fetch the girl from her room. "You're right, of course; Cleio should be here, in spite of her... unseemly appearance. Her grieving shows her to be a woman, after all, but I've raised her almost as a son, you know. I made sure she learned to read and write. I sent her to the same tutors as Cleon. Of late she's been reading Plato with him, both of them studying with Mulciber..."

"Yes, I know."

Cleio entered the room, her mantle pushed defiantly back from her shorn head. Her cheeks were lined with fresh, livid scratches, signs that her mourning had continued unabated through the day.

"The Finder thinks he knows who killed Cleon," Sosistrides explained.

"Yes, but I need to ask you a few questions first," I said. "Are you well enough to talk?"

She nodded.

"Is it true that you and your brother went to your regular morning class with Mulciber yesterday?"

"Yes." She averted her tear-reddened eyes and spoke in a hoarse whisper.

"When you arrived at his house, was Mulciber there?"

She paused. "Yes."

"Was it he who let you in the door?"

Again a pause. "No."

"But his slave was out of the house, gone for the day. Who let you in?"

"The door was unlocked... ajar..."

"So you and Cleon simply stepped inside?"

"Yes."

"Were harsh words exchanged between your brother and Mulciber?"

Her breath became ragged. "No."

"Are you sure? Only the day before, your brother had publicly rejected and humiliated Mulciber. He returned his love poems and ridiculed them in front of others. That must have been a tremendous blow to Mulciber. Isn't it true that when the two of you showed up at his house yesterday morning, Mulciber lost his temper with Cleon?"

She shook her head.

"What if I suggest that Mulciber became hysterical? That he ranted against your brother? That he threatened to kill him?"

"No! That never happened. Mulciber was too – he would never have done such a thing!"

"But I suggest that he did. I suggest that yesterday, after suffering your brother's deceit and abuse, Mulciber reached the end of his tether. He snapped, like a rein that's worn clean through, and his passions ran away with him like maddened horses. By the time you and your brother left his house, Mulciber must have been raving like a madman –"

"No! He wasn't! He was –"

"And after you left, he brooded. He took out the love poems into which he had poured his heart and soul, the very poems that Cleon returned to him so scornfully the day before. They had once been beautiful to him, but now they were vile, so he burned them."

"Never!"

"He had planned to attend the games at the gymnasium, to cheer Cleon on, but instead he waited until the contests were over, then sneaked into the vestibule, skulking like a thief. He came upon Cleon alone in the pool. He saw the statue of Eros – a bitter reminder of his own rejected love. No one else was about, and there was Cleon, swimming face down, not even aware that anyone else was in the courtyard, unsuspecting and helpless. Mulciber couldn't resist – he waited until the very moment that Cleon passed beneath the statue, then pushed it from its pedestal. The statue struck Cleon's head. Cleon sank to the bottom and drowned."

Cleio wept and shook her head. "No, no! It wasn't Mulciber!"

"Oh, yes! And then, wracked with despair at having killed the boy he loved, Mulciber rushed home and hanged himself. He didn't even bother to write a note to justify himself or beg forgiveness for the murder. He'd fancied himself a poet, but what greater failure is there for a poet than to have his love poems rejected? And so he hung himself without writing another line, and he'll go to his funeral pyre in silence, a common murderer –"

"No, no, no!" Cleio clutched her cheeks, tore at her hair and wailed. Eco, whom I had told to be prepared for such an outburst, started back nonetheless. Sosistrides looked at me aghast. I averted my eyes. How could I have simply told him the truth, and made him believe it? He had to be shown. Cleio had to show him.

"He *did* leave a farewell," Cleio cried. "It was the most beautiful poem he ever wrote!"

"But his slave found nothing. Mulciber's poems to Cleon had vanished, and there was nothing new –"

"Because I took them!"

"Where are they, then?"

She reached into the bosom of her black gown and pulled out two handfuls of crumpled papyrus. "These were his poems to Cleon! You never saw such beautiful poems, such pure, sweet love put down in words! Cleon made fun of them, but they broke my heart! And here is his farewell poem, the one he left lying on his threshold so that Cleon would be sure to see it, when we went to his house yesterday and found him hanging in the foyer, his neck broken, his body soiled... dead... gone from me for ever!"

She pressed a scrap of papyrus into my hands. It was in Greek, the letters rendered in a florid, desperate hand. A phrase near the middle caught my eye:

> One day, even your beauty will fade;
> One day, even you may love unrequited!
> Take pity, then, and favor my corpse
> With a first, final, farewell kiss...

She snatched back the papyrus and clutched it to her bosom.

My voice was hollow in my ears. "When you went to Mulciber's house yesterday, you and Cleon found him already dead."

"Yes!"

"And you wept."

"Because I loved him!"

"Even though he didn't love you?"

"Mulciber loved Cleon. He couldn't help himself."

"Did Cleon weep?"

Her face became so contorted with hatred that I heard Sosistrides gasp in horror. "Oh, no," she said, "he didn't weep. Cleon laughed! He laughed! He shook his head and said, 'What a fool,' and walked out the door. I screamed at him to come back, to help me cut him down, and he only said, 'I'll be late for the games!' " Cleio collapsed to the floor, weeping, the poems scattering around her. " 'Late for the games!' " she repeated, as if it were her brother's epitaph.

*

On the long ride back to Rome through the Campanian countryside, Eco's hands grew weary and I grew hoarse debating whether I had done the right thing. Eco argued that I should have kept my suspicions of Cleio to myself. I argued that Sosistrides deserved to know what his daughter had done, and how and why his son had died – and needed to be shown, as well, how deeply and callously his beautiful, beloved Cleon had inflicted misery on others.

"Besides," I said, "when we returned to Sosistrides' house, I wasn't certain myself that Cleio had murdered Cleon. Accusing the dead tutor was a way of flushing her out. Her possession of Mulciber's missing poems were the only tangible evidence that events had unfolded as I suspected. I tried in vain to think of some way, short of housebreaking, to search her room without either Cleio or her father knowing – but as it turned out, such a search would have found nothing. I should have known that she would keep the poems on her person, next to her heart! She was as madly, hopelessly in love with Mulciber as he was in love with Cleon. Eros can be terribly careless when he scatters his arrows!"

We also debated the degree and nature of Cleon's perfidy. When he saw Mulciber's dead body, was Cleon so stunned by the enormity of what he had done – driven a lovesick man to suicide – that he went about his business in a sort of stupor, attending the games and performing his athletic feats like an automaton? Or was he so cold that he felt nothing? Or, as Eco argued in an extremely convoluted series of gestures, did Mulciber's fatal demonstration of lovesick devotion actually stimulate Cleon in some perverse way, inflating his ego and inspiring him to excel as never before at the games?

Whatever his private thoughts, instead of grieving, Cleon blithely went off and won his laurel crown, leaving Mulciber to spin in midair and Cleio to plot her vengeance. In a fit of grief she cut off her hair. The sight of her reflection in Mulciber's atrium pool gave her the idea to pass as a boy; an ill-fitting tunic from the tutor's wardrobe completed her disguise. She carried a knife with her to the gymnasium, the same one she had used to cut her hair, and was prepared to stab her brother in front of his friends. But it turned out that she didn't need the knife. By chance – or guided by Eros – she found her way into the courtyard, where the statue presented itself as the perfect murder weapon.

As far as Cleio was concerned, the statue's role in the crime constituted proof that she acted not only with the god's approval but as an instrument of his will. This pious argument had so far, at least as of our leaving Neapolis, stayed Sosistrides from punishing her. I did not envy the poor merchant. With his wife and son dead, could he bear to snuff out the life of only remaining offspring, even for so great a crime? And yet, how could he bear to let her live, knowing she had murdered his beloved son? Such a conundrum would test the wisdom of Athena!

Eco and I debated, too, the merits of Mulciber's poetry. I had begged of Sosistrides a copy of the tutor's farewell, so that I could ponder it at my leisure:

> Savage, sullen boy, whelp of a lioness,
> Stone-hearted and scornful of love,
> I give you a lover's ring – my noose!
> No longer be sickened by the sight of me;
> I go to the only place that offers solace
> To the broken-hearted: oblivion!
> But will you not stop and weep for me,
> If only for one moment...

The poem continued for many more lines, veering between recrimination, self-pity, and surrender to the annihilating power of love.

Hopelessly sentimental! More cloying than honey! The very worst sort of dreck, pronounced Eco, with a series of gestures so sweeping that he nearly fell from his horse. I merely nodded, and wondered if my son would feel the same in another year or so, after Eros had wounded him with a stray arrow or two and given him a clearer notion, from personal experience, of just how deeply the god of love can pierce the hearts of helpless mortals.

The Haunting of James Elstead
Michael Wilcox

The Haunting of James Elstead
Michael Wilcox

"Mr Elstead, would it be possible for you to come to North Shields police station sometime today?"

"I'm rather busy."

"I think you should, sir."

James Elstead's first morning as manager of the Whitley Bay branch of the Friendly Mutual Bank was a triumph of ambition over talent. He had carried his demanding wife's breakfast upstairs to her separate bedroom as usual, dodged the chaos of his four teenaged sons, who were used to looking after themselves at this time of day, and put a fresh carnation in his button hole before driving away from his new Ashington maisonette. But what he was not expecting that morning was a phone call from the police. Nor had he the slightest idea what it could be about.

When he arrived at the police station, he was introduced to Detective Inspector Rice, who greeted him cordially. But Elstead noticed how every police officer he encountered on entering the building had viewed him curiously, as though he was the centre of intense speculation. He was shown into a small interview room where a video recorder and television had been set up. In front of the screen was a single chair.

"We've got something we think you should see, Mr Elstead."

"Really?"

"It takes about half an hour. We'll leave you in peace."

"I've got to be back at the bank by one thirty."

"One thing at a time, sir." D I Rice pressed the start button and the screen began to flicker.

"We've all seen it anyway."

Rice left the room. The solitary Elstead saw two teenage boys, recorded by what appeared to be a single hidden camera, enter a

425

bedroom. They were in high spirits and shared a bottle of wine between frantic kisses as each tore off the other's clothes. At first, Elstead couldn't understand why the police wanted him to watch what rapidly turned into the crudest pornography. He was about to leave the room to tell D I Rice that he'd got the wrong man when he stopped and took a closer look at the screen. James Elstead, the blood draining from his head, realised that one of the boys was him, as he once was, thirty years ago. He settled again in his chair, leaning forward, his mouth dry and open. Who was the other boy? Where did this happen? The boys didn't speak much and the sound was poor, but he thought he heard himself repeat his partner's name at one point. "Peter... Peter..." Then he remembered. The Edinburgh Festival. He was in a school production of *A Man for all Seasons*. The bar. The invitation. The party. The precocious Scottish boy who loved cock. A classic teenage one-night stand. They never stayed in touch. But whose party was it? Some rich bloke in The Kenilworth. A doctor in the Festival Chorus. Gradually, it came back to him. But his memories were soon distracted by what was happening on the screen. How uninhibited they were. What a brilliant partner Peter had been! The two boys were evidently so happy together, like two randy puppies in a basket. Compared to this, how dull his life had become. The dutiful husband, ignored and despised by his sons, driven by a fiercely ambitious wife. How slim and lithe he was then. How he was overweight and his hair was grey and receding. The tape came to an end, leaving the screen in a blizzard of snow.

James Elstead sat motionless, his confused head spinning, his stomach tense. Then he noticed a dark, damp spot on his grey trousers, evidence of his aroused state. Shit! He adjusted himself, got out his handkerchief and tried, without success, to wipe away the dampness.

D I Rice entered with a glass of water. Elstead blew his nose and left his other hand on his lap.

"I thought you might need this."

He held out the glass. Elstead took it and sipped, trying not to show how his hand was shaking. In a moment unworthy of even a modest amateur dramatic society, he spilled some water on his trousers, handed the glass back to Rice and mopped his soggy lap, crushing his wilting carnation in the process.

"Never mind, Mr Elstead. Take your time.

"Why have you shown me this?"

"It *is* you."

"How do you know?"

"It has your name on it, sir. And the date. How old were you in 1974?"

"Sixteen? Seventeen?"

"And the other lad?"

"I've no idea. Who was it?"

Rice looked at the neat writing on the box.

"Peter McTeer, apparently."

"I don't know."

"He looks younger than you."

"Hard to tell at that age."

"Yes. I know... I know..."

James Elstead started to feel distinctly uncomfortable and shifted around in his seat. Rice stared at him with an irritating look of silent amusement, was this a formal police interview? He hadn't been cautioned. There was no other officer present. He decided to go on the offensive and picked up the video box. He noticed a third name. Dr Thomas Little.

"Where did you get this?"

Rice hesitated. "Our inquiries into another matter. You know... it's not everyday you see your new bank manager in such surprising circumstances, even if it is in a former life."

Elstead looked up sharply at Rice.

"Are you one of our customers?"

"Yes. I was coming to see you anyway."

"What about?"

"A substantial loan. I need an extension. It leaks. My roof."

"My diary's in my office. Perhaps you could call me and make an appointment?"

"Mr Elstead, I need to know more about the circumstances in which this video was made. "

"Are you asking me to make a formal statement?"

"What can you tell me about Peter McTeer?"

"The other boy?"

"Yes."

"I can't tell you anything. I didn't exactly know him. Not personally. We met at a party. That's the only time we spent together."

"Did you stay in touch?"

"No."

"Did you ever see him again?"

"No."

"I want you to go home and write down everything you remember about your encounter with Peter. I mean everything. Where you met. Who was with you. What happened. The whole thing. Will you do that for me?"

Elstead's mind was still racing. Should he get legal advice?

Would he be incriminating himself in any way? It seemed easier to agree to do what he was asked and get the hell out of there. He nodded his head and stared at the floor.

"You were, of course, committing a criminal offence back in 1974. Technically speaking. You do realise that?"

Elstead remained silent.

"But I don't think," continued Rice, "that we need be too concerned about that now, all things considered. Quite a lad, that Peter. Out of the 38 videos we confiscated, he appears in 29 of them. Occasionally, he winks at the camera. He knew perfectly well what was going on."

Half an hour later, James Elstead was back behind his desk at the Friendly Mutual Bank. He shut the door and asked not to be disturbed. He drank bitter coffee from the machine and threw his damaged carnation into the basket. It was bad enough being confronted by such unwelcome glimpses of his secret past, but the knowledge that he had been set up by that posh Edinburgh doctor and his fallen cherub was profoundly humiliating. That he might also have been an unwitting porn star amongst the more bent members of the Edinburgh Festival Chorus was truly grotesque.

Elstead dumped the rest of the undrinkable coffee and entered his private password into the computer. He ran a credit check on Detective Inspector Rice, examining all the information that the bank had in its files. Rice was 42 and unmarried. He lived with his elderly mother. There was nothing exceptional about his standing orders or direct debits. His two accounts were in credit and had long and blameless histories. Elstead then ran a check on Ruth Elizabeth Rice. Her current account was regularly topped up by payments from a host of investments. She was holding far too much at a negligible rate of interest and needed immediate professional advice. Compared to her son, she was seriously well off. Why did he need the hassle and expense of a loan when his mother had so much unused capital? Elstead wondered who owned the house. He also wondered why North Shields police station had videos belonging to an Edinburgh based doctor.

He grabbed the local telephone directory and searched for Dr Thomas Little. There he was, at a posh address in Marine Avenue, just a few minutes walk from the bank. It must be the same man. And what about Peter McTeer? He'd be about 45 years old. Elstead started a search on the computer, limited to the Lothian district of Scotland and his target's age group. A number of names were offered, but none quite fitted the profile he was seeking. He widened his search to include the whole of Scotland. He was offered hundreds McTeers, especially around Glasgow and the West coast. Then an unusual entry caught his eye: "UNSOLVED MURDERS". He opened the file. Someone had researched Scotland's unsolved murders. Elstead was surprised at how many there were. Seconds later, staring back at him from a screen for the second time that day were the unforgettable features of Peter McTeer. But it was not Peter the young lad. Instead, an older, world-weary face, with passionless eyes and a broken front tooth, glared at an unwelcome camera.

Twenty years ago, McTeer's body had been discovered accidentally by divers, trussed up and weighted down, at the bottom of Loch Rannoch. He was just 24 years old. Elstead sat back. My God! Peter had been only 14 years old in the video. He had no idea the boy had been so young. Presumably, D I Rice had full details of the McTeer case at his disposal. But, if so, had he contacted the Lothian police now that a new lead had been established? From the policeman's conduct, it seemed more likely that he didn't know about the murder. That would explain why Rice's interview earlier in the day had been so astonishingly casual. And nowhere in McTeer's case file was there any mention of Dr Little. The victim's biographical details were centred around his extended family and associates in Glasgow. Elstead concluded that the Lothian police hadn't been involved in the investigation of the young man's murder. The file concluded that the Glasgow police had presumed that Peter McTeer was the victim of an underworld killing, but had not uncovered any convincing motive for his violent end.

To the surprise of his staff, James Elstead left his office for the second time that day. Sooner or later, the police would make the necessary connections and get to Dr Thomas Little. Elstead feared that he would also be interrogated more rigorously and that his job and career would not survive a public scandal. He approached a grand, detached house in Marine Avenue and saw an old man pottering about in the garden. Before making his presence known, he watched Dr Thomas Little, now bent and frail, tidying his borders. At the sound of the front gate closing, the old man stopped work and eyed James Elstead with alarm and mistrust.

"Dr Little?"

"Yes."

"I'm James Elstead."

"Who?"

"James Elstead. Thirty years ago, you made a secret video of me having sex with Peter McTeer."

"Did I?"

"I had to watch myself at the police station this lunch time. I need to talk to you."

Reluctantly, Dr Little invited Elstead into his palatial house. He explained how the police had raided him some weeks earlier for downloading pornography off the internet. His computer, photographs, magazines and videos had all been taken away for examination.

"They were very thorough. And polite. They gave me receipts for everything. I was a fool."

"Tell me about the murder of Peter McTeer."

"Tell you what? I know nothing."

"Have the police ever asked you about it?"

"No. Why should they?"

"Because you have over twenty videos involving the victim of an unsolved crime. I don't think they've made the connection yet. But they will."

Dr Little's head fell. Elstead observed the extreme distress his questioning was causing, but did nothing to ease the inner suffering of the old man. Finally, fixing Elstead with a resentful glare, Dr Thomas Little started to tell his story.

"I hadn't seen Peter for some years. Our relationship came to a sticky end. He tried a bit of amateurish blackmail. I made sure he wasn't welcome in Edinburgh after that."

"Was that long before his death?"

"Three years?"

"So your relationship with Peter lasted for six or seven years?"

"I suppose so."

"After he tried to blackmail you... did you see him again?"

"He contacted me shortly before he disappeared. We met up in the Botanical Gardens. He was very frightened but he wouldn't tell me much. He wanted somewhere safe to stay in Edinburgh, but I wasn't having any of that. Two years later, they found his body."

"And you never made a statement to the police?"

"Good God no!"

"And they never came to interview you?"

"No. I told you."

Elstead watched the old man's unease before saying, "They are going to. Dr Little... sooner or later."

"Only if you tell them."

"I won't do that."

"No. I don't think you will. Ghosts from the past are best left undisturbed."

"It was not primarily my past I was forced to watch today, sir, it was yours."

"Mr Elstead, why are you here?"

"I have a wife and family. I have a good job. I got up early this morning, feeling on top of the world. If I'm to be publicly humiliated, I'll lose the lot."

"What do you want me to do about It?"

"Tell them nothing. We may be lucky. I expect you'll have your moment in court and get a fine for down-loading child pornography. They'll put you on the sex offenders' register. Personally, I won't lose any sleep over that, after what you did to me."

Dr Little went pale.

Elstead continued, "I am one of your victims, Dr Little."

"I think that's being a bit melodramatic. You seemed happy enough at the time, I seem to remember."

"I didn't know about the hidden camera and the video. You used me."

"What are you going to do about it?"

"I'll spend the next couple of years with my fingers crossed, always expecting a knock on the door. Maybe I'll hear nothing more. Who knows? Now, I've got to get back to work. My staff's already wondering what the hell's going on."

Indeed they were. On his return, Elstead was aware of curious glances from colleagues he hardly knew. Without stopping, he went to the sanctuary of his office, collapsed into his managerial, leather chair and closed his eyes. For the rest of the day, he could not bring himself to listen to any of the recorded messages that queued for his attention, or read any of the memos piled on his desk. So... D I Rice wanted a written statement?

He'd have to wait. Was he even obliged to provide one? Elstead thought he should seek professional advice, but even that would have to wait until the following morning.

A week later, James Elstead was interviewed at length, in the presence of his solicitor, by senior officers from Glasgow. A full, written statement was prepared and signed. Meanwhile, an abandoned car was attracting attention at the former fishing village of Craster on the Northumbrian coast. The police identified it as belonging to Dr Thomas Little of Marine Avenue, Whitley Bay. The doctor's body was recovered from the rocks below Dunstanburgh Castle. James Elstead requested and was given a transfer to another branch of the Friendly

Mutual Bank, to the dismay of his wife, who had no idea why her husband had accepted demotion to assistant manager. His four sons regarded his demotion as further proof of the sad state of their father. Whether D I Rice got his loan, James Elstead neither knew nor cared.

Jolly Well Played, That Man
Graeme Woolaston

^

Jolly Well Played, That Man
Graeme Woolaston

I got the cricket bat in, of all the improbable places, Glasgow. My work took me to many British cities. On that day I'd decided I needed a new rucksack. I went into the first sports shop I came to, a few hundred yards from my hotel. The first thing I saw was a rack holding at least a dozen cricket bats. Till that moment I'd had no idea cricket was played in Glasgow or anywhere within a hundred miles of Glasgow, but then I couldn't name any cricket team within a hundred miles of here except the counties.

The decision to buy the bat there came to me instantly. Equally instantly I saw the risk. In that city I had a highly distinctive accent. But within seconds I calculated that even if a murder in Gloucestershire were reported in the Glasgow press, an unlikely eventuality, no one in the shop would connect the instrument used assuming it could be identified – with a customer from six months previously.

'Is it for yourself?' a handsome assistant asked. My immediate reaction was that he was being sarcastic at the expense of my receding hair and my waistline. Then I realised he'd intended no rudeness. In reality it was something of a compliment.

I invented a teenage nephew as tall as myself. The bats, I discovered, came in widely differing weights. I bought the heaviest. Then I asked about cricket bags. Four were stacked on a shelf behind me. I chose, to the assistant's obvious disappointment at my lack of taste, one with a common brand name. I left the shop still without a rucksack, but with a cricket bat inside a bag where it would remain till the night it was needed.

My alertness about the brand name paid off two weeks later in Worcester, where I was able to buy a bag identical in every detail. Once again it was a present for my nephew.

The groundsheets – two of them – were bought separately, in

camping shops in Bath and Exeter. I was afraid that buying two at once would arouse suspicion.

The one other vital piece of equipment was shoes.

These I acquired on a busy market day in Cambridge, when the assistants were harassed by the crush of customers. They were cheap, nasty, and utterly indistinguishable, while they remained unworn, from a million other pairs.

I lived, fortunately, in a small cul-de-sac. A normal street would have meant too many potential eyes and ears detecting my movements. In fact there were only five other houses. Despite the smallness of our community none of us were over-friendly with our neighbours, though we were always polite. In summer we discussed our gardens and the weather. In winter, on the rare occasions we met, we discussed the weather. I had no idea of my neighbours' politics. A pleasant family two doors down seemed to be the only parishioners the rector had amongst us. The rest were apparently as godless as myself.

Perhaps I exaggerate the limits of our conversation. Because I was a middle-aged bachelor living alone I detected, from those tiny nuances of accent for which we English all have acute antennae, that I was viewed as an eccentric, possibly some kind of artist manqué, almost certainly a homosexual, and quite probably a serial murderer. My neighbours were tolerant people, and I suspected the latter was the option they found easiest to live with.

Everyone was aware that my hobby is astronomy. Hence the reputation for eccentricity. I made sure, that spring, my immediate neighbours knew I'd bought a new telescope. On one occasion when we were discussing slugs over the garden fence I showed it to them. It was obvious that the slugs were vastly more interesting. This necessity to show the telescope distressed me slightly. I didn't want to be thought of as a bore.

'What unusual hours you keep!' was the remark related neither to the weather nor the garden which was most frequently addressed to me. In other words, I heard it about once every two years. I blamed them on my insomnia, which also explained my interest in the stars. 'It gives me something to do at night,' I explained. I was sure they didn't believe me, but took it to be a cover for my serial murders. The irony was, it was the truth. Since my early thirties my nights had been long and usually solitary.

He was the centre of the eighteen months which necessitate that 'usually' instead of 'always'. God knows what my neighbours made of him. Though he was in fact less than a decade younger than me his stunning looks made the age gap seem much greater. I didn't let him talk to my neighbours, which, being so open and voluble, he'd have been happy to do for hours. I asked him once if he had any American ancestry. He was astonished by the question, and I had to explain what had prompted it. He roared with laughter. He laughed easily, and a great deal.

Of course his regular weekend appearances must have confirmed my reputation as a homosexual. Even the dimmest of my neighbours, intent on eliminating their slugs, couldn't have failed to notice this beautiful young man. Indeed, one summer's day my immediate neighbour's wife went so far as to flirt with him – out of earshot of both her husband and myself – asking him why he never sunbathed in the garden. The reason was, because I forbade it. This had triggered one of the blazing rows which obliged me to play loud classical music to prevent anyone overhearing. I told him that in this small town, and given the nature of my business, I simply couldn't risk making my sexuality blindingly obvious.

When he calmed down, he accepted this. But I had much greater difficulty calming him down when I refused to let him go to church. It would have been out of simple curiosity, since, like me, he had no religious beliefs whatsoever. He admired the architecture of our fourteenth-century parish church, which I had no problem with. But going to a service, 'just to see what it's like these days' as he put it, was out of the question. That weekend he stormed off, and it was two weeks before he returned.

What did he get out of those eighteen months? Well, I was in much better shape then than even half a decade later, and after my many experiences in my twenties I was first-rate in bed. And, being carless, he loved the trips we took every weekend, come rain or sun, over Gloucestershire and Worcestershire, through the Malverns and the Cotswolds, and even, if we set off early enough, to the monuments on Salisbury Plain. And I introduced him to the pleasures of stargazing.

When he no longer arrived on a Friday evening, and we no longer drove off in the mornings, my neighbours no doubt assumed I'd just added him to my tally of murders.

In itself the break-up didn't surprise me. It was the reason. He suddenly decided he wasn't queer after all, and got married, in church, to a loathsome Welshwoman. I would, of course, have automatically hated the person who took him from me. But her grotesque accent, which she made no effort to modify, grated on my ears as much as her looks offended my eyes.

I went to the wedding, because I was certain the marriage wouldn't last and I didn't want to give him unforgiveable grounds for offence. I was right. Within five years they were separated. Unusually for a woman, she didn't make sure she got the house, so he went on living twenty miles from me and she returned to some God-forsaken valley where she could enjoy the company of unemployed miners.

After him, there was nothing. I don't mean there weren't sexual encounters, though as I aged they increasingly took the form of games rather than actual sex, games which required me to play loud classical music to disguise their nature. Perhaps that music added to my reputation among my neighbours as someone with an interest in the arts. If so, the irony is that I can't stand it, which is why I only ever used it for concealment.

I mean there was no fullness in my life, and by the time he was into the third or fourth year of his marriage I knew there never would be. He had given me something I hadn't needed and then taken it away to leave me with a need which could never again be satisfied.

I don't mean that I loved him. I have no belief in love. For me, the most meaningless sentence in the English language is 'God is love'. For me that translates as, 'a being which does not exist is an emotion which is an illusion'. And just as I don't believe in love, so I don't believe in hate. I didn't decide to kill him out of hate. The decision came to me, like the choice of the cricket bat three weeks later, in an instant. I suddenly realised my life would be unendurable while he still lived, and therefore he had to die.

There is neither love nor hate. There is only necessity. After his separation we began to see each other again from time to time, as friends. He remained carless, partly for financial reasons and partly out of a simple lack of organisation. He was supremely impractical in day-to-day matters, which is perhaps why he married. So either he took the train to see me, or, more commonly, I drove across to pick him up. We resumed, on an occasional basis, our drives round the countryside. On one of these I asked if he'd like to join me on a stargazing trip in late October, when the Taurid meteor shower would coincide with a new moon. He knew about my new telescope, and agreed with some keenness.

Since the spring I'd been regularly driving off from home at nightfall during the last and first quarters of the moon, returning at about one in the morning. I apologised to my immediate neighbours if I disturbed them, stressing that I tried to be as quiet as possible. The power of my new telescope, I truthfully explained, was wasted in the light pollution in town. They assured me I didn't disturb them in the slightest, which I was sure was a lie. But it meant that there would be nothing to arouse their suspicions nothing, indeed, that wasn't routine – in the pattern of my movements the night of the murder. On my stargazing nights, if they were looking, they saw me carrying my telescope out to the car in a smart new cricket bag, and if they chanced to catch my return they saw me carry it indoors. This, of course, was the bag I'd bought in Worcester.

The irony was that I didn't get as many opportunities to stargaze that autumn as I would have wished. I was too busy trying to find the right spot. It had to be somewhere not frequently used by walkers, since it was essential to my plan that his body shouldn't be found for at least some days. In addition it had to be near a road where there was very little traffic at night. There was nothing particularly conspicuous about my car, but the danger that someone might recall seeing a car answering its description parked close to the murder scene on the night in question was one I couldn't eliminate altogether. Similarly, I could only minimise the risk of leaving behind distinctive tyre marks, if suspicion were ever to fall on me. It took me three weeks to find a clearing in a wood on a hilltop which met these criteria.

My final preparations were simple. In various shops in various towns I bought a set of new clothes all of which were either identical with or nearly indistinguishable from clothes I already owned. I drove to a deserted stretch of road where, observed by nobody, I lined the car's boot with one of my two groundsheets, folded double. Over a period of a week or so I collected a number of heavy stones that I found by the roadside and stored them in the boot. In a holdall I packed the clothes which matched my new purchases, together with a pair of shoes, and one afternoon I stuck it on the back seat of the car. And I put the second groundsheet and a pair of gloves in the cricket bag bought in Glasgow. Everything was now ready.

The biggest problem of all, of course, was phoning him to finalise arrangements. Naturally, I couldn't call him at home, so I rang him at his office early one afternoon, hoping its telephone system wouldn't be sophisticated enough to record which incoming calls were taken at which extension. He was surprised to hear from me during the day. I explained I was in Cheltenham where I had a business dinner that evening. The former was true, but within the hour I would be in Bath, which was where I actually had an appointment. Even if the call could be eventually be traced I made it from a phonebox well away from the city centre, avoiding security cameras.

I paid urgent attention to his exact words. I knew he worked in a large open-plan office, and indeed behind him I could hear the noise of conversation, phones ringing, and printers. Nonetheless it was conceivable that a colleague might overhear him and later, when questioned by the police, make a connection between this call and what had happened. Therefore, if he said anything at all which linked him clearly to me, our nighttime foray would indeed have to be for nothing more dangerous than trying to spot meteors.

He didn't.

We agreed to meet halfway between our respective homes, at a railway station among fields almost a mile from the village it serves. I'd made this choice weeks earlier. I knew that almost inevitably someone would remember seeing him on the train and seeing him alight there.

It was his movements after then that had to remain a mystery. So there was no question of my car being in the station carpark beforehand. Equally, I didn't want him hanging around too long in case that would also jog someone's memory in due course. Timing was of the essence. I discovered there was layby from which I could see the train on its way. From the timetable I learned it passed there exactly three minutes before it arrived at the village. By experimentation I found that because of winding roads it took me six minutes to make the drive. The three minutes difference wasn't quite enough to be certain every other alighting passenger would be gone. I decided to extend it by a further two minutes.

There was at least one problem I didn't have to contend with, one which would have complicated my plan so seriously I might have had to abandon it. Those were the days before mobile phones, so there was no danger that he might be prompted to ring me with some absurd 'Hi – I'm on the train.'

The final factor had to be left to chance, or else the murder would need to be postponed for perhaps two or three months. Would the skies be clear? Obviously, if they weren't, our trip was off.

As darkness came on that autumn afternoon they were as clear as any stargazer could possibly have desired. Therefore, at my usual time in the evening, any neighbour who happened to notice my movements would have seen me walk to the car carrying, as usual, a cricket bag. What he or she could not have known was that every item of outer clothing on me was brand new, and that for the first time ever I was wearing the shoes I'd bought in Cambridge. The bag, of course, was the Glasgow one.

And thereafter, as they say, it went like clockwork. The train was on time. Five minutes after he alighted, I collected him with profuse apologies which he brushed aside with a laugh. There wasn't another human being in sight. The drive took about thirty minutes, which puzzled him, but I assured him that the hilltop spot was perfect for observing the meteor shower – which, indeed, it would have been.

I parked on the side of the road, trying to keep the tyres off earth. He teased me about my poor parking. We set off along a track through scattered trees which led to the clearing. It was a walk of seven minutes. Once we were there I opened my bag and brought out the item which lay on top – the second groundsheet. He helped me spread it over the damp grass, and then sat down, craning his head backwards to look up at the sky.

'It's months since I saw the Milky Way,' he remarked. Those were his last words.

Once the bag was open I had no choice but to proceed. This was deliberate. I'd been afraid that at the last moment my nerve might fail me, so I created a situation which would have been impossible to explain away. Why no telescope in the bag? Why, instead, a cricket bat? As I took it out with my now gloved hands it still had the Glasgow price tag dangling from it.

He lowered his head to look forward. I didn't want him to suffer, so from behind I hit his skull as hard as I could. It wasn't enough. He crashed forward soundlessly, but on the groundsheet twisted his head to look up at me. His face was expressionless, as if he had yet to register that something odd was happening.

The first blow had been with the flat of the bat. Now I twisted it in my hands and brought it down sideways, once again as hard as I could, on his forehead. It bent inwards, and at the same moment his eyes rolled upward. Clearly he was already beyond suffering. To be sure of his death – and to make recognition more difficult – I smashed the bat down repeatedly on his face, and especially his mouth. I did the job well. The police couldn't even identify him from dental records. They had to use the then relatively new technique of DNA matching.

I wanted to rest, but the longer the car remained parked on the road, the greater the danger that someone might notice it. So at once I began undressing him. I'd done this many times before, of course, but a dead man is very heavy, and it was a struggle to get his clothes off. But it had to be done. All of them had left detectable traces in my car, and moreover his being found stripped was essential to my cover story if he had mentioned to anyone at all, however casually, that that evening he planned to go stargazing. I stuffed his clothes into the cricket bag, leaving him his shorts because they posed no danger and to give him some dignity. Then, with an almighty effort, I managed to raise the side of the groundsheet and toss him off it. I gave him such momentum he rolled over twice, ending in some bracken.

I wanted time to think, but there wasn't any. I pushed my gloves and the groundsheet on top of everything else in the bag, and set off back to the car.

Now came the most dangerous moments of all. If I'd been seen then, I'd have been finished. I stripped myself to my shorts, adding my bloodstained clothing to his. It was becoming difficult to get everything into the bag.

Before I finished I took the holdall off the back seat and dressed in the clothes which it held. Once that was done I could return to the business of getting the cricket bag shut. At the expense of a great deal of shoving I managed this. It went into the boot lined with the first groundsheet to prevent forensic contamination. Finally, I changed my shoes, making sure that the pair I was putting on touched nothing but dry tarmac. The shoes which had left the trail of prints leading to this spot would never be seen again.

I got into the car and drove off. In the five minutes or so I'd been by the roadside no car had passed. I glanced at my watch. It was little more than an hour since I'd left home, and therefore I had some time to kill – the instant I thought of the expression I laughed – before I could return.

I realised I'd made one mistake in my preparations. I'd forgotten to bring with me the groundsheet I normally used when stargazing. Therefore when I reached one of my regular observation points I had to risk sitting on damp grass. The meteor shower proved to be disappointing, and I was frustrated by being able to study the sky only with the naked eye.

But during the two hours I sat watching the slow rotation of the stars I understood with a clarity I'd never known before the absolute impossibility of God. Of course, even the slightest dabbling in astronomy destroys forever the Christian concept of God. As you peer at the distant galaxies, looking back millions of years to when their light began its journey to you, the idea that the creator of this vastness would choose to identify itself with one species on one planet in one solar system in one galaxy in one cluster of galaxies is so absurd it can only be laughed at.

But that night even the Jewish and Islamic concept of God as the unknowable, the all-other, was equally impossible. This I grasped not from what I saw above me, but from what I felt inside me. I realised that with what I'd done I'd achieved what I'd wanted. My life was indeed once again endurable.

At my usual hour I drove up to my house and parked as quietly as I could. If any of the neighbours happened still to be up and about, and witnessed my return, they would have seen only what they always saw – me carrying a cricket bag indoors.

My next problem, of course, was getting rid of that bag and its contents. I kept the cricket bat as a souvenir. Thereafter, my local knowledge came to my aid again. Two nights later I went off with the bag and drove some twenty miles to where a disused quarry had long been flooded. By the side of the road I stuffed the groundsheet that had lined the boot into the bag and then added four of the heavy stones I'd collected. There was no room for more. I squeezed out as much air as I could and walked the short distance to the edge of the quarry, relying on the strengthening moon for light. The splash as the bag went in and sank would have been audible for some distance, but the nearest habitation was over a mile away and there was a thick wood in between. A hawk-eyed neighbour might have noticed my empty-handed entry home that night.

He was found two days later. Early decomposition, together with the mess I'd made of his features, prevented identification for a further three days.

Inevitably, detectives came to interview me. They were two young men in ill-fitting dark suits which together with their inadequately shaved faces made them look more like some cheap film's idea of gangsters than policemen. They called me 'sir' with every utterance. They knew about the queerness in his life and already had a good idea of his relationship with me. In any case there was no need to be dishonest about our history. I allowed myself perhaps only an over-emphasis on the fact that in recent years we'd grown apart, since I had no acting skills and didn't dare risk trying to feign grief at the death of a close friend.

They asked about my movements on the night of the murder, and were visibly surprised when I potentially incriminated myself by saying I'd been out in the car. In response to their questions I showed them the bag with the telescope and groundsheet. Where exactly had I been? I named my second location. Was there anyone who could corroborate my story? I gave them the names of my neighbours and said it was possible they'd heard both my departure and my return some time after midnight. I learned two days later that after interviewing me they did indeed go next door. They stayed just five minutes. All my preparations paid off. My neighbours confirmed that I was indeed in the habit of going out with my telescope on nights when the skies were clear and there was only a small moon.

It soon became obvious to me that the detectives had, quite literally, not a clue as to the truth. They didn't even ask the question I'd carefully planned for, so I myself had to raise the subject.

'I read in the paper,' I said, 'that he was found half naked?' I'd made absolutely certain that I had indeed seen this piece of information in print.

'Stripped to his shorts, sir.'

'So was there any evidence of – sexual activity?'

The question seemed to alert them.

'No, there wasn't, sir. But why do you ask?'

'It's just that that could have been a reason for him being there.'

That surprised them. One of them made his next remarks with undisguised distaste: 'The examination was purely routine, sir. We were inclined to rule out open-air activity, at this time of year.'

'And why go to such an out-of-the-way spot?' the other asked.

Now I risked acting. I pretended a measure of embarrassment.

'Because he was very fond of – rather noisy sex.' I cleared my throat. 'Have you any idea what kind of instrument was used in the attack?'

'We believe, a heavy piece of wood.'

'Could you give me a moment?'

As I went upstairs I mused on the fact that if he had said something beforehand about taking part in a stargazing expedition I would have suggested to the police that this was merely a cover for what he'd really planned. But my precaution on that matter had turned out to be unnecessary.

I returned with an item which the detectives handled with open puzzlement.

'Would something like that have been enough to have done the damage?'

The detective holding it waved it in the air and looked enquiringly at his colleague.

'I don't think this is nearly heavy enough, sir. The force used would have had to have been incredible.' If my embarrassment a minute or two earlier had been faked, his certainly wasn't. 'What exactly is this, sir?'

'It's an American fraternity paddle.' They were obviously none the wiser. I explained its role in sadomasochism, the effect it produced when applied with vigour to buttocks in 'the position'. Their faces became studies in professional suppression of reaction.

'I'm afraid,' I concluded, 'that he really liked being treated in that way.' This was completely untrue. He found my sadomasochism a turn-off, and never wanted to hear any details about it. 'If there was nowhere indoors that was suitable – you know, because of the noise – he and his companion might have chosen a deserted spot where they could really go at it.'

We continued talking about paddles and other toys that might be converted into lethal assault weapons. Throughout all this there was one beautiful touch. Before the police arrived I hadn't been able to resist hiding the cricket bat under the sofa. There was, of course, a chance that one of them might drop something to the floor and, stooping, spot it. In the whole business this was my only touch of recklessness, but in retrospect I loved it. All the time they questioned me, the murder instrument was lying eighteen inches below their fat backsides.

When they left they said they might be back with further questions, but I doubted it. I knew my carefully planned trick had worked. He hadn't just been a queer; he'd been a queer who liked being whacked and humiliated. Even before I'd closed the door I'd seen their commitment to solving the crime withering away in front of my eyes.

I was right. The murderer was never caught.

The body wasn't released for burial for some weeks. I went to the funeral, a wretched affair since the clergyman had known nothing of the man over whom he intoned the Anglican rite. The loathsome Welshwoman wept profusely. Thankfully, none of his family knew of my existence, so I didn't have to offer them condolences beyond the standard mumblings called for on these occasions. Their distress was obvious, which in turn distressed me. Outside of sexual games, I have never taken any pleasure in hurting people.

Now my own death is close, and will have happened before this writing is found. What my executors choose to do with it is their business. They might, if they wish, semi-fictionalise it by, for example, changing the location of these events to a completely different part of the country. But at least it will explain to them why they found a bloodstained cricket bat with a price tag from a Glasgow sports shop propped up at the back of my wardrobe.

I've been aware of the approach of death for some months. I have no fear of it. I know that eight seconds after my heart finally gives away under the stress of supporting my cancer-ridden frame all detectable electrical activity will cease in my brain. Just eight seconds after that final heartbeat, and I will no longer exist.

If I suspected for one moment that there might be some survival of death I would be a great deal more anxious. But I've never forgotten what I perceived with such brilliance on that starlit night twelve years ago. There is no God of Love. There is no God of Justice. And there is, most certainly, no God of Mercy.

Acknowledgements

I would like to thank all the contributors to *Death Comes Easy: The Gay Times Book of Murder Stories* for their excellent short stories, with one exception, all especially written for this collection. I would also like to thank those writers invited to contribute (Jake Arnott, for example) who had the courtesy to let me know that they didn't have time to participate in the book.

I would like to make an especial note of thanks to Sebastian Beaumont (who wielded the word processor), Pamela Hinchliffe for checking details of particulars of murder, Tim d'Arch Smith for finding relevant texts and to those friends (Keith and Teresa Hayes, Michael Lowrie, Gary Pulsifer, Richard Smith, Tony Warren) for support at a particularly difficult time in my life.

'Death by Eros' by Steve Saylor was originally published in *Past Poisons: An Ellis Peters Memorial Anthology of Historical Crime* (Headline, 1998).

Peter Burton
Brighton, 2003

Further reading

This is not a bibliography of tales of murder (fact and fiction) within a gay context. There is a vast literature on the subject, arguably enough to fill a fair sized volume of its own. Thus, what follows is a basic checklist, the aim of which is to point the interested reader in the direction of some of the writers and some of the books in this popular genre. Editions cited are those on my bookshelves, not necessarily firsts:

Bataille, Georges: *The Trial of Gilles de Rais* (Los Angeles, Amok, 1991) (Also see – Benedetti, Jean: *Gilles de Rais: The Authentic Bluebeard* [London, Peter Davies, 1971])

Bell, Arthur: *Kings Don't Mean a Thing: The John Knight Murder Case* (New York, William Morrow, 1978)

Berendt, John: *Midnight in the Garden of Good and Evil* (London, Chatto & Windus, 1994)

Capote, Truman: *In Cold Blood: A True Account of a Multiple Murder and Its Consequences* (London, Sphere Books, 1981)

Cullen, Robert: *The Killer Department: Detective Viktor Burakov's Eight-Year Hunt for the Most Savage Serial Killer in Russian History* (London, Orion, 1993) (Also see – Lourie, Richard: *Hunting the Devil: The Search for the Russian Ripper* [London, Grafton, 1993])

Leopold, Nathan F: *Life Plus 99 Years* (Lonon, Victor Gollancz, 1958) (Also see – Levin, Meyer: *Compulsion* [London, Corgi Books, 1959])

Lucie-Smith, Edward: *The Dark Pageant: A Novel about Gilles de Rais* (London, Blond & Briggs, 1977)

Masters, Brian: *Killing for Company: The Case of Dennis Nilsen* (London, Jonathan Cape, 1985) *The Shrine of Jeffrey Dahmer* (London, Hodder & Stoughton, 1993) (Also see – Norris, Dr Joel: *Jeffrey Dahmer* [London, Constable, 1992])

Orwell, George: 'Decline of the English Murder' (London, *Tribune*, 15 February 1946)

St James, James: *Disco Bloodbath* (London, Sceptre, 1999)

Wilde, Oscar: 'Pen, Pencil and Poison: A Study in Green' in *Complete Works of Oscar Wilde* (London, HarperCollins, 1994)

The number of murder mysteries with gay detectives and/or gay victims is immense and the following authors are just a tiny few whose work is worth pursuing: Jake Arnott, Edgar Box (Gore Vidal), Jack Dickson, Hugh Fleetwood, George Dawes Green, Joseph Hansen, Patricia Highsmith, Jonathan Kellerman, Val McDermid, John Preston and Ruth Rendell (also see – Introduction/*Death Comes Easy*).

About the Authors

Tim Ashley is an ex-banker and an ex-international entrepreneur. He has written two novels and two screenplays in the last two years, but 'Best Eaten Cold' is his first published work of fiction.

Sebastian Beaumont is the author of five novels, including *Heroes Are Hard to Find*, *The Cruelty of Silence* and *The Linguist*. His short stories have been variously anthologised. He was brought up in Dumfriesshire, Scotland. The school he attended there was closed down after one of the pupils drowned in the river.

Perry Brass is the author of *Warlock: A Novel of Possession*, *Mirage*, *Out There: Stories of Private Desires*, *The Harvest*, *How to Survive Your Own Gay Life* and *Angel Lust: An Erotic Novel of Time Travel*. He has been nominated for several Lambda Literary Awards (in the categories Poetry, Religion and Science Fiction & Fantasy).

Scott Brown first appeared in print with 'Justice Armstrong-Jones' in *Bend Sinister: The Gay Times Book of Disturbing Short Stories*. 'The Collection Box' is his second published story. He is working on more stories and a novel.

Jeffrey Buchanan is a New Zealander who has lived most of his working life in Papua New Guinea, Fiji and the Middle East where he has worked as a development specialist. He has published two novels, including *Sucking Feojas* (GMP), short stories and academic works.

Peter Burton's books include *Rod Stewart: A Life on the Town*, *Parallel Lives*, *Talking To...* and *Amongst the Aliens: Some Aspects of a Gay Life*. He has edited *The Black Tent and Other Stories*, *The Boy from Beirut and Other Stories*, *The Mammoth Book of Gay Short Stories* and *Bend Sinister: The Gay Times Book of Disturbing Stories*.

Richard Cawley had a successful career as a designer for a fashion house before becoming a food writer (nine cookbooks) and television chef on such programmes as *Ready Steady Cook* and *Can't Cook Won't Cook*. He is the author of one novel, *The Butterfly Boy*. His first short story appeared in *Bend Sinister: The Gay Times Book of Disturbing Stories*.

Robert Cochrane is a poet, publisher and journalist. Since 1991 he has been Commissioning Editor of The Bad Press and has published Chloe Poems, David Robilliard and Aiden Shaw amongst others. The author of two previous collections, his most recent book is *Winters at the New York Hotel*. He has edited a selection from the work of World War I poet James Lyons and contributes lyrics to the band Blue Eyed Black.

Bryan Connon is best known as a biographer and his books include the acclaimed *Beverley Nichols: A Life* and *Somerset Maugham and the Maugham Dynasty*.

Jack Dickson is the author of *Oddfellows*, *Crossing Jordan*, *Freeform*, *Banged Up*, *Some Kind of Love* (the latter three featuring private investigator Jas Anderson), *Out of This World*, and the television film *The Sucker Punch*.

Simon Edge is a journalist and critic. A one-time editor of *Capital Gay*, he has written for the *Guardian*, the *Independent* and the *London Evening Standard*. He now writes for the *Daily Express*.

Joanne Elliott is a freelance illustrator who has had short stories published in magazines as diverse as *Just Seventeen* and *Reader's Digest*.

Nigel Fairs, once an actor, has had twenty-six of his plays produced, including *Sauna*, *In Conversation With an Acid Bath Murderer*, *Unsex Me Here* and *My Mother Was An Alien – Is That Why I'm Gay?* His third *Tomorrow People* audio adventure, *Alone*, is due out on CD towards the end of 2003.

Steve Ferris published a collection of short stories called *The Cub-Hunting Season* in 1994 but is still struggling with his first novel. Primarily a painter, he currently works as a supply teacher in a secondary school.

Hugh Fleetwood is a painter as well as a writer and has had several exhibitions of his work in Italy. His novels include *The Girl Who Passed for Normal* (winner of the John Llewellyn Rhys Prize), *Foreign Affairs, The Past, The Witch, The Mercy Killer* and *Brothers*.

C.J. Fortescue works as a law clerk in the Supreme Court in Queensland, Australia. Though writing poems, plays and stories from childhood, 'The Mirror's Kiss' marks Fortescue's publication debut.

Christopher Francis currently works in a nursing home in Ireland. 'Little Jimmy' is his first published short story.

Patrick Gale is the author of ten novels, including *The Aerodynamics of Pork, Facing the Tank, Little Bits of Baby, The Cat Sanctuary, Tree Surgery for Beginners*, the best-selling *Rough Music* and, most recently, *A Sweet Obscurity*.

Drew Gummerson is based in the Midlands, but has lived in the United States, Australia, the Czech Republic and Japan. His first novel, *The Lodger* (GMP) was nominated for a Lambda Award.

Michael Hootman is an arts journalist writing for Brighton's *Gscene* and *Juice* magazines. He is currently working on a novel, *Narcissus Unbound*. When not writing his hobbies include cake baking and crying in his bedroom. Offers of literary representation, criticism, fan mail and love poems should be sent to <u>mikebrighton@talk21.com</u>.

Randall Ivey is the author of *The Shape of Man: A novella and five stories*. His work has appeared in literary journals and magazines throughout the USA and in the anthologies *Sex Buddies: Erotic stories about sex without* and *A View to Thrill*.

Alan James is a graduate from the Royal College of Art and he has exhibited three one-man shows. His first short story, 'Monkey Business' was published in *Bend Sinister: The Gay Times Book of Disturbing Stories*.

Francis King published his first three novels while he was an undergraduate at Oxford and since then has written another forty books. His novels include *A Domestic Animal, Act of Darkness, Voices in an Empty Room, Punishments, The Ant Colony, The One and Only, Dead Letters, Prodigies* and, most recently, *The Nick of Time*.

Simon Lovat is the author of *Disorder and Chaos* and *Attrition*. His short stories have been variously anthologised.

Anthony McDonald is the author of *Orange Bitter, Orange Sweet* and the recent *Adam* (GMP).

Joseph Mills is the author of *Towards the End* and *Obsessions*. He also edited *Borderline: The Mainstream Book of Scottish Gay Writing*.

Patrick Roscoe was born on the Spanish island of Formentera in 1965 and spent his childhood in Tanzania, East Africa. He was educated in England and Canada, then divided several decades between California, Mexico and Spain while supporting the writing of his first books through employment as a prostitute and as an adult film actor. He has since become the author of seven internationally acclaimed novels and short story collections, which have been translated into nine languages and which have earned him renown as the most accomplished and adventurous gay writer working in the English language today. His celebrated novels include *God's Peculiar Care* (1991), *The Lost Oasis* (1995) and *The Reincarnation of Linda Lopez* (2003). His widely published and anthologised stories have twice won the prestigious CBC Canadian Literary Award; they have also received a pair of Distinguished Story citations from *Best American Stories*. His work has been featured in consecutive editions of *Winter's Tales*, as well as in *The Gay Times Book of Disturbing Stories*. Roscoe divides his time between Sevilla (Spain), Havana (Cuba) and Sidi Ifni (Morocco), where he is at work on a new novel for which he seeks a UK agent and publisher.

Steven Saylor is best known as the author of the Roma sub Rosa series of novels set in ancient Rome and featuring Gordianus the Finder, which includes *Roman Blood, Arms of Nemesis, Catilina's Riddle, The Venus Throw, A Murder on the Appian Way, The House of the Vestals, Rubicon, Last Seen in Massilia* and *A Mist of Prophecies.*

Michael Wilcox is a dramatist and his plays include *Rents, Lent, Green Fingers* and *Mrs Steinberg and the Byker Boy.* He is the author of an autobiography, *Outlaw in the Hills,* and *Benjamin Britten.* He was also editor of *Gay Plays* (Volumes 1–5).

Graeme Woolaston is the author of *Stranger Than Love, The Learning of Paul O'Neil* and *The Biker Below the Downs.* His short stories have been variously anthologised.

Also available

Bend Sinister:
The Gay Times Book of Disturbing Stories

Edited by Peter Burton

A deeply disturbing collection

This new collection, nominated for a Lambda literary award, is packed with chills and thrills from thirty gay writers. It ventures into the world of the sinister and the disturbing, with flashes of sheer horror.

Authors include: Sebastian Beaumont, David Patrick Beavers, Perry Brass, Christopher Brown, Richard Cawley, Jack Dickson, Neal Drinnan, Francis King, Simon Lovat, Stuart Thorogood, Michael Wilcox and Richard Zimler.

Across a range of nationalities and approaches, one thing is guaranteed: something out of kilter, something dangerously askew.

"A collection of startling originality... a welcome addition to the canon of gay literature" City Life

"[An] excellent anthology of horror, fantasy and crime... a chillingly good read" ★★★ Big Issue

"A lively, eclectic collection... Highly recommended" The List

"Breathtakingly different... incredible 'tales of the unexpected'" Our World

"A superb collection of disturbing tales" ★★★★ OUT in Greater Manchester

Red

Richard James

A celebration of one man's extraordinary life –
a life that spans oceans and centuries

In part, *Red* is a literary thriller in the European tradition, focusing on mysterious art collectors and the curious machinations of Dr Mabuse (who may or may not be the Devil). But as it moves cinematically from the English Civil War to the Mexican Revolution and from Venice to New York, there is much more to this story.

This is a distinguished debut of great scope and ambition, haunted by cultural ghosts from Virginia Woolf's *Orlando* to Thomas Mann's *Death in Venice*, and reminiscent of the sprawling epics of Michael Moorcock.

"One of this year's most unusual new gay works... strikingly original and lively" – OutUK

"Magical... Red moves through times and places like an Angela Carter novel, carrying an air of mystery... Welcome to a world where nothing is quite what it seems" – What's On

GMP books are available from bookshops including Borders, Gay's The Word, Prowler Stores and branches of Waterstone's. Or order direct (quote BEN427 or RED419)) from:

MaleXpress, 75B Great Eastern Street, London EC2A 3HN

Freephone 0800 45 45 66 (Int tel +44 20 7739 4646)

Freefax 0800 917 2551 (Int fax +44 20 7739 4848)

www.gaymenspress.co.uk